DO THIS FOR ME

ALSO BY ELIZA KENNEDY

I Take You

DO THIS FOR ME

A Novel

ELIZA KENNEDY

CROWN
NEW YORK

Copyright © 2018 by Eliza Kennedy

All rights reserved.
Published in the United States by Crown, an imprint of the Crown Publishing Group, a division of Penguin Random House LLC, New York.
crownpublishing.com

CROWN and the Crown colophon are registered trademarks of Penguin Random House LLC.

Library of Congress Cataloging-in-Publication Data is available upon request

ISBN 978-1-101-90720-7
Ebook ISBN 978-1-101-90722-1

PRINTED IN THE UNITED STATES OF AMERICA

Jacket design by Elena Giavaldi
Jacket illustration by Na Kim

10 9 8 7 6 5 4 3 2 1

First Edition

For Joshua

PART ONE

ONE

THE SECOND-WORST DAY of my life started like most days did, back then: with a dream of my own bizarre and improbable death.

This time, I'd traveled to Antarctica to take a deposition. I was ready with my questions. The stenographer was in place. But the curtains in the conference room wouldn't close. The glare off the snow was blinding. The witness was refusing to testify.

The clock was ticking!

I rushed out and began searching for the reception desk. The hallway turned into a tunnel carved in snow. As I clutched my bathrobe tightly around myself (bathrobe?), I passed a polar bear. But polar bears live in the Arctic, not the Antarctic.

"You're not supposed to be here," I told the bear. It snarled and lunged at me.

I ran and ran. I could see reception up ahead. The bear was right behind me, but I was getting closer. I was almost there. I was . . .

Tumbling into an ice crevasse.

I gasped awake, blinked, calmed my pounding heart. Soon, the outlines of dresser and nightstand and lamp emerged from the gloom. Bathroom door. Window.

I was home. I was safe.

I reached for Aaron, but he wasn't there. I felt a fresh burst of panic, until I remembered: he was on tour. The paperback of *Glow Worms* had just been released. My hand swept the smooth, empty space beside me where he should have been. Morning was when I missed him most. I missed watching him sleep, one arm flung over his head like a boy's. Watching his eyes open. Watching him turn toward me and smile.

He'd been away three weeks. Three weeks without the smell of his coffee drifting up the stairs. Without the sound of his laughter. Without his dark eyes, looking up from a book to greet me after a long day.

But he was coming home tonight. Tour over, show on hiatus—he was done traveling for a while. I only had to wait one more day. Then . . .

One more day.

That meant today was . . . the Day.

The clock blinked to 5:02. I sat up.

I had, what? Six hours until 11 a.m.

The call. The case. My moment of truth.

I launched myself out of bed to pace the carpet. What if we lost? Was it possible we'd lost? I grabbed my phone from the nightstand. I needed to talk to Aaron.

I hesitated.

He was in San Francisco. Did I really need to wake him? We'd spoken last night, before his reading. He was loving and reassuring, as always.

"You killed it, Raney. Those executives fell apart on the stand. The judge was nodding along during your closing argument—remember? You have nothing to worry about."

I had nothing to worry about. Nothing. I climbed back into bed and forced myself to spend half an hour editing a brief my senior associate, Stephen, had sent me the night before. Then I showered, brushed my teeth and brushed my hair. Got dressed: suit, blouse, flats. Knuckles on the bathroom counter, I leaned close to the mirror.

"You killed it," I told my reflection.

My reflection didn't look convinced.

Before heading downstairs I cracked the door to the twins' room, peering through the darkness at their huddled forms. I took a step inside. It was all right: they were breathing. They were fifteen—of course they were breathing.

Still, I'm their mother. I worry.

Maisie's bed was closer to the door. I bent down, brushing a swoop of light brown hair from her warm cheek.

"I love you more than anything in the world," I whispered.

"Then stop being creepy," she said.

From the far side of the room, Kate said, "Seriously, Mom. We've talked about this."

I straightened and stepped back. "I'm so sorry!"

"It's okay." Maisie plumped her pillow. "Just let us sleep."

"No, really. It must be awful," I said. "To be so loved."

Kate flopped onto her back. "Here we go."

"To be the center of someone's existence," I continued. "Showered with affection. Lavished with care. How you must suffer."

Maisie reached for her phone. "Most parents encourage their teenagers to rest, Mom. Just FYI."

"It could be worse," I pointed out. "Instead of lolling in these clean, comfortable beds, you could be toiling away in some sweatshop."

She was texting now, her face reflecting the glow of the screen. "Bed or sweatshop," she remarked. "These are always our only options."

"Hold up." Kate raised her head. "Today's the day."

"*That's* why she's on edge," Maisie said.

"I'm not on edge!"

"LOL," Kate said drily.

"Relax, Mama." Maisie smiled up at me. "You're totally going to win."

"Your oppressed waitresses are going to kick some serious corporate ass," Kate agreed.

"The plaintiffs are *management trainees*," Maisie informed her. "Don't you pay any attention?"

"That's how I know most of them started as waitresses, moron."

"You're the moron! You—"

"Well!" I clapped my hands. "My work here is done."

They stopped squabbling long enough to wish me luck. I blew them a kiss and backed out of the room.

A car came for me at 6:15. The driver was new.

"Where's Kurt?" I said.

"Good morning," the driver said.

Greetings. Right. Very important. "Good morning," I said. "Where's Kurt?"

"Kurt?" The driver steered the car to the end of our driveway. "He got reassigned."

I fell back against the seat. "Are you serious?"

Brown eyes glanced at me in the rearview, then away. The town car floated down the street. Dawn was breaking over the wooded hills. In massive homes, behind gates and circular drives and meticulously curated lawns, my neighbors were waking. Bankers. Hedge fund managers. Doctors. Stretching, yawning, showering, shaving. Buttoning and knotting. Brewing, scrambling and toasting.

The world—my world—was getting ready for work.

But I didn't care about any of that at the moment.

"Tell me," I said to the driver. "I can take it."

He hesitated. Finally:

"I heard it was the yelling."

"What?" I cried, before I could catch myself. More calmly: "That's outrageous."

"Would you mind buckling your seat belt, Miz Moore?"

I reached for the belt, not taking my eyes off the mirror. "I never yelled at Kurt."

"I think it was more a proximity-type situation."

"I yelled near him?"

"He's a sensitive guy, what can I say? You want me to take the Sprain Brook?"

"Take the Sawmill." We passed the country club, the shopping center, the nature preserve. I tried to let it go. I couldn't let it go.

I have a hard time, in general, letting things go.

"I'm extremely careful about raising my voice," I said. "I'm strategic."

I caught the hint of a smile. "You ask Kurt, there's an awful lot of strategy going on back there at six thirty in the morning."

I pulled Stephen's brief out of my bag and found my place. I uncapped my pen. I looked up. "What's your name?"

"Jorge."

"Are you going to have a problem with the yelling, Jorge?"

He pursed his lips. "Nah. I'm tough."

"Excellent." I turned a page and circled a typo.

Looking back on that time—that car trip, that morning, that strange, enraging autumn—I can't help but think: forget death in Antarctica—*I* was the real nightmare. Pestering my children, haranguing my driver . . . who does that?

Funny, though: from the inside, life was good. I was happy. My stresses and challenges seemed to me proof of a full, hectic modern existence—the kind we're all supposed to strive for. Sure, I was headstrong and obsessive and maybe a little prickly sometimes, but I had plenty of good qualities, too. The people and things I cared about, I cared about deeply. I worked hard—always had. I'd gone to the best high school in the country, the best university, the best law school, all on my own. I never drank. Never smoked. Never cheated. Never lied. I never even swore.

I sound so impressed with myself, don't I? Swaggering around with my intensity, my work ethic, my litany of bests and nevers. In truth, I was pretty pleased to be me back then. I had a wonderful husband and two great kids. I had good friends and satisfied clients. I was young (thirty-seven), healthy, wealthy and (I thought) wise.

My life was a story I'd written myself, and it hit all the registers. Early loss, long struggle, triumph over adversity. Sacrifices rewarded, love earned and cherished. I was proud of what I'd accomplished.

It was all going very much according to plan.

I finished editing the brief and glanced at my calendar. The entry at 11 a.m. looked so innocuous. "Clerk call." Two little words.

Tiny assassins.

A lot of what I do is pretty dry stuff. Securities fraud, contract disputes, one faceless corporate entity suing another over a big pile of cash. The case tormenting me that particular morning was different. My clients were a group of women suing a restaurant chain called Gaia Café. It was a ubiquitous, supertrendy lunch spot beloved by vegetarians, vegans and people on the Paleo diet.

Turns out the company's employment practices were straight out of the Stone Age, too. My plaintiffs suffered pay discrimination, pregnancy discrimination, promotion discrimination and persistent, unwanted sexual advances.

All at a place called the Gaia Café.

I'd taken the case pro bono and filed a nationwide class action. The defendant fought us for three years. Their lawyers were weasels and their executives were boors. They offered a joke of a settlement on the eve of trial, which I advised my clients to reject. The trial was a four-month ordeal, widely reported in the press. Our evidence was good, but not great. The judge was sympathetic, but skeptical. We submitted our final papers weeks ago. The previous Friday, I'd received an e-mail announcing that the court would issue its ruling at 11 a.m. on Monday, at which time the clerk would call both sides and inform us of the judgment.

So yes. I was a little on edge.

My phone rang. When I answered, a voice said, "Thanks for asking me about my date last night."

It was Sarah, my best friend. We met in the first class on the first day of our first year of law school (Criminal Law, Prof. Raeling, Room 127, third row center). She stopped practicing a few years ago to stay home and raise her kids. Last spring she divorced her husband, the devious and disappointing Tad. Now she was dating again, fiercely and with great determination.

"My apologies," I said. "How was your date?"

"I got LAID!!!"

Jorge's eyes flickered to the rearview, then away. I relaxed into my seat. "Congratulations."

"He was Latvian." Sarah had a weakness for foreign men. "I've finally invaded the Balkans."

"The Baltics."

"Whatever, nerd. It was superhot. He was like this hairy, sexy wild boar. Snuffling and growling. Rooting away at me."

"Sounds dreamy."

"Right?" I heard dishes rattling. "So are you a mass of jangling nerves right now or what?"

Sarah had followed the Gaia Café case from the beginning. She knew the judgment was coming down today. "I'm fine," I said.

"Liar. How did you die in your dream last night?"

I told her.

"You're a perv," she said.

"I'm not a perv!"

"Of course you are. The ice crack represents your—"

Sarah is wonderful. I hadn't said a word about how nervous I was—she just knew. She also knew that I wasn't going to be cheered by empty phrases and vague promises that everything was going to be okay. I needed to be bantered with. Teased. Distracted.

"You're profoundly disturbed," she said. "This is why you need a therapist."

The car slowed. Traffic was getting heavier as we approached the city. "I don't need a therapist."

"Of course you do." I heard more dishes rattle and, in the distance, a child's shout. "The only reason you took this case is because you're an orphan."

According to Sarah, the only reason I do anything is because I'm an orphan.

"Those waitresses are stand-ins for your lost mother," she continued.

"There are fourteen hundred plaintiffs, Sarah."

"Exactly. You have *serious* mommy issues."

I laughed. She kept going. "You're a wounded bird."

"I thought I was a piece of hard candy with a gooey center." Her usual metaphor.

She didn't miss a beat. "You're a bird-shaped piece of candy. With a broken candy wing."

I heard a crash, then wailing. "Is that the wild boar?"

"If only. It's Mercer. Raney."

We were passing under the George Washington Bridge. "Yes?"

"No matter what happens today? You did a phenomenal job."

"Thanks."

"My pleasure. Now get to work, ya deadbeat!" She hung up.

I glanced at my calendar for the rest of the day. I had (a) a meeting at 12:30 with the ACLU, (b) a partner lunch at 1:30 and (c) conference calls at 2:15, 3:30, 4:15 and 5:00. In addition, I needed to (d) draft a letter to the court in one of my securities cases and (e) speak with a client about settlement.

I also had a new associate joining my team. Amanda something or other. Fresh out of law school, she would need to be welcomed and in-spired. Subtly judged. Intellectually challenged and motivated to begin working the insane hours necessary to justify her exorbitant salary. I hoped she was good.

We left the West Side Highway at Fifty-Fourth Street. I checked my e-mail. I had seven new messages, including one from Aaron.

From: Aaron Moore

To: Raney Moore

Date: Monday, September 18, 6:41 AM

Subject: Missing You

Hey hon. It's the middle of the night here, and I can't sleep. The reading last night was great—lots of kids. This is such a beautiful city. We should come here, maybe after the first of the year? Just the two of us.

     This trip has been too long. Can you tell how much I miss you? I miss our daily life. I miss the girls. I miss making love to you. I can't wait to see you.

Poor Aaron. He hated life on the road. He had trouble sleeping, trouble eating. His homesickness was palpable in every e-mail, text and phone call.

Are you nervous? What a question—of course you're nervous. I'm not. We'll be celebrating tonight. I'm so proud of you.

My phone vibrated twice. High-priority messages. I skipped to the end.

I can see a sliver of the Golden Gate Bridge from my window. It's beautiful, all lit up in the darkness. I'm going back to bed. Call me when you hear from the court!

Love, Aaron

As we pulled up to my building, Seventh Avenue was coming to life. Swerving taxis, rumbling trucks. Honking horns and the charred reek of nuts from the vendor on the corner. I took a deep breath of city air, then walked inside.

I read e-mails through the lobby. Past security. Into the elevator. As the doors closed I put my phone away and closed my eyes and did my thing.

Growing up, I was a nervous kid. Anxious pretty much all the time. One night, when I was nine or ten and couldn't sleep, I started leafing through one of my grandmother's goofy magazines. I came across this . . . relaxation technique, I guess you could call it. It sounds dumb, but I tried it, and it worked. I've been doing it ever since.

At the start of each day, whether I'm in the elevator, walking into court or somewhere else, I close my eyes and think of a box. A treasure chest, actually. (See "sounds dumb," above.) I take my time visualizing it: the rounded top, the water-darkened wood. A massive lock dangling from the rusty hasp.

When I'm ready—when the thing is really *there* in my head—I heave open the lid and fill it with all the bad junk clattering around my brain. My many fears: that I've made a mistake, that I've lost a case, that I'll never win one again. That my loved ones will perish. That the end is near.

I take those worries and insecurities—all that *noise*—and stuff them inside. Then I slam the lid and lock it and put the imaginary key around my neck, where it stays as long as I'm at work.

Ridiculous, I know. But effective. When those doors open on the forty-fifth floor and I stride out, my mind is quiet. I am cool and composed. Invincible.

I am everything everyone believes me to be.

As I was that morning. I walked toward the suite I shared with two other partners, Wally Fanucci and Jonathan Tate. The wood paneling gleamed and the air smelled of lemons. The hallway displayed tokens of the firm's illustrious past—sepia photographs of stern, top-hatted men, documents bearing the faded signatures of famous Americans. My firm is the oldest in New York City, and the best in the world. We have brilliant people, important clients, the most high-stakes and complicated cases. I'd been a partner there since I was twenty-nine. The youngest person ever to make partner in the firm's two centuries of existence.

(Swaggering. Swaggering on . . .)

I walked into my office. Large, clean, spare, bright. Desk, chairs, sofa, bookshelves. The sun was burning mist off the treetops in Central Park. I sat down. Took stock. Woke my computer. Got to work.

Renfield stumped into the outer office around eight. I heard her drop her handbag and kick it under her desk. Her chair creaked. She sighed, which provoked a coughing fit. She swore at her computer. Her chair creaked again. The muttering increased in volume as she approached.

She entered my office. "Jesus. You look terrible."

I glanced up from my screen. "Why thanks."

"That goddamn judge! Did you get any sleep at all?"

"Loads." I held out the brief. "Can you leave this in Stephen's office?"

She took it. "I'll get you some breakfast."

"I don't want breakfast."

"I'll get you a fruit cup."

"I don't want a fruit cup."

"You'll eat a fruit cup." She walked out.

I sent an e-mail to my associates. I skimmed a law review article. The phone rang. I didn't recognize the number, so I let it go to voice mail. I sent an e-mail to Maisie's math tutor. I ordered Kate a new pair of soccer cleats. I scanned the headlines in the *Wall Street Journal*. I read an article in the *New York Times*.

I checked Facebook and Twitter. Aaron must not have been able to get back to sleep—he'd sent a series of tweets within the last hour.

Aaron Moore

@RealAaronMoore

New member of Megaloptera family discovered in China—wingspan over 8 in!!! Check out pic: bit.ly/1AK78k #amazinginsects

7.36 AM - 18 Sept 2017

77 RETWEETS 149 FAVORITES

And:

2 wks till release of Nat'l Climate Survey. So proud of our committee's work! Lots of surprises in store for you #climatezombies

7.42 AM - 18 Sept 2017

102 RETWEETS 319 FAVORITES

I felt a presence in the doorway and looked up. A skinny, bearded IT-type was hovering there.

He cleared his throat. "I need to—"

"I'm a little busy right now. Could you set up a time with my secretary?"

"She's not at her—"

"Renfield!" I shouted. He flinched. She didn't answer. He tried again.

"I need to install a patch in your case management software. If I don't do it now, you're not going to be able to sync your documents with the server and—"

IT people. They unsettle me. I don't like their constant upgrades and routine maintenance. I don't like their jargon and casual superiority. I don't like their lightning-quick evolution, as a profession, from nonexistent to indispensable. I don't like how the first thing they always tell you when you have a problem is to reboot your computer.

And I hate how it always works.

"This will take five minutes, tops," he said.

I threw my hands up and walked out. Renfield came in from the hallway. I gave her an injured look.

She snorted. "I can't go to the ladies' now?"

I took the mail back to my office and sorted it on the sofa. The IT-type left. I began drafting my letter to the court. Two paralegals dropped off a stack of documents. I finished drafting my letter. It was 9:12.

At 9:32, Marty strolled in, carrying a rolled-up sheaf of paper. "Buon giorno!" he cried.

I deleted an e-mail. "What now?"

"I'm learning Italian." He straightened a sofa cushion. "Elliot and I are spending June in Tuscany."

"That sounds nice."

"You think so?"

I deleted another e-mail. "Not really."

(Travel. I don't get it.)

Marty laughed. He braced himself against one of my wing chairs and stretched his calves. He walked to the window and gazed out, tapping his roll of paper against the glass. His bald head gleamed in the hazy morning light.

"Raney Jane, Raney Jane," he sighed. "Your office is so very . . . plain."

Marty was the first partner I worked for when I joined the firm. He was my mentor and my champion and my friend. We'd had this conversation dozens of times. "It's just an office, Marty."

He turned from the window, eyebrows high. "Just an office? This is where you spend most of your waking life. Where's your personality? Where are your personal effects?"

I pointed to the framed photo on my desk—me and Aaron and the girls at the beach, two summers ago.

"Oh, Raney." Marty wandered to the bookshelf. He wandered back, draping himself in a chair and rubbing his head. "Raney, Raney."

Marty does this. He shambles and roams and circles. Around rooms, around people, around points of contention. He is amiable, avuncular, a ray of sunshine.

And in the courtroom, a vicious killer.

Now he beamed at me. "What are you working on?"

He's also the firm's managing partner, which means he's in charge of assigning new cases. "I'm all booked up," I said.

He contemplated the tip of one highly polished shoe. "It's a small lawsuit."

I deleted another e-mail. "No chance."

"It's tiny," he said. "It's gemlike. It's a gemlike jewel of a case."

"I'm swamped, Marty. Honestly."

Renfield barreled in and slapped a FedEx on my desk. "She can't do it! She don't even have time to eat a fruit cup." She barreled out again.

He tossed me the rolled-up document. It was a complaint, of course. "State court," he said. "Deceptive trade practices and false advertising."

I flipped through it. The defendant was Hyperium, the media company. Not one of our regular clients. "Class action?"

"Barely. Best guess on damages is less than a mil."

I looked up. Our firm did multimillion-dollar cases. Billion-dollar cases. Bet-the-company cases. Not piddly little one-offs like this.

"We're too expensive. Why are they coming to us?"

"They aren't coming to us. They're coming to you."

"Why?"

He didn't respond, but his eyes were twinkling. Marty loved to be mysterious.

I glanced at the clock. It was 9:41.

"They won't want me after this morning," I blurted out. "Nobody will."

I can lift the lid of the chest with Marty. He already knows most of what's inside, anyway.

"Raney Jane," he said kindly. "Gaia Café has been decided. You simply don't know the outcome. Why get all worked up over a little informational asymmetry?"

"Don't expect me to think rationally right now, Marty."

"As you prefer, my dear. But about Hyperium."

"Do I have to?"

He shrugged. "I could always give it to Templeton."

Andy Templeton. Another partner. Completely useless. I flipped through the complaint again. Marty watched me.

"They're coming in tomorrow," he said. "Two o'clock. I reserved a conference room."

"I'm not promising anything."

"I knew I could count on you." He slapped his knees and stood up. "How's our celebrity?"

"On his way home."

"Elliot loves the new book, did I tell you? He's up all night reading it." He rubbed his head and sighed. "Our sex life is over. All he wants is Aaron's glow worm."

I laughed. Marty left. I had nine new e-mails. I answered three and deleted the rest.

My husband, Aaron, is a famous entomologist. Which is a real accomplishment, because how many of those can you name? It wasn't always this way. Five years ago he was toiling in obscurity, an adjunct lecturer at SUNY. In his off-hours he wrote a book, *The Love Song of the Pine Weevil*. It was a kind of biography of insects—their evolution and diversity and importance to the planet. It was beautiful, profound and rejected by every major publisher. A tiny academic one finally accepted it, printing two thousand copies for sheer love of the thing, never expecting it to sell.

But it did. Slowly at first. It was reviewed in an obscure online journal. Then another, slightly less obscure. Independent bookstores embraced it. The reviews kept coming—now in actual newspapers and magazines. The book was chattered about on blogs, Facebook, Twitter.

It was photographed in the hands of celebrities and thumbed through by politicians on their summer vacations. It was hailed as a seminal work on humanity's impact on the planet. On the possibility of hope despite the devastating effects of climate change. On living a meaningful life.

At the end of the year, *Love Song* made every top-ten list. Then it won a Pulitzer.

That was a really good day.

Aaron quit his teaching job. He wrote a follow-up, *Glow Worms Sing Country Songs*. (These titles? Not my idea.) It was an instant bestseller. Suddenly, he was everywhere: lecturing, commentating, sparring with climate change skeptics and antiscience nuts. He turned out to be great on camera: witty, persuasive, charming. Last year, PBS gave him his own nature program. Now he's the Bug Doctor. (Again, not on me.)

The accolades kept coming. He was invited to join the National Committee for a Sustainable Climate—the group he mentioned in his tweets that morning. He'd spent much of the summer working on its highly respected climate change report.

In short, Aaron was America's favorite science guy. We were all about the cosmos for a while, we were big picture and macro. But when we returned to Earth, to the minuscule but meaningful, Aaron was our man.

And mine. I stared at my phone. Sarah could tease me, and Marty could reason with me, but only Aaron could soothe me. It was 9:47. Almost seven o'clock in San Francisco.

I reached for the receiver.

I stopped myself. Keep it together, woman.

I pressed the intercom button. Renfield said, "Yerp?"

"Can you order more of those pens I like?"

"You got a whole box last month!"

"I hawk them on the subway during my lunch hour. They're very popular. Who keeps calling?" The phone had been ringing all morning, but she hadn't put many calls through.

"Dunno," she said. "Some guy."

"Careful with the rabid curiosity. We wouldn't want you scaring off clients."

"I ask his name he hangs up, okay? You want me to reach through the line and twist his nuts till he identifies himself?"

Interesting idea. I revised my letter and e-mailed it to the client for comments. I skimmed Marty's new complaint. It was 10:02. I went online and bought a travel guide to San Francisco. It was 10:10. I spoke with a client. It was 10:15. Two paralegals dropped off a box of files. The phone rang—that number again. Renfield brought me a fax. It was 10:20. Jisun, one of my associates, came in with a case for me to read. It was 10:24. I answered an e-mail. And another. And another.

At 10:30, Stephen, my senior associate, ushered a woman through my door. I wanted to be alone, to watch the clock and stew in my own anxiety. But I couldn't show it, so I stood and shook hands with my new employee, Amanda Hewes. Stephen left to jump on a conference call. I promised to e-mail him when I heard from the court. It was 10:32.

Amanda and I sat down. I explained my current caseload and the kinds of things she'd be doing. I invited her to sit in on my noon meeting with the ACLU. It was 10:48.

I was *dying* inside.

I forced myself to focus. Amanda was poised and pretty, with long dark hair and a quick smile. She seemed bright, eager, interested.

"How was orientation?" I asked.

"Good!" she said.

I waited.

"Boring," she admitted.

"Let's get you started on something more interesting." I passed her Marty's new complaint. It was 10:50. "It's a consumer fraud case. Something about cable television. Why don't you draft me a memo? Review the relevant statutes and do a preliminary analysis of the plaintiff's strengths and weaknesses." She smiled, pleased to be given the responsibility.

"Did Stephen tell you we have a decision coming down in," I checked the clock, "nine minutes?"

Amanda was nodding, saying she'd read up on Gaia Café, the issues were fascinating, so timely, et cetera.

The case has been decided, I told myself. You simply don't know the outcome.

Our conversation was reaching a natural conclusion. She was ready to leave and dive into the work I'd assigned her, but now I wanted her to stay. I couldn't bear the thought of being alone. I began asking random questions. Where did she grow up? What did her parents do? It was 10:54.

I knew from her résumé that she was older than the typical first-year associate—twenty-nine. She'd spent time at a nonprofit between college and law school.

"You used to work at the Hogarth Foundation," I said. "Are you a rabid liberal?"

She laughed. "Only in my off-hours."

I liked her more and more. "What terrible things have people told you about me?" I asked.

That threw her, but she recovered quickly. "Oh, you know. The standard insanely demanding-partner stuff. You work too hard, you make other people work too hard, you're a perfectionist. You probably knew all that."

"I know everything." She laughed again. It was 10:57.

Then she said, "How did you figure out how to be?"

"What do you mean?"

She frowned—at herself, not me. "Poor phrasing. There aren't many women partners here, or at any of the big firms. It must have been challenging to navigate this place, and to do it so well. I guess I'm wondering what that was like. How did you know how to present yourself? How to . . . be?"

"I didn't think about it like that," I said. "I was just myself."

It wasn't that simple, of course—as the imaginary key dangling around my neck might suggest. But I tended to deflect this sort of question. I didn't find the subject all that interesting.

Amanda was more persistent than most. "Really? You never felt like you had to—"

The phone rang.

My stomach lurched.

Don't think, I told myself. Don't think, just answer.

"Here we go!" I reached for the phone.

Let me stop, right here.

Let me pause, hand extended toward the telephone.

This was the critical moment. I didn't know it, of course. But of all the moments in that ordinary-extraordinary morning, this was the one I would return to again and again.

What if I hadn't picked up the phone? That question would haunt me in the months that followed. It would come to me unbidden at work, or during sleepless nights in Brooklyn. While I interrogated Sarah, or sparred with Doctor Bogard. As I relaxed in the most luxurious hotel room in the city. As I huddled in Holding Cell J-21 of the Manhattan Detention Complex.

Answering the phone. Such a simple act, to set so much in motion. I could have waited, let Renfield pick it up.

What then? Where would I be?

Who would I be?

Impossible to know.

I hit speakerphone.

"This is Raney Moore."

Silence. A cough. Then:

"Uh . . . hi!"

Not the court clerk.

"Who is this?"

"I got through to you!" A nervous laugh. "I wasn't sure if . . . okay." The caller cleared his throat. "My name is Tom." A pause. "This is Raney Moore? The Raney Moore who's married to Aaron Moore?"

It was one of Aaron's kooky fans. A bug lover. This happened from time to time. I raised my eyebrows. Amanda smiled.

"That's me, Tom. What can I do for you?"

And the voice said, "For starters, you can tell your husband to stop fucking my wife."

TWO

I GRABBED THE RECEIVER and brought it to my ear. "Excuse me?"

"Your husband is having an affair with my wife," the voice said.

"That's not true."

"I'm sorry, but it is."

Amanda was already up, across the room, pulling the door shut behind her. Despite my confusion, I remember thinking, with odd detachment, Good instincts, that's promising.

"They work together," the voice was saying. "She's his producer. They . . ."

What was going *on*? How had I suddenly found myself in this ludicrous conversation with a total stranger? The voice was needling, querulous. I interrupted.

"You've made a mistake. Aaron wouldn't . . . he doesn't do that."

"I'm sorry. I'm sure this is difficult to hear."

I should hang up, I thought. Should I call the police?

"What are you doing, slandering my husband like this?" I demanded. "Who are you?"

"My name is Tom Nicholson. I'm married to Deirdre Nicholson."

My grip tightened on the receiver. She worked with Aaron. He mentioned her from time to time. But so what?

"My wife and I have been having some problems—"

"Are you trying to blackmail us? I can assure you that you've come to the wrong—"

"Listen," said the voice. "Just *listen*, okay? I've had my suspicions for a while. And I'm not proud of myself, but I logged on to Deirdre's e-mail. I found . . . letters. From your husband. Lots of letters."

I leaned back in my chair. I closed my eyes.

I felt a sudden, enormous rush of pity.

This guy, I thought. This poor slob. His marriage is on the rocks, he's casting about for explanations and he latches on to Aaron. Aaron, who writes lots of e-mails to lots of people. To me, to his publisher, to our children. To his mom. Rambling, chatty, friendly e-mails. It's what he does. He can't help it.

So yes, he was a likely suspect—if you didn't know him. If you did know him, you'd know this was impossible. Aaron would never cheat. He's the opposite of a cheater. He's—

"He's in San Francisco," the voice said. "Doing a reading. Right?"

I felt a tightness in my chest, sudden and sharp.

"My wife is with him. He bought her plane ticket. I found a bunch of messages about the trip. They're a little . . . well, do you want me to forward them to you?"

"No," I said.

"Okay."

"I want to speak with my husband," I said.

"You should do that. You should—"

I hung up.

THREE

I RELEASED THE RECEIVER. I sat back in my chair.

My eyes rested on the phone.

The firm is obsessed with technology. We're constantly replacing cell phones, upgrading software, dispensing tablets and laptops like candy at a parade. But we never switch out the office telephones. I'd had this one for years. It was square, clean, functional. Black and silver, with a green digital display. Three separate lines.

My wife is with him.

The keypad was a tidy grid, buttons shiny from use. I looked at the two long columns of speed-dial buttons. I looked at the row of buttons along the bottom: conference, mute, hold, redial.

I found a bunch of messages about the trip.

The black cord lay on the desk, snugly curled in on itself like a sleeping animal. I hooked a finger into it and pulled. The coils stretched. The handset shifted in its base. I let go.

Do you want me to forward them to you?

I picked up the receiver and dialed Aaron. He answered after two rings.

"Hey, Rane!" His voice was easy and cheerful. "I'm at the airport, about to go through security. Did you hear from the—"

"Is it true, Aaron?"

My voice was even, my breathing calm. I noticed these things from a distance, with mild surprise.

"What's that, hon?"

"Is it true?"

"Is what true?"

"Aaron," I whispered.

"Raney? I don't—"

"I just got a call." My mouth was dry. "From a man named Tom Nicholson."

Silence.

"Aaron." I swallowed. "Is. It. True."

More silence. It lasted four or five seconds.

It felt like four or five years.

"Yes," he said.

And the breath left my body.

Yes. He said yes.

"Okay," I said.

Aaron couldn't say yes. He wouldn't.

But he just did.

I heard him exhale shakily. "Oh, damn. Damn. Goddammit. It's true."

"Okay," I said again.

"Raney? Raney! Please don't—"

I hung up.

FOUR

I RELEASED THE RECEIVER.

Yes.

I breathed. Maybe I blinked.

Yes.

After a while (one minute? ten? an hour?), I realized I was in pain. I investigated.

I was clenching my muscles. All of them.

I relaxed. I moved my toes inside my shoes. I tapped the arm of my chair with one finger. Everything appeared to be in order.

It's true.

The clock read 11:04.

Now, *that* was surprising. That, I marveled at.

It had only been seven minutes!

Your husband. My wife. Affair.

How sure I had been that those words didn't apply to me. Couldn't apply to me. Until I heard them, seven minutes earlier (seven minutes!), they had never, in almost sixteen years, crossed my mind.

Affairs? Sure, they happen. To colleagues. Neighbors. To Sarah and Tad. Not to us.

So, no. I wouldn't have believed it, couldn't have believed it. Not even after the voice said

San Francisco
bought her plane ticket
I didn't believe it. Until Aaron said
Yes.

My breath left me again. I felt hollow, sucked dry. If you opened me up, you would have found a vast black bottomless void.

I looked around. How strange that my office was still standing. That the entire building hadn't exploded, or quietly collapsed into dust. Even though my life was gone.

I pushed back my chair and stretched out on the floor. I screwed my eyes shut. Into my frantic mind came a memory of a yoga class Sarah had nagged me into taking the year before. Hey, I thought. This is a yoga pose. I'm exercising right now. Inadvertently, but still.

Random thoughts, bouncing uncontrollably around my head. I stood up. Paced to the window. Paced back.

"This isn't happening," I said. "This can't be happening."

Aaron. My home and safety. My sweet loving caring funny everything. All morning, as I'd tried to suppress my anxiety, he'd been in the background, supporting me. He was everything to me.

But apparently, I wasn't everything to him.

I sank into my chair. "Breathe." I put my head between my knees. "Breathe." Blood throbbed in my ears. Images flared across my mind. Aaron, in bed. A shadowy form beside him. He turns to her. They begin—

"No. No no no no no nonononono." I felt tears ignite behind my eyes and push forward, hungry for air.

That's what did it, what made me pull myself together. Crying at work? Not going to happen.

I took a deep breath. I smoothed back my hair and adjusted my collar. Placed my hands flat on the desk.

The clock read 11:12.

I thought, *Hey hon.*

Then I thought, *It's the middle of the night here, and I can't sleep.*

The clock read 11:13.

I thought, *Can you tell how much I miss you?*

Then I thought, *I can't wait to see you.*

The clock read 11:14.

I thought, *Love, Aaron.*

And I completely lost my mind.

Rage exploded inside me. It filled me to the fingertips and the roots of my hair. It screamed and shook. Pounded its fists against my rib cage. Shed tears and spat venom.

I bent my head and gripped the edge of the desk. Fury tore at every other emotion I'd felt in the last few minutes. The fear, confusion and heartbreak. The hopelessness and disbelief. My anger was bigger than all that. It incinerated everything in its path.

It burned and burned.

After a long time, it quieted, receding to a little ember pulsing in my chest.

I straightened up. Smoothed my hair again.

I was calm. No. More than calm. I felt purified. Focused. Powerful.

Love, Aaron. The final words of every e-mail he'd ever sent me— even the shortest ones. The words scrawled at the bottom of the notes he used to slip into my lunch every day, back when we were struggling to pay off our student loans and save for a house. The words that ended the message he'd sent me a few hours ago, shortly after he'd violated his wedding vows.

Love, Aaron. Love Aaron.

I loved Aaron. What did Aaron love?

I pulled a legal pad toward me and made a list of the things my husband held dear.

(a) family
(b) scientific credibility
(c) public persona
(d) social—

My phone rang. I hit speakerphone. "This is Raney Moore."

A reedy voice said, "Good morning, counselor. This is Dale Ferguson from Judge Cleary's chambers."

"Hello, Dale."

"Hello. Per my e-mail on Friday, I'm calling to inform you of the judgment in 15-CIV-9121, *Ramona Whelan et al. v. Gaia Café, Inc.* Judge Cleary has found in favor of the plaintiffs on all counts of the complaint."

The plaintiffs. That was us.

All counts. That meant we won.

We won everything.

"Okay," I said.

"The judge will be filing his findings of fact and conclusions of law this afternoon. I'll e-mail you a copy."

"Thank you, Dale." I hung up.

Where was I?

(d) social connectedness

(e) the comforts of home

The clock read 11:26. I pressed the intercom button.

"Yerp?"

"Would you come in here, please?"

My eyes rested on the family photograph on my desk. The four of us were stretched out on a blanket, ocean and sky behind us. Aaron, then me, then Maisie, then Kate. All squashed together, all laughing. Because instead of summer sunshine we had pouring rain and lashing winds. We were freezing to death in our swimsuits. Still, we had so much fun that day.

I opened a drawer and removed a pair of scissors.

Renfield appeared. "What's with the please? You having a religious experience or something?"

"I need you to do a few things for me." I removed the back of the picture frame.

She licked her thumb and turned to a fresh page of her steno pad. "Shoot."

"First, find Stephen and tell him that Judge Cleary ruled in our favor on all counts."

"Oh my Gawd! Congratulations!"

"Thank you. Ask him to tell the rest of the team, and to call Ramona and give her the news." Ramona was our lead plaintiff. "He should also ask the communications department to prepare a press release. I'd like to review it before it goes out."

Renfield put her fists on her hips. "Why aren't you more excited?"

I glanced up from the photograph. "Why aren't you writing this down?"

"All right, all right." She started scribbling again. "Jeez."

"Second, call Darryl and ask him to come up here immediately."

"Which Darryl?"

"Darryl from Litigation Support."

"Doggie Darryl," she muttered, writing. I removed the photograph from the frame.

"Third, print me a copy of that spreadsheet you created last year—the one with all my personal account numbers and passwords. Fourth, go on the Internet and find the top three nonprofit organizations devoted to denying the existence of climate change."

Renfield's thick eyebrows twitched, but she kept writing. I made my first incision, guiding the scissors carefully to separate Aaron's sandy foot from mine.

"Fifth, go into my e-mail and find Aaron's flight information." I rotated the photograph. "Sixth, find a highly rated, non-sleazy Westchester realtor who can meet me at the house this afternoon." Snip—off with his thigh.

"What're you doing to that picture?"

"Seventh, get me a list of the top five divorce lawyers in the city."

"*What?*"

I was in a tricky spot, angling the scissors around the brim of Aaron's baseball cap. "Divorce lawyers. Ask other secretaries. Check the *Law Journal*'s best-of issue. Schedule consultations with whomever you find. My Wednesday afternoon is wide open."

Silence. I looked up. She was glaring at me.

"Quit joking," she said.

"I'm not joking."

I made a final cut. Aaron fluttered away, landing facedown on the blotter. I aligned my wastebasket with the edge of the desk and swept him into it.

"What the hell's the matter with you?" Renfield demanded. "First you act like you don't care about winning that stupid case, now you're—"

"He broke my heart," I said.

She inhaled, her enormous nostrils flaring. I centered the three of us against the glass. I replaced the back of the frame. I returned the photo to its spot on the desk.

"The guy," she said. "The guy who wouldn't leave his name."

"He's the woman's husband."

She stepped back, shaking her head. "It's gotta be a mistake."

"It's not."

"Aaron wouldn't . . . he's not like that."

"I don't want to talk about it."

"But—"

I dropped the scissors into the drawer and slammed it shut. She flinched. Something deep inside the desk rattled and fell.

"I love you," I said. "And you know I love you. But if you ask me another question, if you say another word, if you do anything other than leave this office and *immediately* begin doing what I've asked you to do, I will fire you."

I waited. She studied her steno pad. She bit her lip.

"Please go," I whispered.

At last, she did.

The phone rang. It was Aaron. I called after her, "He goes straight to voice mail!"

I took a deep breath and surveyed my office. My sanctuary. Of course it hadn't crumbled and collapsed. Nothing had changed. I had simply been laboring under—what was Marty's phrase? An informational asymmetry. About my husband. About my life.

Now, that asymmetry had been corrected. I was in control again.

And I knew exactly what to do.

Two paralegals appeared in the doorway. The boy was tall and lanky, his loud tie a protest against the firm's conservative dress code. The girl was tiny, with a neat ponytail, a brown corduroy skirt and canary-yellow shoes. She said, "We have a binder for you?"

I leaned back in my chair, regarding them. "Why do paralegals always travel in twos?"

The boy paralegal hesitated. "Is this a riddle?"

My cell phone rang. Aaron. I switched it off. "That's a three-inch binder you've got there," I said. "It's a one-person job. Why does it take two paralegals?"

They glanced at each other.

"Because we're afraid of you," the girl admitted.

I pointed at the sofa. "Stick around. I could use your help."

Renfield returned. "Here's your spreadsheet. I found his travel information, too."

"Good. Cancel his flight." She left. The phone rang four times, then stopped. I skimmed the spreadsheet, striking half a dozen entries—my phone, the girls' phones, my credit cards. I came around the desk and passed a page to each paralegal.

"You have your phones with you?" They nodded. "Excellent. This list contains my family's complete financial and administrative information. Credit cards, utilities, insurance, et cetera. It includes all relevant customer service numbers, account numbers and access codes. Whatever hasn't been crossed out needs to be canceled right away. Work your way down the list. You'll have to impersonate me or my husband at times—you have my permission to do so."

"Why?" the boy paralegal asked.

"I beg your pardon?"

"I mean, like," he faltered under my stare, "why are we doing this?"

"Do you need a reason?"

"No, I—"

"Do you need a reason, other than because I'm asking you to do it? A reason other than," I smiled at him, "because I said so?"

"This kind of thing is why we travel in pairs," the girl murmured.

"Get cracking," I said. They bent their heads and started dialing.

Renfield came back. "I can't cancel. He already checked in."

"Can you reroute him? Kick him into coach? Order him the vegan meal?" She shook her head. How frustrating.

Renfield left. Darryl arrived. He managed logistics for our trials: organizing temporary offices in cities across the country, managing the movement of people, equipment and tons and tons of paper. He was short, stout, goateed. The Weimaraner on his sweatshirt peered out at me balefully.

"Darryl!" I waved him in. "What moving company do we use here in New York?"

"Citywide," he replied.

I wrote my address on a legal pad, tore off the sheet and held it out to him. "Have them send a large truck and two dozen men to this address immediately. Tell them to call me when they arrive."

He looked dubious. "What if they can't—"

"Then the firm will never hire them again," I said.

Darryl left. Over on the sofa, each paralegal held a phone to one ear. Neither was talking.

"What's going on?"

The girl jumped a little. "Um, we're on hold?"

"Yeah, hi," said the boy. "I'd like to cancel my credit card?"

This was taking too long. I needed more hands.

"Who's the paralegal who's addicted to Adderall?" I asked.

"Therese," the girl said instantly.

"It's a boy."

"Alex."

"Curly hair?"

"Oh," she said. "That's Cameron."

"Renfield!" I shouted. "Get me Cameron!"

The boy paralegal caught my eye. "They're asking why I want to cancel the Visa."

"Say you prefer MasterCard."

"I prefer MasterCard," he said into the phone.

"Yes, hello!" said the girl paralegal. "I'd like to suspend my Internet service?"

Renfield brought in the list of antiscience groups I'd asked for. I skimmed the page. The Institute for American Science, American Priorities USA and the Galileo Institute.

The Galileo Institute. You had to admire the chutzpah.

"I, uh, lost my cell phone?" The boy paralegal glanced at me. I nodded. "Can you shut it off right away?"

A few minutes later, Cameron shot through the door. He was tall, scarecrow thin, wrists and ankles sticking out of his clothes. Corkscrew blond hair and round blue eyes. He'd helped me prepare for an emergency hearing a few weeks earlier, and I'd been impressed by his enthusiasm and resourcefulness—not to mention his imperviousness to fatigue.

He was definitely an oddball, though. He loped across the room, hopped onto one corner of my desk and bent toward me confidentially.

"Greetings, Boss. I heard you were in desperate need of my services."

I handed him the list and the American Express card I shared with Aaron. "Call each of these organizations. Tell them you're Doctor Aaron Moore, and you want to make a donation of twenty-five thousand dollars to help combat the fake media's pernicious lies about so-called man-made climate change."

Cameron glanced at the sheet of paper. "These people are psychopaths."

"Technically they're delusional paranoiacs," I said. "And therefore ideal for my purposes."

"Whoakay." He slid off the desk and pulled out his phone. The other paralegals made room for him on the sofa.

I turned to my computer. I had eleven new e-mails. I answered three and deleted eight. The phone rang four times. I reviewed my list of what mattered most to the person who used to matter most to me.

Social connectedness. Public persona.

I called up Gmail and typed in Aaron's address. I tried a few passwords. None worked. Same with Twitter. What other accounts did he have? Facebook. Instagram. I tried them. Couldn't get in.

"Renfield!" I hollered. "I need that guy who was in here earlier!"

"Darryl?" she hollered back.

"No! The nerdy guy!"

"This is a law firm! You wanna be a little more specific?"

"The IT guy!"

"Do I want it canceled completely?" The girl paralegal looked at me. I gave her a thumbs-up. "Yes, I do," she said.

"Yes, ma'am," Cameron said into his phone. "I'm *that* Aaron Moore."

A few minutes later, the IT-type arrived. I gestured to a chair. I tried a welcoming smile. He looked concerned. "Are you okay?"

So much for pleasantries. "If I give you an e-mail address, can you figure out its password and the passwords of any related social media accounts?"

"That's illegal," he said.

"The question is illegal?"

"No, but doing it is."

"I didn't ask you to do it. I asked you if you could."

He considered a moment, then shrugged. "Probably."

"Good," I said. "Will you?"

"No!"

"Why not?"

"Because it's illegal."

"Please." I laughed. "Who's the lawyer here?"

"That's right, Betty," Cameron said. "Twenty-five *large*."

"Do this for me," I said. The IT-type shook his head. My phone rang four times. "What's your name?"

"Chase."

"Do you enjoy being employed, Chase?"

He scoffed. "You can't fire me for this."

Probably not. But I was crazed with fury and on a mission—I wasn't going to let the norms of civilized behavior slow me down.

So I leaned over my desk, locking my eyes on his. "Can't, Chase? I *can't*? I am a partner of this firm. This vast, powerful firm." I reached wide with my arms, embracing the office, the floor, the entire building. "A firm that employs the finest legal minds in the world. A firm that consistently tops the national rankings in every metric that matters. I didn't get here through can't, Chase. None of us got here through can't. I think it's safe to say that at this firm, we don't *do* can't."

"Disconnect it immediately," said the girl paralegal.

"Because I don't need it anymore," said the boy paralegal.

"Yes, sir!" Cameron cried. "You're talking to the Bug Doctor!"

Chase looked uneasy, but he held firm. "Just because you're a partner doesn't mean you can—"

"Oh, but Chase. It does. It does mean that. Unlike you, I'm not an employee. I am an *owner*. I own this firm. See this?" I picked up my stapler. "I own this stapler, Chase. I own all the staples in this stapler." I waved it in the air. "I own *all* the staples in *all* the staplers in this *entire building*."

"Publicize my donation on your website?" Cameron's eyes flicked over to me. I nodded. "You betcha, Wayne!"

"They're my staples, Chase. All of them. And I can take them away. I can take everything away."

Cameron read my credit card number into his phone. The girl paralegal and the boy paralegal ended their calls, turned to each other and high-fived. I had managed, through my urgency and intensity, to get them into the spirit of the thing. I was good at that—at rousing people to extraordinary effort, convincing them that what they were doing was necessary, meaningful. Even when they had no clue what was going on.

I watched the IT-type. I waited.

Finally, he relented. "Give me the e-mail address."

I stepped back from my desk. Chase sat down at my computer and typed a string of numbers into the address bar. The screen filled with flashing Cyrillic script.

"Don't look," he muttered. I turned away. The phone had stopped ringing. I wandered to the window and surveyed the city.

I felt fantastic!

All my life, I'd taught myself never to surrender to anger. Sure, I'd faked it sometimes. Anger can be a handy rhetorical strategy, a useful bargaining technique. But I always kept the real thing at bay. I thought anger, like any strong emotion, would cloud my judgment. That if I gave way, some primal part of me would take over, and I wouldn't be able to wrest my true self back.

It wasn't like that at all! I was in my element, doing what I do best. Giving orders. Strategizing under pressure.

I was leaning in. With a vengeance.

Renfield brought in a stack of expense reports. I sat in an armchair and started reviewing them. One of my partners, Wally Fanucci, stuck his grinning red face through the doorway.

"Moore!"

"Fanucci!"

"Gaia Café! Huzzah!"

"Thanks."

"Hell yeah! Way to stick it to those pasture-raised sonsabitches." Wally surveyed the busy room, gripping the doorframe with a meaty hand. "Another case blow up?"

I wasn't ready to explain. "Something like that."

He made the sign of the cross and disappeared.

A few minutes later, Amanda walked in. She looked at the paralegals on the sofa and the IT-type behind the desk. "Is this the ACLU meeting?"

I'd forgotten about my twelve thirty. "Renfield! Where are those useless do-gooders?"

She poked her head through the door. "Emily called. They're ten minutes away."

"You're in." The IT-type pushed away from the desk. "And I was never here."

Cameron ended a call. "Done, Boss."

"I'm done, too," said the boy paralegal.

"What's next?" said the girl.

What's next? I thought.

Anything. I could do anything.

"How hard would it be to hire a couple dozen clowns on short notice?"

"For a woman who can charge seventy-five grand to her Amex?" Cameron said. "It would be child's play."

"Then I want clowns. As many clowns as possible, meeting my husband's flight."

All three of them started typing furiously. I turned to Amanda. "I got involved in this lawsuit a few months ago. I think you'll find it very rewarding."

She looked so lost. "It involves clowns?"

"No. The ACLU." The IT-type had arranged Aaron's accounts in a series of cascading windows on my screen. His e-mail was on top.

Seeing it—something so private, now exposed—made me hesitate. What if Tom Nicholson was wrong? What if Aaron thought I was asking about something else?

What if it was all a big mistake?

I scrolled down his in-box. It took no time at all to find an e-mail from DNicholson, sent yesterday afternoon:

Flight just landed. Be at the hotel in 45. Can't wait to see you. xoD

Were there more? Her husband said there were. I didn't want to see them. I couldn't. I—

"Raney?" said Amanda.

I looked up from the screen. "Does anyone know how to delete a Gmail account?"

"That's pretty dire, Boss," Cameron said. "Are you sure you want to?"

"Do *not* ask her that," the boy paralegal muttered.

The girl paralegal came around the desk and walked me through the process. Two minutes later, Aaron's account was gone.

"Permanently?" I asked.

She nodded, eyes grave.

The phone rang. Renfield poked her head in. "Jim Schleifman's on one."

Jim was the client I was supposed to speak to about settlement—

(e) on the morning's to-do list, before I scrapped the list in favor of a scorched-earth campaign against my husband's existence. Still, clients were clients. I hit speakerphone. "Big Jim!"

"Raney!" he shouted. He always shouted. "What the hell?"

"Sorry, Jim. The morning got away from me."

"Happens to the best of us. Give me the good news."

I told him the plaintiffs in his case wanted thirty million. He swore viciously. I said I could get them to twenty-seven. He swore harder. I had an idea. The boy paralegal was staring into space. I hit the mute button and snapped to get his attention.

"There's a car in the long-term lot at JFK. I want it towed." I gave him the make, model and license plate number. Then I unmuted the phone and explained to Jim why twenty-seven was a good deal. After another torrent of profanity, he assented. I called one of my associates, Jisun, and asked her to start drafting the papers.

"I have some questions about the Hyperium memo," Amanda said. "But . . . maybe now isn't a good time?"

I clicked over to Aaron's Twitter account. "Now is always a good time."

The boy paralegal put a palm over his phone. "They won't tow unless someone is there waiting."

"Renfield will order you a car." He left.

I turned back to my computer. Aaron had 3.2 million followers. Popular guy.

"I'm wondering how much detail you want regarding the liability of the Hyperium subsidiaries that are named as defendants," Amanda said. "Should I . . ."

A box at the top of Aaron's feed asked:

What's Happening?

I clicked on it and began to type.

Anybody know where I can find a reasonably priced hooker to take a dump on my face?

I deleted it without posting.

". . . and I wasn't sure whether you wanted a full analysis of . . ."

I know the big debate is cows vs. horses. But trust me: for depth of penetration, nothing beats a sheep.

I deleted that one, too.

"Don't worry about corporate structure at this point," I told Amanda. "We can ask them about it tomorrow."

My tweets were too wacky, too out there. Aaron was widely admired, even beloved. If he started tweeting about appalling sexual fetishes, everyone would know he'd been hacked.

I needed something more subtle.

"I was also wondering whether you'd like me to separate out the analysis of—"

"That congressman," I said. "With the Twitter scandal. Who was that?"

"Uh, all of them?" Cameron said.

"I mean the guy who sent crotch shots to random women. Then he ran for mayor."

"Anthony Weiner!" they all said at once.

"Weiner!" I snapped my fingers. "What did he do, exactly? The first time, I mean."

"I think he meant to send the pictures as direct messages, but accidentally posted them to his public feed," Amanda said.

"Accidentally posted them to his public feed." I started typing. "To answer your question, keep the analysis high level. At this point, I only need to know whether there's any credible basis for dismissing the complaint."

I finished typing a new tweet. I read it.

I thought, I can't post that.

I thought, *Love, Aaron.*

I thought, *xoD.*

I hit Tweet.

Aaron Moore
@RealAaronMoore

Hey @DavidHKoch Thanx for the $$! You & Chas shd be pleased w/ final NCSC report. Scrubbed the heck outta that data!

12.02 PM - 18 Sept 2017

I counted to fifteen. Then I typed:

Sorry folks—not for public consumption.

I hit Tweet a second time.

I was pierced with doubt.

This was a waste of time. Nobody was going to believe that the environmental movement's newest hero was secretly in the pay of Republican supervillains. It was too implausible.

I should have stuck with sheep sex.

The ACLU people arrived. Emily bounced into the room, hugging Renfield and throwing herself into a chair. She used to work at the firm, so she was very much at ease here. Her boss, David, followed her in. He was a mild-mannered guy, an ACLU lifer. He always seemed a little uncomfortable when he visited our offices. Hesitant, peering around, as if he expected to pass an open doorway and spot a herd of plutocrats smoking cigars and deciding the next election.

That would never happen. We keep those doors locked.

"Your chairs suck, Raney," Emily complained. "Ten seconds and my ass is on fire."

"Should I buy new ones, or throw more money at your useless expert?" I held up the report they were here to discuss.

David looked stricken. "Are there problems with the draft?"

Emily laughed. "No worries. 'Useless' is high praise in this room."

I introduced them to Amanda. David glanced back at the sofa. The girl paralegal was typing rapidly. Cameron was staring at the ceiling, one knee jiggling up and down.

"Em, give Amanda an overview of the lawsuit. Then we can talk about the report."

"So here's the deal," Emily said. "Anybody who's accused of a crime is constitutionally entitled to an attorney, right? Well, New York's system of appointing counsel to the poor is fucked, and we're going to sue the shit out of them."

She launched into an explanation of the right to counsel, *Gideon v. Wainwright* and flaws in the state's indigent defense system. I checked Aaron's Twitter account. A box at the top of his feed said, "View 67 new Tweets."

I clicked on it. A series of messages unscrolled on the screen.

Science Times
@ScienceTimes

Is this a joke? RT @RealAaronMoore: Hey, @DavidHKoch Thanx for the $$! You & Chas shd be pleased w/ final NCSC report . . .

Faru Marzeen
@Amazing_Faru

Whats @RealAaronMoore doing tweeting at #greatsatan @DavidHKoch re upcoming climate change report? Scrubbing data? WTF?

They went on and on. People wondered if it was a gag, a parody, a viral marketing campaign for *The Bug Doctor.* As I skimmed the tweets, four more arrived. Then six. Then nine. Then eleven.

One was from a science journalist with whom Aaron had become friendly.

George McHenry
@McGeorge

Hey, @RealAaronMoore, people are confused. Can you explain this?

Eight more tweets appeared. Then nineteen. Then twenty-three.

Stop this, I told myself. You could ruin him.

Ruin? my anger said. Like he ruined your marriage? Like he ruined your life?

Right. I typed:

That was a private message. I have no further comment.

I hit Tweet.

"The idea is we're going to represent defendants in their criminal cases?" Amanda asked.

"We don't do criminal defense," I explained. "This lawsuit is aimed at systemic deficiencies."

HuffPostScience
@HuffPostScience

@RealAaronMoore, are you admitting you tried to dm the Koch brothers?

I replied:

I'm not discussing a nonpublic communication.

People jumped all over that, of course.

What do u mean nonpublic? Its in ur public feed!

This is satire. It doesnt sound like him.

I always thought there was something suspicious about him. The way he burst out of nowhere with #LoveSong?

Nah. Hes been hacked

A botanist named Viv Westman, whose hippy-dippy flower book Aaron reviewed unfavorably a few months ago, weighed in.

Concerned abt troubling Qs raised in @RealAaronMoore's apparent twitter misfire.

McHenry tried to help Aaron out.

You need to clear this up, @RealAaronMoore. It looks bad.

I responded:

Good idea, George.

I deleted the original tweet.

Amanda asked a question about the Sixth Amendment. Emily responded. I clicked over to Aaron's Facebook page, where his tweets were appearing in a steady stream. I posted an update:

My Twitter has been hacked! Disregard all tweets!

Cameron was waving to me from the sofa.

"Strippers!" he whispered loudly.

David looked back at him, startled.

"What?" I said.

"Hire a bunch of strippers! To go along with the clowns!"

David gaped at Cameron, then at me.

Tempting, but a little too on the nose. I shook my head.

I toggled back to Twitter, checking the Mentions tab, which collected all references to Aaron across the site. By deleting the original tweet I had, of course, thrown gasoline on the fire.

HE DELETED THE TWEET!!! HE DELETED THE TWEET!!
#coverup

No worries—I got a screenshot. ow.ly/JxQmR

Is this for real?

OMFG check out this press release from Galileo Fdn . . .
Moore donated 25 grand! ow.ly/JxQmR

I clicked on the link, which took me to a press release touting the large contribution and quoting glowing praise from "Aaron." I hadn't realized how nicely those donations would dovetail with Aaron's Twitter snafu.

I cant believe this is happening. #heartbroken

Is that the $$ you got from the Koch bros, @RealAaronMoore? Decided to funnel it back to the cause?

He's saying on FB he's been hacked.

Yeah right. The first refuge of the twitter fuckup. #dmfail

I clicked back to Aaron's home screen and wrote:

My message has been grossly misinterpreted and taken out of context.

George McHenry quickly responded.

Explain the context, Aaron. That's all people want.

I smiled. Then I looked up. Emily's eyes slid away as she explained to Amanda, "We retained an expert to do a survey and identify state-wide problems. This is his preliminary report."

Back in Aaron's main feed, a handful of people were arguing that it must be a hack or a bad joke. They were being shouted down by the taunters and the mockers, as well as by more concrete evidence.

OMG another donation! RT: @AmerPriorities: Bestselling scientist Aaron Moore donates $25,000 to the cause of fighting liberal hysteria with #RealFacts.

Last chance, @RealAaronMoore. Explain yourself.

I wrote:

I refuse to be bullied. This is #fakenews!

I clicked back to Aaron's Mentions. They'd exploded with hundreds of tweets discussing, excoriating and defending @RealAaron Moore. As I scrolled, ten more appeared. Twenty-two. Forty-seven. Some people were amused. Others were concerned. More were offended, horrified.

I kept refreshing the screen. The tweets kept coming.

I thought about the woman who posted a terrible AIDS joke and became an international pariah. The man who lost his job when a sexist remark went viral. The comedian scorned for offensive jokes about gay people. I'd read about these unfortunates. I'd pitied them. Their punishments seemed so wildly disproportionate to their crimes.

I just added my husband to their ranks. How did I feel about that?

Be at the hotel in 45.

I felt fine, thanks.

The phone rang. Renfield stuck her head around the door. "The movers are on line one."

Emily couldn't keep quiet any longer. "Movers?"

I picked up the phone. "Hello. Who's this?"

"My name is Arnault," said a gravelly, accented voice.

"You're at the house, Arnault?"

"Yes, madam."

"Good. The security code is 2739. I want you to do three things. First—"

"Wait, please. I find a pen."

"With any luck, the state will make changes based on initial discovery," David was telling Amanda.

I jumped in. "If they don't, we'll be prepared to move directly to trial."

Arnault came back on the line, and I finished instructing him. "Any questions?"

"No, madam."

"Excellent. I'll be there in two hours." I hung up.

What an asshole. #deadtome

A traitor. In it for the money.

Lets burn his stupid-ass books.

"Raney?" Emily said. "What's going on?"

I swiveled away from my computer and picked up the report. "What do you mean?"

"I mean that I know you, okay? I know this place. Those elevator doors open into Crazytown, and there's no going back. But this is different. Clowns? Movers?" She looked around, bewildered. "What the fuck is happening here?"

I understood. I did. From the outside, things probably seemed strange.

But from where I was sitting, everything was great. I'd never felt better.

"We could come back another time," David suggested.

"Of course not." I opened the report. "Let's dive in."

FIVE

TWENTY MINUTES LATER, Amanda showed Emily and David out.

"Paralegals." I swiveled my chair to face them. "Give me a status report."

"We canceled your electricity, heating oil, telephone, Internet, cable television, garbage collection and home alarm system," said the girl paralegal. "Your husband's cell phone was cut off. And Jamie says the car is at Murray's Auto Body in Bedford Village."

"Jamie?"

"The, um . . ." She pointed at the empty space next to her on the sofa.

"Jamie." I nodded. "Right. What else?"

It was Cameron's turn. "We canceled two debit cards, three Visa cards and a Discover. When his flight lands, your husband will be met by eleven clowns and a videographer." He paused, with a slight smile. "In case you want documentation for posterity."

"Good thinking. How would you both like to do a little shopping?"

I handed them a (functioning) credit card and an address in Brooklyn. They trooped out. Marty entered. "Congratulations!"

"What for?"

He gave me a puzzled look. "Gaia Café, of course."

Oh, that. I reached under my desk for my bag. "You were right all along."

"You know how much I love saying I told you so." Hands in his pockets, he rocked back on his heels. "What are you and Aaron doing to celebrate?"

I leafed through a few file folders. "Getting a divorce."

"Naturally." He walked out, chuckling.

Next came Amanda, knocking hesitantly on the doorframe. I tossed a sheaf of papers into my bag. "I'm taking the rest of the day off. You're clear on what I need for the Hyperium meeting tomorrow?"

"I think so. I'll e-mail you the memo tonight." She paused. "Are you . . . okay?"

I was instantly enraged. How dare she ask me that? Who was she? A new associate. A nobody. She had no right to feel sorry for me. She—

Easy, I told myself.

She was innocent. And feeling intensely awkward, no doubt. Stanford Law School doesn't offer a class on how to act when a partner's marriage falls apart in front of you.

"I'm fine," I said.

"Good. I didn't say anything to anyone about—"

"Thank you." I zipped my bag. "I don't care, but thank you."

She nodded. I straightened some papers until she said goodbye and left. I pressed the intercom and asked Renfield to order my car.

Before packing up my laptop, I checked Twitter, clicking on Aaron's direct messages. He'd received dozens—from friends expressing support or confusion, from fellow members of the climate change committee requesting clarification, from the media. A reporter from the Associated Press asked whether he'd really received funding from the Koch brothers. The *Wall Street Journal* queried whether he'd interfered with the results of the NCSC study. A producer from Fox News guaranteed him a fair hearing if he'd be willing to sit for an interview.

And there was this, from Aaron's literary agent, Eve:

Aaron??? Your phone says it's disconnected, emails to your account are bouncing back. Can you please call me?

Renfield came in and watched me shut down my computer.

"The *Times* called," she said. "That reporter who followed the trial. She wants to talk to you about the verdict."

"I'll call her from the car." Renfield handed me a few other messages. I flipped through them.

"I haven't gotten those names for you," she said. "Those divorce lawyers you wanted."

"Okay."

"You can fire me if you want."

I stopped tidying and looked up at her. "You know I'd never fire you."

"Aaron?" she said mournfully. "I can't believe it."

How I longed at that moment to let go. To stand and allow her to wrap her arms around me. To rest my cheek on her shoulder and inhale the musty smell of her cardigan while she patted my back and muttered and swore.

Instead, I picked up my bag.

"Thanks for your help today. See you tomorrow."

Downstairs, Jorge was waiting. He opened the door for me, then hurried around the idling car.

"How you doing, Miz Moore?"

I buckled my seat belt. "Fine. Yourself?"

"Not bad, not bad. Knocking off early today, huh?"

"I've got some personal matters to take care of. I'm leaving my husband."

Jorge twisted around, eyes wide. "You mean like, *leaving* him leaving him?"

"Yes. Could you start driving?"

"Uh, sure." He pulled into traffic. "Where we headed?"

"To my house. Then we'll pick up my daughters from school. Then we'll come back to the city."

"You got it." He glanced at me a few times in the rearview before focusing on the road. I contemplated the sky above the river. Aaron was probably somewhere over Nevada by now. And he didn't have a clue.

I felt a qualm.

This is not how I normally behave. I'm not vindictive and lacerating and cruel. Stranding my husband financially? Dismantling our home? Attacking his reputation? Was I being too extreme?

xoD

Goodbye, qualm.

I switched on my cell phone. The latest of my many, many new texts read:

—WTF Aaron's twitter?

Sarah. I wanted to call her, tell her everything. But I'd barely held it together with Renfield—I would dissolve completely in the face of Sarah's empathy and outrage. I typed a quick message.

—He cheated on me. Not joking. Going to pick up the girls. I'll be in touch.

I took out my stack of messages and started returning calls.

THE MOVERS were finishing up when we arrived. I met Arnault, a tall, somber Frenchman in a red T-shirt and lumbar support belt. Per my instructions, Aaron's clothes and books would be sent to his mother's house in Vermont. The rest of our belongings were in a huge truck parked in the driveway, waiting to follow us into the city. I walked through the empty rooms with the realtor Renfield had found. She raved about the design, the layout, the view. She was sure it would sell in no time.

Back in the car, Jorge tapped the address of Kate and Maisie's school into his GPS, and we were off. I leaned back in my seat, relaxing my muscles for what felt like the first time in hours. The house was dealt with. Soon I'd have the girls, and we could head to Brooklyn, where—

The girls.

The *girls.*

What was I going to tell the girls?

In the last four hours, as I systematically demolished my husband's existence, it hadn't once occurred to me to consider the possible effect of all this on our daughters.

I always think of everything. But I hadn't once thought of them.

I berated myself for a few minutes, silently and viciously. Then I shook it off. I made a mistake. It happens. And it's not like I don't love my daughters. I love them desperately. For the first three years of their lives I woke every night and tiptoed into their room to make sure they were breathing. I still do that occasionally. (Regularly.) My love for them is a little convulsive, a little hysterical. Every moment I'm with them I'm basically physically restraining myself from pouncing on them and smothering them with overwhelming maternal adoration.

They know it, too. This is not that story, okay? This is not the story of an ambitious, soulless career woman who chases every brass ring of professional success to the neglect of her affection-deprived, rudderless and emotionally crippled offspring.

No. This is the story of an ambitious, soulless career woman who chases every brass ring of professional success *and whose offspring are only too aware that she loves them.*

The girls had just turned one when I started at the firm. Most associates—men and women—wait a few years before starting a family. Some put it off until they make partner, or transition to a more forgiving job. I didn't have that luxury, because . . . well, I'll get to that. The point is, most people delay parenthood because law firm life is all-consuming. Six-day weeks are the norm. Sixteen-, eighteen-hour days are standard. Canceled holidays, postponed vacations—those things come with the territory. You are captive to the schedules of the courts, the needs of your supervising partner, the machinations of the opposing side.

From the very beginning, I excelled. I rarely made mistakes. I went above and beyond, over and over again.

(Swaggering . . .)

I was equally committed as a parent. I put the girls to bed every night I wasn't traveling. I got them ready for school every morning. I never missed a birthday party, a school play or a doctor's visit.

How? Sheer force of will. Constant exhaustion. Giving up things other people enjoyed: hobbies, pastimes. A social life. I didn't want to be a great lawyer and a bad mother. I didn't want to be a bad lawyer and a great mom. So I threw myself into both with the same determination. It got easier as they got older. By the time I made partner—

The car hit a bump in the road, jolting me back into the present. Instead of reminiscing about my maternal glory days, I needed to be figuring out how to inform Kate and Maisie that life as they knew it was over.

How do people tell their children that they're getting a divorce? This was too important to trust to instinct. I needed research.

I googled "explaining divorce to children."

The search yielded "about 6,190,000 results."

There's a real dearth of guidance out there, I guess.

The first result was "How to Tell Your Children You're Getting a Divorce: 20 Tips."

Twenty tips? Who has time for that? Retirees, maybe. The incarcerated. Not me.

The next result was from a site called Babycenter.com. Maisie and Kate weren't babies. I wasn't about to start talking down to them.

Next: "Three Things to Tell—"

Forget it. If twenty was too many, three was too few.

"The Idiot's Guide to Telling Your Children About Divorce"? Sorry, no.

The next one looked promising: "Seven Steps for Breaking the News of Your Divorce to the Kids." Seven—a totally manageable number! I skimmed the list as we joined a line of cars in the school drive. The moving truck pulled in behind us. Children streamed out of the main building. I caught sight of Kate, slim and sandy haired, loping along in the company of two boys. I powered down the window and waved her over. She froze. Her eyes widened. She approached slowly, trailed by the boys. They gathered around the car, gawking at me.

"What are you doing here?" she asked.

"Picking you up from school, of course."

"But—"

"Let's go." I was on edge about our looming conversation.

"Yo, Kate's mom," said one boy.

"Sweet ride," said the other.

Arnault had left the truck to consult with Jorge. "What's in the truck?" Kate asked.

"All our earthly possessions. Where's your sister?"

"I'll text her." Kate pulled out her phone. The boys were still staring at me.

"Kate, who are these people?"

"Strangers who pay me to sleep with them," she replied, eyes on her screen.

I sighed. "Get in the car."

"No worries, Kate's mom," one boy told me. "She's totally joking."

"Yeah," said the other. "She pays us."

They guffawed. Kate punched one of them in the chest. "Bye, losers." She opened the door and took the backward-facing seat, across from me. "I thought we were taking the bus home today."

"We're not going home. We're moving."

"When?"

"Now."

"Where to?"

"Brooklyn."

Kate opened her mouth to ask another question, but thought better of it. Kate has excellent instincts. She buckled her seat belt. She swiped her hair from her forehead and straightened the pleats of her skirt. She pulled a book out of her bag.

The door opened and Maisie stuck her head in. "Who died?"

"Nobody."

She threw her backpack inside and clambered after it, settling next to Kate. Although "settling" is the wrong way to describe anything Maisie does. She is frenetic, agitated, constantly in motion. She is Kate reflected in a cracked mirror, disheveled, fritzy and distractible.

"You wouldn't be here if someone wasn't dead," she insisted.

"Weren't dead," Kate said.

"Shut up. It's Nana, isn't it."

"It's not Nana."

Maisie pressed. "But it's somebody. The way you answered it has to be somebody."

"Nobody died!" I cried. "I promise you, nobody died."

She pursed her lips, unconvinced. She dragged her backpack up from the floor. Half the contents spilled out.

"Dumbass," Kate muttered.

"Anal cleft," Maisie muttered back.

"Enough!" I snapped.

"We all set, Miz Moore?"

"Yes, Jorge. We're going to Brooklyn. Park Place between Vanderbilt and Underhill."

Kate cocked her head. "Your old house?"

"That's where we live now."

Maisie gasped. "Our house burned down!"

I hadn't even begun, and already this conversation had gone off the rails.

The car pulled away from the curb. Kate was frowning at her phone. "What's with Dad's Twitter?"

Maisie read over Kate's shoulder. "Yikes."

I needed to Explain the Decision Using Neutral and Productive Language. Then I needed to Stress the Love. After that I needed to—

"Mom?"

I tossed my phone onto the seat. I didn't need guidance. These were my daughters. My people. They were smart and kind and good. They were solid and sound. I knew how to talk to them.

"I have some bad news," I said.

They waited.

"Your father and I . . ."

Courage, I told myself.

"We're . . . splitting up."

"Huh?" said Maisie.

"What?" said Kate.

I tried again. "We're . . . we're separating."

"Ha ha," Maisie said.

"Seriously, Mom." Kate smirked. "Don't quit your day job."

They didn't believe me? "I'm not joking."

Silence. They exchanged a look. Kate tried again, but she was less certain this time. "Cut it out, Mom. You're being weird."

"We're going to stay in Brooklyn while I figure out our next step. I'll find a good school for you in the city, and—"

Maisie was shaking her head. She waved her hands, silently begging me to stop. But I had to get through this.

"I know it's sudden. I know it's a surprise—a shock, even. I want to stress how much your father and I love—"

"No!" Kate cried. "This is not—no!"

Maisie had drawn back in her seat, staring with scared eyes. Kate was angled forward, hands on her knees.

"This morning, you came in and woke us up. That was, what, nine hours ago? Had you and Dad . . . I mean, had this already happened?"

"No," I admitted.

"But now it has? How is that possible?"

"I can't give you the details right now."

"Shouldn't Dad be here? When Audra's parents split up, they sat her down together and—"

"Oh my God." Maisie began to shake. "Oh my God."

I reached for her. "Breathe, honey. You have to breathe."

"This is nuts!" Kate cried. "This doesn't just happen!"

"I'm afraid it happens all the time."

"No!" she shouted. "Not you guys. Most people's parents fucking hate each other."

"Watch your language, Katherine."

"You and Dad are *happy*."

"Why are we here?" Maisie wailed. "What's going on?"

"Maisie, please calm down. Your asthma—"

"Why, Mother?" Kate said. "Why is this happening? Why why why why whywhywhywhywhy?"

I scrabbled around inside Maisie's bag and found her inhaler. I should have known their first question would be the one I couldn't answer. Maisie pressed the pump and took a deep breath. I couldn't tell them the truth. Kate was so judgmental. Maisie so emotional. Their father's infidelity could have serious repercussions in their lives and romantic relationships. I wasn't going to have that on my hands.

Especially since none of this was my fault.

Kate crossed her arms. "There are only so many reasons people divorce."

Maisie nodded and wiped her nose. "They aren't like Jordan's parents, who can't stand each other."

"Nobody's an alcoholic," Kate said, "like Sam's dad."

We were stuck in traffic. I willed the car to go faster. I willed a huge distraction, like an earthquake or an alien invasion. Because I'd forgotten who I was dealing with. My daughters were inquisitive, obstinate, relentless.

And smarter than Aaron and me combined.

"Could it be money problems?" Kate asked.

Maisie shook her head. "I checked our balances this morning."

"Maisie Clare!"

"Sorry, Mom! I get anxious."

Kate peered at her phone. "Growing apart? We would have seen that coming."

I stared at her. "Are you . . . *googling* this?"

I reached for the phone, but she held it away. "Religious or cultural differences?"

"Impossible," Maisie said. "They agree about everything."

I was helpless. A fox cowering under a hedgerow. I could hear the beat of hooves and the baying of hounds, growing ever closer. "Girls, I don't think—"

"Abuse?" Kate continued. "No way. Lack of communication? They never shut up. Midlife crisis, nah, gambling, ditto, sexual—"

She broke off.

"What?" Maisie said. Kate looked at me.

"Don't," I whispered.

"Infidelity," she said.

Silence.

"No way." Maisie almost laughed. "Not Daddy."

"Mom?"

I could have lied. I'd been lying all day. To my employees. To Aaron's Twitter followers. To the Visa Network.

But I was tired of lying. And I couldn't lie to my children. Not about this.

So I nodded.

Maisie buried her face in her hands. Kate threw her phone across the car. "That asshole!"

"Kate, please."

"How could he do that to you?"

"I can't believe this is happening!" Maisie sobbed.

I opened my arms. They unbuckled their seat belts and flew across the car. I tried to console them. They tried to console me. We all failed.

After a while, Maisie said, "Where is he now?"

Kate turned on her ferociously. "Who gives a shit?"

"He's flying home," I said.

They had more questions: Who was she? How did I find out? Had I talked to him? What did he say? I evaded them all. Eventually, we were quiet. I had a girl on either side of me, my arms around their shoulders. I tipped my head back and closed my eyes, utterly spent.

What have I done?

My phone pinged. I ignored it. The girls gazed out at the traffic. Jorge, unwilling witness to the day's circus, kept his eyes fixed on the road. No doubt I'd have another new driver in the morning. I couldn't blame him.

WE ARRIVED in Brooklyn at six thirty. The beautiful late-summer day had turned into a crisp early-fall evening. The old neighborhood was looking good. There was a new coffee shop on Washington Avenue, a juice bar. A condo building had arisen on the corner of my block, silver skinned and futuristic. We turned onto Park Place. The houses were all brownstones, models of thoughtful, historically sensitive renovation.

Until we got to mine.

What an eyesore. Peeling paint, broken windows. A relic of dirty old irascible Brooklyn. My parents bought it forty years ago, before I was born. They ran a legal clinic out of the parlor floor, helping addicts, welfare moms, the poor. They died when I was three. Car accident. My grandmother left her retirement community on Long Island and moved in to take care of me. She lived here until she passed away, ten years ago. That's when I should have had it cleaned it up, put it on the market. But I never seemed to find the time.

A man was crouched at the base of the stoop, his back to us. Faded jeans and filthy sneakers. Homeless, no doubt. Possibly deranged. I braced myself.

He straightened and turned. He was slim and bearded and wore a T-shirt that said THIS IS WHAT A COOL CAT LADY LOOKS LIKE.

"What are you doing?" I said.

He adjusted his glasses. "Checking out these steps. There are some big cracks and gaps, and I'm hoping to . . ." He trailed off. "Hey. Are you the owner?"

I crossed my arms.

"I live next door," he said. "My name is Wade. I—"

"I know who you are. You keep sending me letters."

"I'd really like to talk to you about—"

"The house isn't for sale."

"But it's falling apart. It hasn't been occupied for years."

"It's occupied now." I marched past him up the steps. The girls trailed behind me. The moving truck pulled up.

"You need me to stick around, Miz Moore?" Jorge was standing on the sidewalk next to the perplexed hipster.

"No, Jorge. Thank you."

"You bet." He shifted from one foot to the other. "So, good luck with everything." Kate and Maisie waved to him.

Arnault and his team began unloading boxes onto the sidewalk. A cab stopped, and Cameron and the girl paralegal tumbled out, dragging grocery bags. Everyone followed me inside. The wallpaper was peeling, and the pendant lamp was thick with dust. But it still smelled like it did when I grew up there—floor wax, damp and Grandma's lavender perfume.

Cameron inhaled deeply. "Eau de Creepyville."

"Where shall we begin?" Arnault inquired.

The paralegals put away groceries. The movers went room by room, unrolling rugs, hefting furniture, hanging art—reconstructing our suburban home in this decrepit space.

In a few hours, they were finished. I thanked everyone and sent them on their way. Kate, Maisie and I headed up to an eerie facsimile of their bedroom—beds, desks, nightstands, all in place. We talked. They cried. Finally they fell asleep, miserable and exhausted.

I couldn't face the master bedroom, so I climbed the stairs to a room on the fourth floor, now occupied by odds and ends and an ancient leather sofa. My childhood bedroom.

Outside, night had fallen. Neighbors were dragging garbage bins to the curb. A woman walked her dog. A teenager glided by on a skateboard, texting.

I glanced at my phone. It was 10:59.

Twelve hours.

Twelve hours, and I'd botched everything.

My rage vanished, leaving me defenseless against a wave of regret. I'd deprived Aaron of his family. Dismantled his everyday life. Diabolically undermined his professional credibility.

And the girls—what had I done to them? Tearing them out of their lives, revealing a horrible truth about their parents' marriage they should never have had to deal with.

I had been deranged, despotic, unforgivably cruel.

But look at what Aaron had done! How could he?

I picked up my phone and scrolled through the day's many e-mails. Back to the beginning.

Hey hon. It's the middle of the night here, and I can't sleep.

I read it carefully, searching for signs. Where had we gone wrong? How had I lost him?

> We should come here, maybe after the first of the year? Just the
> two of us.

I reached the part I'd skipped earlier, already absorbed by the demands of the day.

> I used to think going on a book tour would be so much fun. Doing
> readings, meeting booksellers, talking to readers. Now I know
> better. The people couldn't be nicer, but it's exhausting. And
> isolating. I'm a version of myself that I don't quite recognize. I feel
> disconnected from real life. Too far away from you.

There was more, but I couldn't go on. I dropped the phone, and at last I let go. Alone in my childhood room, gasping for breath, shaking as I sobbed, I cried, and I cried, and I cried.

PART TWO

SIX

I WOKE JUST before five, gasping for breath. Someone had been chasing me through a crumbling medieval fortress. As usual, it hadn't ended well.

I rolled over on the punishing sofa and reached for my phone. I had nineteen e-mails, which I dealt with as the sky grew light and the city woke up outside my window. At eight I ordered a car and roused the girls. I helped them find clothes and showed them how to use the wonky second-floor shower. They were sleepy and subdued. I was patient and loving.

Inside I was burning all over again.

The sadness and hurt of the night before had been swept away, the guilt and regret obliterated by my renewed rage. Aaron had lied to me. Aaron had betrayed me. How could I have thought, even for a moment, that I'd gone too far?

While the girls got ready, I googled him. As I typed his name into the search bar, autocomplete made this happen:

Aaron Moor**e**
Aaron Moore **twitter meltdown**   Aaron Moore **fraud**   Aaron Moore **traitor to science**

Excellent.

We trooped downstairs. The kitchen was as shabby as the rest of the house, but slightly less gloomy. Grandma's flowered curtains still hung in the windows. The yellow of the cabinets shone through the grime. The place smelled faintly of apples.

The girls slumped at the table. "I'm starving my face off," Kate mumbled.

"Same," said Maisie.

None of us had felt like eating the night before. I opened the refrigerator to see what the paralegals had bought for us.

"We've got California rolls, marshmallows and a southwestern tofu wrap."

I needed to go to the grocery store myself next time.

"How did you sleep?" I asked. Maisie snorted. Kate executed a class-A eye roll. "What's wrong?"

Kate sniffed at a piece of California roll and dropped it with disdain. "Uh, everything, Mom. It's freezing in this dump. It smells bad. And we had company. Scratching in the corner, all night."

I searched the cupboards for a water glass. "Rats. They've always been a problem."

Kate turned to Maisie. " 'Rats,' she says. Like her children spent the night in a room infested with, I don't know. Kittens. Cuddly bunnies."

"I can't have them killed," I explained. "Their parents and I grew up together."

My daughters stared at me. "That was a joke," I added.

Kate raised her eyebrows. "It was super funny."

Mutiny was in the air. Fortunately, I heard two quick taps of a horn and hustled the girls out of the kitchen. I had a busy day ahead of me. The car would drop me at the office, then take the girls to Westchester. My plan had been to find them a school in the city, bidding farewell to our former life completely. But last night they begged me to let them commute, and I relented. For now.

Maisie pulled on her coat. Kate slung her bag over her shoulder. I ushered them through the foyer and into a gray, rainy day. I glanced at my calendar as I locked the door behind us. I had (a) half a dozen conference calls, including the ones I'd had to cancel the day before. I also had (b) a team meeting, (c) the Hyperium interview at two, (d) a meeting with—

"Hello, Raney," said Aaron.

I clutched the railing. My phone flew into the air and clattered down the steps, coming to rest at my husband's feet.

"Dad!" Maisie ran toward him and threw herself into his arms. I made my way down to the sidewalk.

Kate followed. "Traitor," she hissed at Maisie.

Aaron's eyes met mine. "We need to talk."

What a handsome man my husband had become in the last few years. He was unshaven that morning, rumpled, bedraggled by the rain, but he still looked good. Age had clarified his features, rubbing away some of the softness to reveal the strong lines underneath. The gray in his dark hair gave him dignity.

He had been appalled the first time he saw himself on television. Hired a trainer and a nutritionist. Switched his thick plastic frames for contact lenses. Started dressing better.

Red flags. Red flags and warning signs.

I picked up my phone. "Let's go, girls. We're going to be late."

Aaron moved toward the car. "I'm coming with you."

I stared at him. "What makes you think that's in any way an option?"

"Raney, please. You can't freeze me out like this."

Watch me, pal. I held the door open for Kate and Maisie, who hustled in without complaint. Aaron followed. As soon as he was inside, I slammed the door and tapped on the driver's-side window. Jorge lowered it with a cheerful grin, which died when he saw my face.

"Can you take the girls to school? I'll find my own way to work."

He nodded, bewildered. I set off toward Vanderbilt Avenue.

I heard a door slam, the car pull away. Then Aaron was beside me.

"I'm due at PBS in an hour," he said. "I need you to come with me."

I laughed.

"Raney, listen." His voice was tense, urgent. "I know we have a lot to talk about. I have so much to explain and make right. But I also have an emergency on my hands. I don't know if you fully understand what you did yesterday, but things are bad. What you wrote is everywhere. And it's not going away."

Rain was falling steadily. I pulled a newspaper out of my bag and held it over my head.

"There's a team of lawyers waiting to talk to me. They're extremely interested in hearing more about my apparent involvement in a vast, right-wing conspiracy. Are you listening, Raney? You have to tell them it wasn't me."

"I have to," I said. "This is something I have to do."

"Honey, I'm pressed for time here, and you're the only person who can—"

"That's an interesting approach, Aaron. You know how much I love it when men tell me what to do."

He hurried to keep up. "Dammit, Raney! I'm not some man—I'm your husband."

Not for long. We made it to Vanderbilt. No cabs in sight. I took a right, toward Atlantic.

Aaron passed a hand over his face. He took a deep breath. "Let me try again. What happened yesterday, what I did to you . . . it was the worst. I'm the worst. When you called? It was like waking up from a dream. I was horrified by what I'd done. I'm a selfish, miserable bastard, and whatever I'm about to lose, it's entirely my fault."

Sounded about right to me.

"The hardest part? Knowing that I hurt you. It was the last thing in the world I meant to do. I wanted to talk to you, abase myself, try to make you feel better. But I was thousands of miles away, and I couldn't get through to you. Finally I said, She's angry. Give her some space. But when I landed, my phone didn't work. Then, at baggage claim . . . *clowns,* Raney? They followed me through the airport. When I reached the parking lot, the car was gone. I managed to get a cab home, where I found the FOR SALE sign. And a completely empty house."

I crossed Dean Street, stomping through a wide black puddle.

"I had to borrow money from the Kratensteins to pay for the cab, because my credit cards were declined. I used their phone to get in touch with Yael, who came and got me. On the way to his apartment, he told me what was happening online. I know you're upset, you have every right to be, but . . . Jesus, Raney."

We reached Atlantic. Still no cabs. I headed toward Flatbush.

"There I was, sitting on my assistant's futon, staring at his laptop, surveying the ruins of my life. I'm reading the tweets, I'm reading the tweets about the tweets, the blog posts, the commentary. And yes, I am the worst husband in the entire world. But it's also quite possible that you've *completely* destroyed my reputation. You need to make this right."

"Stop!" I shouted. "Stop talking!"

He fell silent. A few passersby eyed me apprehensively.

"I won my case, Aaron. Gaia Café. All counts. Total victory."

"Oh." His expression changed from frustration to delight. "*Oh!* That's great! I—"

"I was so anxious yesterday morning. Desperate to talk to you. But I held off. 'Be considerate,' I told myself. 'He's exhausted.' And all the while, you were . . ."

He reached for me. I stepped back, wiping the tears away.

"You were right, Aaron. I killed it. But you know what? It didn't matter. Because I didn't care."

He reached out again, and my anger flared up, hotter than ever. I pushed him away, hard.

"You *ruined* it, Aaron! You ruined a really great day. And a really great marriage. How could you give up everything we had? Our past, our life, everything that's ever happened to us."

"Don't say that, Raney. We can—"

"How many times? How many times have you been unfaithful to me?"

He bowed his head. He couldn't even look at me. "Once. This was the first—the only time."

I kept moving. He followed. "The first time. So you would have done it again."

He studied the ground as we walked. "I . . . I don't know."

"Was she there when we spoke on the phone, Sunday afternoon?"

"She was . . . downstairs. In the lobby."

"Was she there when you wrote to me? She must have been. When you sent that e-mail about San Francisco. The lights on the bridge. How we should visit. Was she sleeping? Was she *sated*?"

He nodded miserably. I longed to hit him, scratch him. Make him hurt. I stepped into the street and looked up and down. Still no cabs. "Were you in bed with her when you wrote it?"

"Raney . . ."

"Where were you?" A woman pushing a stroller swathed in plastic turned to stare. I stared back, hard.

"I was . . . I was at a desk. There was a desk in the room. I was there."

"Could you see her from where you were sitting?"

"No."

"How far were you from the bed?"

I was interrogating him. I couldn't help it. I didn't really want answers. I wanted to wake up from this nightmare.

"Raney, this isn't—"

"How far from her were you when you were lying to me?" I shouted. "Lying about how much you missed me. Lying about how much you loved me."

"I wasn't lying! Everything I wrote was true."

"Did you get back into bed after you sent the e-mail? Did you . . ." I couldn't go on.

"Raney, please," he said softly. "This isn't what we should be talking about."

"When did it happen, Aaron?" I was piteous, whimpering. I hated myself for it, but I couldn't stop. "When did you stop loving me?"

"Oh, honey." He reached for me again.

I knocked his imploring hand away. "Don't touch me."

We were facing off in the middle of the sidewalk. Waves of commuters broke around us with huffs and grimaces and little sidesteps of irritation.

"I didn't stop loving you. I couldn't. I . . . screwed up. I really, really screwed up. Let's back up, okay? Let's . . . start over."

"Start over? We're done."

I began walking again. So did he. "We're not done. We're going to figure out how to fix this. We're going to talk it out, deal with our problems once and for all, and—"

"Problems?" I stopped again. "We don't have problems, plural. We have one problem, Aaron. You, cheating on me."

"What I did was wrong, Raney. It was awful." He hesitated. "But—do you really think we're fine? That things haven't changed between us?"

"Ohhh." I nodded slowly. "I get it. You're deflecting blame. You're trying to shift the responsibility for this away from yourself, and onto me."

"No! What I did was horrendous. But look at how you reacted, Raney. You went ballistic. That's hardly the sign of a healthy relationship."

I stepped past a line of parked cars on Flatbush and raised my arm. "Do you know what I haven't heard this morning, Aaron? Not through all your demands, your accusations and your self-pity? I haven't heard an apology. Not one. This has been all about you."

A cab slowed down and pulled toward me. At last.

"I tried to apologize!" he cried. "But you wouldn't talk, and you wouldn't listen, and . . . and you're the one who made it all about me by going fucking nuclear on the Internet!"

I opened the door of the cab and got in. He grabbed on to it.

"Raney, please. We'll talk about this, we'll talk about everything. But right now I really need you to clear my name."

"You're a talented guy. I'm sure you can handle it." I yanked the door shut and leaned forward to direct the driver. That's how I stayed, eyes to the front, on the edge of the seat, willing myself not to look out the window until we pulled away.

SEVEN

I DIDN'T WANT to go out that night, but my roommate insisted.

"It's the party of the year!" Leila cried.

"It's only September," I pointed out.

"You're hopeless, Raney. You do know that, right?"

I opened a book. She reached across my desk and slapped it shut.

"You're coming with me." She looked me up and down. "And I'm dressing you."

Leila took me to a finals club—Harvard's version of a fraternity, meaning the men were both drunk and pompous. She quickly disappeared with a guy she had a crush on, leaving me to wander through oak-paneled rooms full of people dancing and drinking and flirting. I felt so out of place.

Someone caught up with me as I was hunting for my coat. "You're not leaving, are you?"

I straightened up. He had dark hair, glasses, a round, boyish face. He was wearing a green flannel shirt.

"Do we . . ."

"Know each other? Nope." He smiled. His eyes were bright behind his glasses.

Boys. They perplexed me. I had friends who were boys. We got along great, as pals. That was me—pal Raney. But romance, attraction, all that tender, sloppy stuff? So far it had been in short supply. An awkward date here, a fumbling encounter there. Suitors weren't exactly lining up.

Which was fine! I was in my sophomore year of college. I had important things to deal with. Internships and scholarships and student loans. Preparing for law school. Doing whatever I could to keep my fretful and increasingly frail grandmother from worrying about me too much.

Better not to be distracted. Better to keep my head down. So I kept my head down.

Now, my eyes strayed to the pile of coats.

"I found something in the backyard," the boy said. "Come look."

After an instant of silence, we started laughing at the same time. He clapped a palm to his forehead.

"That came out *so* wrong. I'm not a murderer or a weirdo, I promise." He paused. "Well, maybe a little bit of a weirdo."

There was a hole in one elbow of his shirt. His shoes were muddy. He didn't belong here, either. But he didn't seem bothered by that.

"Come on!" he urged me. "Before it flies away."

He led me through the house and out the back door, past a crowd of smokers and a boy throwing up in the bushes. He knelt beside a large tree in a far corner of the yard. I crouched down as he pushed aside a few blades of grass. "Look."

I squinted. In the dim light from the house I could barely make it out.

"It's . . . a bug," I said.

"Isn't it beautiful?"

I gave him a sideways glance. Where I came from, people didn't sit around admiring bugs. They reached for a rolled-up newspaper. Was this guy joking? No, he seemed entirely earnest.

So he really was a weirdo.

I bent closer, to be polite. The thing was large and shiny black. It had bright-orange markings on its back that reminded me of a tie-dyed T-shirt, and orange blobs on its antennae.

Actually, it was kind of beautiful.

"It's an American burying beetle," he said. "They're carnivorous—I think it's going at a piece of hamburger right now. I have no idea what it's doing here—its closest habitat is western Mass."

He explained its markings, how it flew, how it fought and mated and why it was endangered. He spoke in a low voice, as if he didn't want to disturb it.

He watched the insect. I watched him. I liked his glasses and his too-big shirt. I liked his sincerity. He was the very opposite of the cool, ironic kids who surrounded me every day.

Eventually we stood up. He frowned and pressed gently at a spot on the tree.

"Someone drove a nail in here. Maybe they were trying to get syrup."

"You can do that?"

"Sure. It's a sugar maple."

Syrup comes from trees? I probably would have realized that if I'd thought about it for half a second, but I never had. To cover up my city-girl ignorance, I quickly pointed at another tree. "What's that?"

"An English oak," he replied.

"And that one?"

"An elm."

We made a game of it, going around the yard, me pointing, him answering. He was shy about it, a little abashed—but he always knew the answer.

"What's that?"

"A rhododendron."

"What about that?"

"Japanese knotweed. An invasive species." He glanced at the house. "Like the jokers who hang out here."

It wasn't much of a game, because he knew everything.

"What's that?"

"A sparrow. No, wait. A wren."

I pointed at the sky. "That?"

"Ursa Major."

Under a bush. "That?"

"Dog shit."

I laughed. "That?"

"A beer can," he said. "Pabst Blue Ribbon."

We circled back to the sugar maple. I was so impressed. "How do you know all this stuff?"

"I grew up not too far from here. And this is what I study. The natural sciences. Insects."

I nodded at the beetle, which was still scrabbling quietly in the dirt. "Are you going to rescue this guy?"

"Nah. Why interrupt a good meal?"

I had nothing else to say, and my awkwardness returned full force. What was going to happen? Should I say something? Should I go?

I should probably go.

"You study at Widener, right?" he said. "In the big reading room?"

"All the time. I've never seen you there."

"Yeah, well." He smiled. "You don't look up much."

More awkward silence. The smokers let out a shout of laughter.

"What do we do now?" I asked at last.

"Get married," he said.

"What?"

He grinned, raising his hands helplessly. "Sorry. I should have told you. When two people come across an American burying beetle eating trash in the backyard during a stupid party? They're linked for life."

I bit my lip to keep from laughing. "Is that right?"

"There's nothing we can do about it. But we don't have to get married right away. We can get a drink first."

"That sounds like a good idea," I said.

He smiled at me. "I'm Aaron, by the way."

I smiled back. "I'm Raney."

IT WAS past ten by the time I stepped out of the elevator on forty-five. I'm usually one of the first partners to arrive each day, greeted only by cleaners and the occasional associate, wan and itchy eyed after pulling an all-nighter. But that morning, the secretaries were already at their stations. Paralegals were hurrying through the halls. My partners were shouting, laughing and bargaining behind their closed doors.

People greeted me briefly, eyes averted. They must know, I thought. I wasn't surprised. I'd long ago recognized the futility of trying to keep anything a secret around here.

Renfield was on the phone when I breezed past her desk. Inside my office, I dropped my bag. The rain had stopped, but fog hung low over the park.

Renfield clomped in with a revised draft of yesterday's brief, a stack of mail and a fluffy white towel. She stood behind me and dried my hair as I went through everything.

I finished and gestured to a chair. She sat down.

I said, "What do you do when you feel sad?"

"Steal a copy of *The Thorn Birds* and reread all the carnal passages," she replied.

"You steal a copy?"

"Yep."

"Every time?"

"Yep."

"Why not keep one at home?"

"Tried it," she said. "Doesn't have the same effect."

I mulled that over. "What do you think *normal* people do when they feel sad?"

She puffed out her cheeks. "Damned if I know."

"Find out for me, will you?"

She made a note in her steno pad, hauled herself upright and left.

I got to work. I conferenced. I called. I read and wrote. I met with my team and congratulated them on Gaia Café. I reviewed the settlement agreement I'd asked Jisun to draft the day before. Paralegals came and went.

It was an ordinary day, full and productive. The kind of day I loved. But I felt lifeless. The world had drained of color.

At one thirty, the phone rang. I glanced at the display. It was Aaron.

Renfield answered. She was brusque, businesslike. Love for her bloomed in my heart.

Line one started blinking. I thought about ignoring it, but that felt like an admission of defeat. So I picked up. "I see you got your phone back."

"I am sorry, Raney," Aaron said. "I am so sorry. I intend to spend the rest of my life telling you how sorry I am, and trying to make it up to you—if you'll let me."

I glanced out the window. Rain was falling again.

"Are you listening? I am so, so sorry."

This was the Aaron I knew. Not ranting and raving. Not a phony or a liar. He was sorry. I could hear it in his voice, the way his words came tumbling out.

"This morning was awful, and that was my fault. I was exhausted, panicking about what had happened . . . but none of that matters. We have to find a way through this. I can't lose you."

Step back, I thought.

Step away from the brink.

He did a horrible thing. But he's sorry. And didn't you get your revenge?

Don't let a solitary lapse ruin almost sixteen years of happiness.

"There was one thing you said, and I have to tell you again, to make sure you know. I love you, Raney. I never stopped loving you. I couldn't."

Sixteen years of happiness. More—twenty years since we met at that party. Since we fell in love. Twenty years, and Aaron did this to me. He lied. He presented a version of himself—an honest man, a faithful husband—that was deliberately misleading.

I should forgive? *I* should let it go?

"What I did was the worst. But people get over this, Raney. We can get over this. We're strong. If you—"

"I have to go."

I hung up. I tilted my chair back and gazed at the ceiling.

I was confused.

I had assumed Aaron's betrayal meant he was rejecting me. Now he was saying he still loved me, and I believed him. If he wanted to leave me, he wouldn't be begging my forgiveness. He'd be off with Deirdre, doing whatever cheaters do. Having intercourse. Reading love poetry. Slurping champagne from each other's orifices.

So, fine. Love triumphs. Then why did he cheat?

And what was I supposed to do about it?

There was a knock at the door. Amanda poked her head in. "They're here."

WHEN WE arrived in the conference room, Marty was chatting with two other men.

"There she is!" he cried, in his cheerful, Martyish way. "Raney, this is Michael Singer, from Hyperium's legal department. Michael, meet my partner, Raney Moore."

One of the two men held out his hand. "Call me Mickey."

His colleague stepped forward, fresh-faced and eager. "Xander Corwin. It's a pleasure."

Mickey and Xander. I felt like a guest on Mr. Bobo's Clown Show.

"We've actually met before," Singer said. "I used to work at Brown and Taft. You deposed a witness of mine in the Permasoft litigation, about five years ago."

"Did I? I don't remember."

"I wish I could forget. You destroyed him." Then he laughed, without a trace of bitterness. I was so surprised. I could never be that amicable with a lawyer who'd outgunned me. But then, Singer didn't seem like a typical New York litigator. No sagging gut, no purplish eye bags. No aura of impenetrable malaise. He was my age, maybe a few years older. His blond hair was scruffy around the ears. He seemed relaxed, slightly mischievous. I wondered why I didn't remember him.

"Congratulations on Gaia Café by the way," he said. "I read about it this morning."

I thanked him, and we all sat down. Amanda readied her legal pad. I glanced at the memo she'd written.

"Why don't you start by telling me how Hyperium managed to make a mortal enemy of Mrs. Maxine Tierney of Babylon, New York."

"You bet." Xander hitched up his chair. "Mrs. Tierney is a customer of Long Island HighSpeed, one of our cable subsidiaries. A few years ago, LIHS offered a promotion to new customers. It was basic stuff: sign up now, get fifty percent off your first two years of service. After that, the rate reverts to normal. Mrs. Tierney subscribed—as did about nine hundred other people. Two years pass, the promotional period ends and her monthly bill increases. She calls to complain. She says she was promised the rate would never change, we're cheating her, so forth and so on. Chances are, she forgot what she was told. LIHS explains but says they can't adjust her bill. Two months later, this lawsuit lands on our desk."

"What was the increase in her rate?"

"Forty dollars per month," he replied.

I shot Marty a glance: *Are you hearing this?* No reaction.

"As you can see, it's a proposed class action," Singer noted. "Her lawyer obviously hopes to find other disgruntled customers and earn a nice fee."

"A class action," I said. "Consisting of, at most, nine hundred people."

Xander nodded, eyes darting to Singer.

"Each of whom could claim damages of, at most, forty dollars a month."

Xander nodded again. I paged through the complaint.

Finally, he asked, "Do you have any other questions?"

"Only one." I pushed the document away and smiled at them. "Do you gentlemen have me confused with someone else?"

"Raney," Marty said. It was a warning. I ignored it.

Because how dare they? How dare these clueless lawyers waltz in here and offer me this ridiculous case like it was some kind of gift? In normal circumstances I would have swallowed my annoyance and declined their munificence with every appearance of regret.

But these weren't normal circumstances.

"Let me dispel your confusion," I said. "I am a highly experienced litigator. I specialize in complex commercial lawsuits, multidistrict securities fraud cases and white-collar criminal appeals. I've argued before the Supreme Court three times. I've won twice. In other words," I controlled my temper with effort, "I'm not some solo practitioner operating out of the back of a shoe repair shop, which is more or less the caliber of lawyer you need to bring this penny-ante nuisance suit to a successful conclusion."

Xander looked terrified. I wasn't finished.

"But you must know this. It can't actually be a surprise to you. So I'm curious: Why are you insulting me by offering me this joke of a case?"

That, I figured, should do it. They would leave, angry or shamefaced. Marty would rebuke me. Then I could go back to tending the charred wreckage of my personal life.

That's not what happened.

"Insulted?" Singer said. "You should feel flattered."

The nerve of this guy. "And why is that?"

"We're here because we're reconsidering our relationship with Rayburn Walsh."

I was about to let rip with another tirade. That stopped me.

Rayburn Walsh was Hyperium's main outside law firm. They ran the corporation's major litigations—work that earned them tens of millions of dollars in fees every year.

Hyperium was shopping for new outside counsel. This was a test case, a low-stakes matter that would allow them to see how we perform.

Why had I not figured that out? What was wrong with me?

I wasn't focused, that's what.

Aaron's fault.

"Rayburn botched a document production in a trademark case a few months ago," Singer explained. "But we were already thinking about making a change. Our CEO wants new energy. Someone incredibly important and extremely impressive." He smiled, all innocence. "Naturally, we came to you."

He was mocking me! But I had it coming.

"Then why give me this dog of a case?" I complained. "How about something fun?"

I got that big, friendly laugh again. "We just need to assure the board that we've done our due diligence. Keep it simple and make it snappy. Crush them with discovery, or work out a decent settlement. Then we can move on to the good stuff. What do you say?"

I said yes, of course. We spent half an hour discussing logistics. My new clients prepared to leave. Xander still looked traumatized. Not Singer.

"Shoe repair." He raised his eyebrows. "This is going to be interesting."

Amanda showed them out. Marty folded his hands over his belly.

"Well," he said. "That was bracing."

Now I understood his mysterious behavior the day before. "You might have warned me, you know."

"They wished to raise the topic themselves. If it was a test, you passed."

I pulled Amanda's legal pad toward me. Her notes were orderly and thorough. "Still, Marty. This case."

"It's a stinker," he agreed. "But if we can steal Hyperium away from those know-nothings at Rayburn?" His eyes gleamed. Then they went soft.

This was the part I'd been dreading.

"I'm fine," I said.

"Do I need to worry?"

"Of course not."

"Well I do," he said. "I worry."

"Don't, Marty. I'll be okay."

He stood up and came around the table. "Anything you need, Raney Jane. You know I'm here." He gripped my shoulder and left.

AT FIVE O'CLOCK, I finished a call and pressed the intercom. Renfield entered.

I leaned back in my chair. "Tell me what you found out."

She flipped back a few pages in her steno pad. "Number one thing people do when they're sad? Get drunk."

I was afraid she'd say that. "Number two?"

She pulled a stubby pencil from behind her ear and made a note. "Take pills."

"Also no good."

"I know, I know." She crossed it out. "Number three. Listen to sad songs."

"What, like funeral dirges?"

"Thought you'd ask." She bustled around the desk. "I made you a playlist."

I moved aside so she could sit down at my computer. "You know how to make a playlist?"

Renfield clucked her tongue. "You don't have the right program. I gotta download it."

I watched her work her magic. "I've never made a playlist."

"You don't say. Here we go." She pressed a key. We listened to a few songs.

"What is this supposed to be doing for me?"

She scratched her ear with her pencil. "Hearing someone else express their sadness might help you get in touch with your own."

Exactly what I was trying to avoid. "Let's move on."

She took up her notebook with a martyred air. "Number four. Talk to a therapist."

A therapist. Sarah saw a therapist. So did Rahsaan, one of my associates. I reached for my phone.

He loped into my office a few minutes later. Rahsaan was brilliant, elegant, impossibly handsome and profoundly neurotic.

"Explain therapy," I said.

He sank into a chair. "My shrink is the greatest. I tell her everything."

"Has she helped you with a specific, concrete problem?"

Rahsaan placed a finger over his lips, pondering. "Our discussions are usually more global than that, but sometimes. She'll drop an insight that clarifies a situation I've been stressing over, or offer a fresh perspective. When Glen and I were having problems, she gave me some exercises that helped us—"

"Exercises?"

"Yeah. Kind of like homework."

I thought therapy was all talk—I didn't know there were activities. Things to *do*. This sounded very promising.

Rahsaan gave me a few more details. When he left, I summoned Renfield back in.

"Find me a therapist," I told her. "The best in Manhattan."

EIGHT

"HONEY, I'VE BEEN so worried! Come in, come in."

Sarah pulled me through her front door and into a fierce hug. I relaxed in her arms, momentarily forgetting why I'd come.

Then she released me and squinted into the dark street. "What time is it?"

"A little after four," I said.

"In the morning?" Her sleepy eyes widened, and she glanced fearfully over her shoulder. "Oh Jesus. The kids."

Sarah lives in a narrow brick town house in Cobble Hill, a few miles from the house on Park Place. I'd been awake all night, waiting for a report from the firm's research librarian. When I got it, I rushed right over.

"I'm sorry," I said. "I wasn't sleeping, and—"

"No no, it's fine. But keep your voice down, okay?" She ushered me through the foyer. "I must have tried calling you every ten minutes yesterday. What happened?"

"Why's Auntie Raney here?"

"Oh no," Sarah murmured. "Jesus please no."

Della and Mercer were watching us from the top of the stairs. Sarah smiled brightly and made herding motions at her children.

"Everything's fine, babies! Go back to bed."

"But what's she doing here?" Della persisted.

Della is smart and serious and dogged. She looks like her father, Tad: tall and red-haired. She's nine. Maybe ten.

"I need your mom's help with something," I explained. "It's urgent."

"What's 'urgent' mean?" Mercer asked.

Mercer is sweet and sensitive. He looks like Sarah: plump and comfortable, with curly dark hair and dark eyes. He's five. Maybe six.

"Requiring immediate action or attention," I said.

"Like my need for you to go back to bed," Sarah added. "I'm serious, babies."

They disappeared. She tightened the belt of her robe and headed down the hall. In the kitchen, she put her arms around me again. "What can I do?"

"Call your therapist for me."

"Doctor Feuerstein?" She released me and wandered over to the stove. "Do you want to start seeing him?"

"No. I want to see Doctor Bogard."

"Who's Bogard?"

Sarah's kitchen was a mess—sink overflowing with dishes, counter strewn with crumbs. I opened the dishwasher. "Bogard is the therapist I want to see. Renfield found him, but he's not accepting new patients. I need Feuerstein to persuade him to take me on."

"Are they in the same practice?"

"No. They went to school together." I rinsed a glass and slotted it into the dishwasher.

"Graduate school?"

"Grade school."

She'd been rooting around in a drawer. She looked up. "How do you know that?"

"I did a little research."

"Into my therapist? That's kind of creepy, Raney."

Kind of? She had no idea. When I realized I needed help getting to Bogard, I zeroed in on Sarah. She has an army of medical professionals tending to her every need. She must know someone who knows someone who . . . et cetera. I called Norton, my favorite librarian. He has ways of gathering intelligence about people. I don't ask too many questions. But at some point I'd have to warn Sarah that her dentist had an alarming history with law enforcement, and her podiatrist was up to no good online.

Not now, though. I needed her to focus.

Della and Mercer wandered into the kitchen. "Oh, babies!" Sarah groaned. "No!"

"We couldn't fall back asleep," Della said.

"This is a disaster. The entire day is shot." Sarah slumped at the table and covered her face. "I'm not going to make it!"

Mercer put his arms around her. "Sorry, Mommy."

I finished loading the dishwasher, found the soap and started a cycle. The children climbed onto stools at the breakfast bar and looked at me expectantly. I opened the refrigerator and pulled out a loaf of bread, butter, jam and milk.

"You're always telling me I need a therapist," I said. "Now I've found one, but I need your help getting to him."

"Why this particular guy?"

"He's the best."

"Therapy is about communication styles, Raney. How well your personalities fit. It isn't a competition."

I slammed the refrigerator door. "This is New York City, Sarah. Everything is a competition."

I washed and sliced strawberries. I poured milk. I toasted bread, spread it with butter and jam and cut off the crusts. I put plates and cups in front of the children. I grabbed a sponge and attacked a hardened glob of ketchup on the countertop. I rinsed the sponge, leaned back against the counter and crossed my arms.

"Do this for me," I said.

Sarah sighed. "You're never going to let up, are you?"

"I will hound you until your dying day."

She reached for her phone. "I'll leave a message with his service."

The children ate. I began organizing Sarah's cupboards.

"Thanks for breakfast, Auntie Raney," Della said.

"You bet." I flattened a stack of boxes and threw them in the recycling bin. "It's been a while since I've seen you guys. What's new?"

"No, it's not an emergency," Sarah said into the phone, shooting me an annoyed look.

"I like dinosaurs," Mercer offered.

"Yeah? Which is your favorite?"

"T. rex!" he roared.

"Nice. What about you, Della?" I tugged on a drawer handle.

"I'm really into outer space," she said. "We're studying it in school."

"Is that right? Astronomy and astrophysics are fascinating. Keep it up. Don't let anyone discourage you."

"I've been a patient for fifteen years," Sarah said. "I promise you I'm in the system."

"Why would anyone discourage me?" Della asked.

I tugged harder on the handle. It wouldn't budge. "Because you're a girl."

"I can't do science because I'm a girl?"

"Of course you can. And you can excel." I gave up on the drawer and opened a cupboard. "But it won't be easy. You'll face a lot of obstacles. People who think you aren't good enough. You'll have to find a way to deal with the pressure."

"I thought science was fun," she said. "This doesn't sound like fun."

"It's not only science. It's almost every field. Unfair as it is, Della, men still rule the world. If you want to succeed, you're going to have to work harder than they do."

Sarah ended her call. "What an ordeal. But he'll call me when he gets in." She yawned and scrolled through her texts.

"You can do this," I told Della. "You just have to drown out the distractions. Toughen up. Never let them see you cry."

"But," Della looked troubled, "I cry all the time."

"That needs to stop," I said.

Sarah looked up from her phone. "What are you two talking about?"

Della's eyes were round and wounded. "Auntie Raney says I can't cry anymore. And she made science sound awful!"

"Wait," I said. "That's not what I—"

Too late. Sarah had gone full mama grizzly.

"What the hell's wrong with you?"

"I was just saying—"

"Come here, baby." Sarah held out her arms, and Della slipped into them. "You can cry whenever you want. And science is great! Remember chemistry camp? You had so much fun!"

Mercer finished eating, and the kids wandered off to the playroom. I cleared the dishes. I could feel Sarah's eyes on me. At last, she spoke.

"Did my daughter really deserve one of your psycho pep talks at four in the morning?"

"She needs to know what it's like out there, Sarah."

"She's *eight*, Raney. I think we have a little time before we have to welcome her into the wonderful world of gender inequality."

Eight. Della was eight.

Maybe I should have dialed it back.

"I'm sorry. I wasn't thinking." I started wiping down the counter.

"Can you please stop cleaning? You're making me crazy."

"I can't sit around doing nothing!"

She softened. "That's what most people do at the ass crack of dawn, honey. We ease into the day."

That sounded like useful information. But I had too much energy to put it into practice. I pushed aside a collection of bottles and tins to clean underneath. I picked one up, and it gave off a spicy scent.

I turned to her, scandalized. "You keep marijuana in the kitchen?"

"Calm down, J. Edgar. It's chai."

"What's that?"

"You seriously don't know what chai is?" Sarah hauled herself out of her chair. "I'll make some. I'm about to fall into a coma just watching you."

She made chai. (It's a kind of tea. And delicious.) She led me into the sunroom, pushed me into a chair and gave me a mug. She pulled up an ottoman and sat down.

"Now," she said. "Tell me everything."

I did. And she was empathetic and outraged and loving, exactly as I knew she'd be.

Until I got to the part about how I'd reacted.

"Wait," she said. "That was you?"

"I lost my temper."

"I thought he had a breakdown or something. Holy shit. That was *you?*"

"Do you think I overdid it?"

"Hell no! He's lucky you stopped short of castration. Although he might have preferred that, careerwise. Wow." She shook her head in wonder. "You took him down, Raney. I'm proud of you. Terrified, but proud. What did you do to the woman?"

"Nothing."

"I'm surprised she's not in witness protection." Sarah stood up, waggling her empty mug. "This is doing nothing for me."

Back in the kitchen, she started futzing with the espresso maker. "She's irrelevant," I said. "Aaron is the one who broke a promise to me. She didn't owe me any duty not to sleep with my husband."

"That's a very legalistic way of looking at it."

"I am a lawyer, after all."

"So am I, but remember when I found out about Tad and his little dog walker? She was a homewrecker. She'd stolen something that belonged to me. I eventually realized I didn't want what she'd taken, but at first?" Sarah knocked back her espresso. "Hoo boy."

She rinsed our tea mugs and set them on the rack. "Anyway, therapy is a great idea. You should do more. You need one of those whatchamacallits, from a car dealership. A twenty-point inspection. When was the last time you had a physical? I'll give you the name of my internist."

Thanks to Norton, I knew the name of Sarah's internist, and a whole lot more. I wasn't letting that guy within a mile of my internal organs.

"Aaron said we have problems. Can you believe that?"

"Everybody has problems. That's no excuse." She began preparing another espresso. "How was the sex?"

"Fine," I said. "Good."

"Still twice a week?" I nodded. "That's impressive."

"Right? It couldn't have been the sex."

So what was it? Aaron and I were solid. We were sound. We were the ones everyone said would last.

I simply didn't understand.

"When you told me," Sarah said, "I was blown away. I thought, Aaron? He's so not that kind of guy. But that's habit talking. Every guy is that kind of guy—or could be, given the opportunity."

"I'm so angry," I said. "I can't seem to control it."

She sipped her new espresso. "Of course you can't. You're like a car that's been sitting in the garage for a while. The first time you start it up, the engine is going to flood or backfire or whatever."

"What's with the automotive metaphors today?"

"Remember that safety engineer I went out with last week? He was a real chatterbox in bed."

"I thought I was done," I said.

"Done?"

"With that part of my life. Romance, love, companionship—I thought it was all wrapped up. Now I find out that all along, I should have been sitting on the porch of my cabin, shotgun across my lap, ready to defend against all comers."

Sarah reached over and rubbed my arm. "You're never done, honey. Nobody tells you that, but it's true. You're never done."

NINE

"YOU'RE A DIFFICULT man to get ahold of," I told Doctor Bogard.

"You're a difficult woman to get away from," he replied.

Fair enough. I'd gotten the call from Doctor Feuerstein's reception-ist at ten, saying Bogard would take me on. I immediately phoned his office. His receptionist said he could see me in six weeks. I said that wasn't going to work for me. She said it was the best she could do. I kept talking. I didn't try to intimidate or hassle her. That never works with receptionists—they're too powerful. Instead, I coaxed and flat-tered. I referenced my Brooklyn roots. I might have let a ghost of the old accent creep in.

Little by little, Tilda softened.

She said she was sorry but . . .

I kept talking.

She said she wished she could . . .

I kept talking.

She said she'd call me back.

At one o'clock, I was sitting across from the great man himself.

I'd never met anyone who looked so much like a lizard. Bogard had a bald, palely freckled head. A wide, lipless mouth. Long fingers with broad tips. He was a slim little lizard man, dressed in a gray suit, sitting neatly in a gray chair.

"What can I do for you, Ms. Moore?"

"My husband cheated on me, Doctor Bogard."

He nodded slowly, almost rhythmically. "And how does that make you feel?"

This struck me as somewhat clichéd, coming from "Manhattan's best." I said, "I'm sad, obviously. And angry. Very angry."

"You're here to work through those emotions," he suggested.

"No. I'm here to find out why he did it."

"You're asking me?" His nearly invisible eyebrows rose. "I don't know the guy."

We were facing each other in matching gray chairs, atop a tufted gray rug. I realized I was clutching the armrests. I released them.

"Here's the thing, Doctor Bogard. I know myself. Talking about my emotions won't help me. I keep them locked up most of the time."

"Locked up?"

"In an imaginary box. A treasure chest, actually."

"That's interesting," he said.

"No it isn't. My point is, talking, unpacking, delving, working through, processing—whatever mumbo-jumbo psychotherapeutic term you want to use? That's not how I function. What helps me is information. Clarity. Thus my plan."

"Sorry . . . plan?"

"For understanding why Aaron betrayed me. For getting rid of him."

The doctor pressed his fingertips together, scrutinizing me over the little triangle they made. "Getting rid of him—that's the goal?"

"Yes. And to do that, I have to know why he cheated."

"So ask him."

"I will. But maybe he doesn't know why he did it. Maybe he was subconsciously motivated. That's why I'm looking for a broader perspective. You don't know my husband, Doctor, but you know people."

"You want me to tell you why people cheat? You need somebody else for that. A priest, maybe. A talk-show host. A country-western singer. I can't talk to you about people in general. I can only talk to you about you."

This was disappointing. "So you can't help me?"

"Maybe, maybe not. Tell me about your marriage."

"We got along, Doctor. We talked. We enjoyed each other's company. We valued each other's opinions and respected each other's minds." I hesitated, thinking. "There are troubled marriages out there, right? The ones that are obviously rocky. Then there are the ones that seem fine on the outside, but are waiting for one problem, one little match that will blow the whole thing sky high. My marriage wasn't either of those. Sure, we bickered from time to time, we sniped. But we always worked it out. We didn't . . . go off and sleep with other people."

"Or so you thought," he said.

By this point I'd dismissed Bogard, dismissed the whole enterprise. But the challenge in his tone made me pause.

"You're coming in here, telling me how you work, what you need," he observed. "Here's what I think. You didn't know your husband, Ms. Moore. Not entirely. What makes you so certain you know yourself?"

That set me back a little. "Touché."

"My advice?" Bogard continued. "Forget about what you think you need to get through this. Forget about people in general. Let's find out if there are things about *you* that you aren't aware of—things that might lead to the clarity you seek. How does that sound?"

WE SPENT the rest of the hour on my childhood, work, the girls. I walked out feeling better than I had since Monday morning. Bogard hadn't given me any exercises, but maybe he'd have insights. Or lead me to epiphanies. Who doesn't love a good epiphany?

I'd just gotten back to the office when Aaron called. "Do you have a minute?" he asked.

I woke up my computer. "Not really."

"How are you?"

"Superb. Yourself?"

"Raney, talk to me. Tell me how you're feeling."

"Not your concern anymore, Aaron."

"It will always be my concern."

"You have a funny way of showing it."

We went back and forth like that for a while. It soon became clear that my well-being was not the sole reason he'd called. The Committee for a Sustainable Climate had announced an investigation into his ties to conservative interest groups. Sponsors were pulling out of *The Bug Doctor*. The network was pressing him for answers.

"I don't want to get you involved," he said, "but if you spoke to a few people, privately, and said, I don't know, that you were playing a joke on me, and it got out of hand—"

"You want me to lie for you."

"Yes!" he cried. "Yes, Raney. I want you to lie, in order to correct all the lies that got me into this mess!"

I began deleting e-mails. "Why don't you ask your girlfriend to help you? I hear she's pretty good at lying."

"This is a nightmare," he muttered.

"Admit it, Aaron. You don't want to get me involved because then people would know the truth about what you did. You wouldn't be a leader of the scientific resistance anymore. You'd be just another man who couldn't keep it in his pants."

"Believe it or not, Raney, I'm trying to protect you. Some of the things you did . . . you could get in real trouble."

"Yeah? Sounds like I'd better get a lawyer." I hung up.

I took a few deep breaths, feeling my fury subside. Then I focused on the issue at hand. Who had been the most enthusiastic of my aiders and abettors on Monday?

I pressed the intercom. "Get me Cameron."

A few minutes later, he strode in, took a seat, smoothed his tie and bent his long torso toward me, the picture of paralegalistic attentiveness.

"I have a project for you," I said.

He whipped out his phone. "Lay it on me, Boss. Your command is my wish."

"I want you to learn everything you can about infidelity."

He typed, chewing his lower lip. Then he looked up. "Is that it?"

"Do you need more?"

"No, but as a research assignment, it's somewhat . . . lacking in structure."

"I don't want structure. I want comprehensiveness. Breadth and depth. Don't be constrained by traditional resources. Consider science. Social science. History. Religion. Literature." I paused. "Country-western music."

Cameron's brow twitched, but he kept typing.

"Bring me regular updates. You should come and go from this office as you please."

His narrow face grew crafty. "I might have a difficult time executing this task alongside my onerous paralegal workload."

"Consider yourself relieved of all other duties."

He bounced out of the room, shining with happiness. I was feeling better, too. Aaron's infidelity was a puzzle, nothing more. Solve it, and I could move on.

I heard Wally Fanucci yukking it up with Renfield in the outer office. He ambled through my doorway. "Moore!"

"Fanucci!"

"I heard about Aaron." Wally flung his bulk onto the sofa. "Fucking rim job."

I didn't know what that was, but he seemed to be expressing condolences. "Thanks."

"Seriously, Raney, I'm sorry. Heard you did a number on him, though. That must have felt good."

I turned from my computer and looked him up and down. "Wally. You're a man."

"So they tell me."

"Give me some insight. Why did Aaron cheat?"

He considered the question. "Best guess? He wanted to sleep with someone else."

"Thanks, genius."

"Hell, I don't know, Raney! Obviously something was wrong."

"Why do you say that?"

He stretched his arms along the back of the sofa. "Contrary to popular belief, most men don't have affairs for the hell of it. They're prompted by some crisis—midlife, existential, what have you. A long-standing problem. A need that goes unfulfilled."

Problem. Aaron had said something about problems.

But he was wrong.

"Men have affairs all the time," I pointed out.

Wally readily assented. "We're assholes. Still, we're not without our reasons. They may not be valid reasons, but they do exist. Much as we may talk about it, and dream about it, we're not going to go out and fuck another woman simply because we want to."

Our other suitemate, Jonathan Tate, stuck his sharp, excitable face through the door. "Great news! The Supreme Court agreed to hear our challenge to the Carter-Cyrulnik Act."

Wally surveyed him with genial scorn. "Fuck the Supreme Court, fuck Carter-Cyrulnik and fuck you, you fucking nerd. We're talking about important shit in here, d'you mind?"

"My marriage," I explained.

Jonathan winced. He'd heard the news, too. "I'm so sorry, Raney. Is there anything we can do?"

"Did you really say you owned all the staples in the building?" Wally asked.

I sighed. "I was under duress, okay?"

"The Twitter thing." Jonathan shook his head admiringly. "That was inspired."

"You want to do something for me? Help me figure out why Aaron was unfaithful."

Jonathan lounged against the wall. He considered me through his round spectacles. Finally, he said, "I suspect it's because you're a massive ball breaker."

"What?"

"Massive, relentless and highly effective," he added.

"I am not!"

"True," Wally conceded. "You occasionally relent."

"You guys don't know me the way Aaron does. I'm a loving and supportive wife. I listen to his troubles. I worry about him. We have sex all the time."

"Oh, God!" Jonathan clutched his head. "I didn't need to know that."

Neither did Wally, apparently. "As the youth say: TMI, Moore. TMI."

"Whatever. Bottom line? I'm not a . . . what you called me. What else?"

Jonathan removed his glasses. Polishing them on his tie, he mulled over the question.

"You've let yourself go a little bit," he said.

Wally whistled. "Brave man right here."

Brave? Not really. Jonathan knew he couldn't hurt my feelings, just as I couldn't hurt his. We were all that way, those of us who had come up through the associate ranks together. We'd spent hours parsing ambiguous praise from our overlords, arguing arcane points of procedure and supporting one another in times of trouble—the death of my grandmother, the end of Jonathan's first marriage, the mistake that nearly got Wally fired. We were a family, a diverse, slightly demented tribe with vicious in-jokes and perpetual grievances and undying loyalty. Complete honesty was what we wanted, and what we knew to expect from each other.

"So I'm no beauty queen," I said. "It's not like anything's changed."

Jonathan wasn't buying it. "We're getting older. Everyone needs to make more of an effort. I remember a time when you were almost—*almost*—fuckable. Now look at you. No makeup. Boring clothes. Your hair is, like . . . I don't even know what that is."

"You're being so sexist right now," I told him.

"Uh, sorry, no. Sexist would be me pussyfooting around and *not* telling you the truth, because you're a girl and you might get your feelings hurt." He jerked his head toward Wally. "I'd be equally straightforward with this foul slob."

"I'm as beautiful as an angel," Wally said.

"You have a busted face and clown hair," Jonathan informed him.

"How you convince your wife to sleep with you is an utter mystery to me."

Wally smiled at him serenely. "I'll give you a hint, my boy. One word. Four syllables. Rhymes with 'schmunnilingus.'"

"You *are* being sexist," I said. "Listen to what you're saying, Jonathan. I'm a woman, and my life has gone haywire. Why? Because I don't pay enough attention to my appearance. I'm supposed to change, to make myself more attractive—if not for Aaron, because of Aaron."

"Duck and cover, Tatey," Wally advised him.

"That's not what I'm saying," Jonathan said. "I'm saying—"

"It's outrageous," I said. "I reject it. I reject that narrative."

"Good for you," Wally said. "You're right—we only see one side of you. To Aaron, you may have been the shit. You may have been the hottest thing going."

"Exactly!" I paused. "But then why did he cheat?"

Wally glanced at Jonathan, Jonathan at Wally. They turned to me, helpless.

"We have no idea."

TEN

I WAS HURRYING down Chapel Street when my phone rang. I fished it out of my backpack. "I'm almost there."

"What about *O Brother, Where Art Thou?*" Aaron said.

I entered the shop and scanned the shelves. "Checked out." I'd walked too fast, and now I started to cough.

"Are you still sick? What did the doctor say?"

"I haven't gone yet."

"Raney," he chided me. "You're not taking care of yourself."

"What's the point, when you're not here?"

I'd meant to sound playful. It came out pathetic. "Sorry. I didn't mean—"

"It's okay," he said. "I feel the same way."

I was in a video store in New Haven. Aaron was in a video store in Palo Alto. Both are long gone, no doubt. But for a few months back in 2001, we more or less kept them in business.

"How's the weather?" I asked.

"Warm. Sunny. I hate it. Do they have *Scream 2?*"

I asked. The guy behind the counter shook his head. "Checked out," I told Aaron.

We were renting a movie. Specifically, we were renting two copies of the same movie, which we would then take back to our separate apartments and watch, staying on the phone the entire time. That way, we could talk, and laugh, and pretend that the other was right there beside us, instead of three hours and three thousand miles away.

"What about *American Beauty*?" I said.

"We saw it in the theater, remember?"

In the four years since we met, Aaron and I had been pretty much inseparable. Evenings, weekends, holidays and school breaks—if we weren't in class, we were together. After we graduated, he followed me to Yale and did a year of postgraduate work while I started law school.

Now we were apart. A month earlier he'd moved to California to start his Ph.D. program. The change was abrupt, and upsetting. We had postcards and letters, e-mails and phone calls. We'd have visits, too, but those hadn't started yet.

In the meantime, Aaron came up with Transcontinental Movie Night. This would be our seventh venture. It was fun, for the two hours it lasted. It provided the illusion of normalcy, of togetherness. But when the credits rolled, and we hung up, the separation was worse than ever.

"I hate this," I whispered.

He sighed. "Me too."

His departure had made me realize that my life, which had seemed continuous, coherent, was actually two lives: the life before Aaron, and the life that started when he came up to me at that party. The life before was . . . well, it was a little dull. I had friends. I had a species of fun. But my attention was always focused on what was coming. The next exam, the next scholarship application, the next acceptance letter.

Aaron made me ease up and look around. He made me laugh. He showed me a world I'd been too busy to notice. I still worked hard, I still focused on the future, but when I was finished, Aaron was there.

Until now.

"How could you leave?" I blurted out.

The guy behind the counter looked up. I pushed through the door, brushing away my tears.

"Oh, Raney." Aaron's voice was so kind. "I didn't leave. Not really. This is temporary. It's—"

"I don't know what I'm doing without you!"

"We should have picked the same school," he said. "What were we thinking?"

I slumped down on a bench. "We weren't."

"I'll come back." He sounded resolute. It cheered me, even though I knew it was impossible. Stanford had wooed him. He was going to be a star.

"You can't," I said. "You need to be there, and I need to be here. But it's hard."

"Only for a few years. We'll see each other every other month, and be together in the summers. It's bad now, but we'll get used to it."

"No, we won't," I grumbled.

"Okay, we won't. But it will get easier. And one day it will end, and we'll be together."

"You're coming for Columbus Day, right?"

"Already bought a ticket."

"Let's not watch a movie tonight."

"Fine by me," he said. "We'll just talk."

I felt my cough rising up again. I fought it down. I'd go to the doctor tomorrow.

"I'm here, Raney," he said. "I'm not there, but I'm *here*. With you. And I'm not going anywhere."

THURSDAY MORNING. A team meeting in my office.

"Where are we on the Griswold stipulation?" I asked.

Stephen consulted his notes. Rahsaan lounged on the window ledge. Amanda perched on the sofa, all eagerness and pen at the ready. Jisun, my fourth-year and secret favorite, sat in the chair opposite Stephen, blade straight and missing nothing.

We discussed the stipulation, then moved on to the next case. I half listened. After thinking over what Wally and Jonathan had said, I'd gone back to Brooklyn last night, taken off my clothes and inspected myself in the mirror.

On the plus side? I was basically normal looking. No strange tics or obvious flaws. My hazel eyes were pretty. I had decent teeth. And despite years of sleep deprivation, lack of exercise and poor eating habits, I managed to look young for my age.

On the minus side? I was basically normal looking. My hair, which used to be strawberry blonde, had faded to a kind of sad beige. It was frizzy and indifferently cut. My face was . . . a face. My body was scrawny in some places, flabby in others. Breasts: meh. Bottom: meh.

Overall assessment: meh.

I wasn't insecure about my looks. I was secure in the fact that I didn't have any. I'd known I was plain since the second grade. That was the year Derek Frasier sat next to me. He was such a cute kid. Black hair, blue eyes. Freckles. He'd always ignored me. One day, he leaned into the aisle.

"I went to the zoo this weekend," he said.

I smiled, surprised, uncertain. "Yeah?"

"Yeah. I saw a frog there that looked just like you."

Then he laughed, showing me his even, white teeth.

I went home that afternoon and spent some time in front of the mirror. I could see what he was talking about. My eyes were too big for my round face. My mouth was wide, my chin pointed. I loosened my tight pigtails so that my hair fluffed out around my face.

Didn't help.

Every girl has this story, right? Every girl has been teased about her face, or her height, or her hair, or her weight. I got over it. My strengths lay elsewhere.

Stephen and Rahsaan were arguing about deposition scheduling. My phone pinged.

—How's everything?

I didn't recognize the number. My stomach did a flip. Was it Tom Nicholson, back to wreak more havoc? I took a deep breath and typed:

—Who is this?

—Mickey Singer. From Hyperium.

What a relief. Now I could be annoyed for a completely different reason. I hate texting with clients. It's too informal. Want to confirm a call or set up a meeting? Fine. But let's not conduct substantive discussions on tiny screens with our thumbs.

He wrote again:

—Have you beaten our foe into submission yet?

What a comedian.

—I spoke with plaintiff's counsel yesterday. He agreed to an extension of our time to answer the complaint. We confirmed with a letter.

—Great. Can you forward it to me?

Singer wanted a copy of a two-line letter memorializing a three-minute conversation? Before I could answer, he wrote again.

—Have your minions had any luck w/ legal research?

I needed to shut this down.

—Will call you with update in 10.

—Why, you miss the sound of my voice?

That made me laugh. My associates looked at me with surprise. I didn't feel like explaining, so I said, "Who wants to help with a presentation for the city bar association on the useless new class action rules?"

"Way to sell it," Rahsaan said. They all laughed. Amanda raised her hand.

"Thanks. Jisun, tell us about progress in the Starworth case."

—I'm afraid I don't remember your voice.

—No? Most people find it appealing. Inspiring.

—Fascinating.

—That too.

—I offered to call because texting is a waste of time.

—What?? Texting is fun!

—You know my hourly rate, right?

—$900 or something outrageous like that.

—$920. Applies to texting.

—Does it also apply to shoe repair? I've got a loafer with a worn-out heel . . .

"—and I told him if they refused, we'd file a motion to compel," Jisun concluded.

I tore my eyes away from my phone. "Nicely done. Let me know if I need to follow up."

—Sorry. Can't help you with that.

—I bet you can. I bet you've got hidden talents.

I studied the bubble of text. Was Singer *flirting* with me? I looked up, feeling absurdly guilty, as if my screen was projected overhead for all to see. My associates were paying no attention, of course.

I started to reply. I stopped.

He wasn't flirting with me. Nobody flirted with me.

Stephen tapped his pen on his legal pad. "That's all I've got."

"Great." I dropped my phone into a drawer. "Thanks, everyone."

A FEW hours later, Cameron entered my office, sat down, clicked his pen and opened a binder with a flourish.

"Infidelity," he announced.

I eased into my favorite thinking posture: chair tilted back, feet on my desk.

"The existing therapeutic-slash-sociological literature classifies extramarital affairs as falling into six different categories."

"Six is a lot," I remarked.

He held up an ink-stained finger. "First, you've got your conflict avoidance affair. This is when one partner doesn't know how to deal with bad shit—can't communicate, can't solve problems—and signals his or her dissatisfaction by having sex with someone else."

"Aaron and I had no communication problems. Next?"

He held up a second finger. "The intimacy avoidance affair. Here, one spouse is terrified of opening up to the other emotionally, so he or she creates barriers to intimacy by having sex with someone else."

"Not Aaron. He's earnest, forthcoming. Totally sincere."

Cameron turned a page. "Okay, how about number three, the exit affair? One partner wants outsies and forces it by having sex with someone else."

"Can't be. He's begging me to take him back."

"Here's number four: the double-life affair. This is when someone has a comfortable, basically content marriage, at the same time that they're conducting a long-term romance on the side."

"It only happened once. And again, that doesn't sound like Aaron."

Cameron made a note. "Number five. The entitlement affair. This is when one spouse is powerful, perhaps well known. He thinks he can do as he pleases, which—"

"That can't be it," I said.

Cameron eyed me uncertainly. "Feel free to speak your mind," I told him.

"Well . . ." He shifted in his chair. "He won a Pulitzer. He's got a TV show. He's kind of famous, right? Maybe he felt like he could—"

"He didn't," I said. "He wouldn't."

Don't think it hadn't occurred to me. Something highly unusual had happened to Aaron. He'd become someone. A well-known writer and speaker. A personality. People cared about what he said, and did, and thought. He had geeky groupies. He was regularly turned into memes.

I saw how the public responded to him—but I also saw how he responded to fame. Far from becoming arrogant, or overly impressed with himself, he seemed uncomfortable. Vaguely embarrassed. He loved his work, he loved insects, and the planet. Adulation was not his thing.

"Let's move on," I said.

Cameron turned another page. "Finally, you've got your sex addicts—people who are psychologically compelled to screw around."

"Impossible. Aaron likes sex, of course, but he had no need to go elsewhere for it. We had plenty of sex. We . . ."

I stopped. I was crossing a line. Of course, I'd recently engaged Cameron to help me burn Aaron's life down, and now I was employing him as my personal infidelity researcher. Crossing lines was becoming something of a habit. Still, this felt different.

"You don't need to hear about my sex life."

"It's no big deal, Boss. We're talking about infidelity, after all. Sex is bound to pop up." Cameron smiled. "No pun intended."

I was confused. "How is that a pun?"

His smile faded. "I . . . I don't know," he stammered. "It isn't."

I frowned at the ceiling. "Nothing in your taxonomy seems to fit my case."

"Have you . . ." He cleared his throat. "I mean, have you asked him?"

I sat up, drawing my chair close to my desk. "Not yet. But I will, obviously. This is a good start. Keep going. Focus on the question of why."

He scribbled quickly. I thought of something Wally had said.

"What's a rim job?"

Cameron's pen froze.

"Cameron?"

"I don't know," he said.

"You've never heard of it?"

"Nope!"

"Sounds automotive, doesn't it?"

"Um, yeah!"

"I should ask my friend Sarah."

"You should," he said. "You should definitely ask Sarah."

THAT NIGHT, Jorge picked me up on the way back from Westchester. "How was your day?" I asked the girls.

"Eh," said Maisie, frowning at her phone.

"So-so," said Kate, staring out the window.

"Is everything all right?"

Maisie drooped against the seat. "This commute is a huge bummer, Mom."

"We spend half the day in the car," Kate added.

Just the opening I was looking for. "Why don't we find you a school in the city? Park Slope has some fantastic—"

"No!"

I backed off. Maisie's attention returned to her screen.

"Dad's been disinvited to a bunch of conferences," she said. "There are, like, a million online petitions trying to get PBS to drop his show."

I pulled a binder out of my bag and opened it. I felt Kate's eyes on me.

"Do you think maybe you should do something about that, Mom?"

Before I could answer, we arrived at the house. A man in a navy jumpsuit was standing on the stoop, nose pressed to the window. I hurried up the steps. "Can I help you?"

He turned to me. Mustachioed. Red-faced. His breast pocket said "Department of Buildings." He was holding a clipboard.

A clipboard. That's never a good sign.

"You the owner?" he said. "Mind if I take a look around?"

FOR THE next hour, I followed the inspector—Tony—as he methodically deconstructed my childhood home. "This roof's a sieve," he declared, pointing at water stains with his flashlight. "And look at the seal on your chimney. Rotted away. That's how come the birds got in."

"Birds?"

He swept the floor with the light. Droppings were everywhere.

"See that?" We were in the second-floor bathroom. Tony pointed at a dark patch on the ceiling next to the shower.

"That's dirt," I said. "The house hasn't been occupied in a while."

"Lady, that's black mold."

I shrank away. "You mean, the really bad kind?"

"Toxic as all get-out." He clambered onto the toilet and scraped a sample into a vial.

There was rot under the floorboards. Cracks in the foundation that Tony could put his hand through, and did (the guy had a real flair for the dramatic). A decaying party wall. The mother of all rat warrens in the backyard. Oh, and a problem with our sewer connection.

We didn't have one.

The beam from his flashlight flickered across the unholy mess in the basement. "I gotta bring the guys over to see this," Tony murmured. "It's like something outta *Game of Thrones.*"

We returned to the stoop, and I tried to summon a bit of my litigator's spirit. "Why wasn't I notified you were coming? Who told you to snoop around on my property?"

"Somebody called it in." Tony was scribbling on his clipboard. "They call it in, I gotta come and inspect."

I glanced at the perfect brownstone next door. That hipster was behind this, no doubt. I'd deal with him later.

I made a final plea to Tony. "I'm renovating. It's going to be good as new in no time."

"Yeah?" He snorted. "Best of luck with that."

I returned to the car. Kate craned her neck to watch as Tony affixed a red sticker to the front door. The words *UNSAFE AREA* screamed out in 48-point type. "What does that mean?" she asked.

"It means the property has been condemned."

The girls gaped at me, horrified. I couldn't blame them. My fury had blinded me to the house's problems when we moved in. But at some point, clarity should have prevailed—enough at least for me to notice that I'd dragged my daughters out of their safe, comfortable home into a toxic, vermin-infested *cesspool*.

What was I doing?

"Jorge, will you please take us to the Marriott on Sixth Avenue?"

"You bet, Miz Moore."

Maisie stared out the window as the car pulled away. "I can't believe you made us live in a condemned house."

"It wasn't condemned when we moved in," Kate pointed out.

"Way to miss the point, genius."

They began squabbling. I sank back into the seat and closed my eyes.

ELEVEN

AT FOUR THE next morning, Sarah opened her front door.

"Careful," she warned me. "You're using up all the punches on your crazy card."

"Can I please come in?"

She glanced behind her, up the stairs. "This really isn't a good time."

"I promise I won't wake the kids. I need your help."

Reluctantly, she stepped back. I headed for the kitchen, flipping the light switch. "How about some chai?"

She slumped into a chair. "This is a nightmare. I'm like a woman in one of those Lifetime movies, held hostage in her own home."

I made two mugs of tea and sat down across from her. "On Wednesday, you told me that Aaron was typical. That every guy is the kind who cheats. Is that true?"

"I can't believe that's why you're here." She rubbed her sleepy face with both hands. "But yes. Not every guy, but many. Many, many guys."

"Many?"

Sarah tasted her chai, grimaced and reached for the sugar. "Look around, Raney. Tad. My father. Half the partners at your firm. Remember Tom Kratchovil, from Con Law? He left his wife for his secretary. Jasmine, from my moms group? Her husband hooked up with a college friend via Facebook. Here's one you haven't heard yet. Remember Heidi Frota? Sat in the front row of our Civil Procedure class?"

"Heidi Frota," I said. "Heidi Frota."

"Tinyface."

"Oh, Heidi Frota! Of course. She married the skinny guy who was always cold."

"They're divorced now," Sarah said. "She caught Scarfy screwing around right after she gave birth."

"Scarfy didn't seem like the type."

"That's what I'm trying to tell you. Nobody seems like the type, because there *is* no type. Still, Scarfy took it to another level. He fucked her lactation consultant."

"What?"

"Scarfy," she paused dramatically, "had *sexual intercourse*," pause, "with Tinyface's *lactation consultant*."

"Ouch," I said.

She sipped her tea. "Ouch doesn't begin to cover that shit."

"Okay, I get it. Men are pigs."

"Women, too."

"Not as often."

"I can think of half a dozen off the top of my head. My neighbor Vanita got drunk at a conference last year and went to bed with her boss. Fiona from my moms group hooked up with a man she met on the Internet. They spend an afternoon at a Midtown hotel every week."

"What is going on with your moms group?"

Sarah reached across the table and flicked me in the head. "My point, Raney, is that people cheat. Not just men."

At that moment a tall man wearing only boxer shorts and a pair of black-framed eyeglasses wandered in from the hallway. He bent down and kissed the top of Sarah's head.

"Holla, ladies. What're we drinking?"

"Who are you?" I said.

He gave me a sunny smile. "I'm Clem!"

"Are you the Latvian?"

"Nope."

"The automotive engineer?"

He reached out and tousled Sarah's hair. "Somebody's been busy!"

She smiled up at him. "Wait for me upstairs, okay?"

"You bet." He shuffled back down the hall.

I was astounded. "Are the kids here?"

"Of course not! They're with Tad."

"Right," I said. "Sorry. So, about what you said. Cheating requires opportunity. Does that mean Aaron was enticed? That he wouldn't have done it, but she—"

"Raney," Sarah said.

"What?"

"Stop."

Her eyes were as kind as ever, but her voice was firm. I drooped a little.

"I want to be here for you," she continued. "When I was going through this shit, you were my rock. But honey? You don't make it easy."

"I don't know what I'm doing," I confessed.

Sarah gave my arm a comforting little shake. "Here's the good news. Nobody expects you to know. And nobody expects you to *do* anything. When really bad things happen, most of us lie on the floor and cry and eat too much ice cream. And we talk, Raney. We share what we're feeling. You're rushing around asking questions and working yourself up, when maybe you should take a deep breath and just . . . be. It's okay to sit and be sad. It's okay to be mortal."

I gazed into my mug. Be normal. Be mortal. Good advice, no doubt. But I wasn't sure I knew how.

EIGHT HOURS later, I left a meeting on the forty-eighth floor and took the stairs back to my office. When I walked into the suite, Renfield was on the phone. She waved. She pointed at my doorway. She scowled. I sidled up and peeked in.

Aaron was sitting on the sofa, reading a book.

He turned a page. The light from the window shone on his dark hair. I pulled back. I hazarded another glance. He checked his watch, then returned to his book.

Most of the time, Aaron loses himself in books, quickly becoming oblivious to the world around him. Not that day. Every few seconds he would look up, check his phone, cock his head to listen to the sounds of the outer office. Then he'd sigh, shift in his seat and start over.

I watched him prop his elbow on the arm of the sofa. Rest his chin in his hand. Drum the fingers of his other hand on the page.

I watched him for a long time. Then I backed out and left the suite.

MY NEXT appointment with Bogard wasn't until Monday. I rushed to his office anyway. His afternoon was booked. I could see from Tilda's face there would be no appeal.

I scanned the waiting room. The only other occupant was a wan, stringy kid slouched in a chair, scratching his throat slowly, deliberately. Possibly pathologically. I sat down.

Ten minutes later, I was sitting down across from Doctor Bogard.

"I have a situation," I said.

"And I have a sudden cancellation." His eyes narrowed. "Go figure."

I remained silent. The check I'd written to the scrawny neck-scratcher was either going to be the best five hundred dollars I'd ever spent, or the worst.

Bogard relented. "Spit it out."

"I love my husband," I said.

He nodded.

"What's with the nod?"

"I thought that might be the case."

"You did? That's nice. If you have any other major insights into my psyche, Doctor, don't be shy. Sharing is caring."

He waved a weary hand. "Talk."

"I walked into my office about twenty minutes ago, and there he was. He didn't see me. I was able to look at him without interference. And by 'interference,' I mean not from him, but from me. From my brain, and my anger, and my hurt. I simply . . . looked.

"And it hit me. I love him. He's a good person, Doctor. So much better than I am. Kinder, more patient, more open to the world. He's funny, generous, endlessly curious. I love his rambling e-mails. I love how good he is with Kate and Maisie. I love how good he is with me. I love him. And I don't know how to stop."

Bogard digested this for a moment. "Your plan for getting rid of him. That involved, what? Gathering information."

"Pestering people," I admitted.

"You said you needed to understand why it had happened. You talked to everyone but Aaron. Asked everyone but Aaron."

As soon as he said that, I knew.

"I didn't ask him because I didn't really want to know."

"Ah."

"I was searching for a plausible explanation. The last thing I wanted was the truth."

"Why is that?"

"Because it's the truth," I said. "It might hurt."

"So you tried to reduce him to a type," Bogard suggested. "A statistic."

"I wanted a tidy resolution. Something that would allow me to say, 'This is not the person I love.' If I could kill my love for him, I could dispose of this mess and move on. But it didn't work. My husband isn't an entitled jerk or a sex-addicted creep. He's not a capital-C Cheater. He's not all men, or some men, or most men. He's Aaron. And I still love him."

We were quiet for a while. Then Bogard spoke.

"What do you want to do?"

I thought about it for a moment. "I want to go home."

"So go home."

"And let him win?"

"Win? It's not a competition."

"Wrong, Doctor. Everything's a competition."

He adjusted his eyeglasses. "I see we have a lot of work ahead of us."

"I don't want to be that woman, Doctor Bogard."

"What woman?"

"You know the woman. The one whose husband betrays her, humiliates her, disrespects her—and she stays. The one we've seen at a thousand press conferences, standing stone-faced as her dearly beloved apologizes to the world for whatever deceitful, depraved thing he did. That's not my story, Doctor. I reject that narrative. But . . ." I stopped, flummoxed. "What *is* my story? I thought I knew how this worked: the faithless man, the devastated wife. Crime, cover-up, revenge. It's different when you're on the inside. I'm a character. And I don't know my lines."

Bogard tossed his notebook aside. "You want some advice? Forget the damned narrative. This predicament you're in isn't some grand plot. It's not about archetypes, or stereotypes, or any other types. It's about you."

His little gray eyes bored into me. "It doesn't take a genius to see that you're someone who likes to be in control. That you are accustomed to managing most situations you find yourself in. I regret to inform you that you cannot do that here. You cannot shape the truth of what happened to your liking. To get through this, you're going to have to deal, head-on, with what actually happened. You're going to have to talk to your husband. And you're going to have to work through how you feel."

Feelings again. There was a print on the wall above Bogard's head. A dramatic swirl of dark and light gray. It was highly stylized, but not abstract—there was a figure captured in the sharp lines and shadows. I squinted, trying to make out what it was.

"Raney?"

"Hmm?"

"What do you think about what I said?"

I sighed. "I don't have much choice, do I?"

"You always have a choice. You can keep avoiding your husband. But confronting him might give you the answers you seek."

The print clicked into place, so obvious once I grasped it. A racehorse, flying out of a gate. It looked so swift, so weightless. So free.

"Fine," I said. "I'll go home."

TWELVE

ON SATURDAY MORNING, the girls and I met Arnault the mover at the house in Brooklyn. He and his team packed up everything and loaded it into the big truck. He offered us a ride in his van, so we crammed in beside him on the bench seat for the bumpy ride home.

When Kate and Maisie saw Aaron waiting on the porch, they jumped out and swarmed him with joy and hugs. Arnault pulled the parking brake and turned to me. His dark eyes were so compassionate, I had to look away.

I followed my daughters up the walk. I looked at the ground, the lawn, the hedge, the house. Finally, at Aaron.

"Hi." He gave me a hopeful smile.

I thought, How do I feel?

How do I feel how do I feel how do I feel how do I—

No idea.

Aaron was in a good mood. Why wouldn't he be? He had his family back, and his professional woes were abating. *Slate* had published a sympathetic article on Thursday. PBS issued a statement of support. He wasn't totally in the clear—the climate panel was still investigating, and his publisher had concerns—but there was a growing consensus that he'd been the victim of a sophisticated hack.

"Nobody knows you masterminded it," Kate had noted at dinner on Friday. "You're lucky people don't know what a psycho you are."

"Yet," Maisie added helpfully.

We spent Saturday reshelving books and hanging up clothes. Kate and Maisie vanished after dinner. I spent an hour organizing my office. Then I knocked on their door.

They were sitting up in their beds, laptops on knees. I stepped inside. "Homework?"

Kate pulled off her headphones. "Porn."

"You're so dumb," Maisie told her.

I sat at the foot of Kate's bed. "Are you happy to be home?"

"In some ways, yes," Maisie began.

"In other ways, no," Kate finished.

"It's weird, being around Dad."

"We're glad to be back. And we love Dad and all . . ."

"But thinking of him doing that? It's . . ." Maisie shuddered, "messed up."

"What's messed up is how you got thrust into the middle of this. You shouldn't have to know these things about your parents. But since we can't fix that, you should try to be yourselves. If you're glad to see him, say so. If you're upset, tell him."

"What's going to happen?" Maisie asked.

"I don't know."

"Are you going to get a divorce?"

Kate threw a pillow at her. "She said she didn't know!"

"We're going to try to work it out. But we need some time. And space. I hope you understand when we're not willing to go into too many details."

Kate put her arms around me. "Are you okay, Mom?"

I hugged her back. "I think so."

In truth, I had no idea.

HALFWAY DOWN the staircase, I paused. From where I was standing, I could see Aaron on the sofa in the living room. The night had turned cool, and he'd lit a fire. I experienced a moment of dislocation, a sense of unreality so strong I reached for the banister to steady

myself. This could be any night. Any ordinary night. I could be coming down from my office to ask Aaron a question, to get a glass of water
or to join him on the sofa.

But it wasn't any night. It was my first night home after our great
upheaval. It was the first night of the rest of our marriage.

I had no idea if it would last.

He'd been watching the flames. Now he saw me on the stairs. "Is
everything okay?"

"I'm scared," I said.

"Me too."

I sat beside him. I could see the weave of his button-down, the scattered threads of silver in his hair. I could smell his familiar blend of
soap and aftershave and . . . Aaron-ness.

He slid onto the floor. He wrapped his arms around my legs, pressing his face against my knees. "You can't leave again, Raney."

"Aaron." I tugged at his arm. "Come on."

"Not until you promise." The lines around his mouth were tight
with anxiety. His dark eyes were shining. He was the guilty party, but
he was suffering, too. I felt a rush of sympathy for him.

Sympathy? I thought. He *betrayed* you, and you want to make him
feel better? He's the wrongdoer. The promise breaker.

What did I owe him? How did this work?

Aaron got up and sat next to me again. He gripped my hands.
"Thank you for giving me another chance. I am going to do whatever
it takes to fix this."

He kept talking. He was horrified. Disbelieving of his own capacity
for awful behavior. Sincerely, comprehensively sorry.

"Aaron, I need to know . . ." I felt so weak for having to ask. "Have
you seen her again?"

"Only once. For a work meeting. But listen. If you want me to quit
the show, I will."

"Of course not."

"I mean it, Raney. You're more important. We're more important."

I could have become his keeper. Insisted on knowing his where-
abouts at all times, monitored his phone calls and e-mail. But some-

how, I still trusted him. And I couldn't ask him to quit the show. He loved it too much.

"I don't want that. But I don't want to hear from her husband again, either."

He looked pained. "You won't. I promise. What else do you need?"

That was the question. I'd come home to talk and to listen. To feel. I'd abandoned my half-baked plan to erase him from my life, but I still needed to understand why he'd done it. Not to kill my love this time, but to save it.

"We have to talk about why it happened. Maybe we can come up with some ground rules. First principles we can use to guide our conversations."

"Ground rules." He liked the sound of that. "Okay. Here's one— maybe the most important one. We love each other."

"We love each other."

"And we're going to fix this."

"We're going to try." He looked crestfallen. "That's the most I can give you right now," I added.

"But we're going to talk through everything."

"In good faith, with complete honesty," I said. "Anything else?"

"Just one thing." The hint of a smile. "No matter how bad it gets, no tweeting."

"Deal's off." I started to get up.

He laughed and pulled me back down. I thought it would be difficult—being next to him, being touched by him. But it wasn't.

"Thank you, Raney," he whispered. "Thank you for coming home."

WE SPENT the rest of the weekend together as a family. It was normal-ish. Normal with a chance of not-normal. Tense around the edges, electric with things not said. After our hopeful start, Aaron and I fell silent around each other. By Sunday afternoon, I was fantasizing about the office the way most people long for vacation. I was at my desk by seven the next day.

Around eleven, Andy Templeton strolled in. "Hey, Moore."

My irritation level spiked. "What's up, Templeton?"

"Not much." He dropped into a chair and grinned at me. "I was passing by, and I saw you in here, hard at work." He stretched out his legs, crossing them at the ankles. "You're always so hard at work."

Andy Templeton and I graduated from law school together. We joined the firm at the same time. He made partner a few years after me. (Not bragging. Stating a fact.) Templeton was friendly and easygoing. Tall and handsome. A phony. A glad-hander. My close personal enemy.

He glanced at the open binder on my desk. "What are you up to?"

"Prepping for an oral argument next week."

He raised his eyebrows. "And you're still reviewing cases?"

He was so obvious, it was almost laughable. "I'm on schedule, Andy. But thanks for your concern."

Renfield clomped into the room. She stopped short when she saw him. Gave the back of his head the finger. Clomped out again.

Templeton picked up a book from a side table and flipped through it. "Marty says you took a case for Hyperium."

Associates think the partners don't gossip. They think we sit up here on forty-five like little gods, pondering eternal questions of law, plotting the downfall of our rivals, hurling the occasional thunderbolt at the mortals cowering below. They're wrong. Sure, we ponder and plot and hurl, but we also chatter like tree monkeys. The whole partnership was talking about my potentially huge, potentially lucrative new client. No wonder Templeton was sniffing around.

"A consumer fraud thing, right?" he continued. "Sounds like real trivial shit. But hey—at least it'll generate income."

In public, my partners spoke in reverent tones about the firm's commitment to pro bono work. But Gaia Café had prompted a lot of grumbling. It was too public and too expensive, costing a few million dollars in attorney time and other resources.

That's not what bothered Templeton, though. He was sorry I'd won.

"Is there something I can do for you, Andy?"

"So many books." He was inspecting my shelves. "You don't do research online?"

"I'm not crazy about computers."

He arranged his bland features in an expression of surprise. "That's not what I heard."

So that's why he was here.

He smirked. "I heard that you are, in fact, *crazy* about computers."

Who told him? The IT-type, maybe. I wasn't concerned. People inside the firm could talk all they liked, but the truth wasn't likely to jump the walls. Those who'd helped me were complicit. Those who heard the rumors would hesitate to repeat them, knowing how the firm deals with employees who talk out of turn.

I should have been more worried. But despite the occasional qualm, I still thought I was justified in what I'd done. My sense of grievance made me feel immune to repercussion.

I wasn't, of course. But I wouldn't know that for a long time.

"Surely you have better things to do than listen to gossip, Andy." I raised my eyebrows. "Or maybe you don't?"

Before he could respond, the phone rang. A few seconds later, Renfield barged in. "Mickey Singer on line one."

Looking thwarted, Templeton followed her out. I picked up the phone. "Hi, Singer."

I heard a heavy sigh. "You don't call, you don't write. I'm beginning to think it's over."

"I left a message with your secretary on Friday."

"You did? See, this is why you should text. We could have been chatting about scintillating legal issues all weekend."

Singer was right—he did have a good voice. Warm. Slightly hoarse. Confiding. I pictured him behind a sleek desk in some modern office, gazing out the window or surfing the Internet while we talked. Surrounded by, what? Pictures of his family? I tried to remember if he'd been wearing a wedding ring.

Why was I thinking about this? I told him about a few helpful cases Amanda had found and recommended we move to dismiss the complaint.

"I love it!" he declared. "Let's celebrate. What are you doing for lunch?"

"You want to celebrate because we're filing a motion?"

"I'm going to let you in on a little secret, counselor. I am one profoundly lazy bastard. If you draft this little motion of yours, I'm going to have to spend time reading it, offering comments, *pretending* that I'm adding value to the process. At the very least, you owe me a sandwich."

Lazy? He was too engaged in our discussion the other day. And he was diligently following up now. Which meant he was one of those self-deprecating types. He probably thought he was oh-so-so charming, with his wit, and his attractive voice. He probably thought he could win people over by writing funny texts.

And . . . demanding sandwiches.

I woke my computer and checked my e-mail. "I don't really do lunch."

"What does that mean? You don't eat?"

"I eat. I just don't make a big deal out of it."

"Different foods, from different food groups, arranged enticingly on a plate," he said. "That's a, quote, big deal?"

Renfield came in with a FedEx. "I feel like this whole food situation has gotten out of control," I said. "The eating. The talking about eating. The trends and the movements and the fetishizing of restaurants. It's food."

"Eating is fun. Talking about eating is fun."

"Eh." I deleted an e-mail.

"Let's make this simple. Don't eat. But come with me. I want the experience of sitting across from you when you're not tearing someone a new asshole."

That made me laugh. Renfield poked her head through the doorway and gawped at me. I waved her away. "Has Xander recovered?"

"He's in an ashram in New Mexico, processing the trauma. But about lunch."

This was the kind of thing Marty was always nagging me about. Taking clients out, wining and dining them. Hyperium was a big deal. I should be wooing this guy.

"I'm a little busy right now," I said. "I have a Second Circuit argument coming up."

"Even better! I'd love to watch you browbeat a panel of federal judges."

I laughed again. Then I looked up. My entire team was clustered in the doorway, watching me.

"I have to go," I said hurriedly. "We'll send you a draft of the motion later this week."

I hung up and rifled through the papers on my desk, feeling the sudden urge to appear meaningfully occupied. "Come on in, everybody," I said. "Come right in."

After the meeting, I scrolled through my texts until I got to the exchange with Singer from the previous week. I found Jonathan in his office, shopping for ties online.

"Fuck paisley," he muttered.

I held out my phone. "Interpret these texts."

"Huh?"

"I want to know if this person is flirting with me."

"He's not," Jonathan said.

"You haven't even looked at them."

"I don't have to." He clicked on a tie. "Nobody flirts with you."

"That's what I thought! Still." I pressed the phone on him.

He took his time reading. At last: "It's possible. What's this about shoe repair?"

"Nothing. That's—"

Wally shambled in. "Greetings, my fuzzy ducklings! What am I missing?"

"Attempted flirtation, by an unknown assailant." Jonathan passed him the phone.

Wally peered at the screen through his reading glasses. "Oh yeah. She totally wants you."

He tried to return the phone to Jonathan, but he pointed at me. Wally's eyes bulged. "These were written to *you*?"

Now I was annoyed. "Is it so unlikely?"

"You don't exactly invite this kind of attention," Jonathan said.

"I know, but you guys act like—"

"Shh, children." Wally adjusted his reading glasses. "Papa's working."

He reread the texts, mouthing the words. Then he nodded briskly. "My ruling stands. He's flirting, for sure."

"No way," I said.

"This shoe business? It's obviously a sex thing."

"It's not. It's—"

"Yup," Wally said. "Hot dog's got a big-time foot fetish. Who is he?"

"Nobody. And he's not flirting."

Wally scrolled up the screen. " 'I bet you've got hidden talents'? Come on. This guy wants a little Raney on his parade, know what I mean?"

"He wants to be singing in the Rane," Jonathan added.

"He wants to Rane you in."

"He hopes his kingdom will—"

"Stop!" I grabbed the phone. "You guys don't know what you're talking about."

Wally looked sly. "Here's a question. Do you want him to be flirting with you?"

"Of course not!"

"Then why," Jonathan inquired, "are you asking?"

"I don't know! I . . . forget it." I went back to my office.

THIRTEEN

"I CAN'T LIGHT the pilot," I muttered.

Aaron glanced around the kitchen. "There must be instructions here somewhere."

The movers were gone. The girls were in the backyard. We were alone in our new house.

The place was elegant, spacious, immaculate. I'd wanted something pristine after growing up in a falling-down house, and enduring years of cramped apartments in New Haven and Manhattan. Six months earlier, we'd found it: a center-hall colonial on a rolling lot. I was a newly minted partner. Aaron was teaching steadily. Still, the mortgage was staggering. Marty told us not to worry. To take the leap.

I tried the pilot again. Nothing.

"I bet there's a manual online." Aaron reached for his phone.

I stretched out on the floor and groaned.

"Uh-oh," he said.

"We have to go back to the city, Aaron. Right now."

He sat down beside me. I felt his fingers stroking my hair.

He said, "Tell me your troubles."

Where to begin? Everything was cascading down on me at once. "One. This is too much house for us."

"We did the math, honey. We can afford it, thanks to you."

"Okay, two. What if I fail? What if they fire me?"

"Isn't the point of being a partner that they can't fire you?"

"No! They can kick me out with a two-thirds vote."

"Three-thirds voted to kick you in, Rane. You've never failed. You won't start now." Aaron paused. "Did you look up that two-thirds thing?"

"Maybe," I admitted. "Here's three: what if the girls hate their new school? Four: what if they love their new school and become shallow, status-obsessed rich kids? What are we doing in this fancy suburb? You grew up on a farm. I grew up in Brooklyn."

"We'll adapt," he assured me. "I'll keep cows on the lawn, and you can run a bodega out of the garage. The neighbors are going to *love* us."

"Aaron."

"Sorry." He stroked my hair. "Keep going."

The back door slammed. Two pairs of light-up sneakers stopped a few feet from my head.

"Where's Monopoly?" asked Kate.

"Why is Mommy on the floor?" asked Maisie.

"Your toys are in your boxes, which are upstairs in your rooms," Aaron told them.

I raised my head so I could see their faces. "You have three acres of lawn and your own swing set. You want to play a board game?"

"Yes," Kate said. "Also, can we share a room?"

"This house is huge," Maisie added. "And scary."

I clutched my head with both hands. "What have we *done*?"

Aaron ushered them out. Then he eased my head into his lap. I looked up into his patient, loving face. "Five. Everything is changing."

"Nothing is changing," he said.

"But—"

"You will not fail. Our daughters will not become assholes. We will make this our home, and we will belong here."

This is what I needed. To talk, to spill everything, while Aaron listened and sympathized and told me how it really was. This is what comforted me.

Though I had a few follow-up questions.

"Will you keep packing my lunch every day?"

"If you want me to."

"Will you include a note?"

He smiled down at me. "Always."

"I love you," I said. "You make me make sense."

He touched my cheek. "It's a tough job, but somebody's got to do it."

"What about the stove?"

"We'll fix it tomorrow. Tonight we're going out."

"Where?"

"There must be a pizza place around here. We'll drive around until we find it." He pulled me to my feet and kissed me. "That'll give me time to tell you this idea I have for a book I want to write. I think you might like it."

MY EYES flew open seconds before the alarm. Aaron was asleep. Chest rising and falling, one arm flung over his head. He was far from me, on the opposite side of the mattress. We usually slept close together, near the middle. But in the days since my return, space had opened up between us in bed. We didn't plan it, but we patrolled it diligently. No stray limbs, no sudden feints. It was wide, white and smooth—a three-hundred-thread-count demilitarized zone.

I left the bedroom. Poked my head into the girls' room. Still breathing.

In the kitchen, I put the kettle on. Checked my e-mail. Nothing important. I placed a call.

Far away, I heard a phone ring. Once. Twice. Then, "Raney?"

"Why did you do it, Aaron?"

"Where are you?" His voice was thick with sleep.

"In the kitchen."

"Why are you calling?"

"We're supposed to be talking," I said. "I thought it might be easier on the phone."

I heard the rustle of sheets. "I'm coming down."

I sighed. "Okay."

I made chai. I flipped the switch on the coffeemaker. I was at the table when he came in. He picked up the tin on the counter, squinting at it curiously. "Since when do you drink chai?"

"Tell me how it happened, Aaron."

He sat down. He ran his hands through his hair, tugging on the ends, a habit in moments of stress. Then he rested his arms on the table and looked at me.

"I've thought about this a lot. The best way I've found to explain the feelings I was having, and the thoughts I was thinking that led me to do what I did, is this: I woke up one day, and you weren't there."

I was confused. "When was this?"

"About two years ago."

"What?"

"We've been together a long time, right? And we've been happy. Those early years, when you were killing yourself at the firm, and I was struggling to finish my dissertation? They were the best times of my life. But they were also a blur. We were always working, always parenting—apart or together. Time passed. The girls got older. You were so successful. Then my career took off. It was unreal, and so exciting. It felt like we had everything we'd ever dreamed of. But one day, it hit me. There was something I didn't have anymore." He paused. "You."

"What are you talking about, Aaron?"

"I'm trying to say that we'd lost each other. As a couple. We were drifting. And yes, I know that's a cliché. But when it's an accurate description of your reality, the fact that it's dumb and trite and what everybody says in this situation doesn't really matter that much."

I was doing my best to remain calm. To fight the enraged howl, lunging upward, begging for release. "I have to tell you, I've never felt that way. We're busy people. Just because we don't spend every waking moment together doesn't mean we're living separate lives."

He pushed his mug aside and reached for my hands. He pressed them together within his. "Life is good, Raney. On the surface, everything's fine. We rarely fight. The girls are great. The machine is running smoothly. Which is what it felt like sometimes. A machine, operating without much spontaneity, or togetherness."

"We're living separate lives? Is that what you're saying?"

"Do you know how many times we've gone out, alone, in the last year? Twice. How many evenings we spend with each other at home? One a week, tops."

"Why didn't you say something?"

"I did. I would say we needed to make more time for each other. And things would be better—until the next work emergency or Maisie meltdown. I started feeling bad about complaining. You're such a superhero. It's one of the things I love about you. But you give it all to the girls and the firm. These last few years, you haven't been sharing your life with me."

"What is it you want me to share? How an associate dropped a ball on something? The joke Wally told at a partner meeting? It's all pretty boring. Especially compared to your life. The books, the show. How am I supposed to compete with that?"

He looked perplexed. "Why would you have to compete?"

"You know what I mean," I said. "My day-to-day isn't that interesting."

"*You're* what's interesting. If you want to share something, I want to hear it. I think you're the most amazing person on the planet."

I shrank away. "So it's my fault. I, what—drove you into her arms?"

He sighed, defeated. "This is what I was worried about. I'm trying to explain, and you only hear excuses. You hear me blaming you."

"Because you are."

"I'm not! I'm saying there was a void in my life—a void that was as much my fault as yours. I didn't try to find you again. I didn't fight my way back."

"Why not? If you loved me, you realized something was wrong . . . why not try harder?"

He bowed his head. "I wish I had a satisfying answer. I was weak. I am weak."

I didn't say anything for a moment. I was gathering my strength.

"She came along," I said. "Tell me how that happened."

He rose to refill his coffee, then returned to the table. Those hang-dog eyes. "The network hired Deirdre to help me develop the show. I was a television rookie, whereas she had a lot of experience as a pro-ducer. She was helpful. And really nice. She—"

I set my mug on the table, a little too hard. "I'm sure she's lovely, but you can skip the specifics."

"I'm trying to answer your question." He was choosing his words with care. "To do that, I have to say a few things about her. Because it explains why . . . I began to look forward to seeing her. Talking with her became a fun part of my day. We became friends. She was hav-ing trouble in her marriage. We discussed it. We started having lunch together. We e-mailed at night and on the weekends. I found myself thinking about her when she wasn't around. I found myself . . ." He buried his face in his hands. "Oh, God. This is hard."

Hard? It was killing me. But he was only giving me what I asked for.

"I love you, Raney. You have to remember that. That's what's real, and important."

I was still struggling to stay calm. "You must have known what you were doing was wrong. Didn't you feel guilty?"

"It's kind of remarkable, the contortions your mind is capable of. The justifications and delusions. How elastic your morality can be when it runs up against your . . ." He faltered, looking down. "Against what you want. How did it happen? Step by very, very small step. Talk-ing. Getting coffee. Getting lunch. Texting. And at every turn, I told myself that I wasn't doing anything wrong. She's my friend. A man and a woman can be friends! I love my wife. I would never do anything to hurt her."

Aaron looked up from his nearly empty cup, eyes pleading now. "I believed all that. It's what I said to reassure myself that I wouldn't really do the thing that I . . . that I increasingly wanted to do."

"And that you ultimately decided to do," I said. "You decided to cheat."

"Decided?" he said, as if confused by the word. "Did I consciously decide?"

"You bought her a plane ticket, Aaron. You had a hotel room."

"I know, but you're suggesting something deliberate. I didn't have a moment where I rubbed my hands together and said, 'Now I'm going to commit adultery!'"

"Still, you wanted to," I insisted. "At some point, you decided to do it. To stop being a faithful husband, and to start cheating."

"I must have," he said sadly. "But I didn't think about it that way."

"SO ACCORDING to him we've changed," I said to Bogard the next day. "I don't buy it—I mean, how convenient, right? But let's say, for the sake of argument, that he genuinely believes this. It still doesn't explain anything, because it doesn't explain him. He's earnest and authentic and good. He's an entomologist, Doctor—he *literally* wouldn't hurt a fly." I paused. "So why did he decide to hurt me?"

"Let's talk about your treasure chest," Bogard suggested.

"Why?"

"It's a fascinating way to compartmentalize yourself, don't you think?"

"More like useless." I remembered I was waiting for client sign-off on a brief. I pulled out my phone. "Look how much good it's done me the last few weeks."

"Your choice of container is intriguing," he noted.

"I was going to go with a Rubbermaid storage locker, but plastic is full of toxins, so . . ."

"Why don't you put your phone away?"

I dropped it into my bag.

"What was happening in your life that you felt such anxiety?" Bogard asked.

I thought about it. "Nothing in particular. I didn't remember my parents' death, so no trauma there." I paused. "I suppose the world did feel . . . precarious. It was just me and my grandmother. We didn't have a lot of money. We lived in a bad neighborhood."

"Why didn't you move?"

"I never asked Grandma about it, but looking back, I think she didn't have a lot of inner resources. Her daughter had died. For her, that kind of ended things. She wasn't one of those sassy seniors who flourish in the face of tragedy. She got the job done—she kept me fed and clothed and safe, she was unfailingly gentle—but her wherewithal was limited."

"Did you feel loved?"

"Sure."

Bogard peered at me over his spectacles. "I sense a 'but' coming on."

"Well, I was just thinking. I did see . . . pictures. From before. Grandma with my mother, with my grandfather. With this crazy old car she had. Smiling, laughing. Happy. I never knew her like that. She was anxious. Tired. I seemed to overwhelm her, though I don't think I was that much trouble. I tried not to be. Anyway, rather than burden her with my troubles, I decided to cope with them on my own."

"Treasure chests hold valuable things," Bogard remarked. "Gold. Jewels. Are you sure it was only unpleasant feelings you locked away?"

"What do you mean?"

"Strong emotions of any kind are powerful. They can be unsettling. Uncomfortable."

I was itching to check my phone again. "If you say so."

"Do you disagree?"

"I'm not a robot, Doctor. I express happiness and contentment on a daily basis. I never locked away my love for the girls. Or Aaron."

"You filled the chest every day before school? And, later, before work?"

I wished he wasn't so fixated on the stupid chest. "Shouldn't we be talking about my marriage?"

"Indulge me."

"I filled it every day, more or less."

"And when your day was done, did you unlock the chest? Did you release all those emotions?"

I thought about it. "Well, no. That would be . . . I mean, that's kind of silly, isn't it?"

"Sillier than locking them up in the first place?"

"I unlocked it with Aaron," I said. "I would tell him things. My worries, and troubles."

"Always?"

"Yes," I said. "Maybe not as much lately, but . . . no. Not true. I did. Always."

Bogard nodded. "Interesting."

FOURTEEN

A FEW WEEKS LATER, I went to the gym at lunchtime. I had always thought exercise was a waste of time. But since my great marital cataclysm, I'd found myself with a ridiculous amount of excess energy. Long walks, taking the stairs—nothing helped. Most nights I spent hours staring at the ceiling, brain whirring, body fizzing with restlessness.

So shortly after returning home, I joined a sleek and intimidating "fitness center" down the street from the firm, signing up for a batch of sessions with a "personal fitness consultant." Jared was a cheerful boy with a blocky blond head. Raised in Wisconsin. Partial to tight T-shirts. Impervious to irony.

"What would you say is your primary fitness goal?" he asked, during our first meeting.

"Cessation of thought," I replied.

His baby-smooth forehead crinkled. "Huh."

I was sure I'd despise him. I was sure I'd despise the entire enterprise—the sweaty, mirrored cave, the throbbing music, the grunters and gaspers and conspicuous preeners. But it wasn't that bad. Jared was patient and encouraging, impressed by my stamina and reluctance to rest between sets (why waste time?).

We were focusing on my lower body that day. "Grasp the bar and raise it slowly, keeping your shoulders relaxed," he instructed me.

"Feet apart?"

"Not as such." Jared loved that phrase.

I put my feet together. I bent. I grasped. I raised.

"Good!" I did it nine more times. "You're feeling that in your glutes, right?"

"My glutes are in my arms?"

His forehead crinkled. "Um, no . . ."

I was wearing baggy sweatpants and one of Kate's cross-country tank tops. As I lifted the bar again, I caught my reflection in the mirror.

Were those my arms? They seemed to have . . . muscles.

"I look good," I blurted out.

"You've been coming every day," Jared said. "It's starting to show."

I lifted the bar again. Then I stopped smiling. This is about sleeping better, I reminded myself. Looks don't come into it.

I thought I knew myself back then. I didn't know myself at all.

ORDINARY LIFE resumed. The girls went to and from school, sports, the homes of friends. I went to and from work. Aaron threw himself into research for his next book.

We kept talking. We let our conversations unfold organically, keeping our ground rules in mind. Love. Honesty. No storming out.

I tended to find myself at one of two extremes. The first was a place of remarkable calm. I had a genuine desire to know how the man I loved had come to do and feel things so foreign to my understanding of our relationship. The fact of his cheating was so unreal that at times I could view his infidelity with an almost detached curiosity. That actually happened? How astonishing.

The second place was darker and all too real. There, I thrashed around in my now-familiar mix of rage, fear and humiliation. How could he? Why would he? Who was he?

Aaron was struggling, too. Intensely guilty, ashamed, forced to articulate the impulses that led him to do what he did. Sometimes eager to take the blame. Sometimes defensive.

Still, we talked.

"What's the thought process that allows you to go from missing your wife's company to copulating with a coworker?" I asked one night.

It was a Thursday in late October, over a month since I'd come home. The girls were upstairs doing homework. Aaron and I were cleaning up after dinner.

He rinsed a saucepan. "Do you want an answer, or are you going on the attack?"

"You were feeling lonely. Why not join a book club? Take up a hobby, like . . . I don't know." I snapped out my dish towel. "Competitive birding. Is an affair really the answer?"

"Of course not. But I didn't want a friend. I wanted romance. I wanted what we'd lost."

"We," I repeated. "What *we* lost. Yet you didn't talk to me. You went elsewhere."

"I tried talking to you. You were always working. Or wrapped up with the girls."

I threw my towel onto the floor. "And you wonder why I feel blamed."

Aaron was in an impossible position, forced to answer my questions, then deal with the inevitable blowback. To his credit, he didn't give up.

"You want me to be honest, Raney. I'm being honest. My affair was wrong. But it was a reaction to what was going on between you and me."

I looked at him closely. My husband. The man I'd known half my life. The man who was my life. So loved, so familiar, so utterly known—and yet so completely strange! How could he be the boy who came up to me at that party, the voice on the phone telling me not to cry, the man sitting on the kitchen floor listening to me catalog my anxieties—and also the man standing before me now, confessing the urges that had led him to sleep with someone else?

I didn't—couldn't—understand.

"This revelation," I said. "About us growing apart. You said it hit you one day. When?"

He shut off the water and dried his hands. "Do you remember Bethany and Georgia's wedding?"

"Of course." They were some of our closest college friends, married two summers ago.

"We were in the third row, remember? The moment the 'Wedding March' started, everybody stood up to see Georgia come sailing up the aisle. I had a really good view of Bethany. She was watching Georgia, too, and the expression on her face . . ." He trailed off. "She was radiant. She was looking at the best thing that had ever happened to her. I was so happy for her. Then I realized something. You used to look at me like that."

I pulled out a chair and sat down. "We are so broken."

"Raney, no!" Aaron sat across from me. "We're not broken. We're . . . dented. We're here because we have something worth saving."

" 'Missing you.' That was the subject line of the e-mail you sent me. How could you write that, when you were with someone else?"

"Because it was still true."

"I bought a travel guide to San Francisco," I said, as if this were a defense against his argument. "I want to spend time with you. I just . . ." I picked at the grain of the table with my thumbnail.

He reached for my hand. I drew it back. "Tell me about Deirdre."

This surprised him. "I thought you didn't want—"

"Specifics," I said. "I know. I changed my mind."

"Okay." He cleared his throat, tugged at an ear. "Well, she's . . . a nice person, believe it or not. She's smart. Funny. She—"

"Is she more attractive than I am?"

"Absolutely not."

That was way too quick. "You're lying."

"I'm telling the truth."

"You aren't attracted to me anymore." It was a statement, not a question. I wanted desperately to be contradicted.

"Of course I am, Raney. I always have been."

"What does she look like?"

He hesitated.

I reached for my phone. "I'm googling her."

"No. Please." He sighed. "This is hard, okay? To tell you about the person I . . . but okay. She's not as attractive as you are. She's different. I mean, a different type of woman. She's . . . I guess you'd say she's full-bodied."

I'd been watching his face closely, intent on what he was saying. Now I recoiled.

"She's my age. She's not . . . I mean, when we first met, I wasn't attracted to her."

Deirdre was a full-bodied woman. I'd watched his mouth form those words, describe her body. A body he had possessed with his own. Caressed and kissed. His mouth on . . . what? Her round breasts. His hands on her voluptuous, feminine hips.

I looked at my hands, clinging to each other on the table. I'd always thought they were my best feature—delicate, with long, slender fingers. Now they seemed bony. Bloodless.

Full-bodied. Is that what he liked? Is that what he wanted, before he got stuck with me?

"Raney?" Aaron watched me closely. "Talk to me. Please."

"Keep going," I said.

"It's hard to explain, but more than how she looked, it was the fact that she was new. Someone different, who was into me. It was fun to feel that I was interesting, that I was important to someone—"

"Wait," I said. "Important? You're important to me."

He gave me an uncertain look.

"Aaron. You're my *husband*. I love you."

"I know. Of course. But day to day, you don't really . . . show it, so much."

I shook my head. I didn't get it.

"You're so self-sufficient," he explained. "It's hard to know when you need me."

"I need you all the time!" Then I thought back to the day everything changed. I'd been waiting for news, missing Aaron, longing for his reassurance. I'd considered calling him—only to talk myself out of it. Over and over.

It had been the idea of him that made me feel strong. Knowing he was in my corner.

"You're there for me in my head," I said, well aware of how inadequate it sounded.

He touched my arm. "I want to be there for you in the real world. All the time, like I used to be. That's what makes a couple."

At which point I was overcome by the unfairness of it all. He loved me for being a superwoman, but also expected me to be a damsel in distress. I was supposed to be myself, but also open and expressive. Strong and vulnerable. Capable and needy.

It was hard enough being me—now I had to be two people?

"I'm sorry I let you down," I snapped. "I'm glad you found a nice full-bodied woman who could be all the things you needed."

His face flushed. "I am trying here, Raney. Trying to apologize and explain. Two tasks, I'd note, that you haven't gotten around to yet."

"Don't change the subject."

"It's the same subject. You tried to destroy me, Raney. Is that how you treat someone you need? Someone who's important to you? There are people who still look at me like I'm the enemy. My motives are going to be suspect for a long time. You did that."

"I was hurt!" I cried.

"I know," Aaron said. "Trust me—you made that very clear."

"NAKED, FATHER RALPH stepped off the veranda to stand on the barbered lawn with his arms raised above his head—"

"Can I help you?" asked the clerk.

I jumped. *The Thorn Birds* slipped from my grasp. I fumbled to catch it.

"No! Thank you. I'm only browsing." I shoved the book back on the shelf and fled the store.

I hurried to the café where I was meeting Sarah. It was a faux-French place, all fogged mirrors and woven bistro chairs. She entered a few minutes later, trailing Mercer.

"No school today?" I said.

"Pinkeye." She shed her hat and coat. "We're under quarantine, but we needed to get out of the house. Right, kiddo?"

He saluted her. "Right, Mom-o!"

Sarah ordered a cappuccino for herself and a hot chocolate for Mercer. I ordered a chai.

Mercer said, "Did you know a kid in my class, his name is Moloch, when he was a baby he ate a stick and that's how he got that voice?"

I looked at Sarah. "Hard to know where to begin, right?" she said.

"His name is Moloch?"

"The evil god of the Hittites," she said. "I had to google it. There's also an Anouk, a Reagan, a Carter and a Xerxes."

"There's not a Xerxes," I said.

"I shit you not, my friend."

"Don't swear, Mommy," Mercer said sternly.

She ruffled his hair. "Sorry, baby."

Our drinks arrived. Mercer disappeared under the table with his cocoa. "You've lost weight," Sarah remarked.

"I've been going to the gym a lot."

"It shows." She sipped her coffee. "Isn't it great when the pounds finally start dropping off? When your clothes get loose, and full-length mirrors don't need trigger warnings?"

"I'm not doing it for Aaron, if that's what you're thinking."

She gave me a baffled look. "I wasn't, weirdo. I hope you're doing it for yourself."

"I'm definitely sleeping better."

"That's good. But there's nothing wrong with wanting to look hot, too. You should capitalize on it." Her eyes lit up. "Let's go shopping!"

Sarah always lamented my, shall we say, no-nonsense personal style. Plain suits, plain blouses, plain shoes. I liked to keep things simple.

Was Deirdre chic? Was she quirky? Did she dress her voluptuous body in sexy clothes?

"I could take you to the guy who does my hair, too," Sarah said. "Sergio is fabulous."

Was Deirdre's hair long and stylishly cut? Did Aaron like to run his—

"Raney?"

I blinked and frowned and stared into my chai. "I'm not really in the mood to indulge myself."

"What a shocker." Sarah blew on her drink. "You would have been a great early Christian. One of those guys who went out in the desert and, like, sat on a pillar for fifty years."

"A stylite," I said.

"You would also be a fabulous *Jeopardy!* contestant," she remarked.

"Do you think I repress my feelings?"

Sarah regarded me over the rim of her cup. "Is that a trick question?"

I pressed my fingertips into my eyes. "I wish I was on a pillar right now."

I felt her hand on my arm. "You know you keep a lot inside, honey. Like right now. Here we are, chatting about gym routines and Jesus freaks, and you're obviously stewing in your own misery."

"What's so great about emotions?" I demanded. "Last time I let mine out, I nearly ruined Aaron's career. I keep a lid on them—I always have. But suddenly everyone wants me to change. Bogard thinks I should open up. Aaron says he needs more of me. What does that even mean?"

I pushed my chair away from the table. Mercer looked up from his cocoa, worried.

"I thought I had a good marriage, Sarah. Then Aaron did a terrible thing. Then I was told that the terrible thing wasn't a freak event, or an aberration—it was the result of *problems*. And those problems allegedly involve me. Aaron committed the crime, but I have to change. Even if I should, even if I can, I don't know how."

Sarah was already coming around the table. She enveloped me in a hug. Mercer reached out and hugged my leg.

"I need to act, Sarah. I need to *do* something. I can't just keep sitting around waiting for Aaron to tell me the next thing that's going to make me feel bad about myself."

Sarah pulled back. "I have an idea. Let's go away. You and me. A girls' weekend. We can do crazy shit like parasailing and zip lining. We'll have so much action you'll want to puke."

I shook my head. "Work is too busy right now."

She was doing her best. And I loved her for it. But I couldn't—or wouldn't—be helped.

She touched my arm. "I know this sucks, but you'll get through it, Raney. I promise."

FIFTEEN

ON THE FIRST of November, the partnership held its monthly meeting. Attendance was light—maybe fifty of us gathered in the conference room on forty-eight. The discussion revolved around planning for the firm's bicentennial gala—a lavish, black-tie affair we were throwing in April at the Museum of Natural History. Partners, associates, general counsels, CEOs, all gathered together to celebrate the firm. It was going to be quite an event.

After the meeting, I headed back to my suite. Renfield was on the phone. I was about to enter my office when I saw Mickey Singer sitting on my sofa, paging through a document.

I stood in the doorway and watched him. His legs were crossed. One elbow rested lightly on the arm of the sofa. He reached inside his suit jacket, took out a pen and made a note.

He was different than I remembered. I must not have been paying attention when we met. Or my rage goggles had blinded me. He was a handsome man. Was he this tan last time, or had he recently returned from someplace warm? I liked his suit. It was an unusual shade of blue.

He raised his head, saw me and smiled. "Hi there."

I felt my face go hot. Did he think I was staring? Because I wasn't staring.

"Do we have a meeting?" I said.

"Nope. I was in the neighborhood. Thought I'd drop this off." He held out the document. "Your motion to dismiss, with my brilliant comments."

He was dropping it off in person? Who drops things off in person? I took the draft from him and walked to my desk, nearly tripping along the way.

"It's excellent," he added.

I sat down behind my desk. My wide, safe, distancing desk. "Thank you. I have a talented new associate."

"Of course." He rose and walked over to the window. "I knew you couldn't have had anything to do with it."

Who drops things off in person? Clients, I told myself. All the time. His behavior is totally normal. Your reaction is what's weird.

Rather than analyze that, I called for backup. "Renfield!"

She stuck her head through the doorway. "Would you like something to drink?" I asked Singer. "Coffee? Tea?"

"I'd love a glass of water, thank you."

He smiled. She melted. Typical.

"I'll have a chai," I said. She disappeared.

"Chai," Singer mused. "Interesting."

"Is it?" I flipped through the document. He'd made a half-dozen notations and rewritten a few sentences.

"Definitely. Why do you call your secretary Renfield?"

I liked his spiky handwriting. "Sorry?"

"Her nameplate says Gloria Chernowsky. Why do you call her Renfield?"

"Literary joke." I held up the pages. "Thanks for this."

Renfield came in with his water. "Thank you, Gloria."

"You're very welcome, Mr. Singer." She headed to the door. Looking at me behind his back, she put a hand on her heart and mouthed, *I love him!*

"What about my chai?" She rolled her eyes and walked out.

"I brought you another present," Singer said. Now I noticed a foil-wrapped package sitting on my desk. "It's from the food truck down the street. They make the best carnitas in Manhattan."

"Thanks." While he was looking out the window, I googled "carnitas." They looked disgusting.

He turned back to me. "There's something I have to tell you."

His expression was grave. My stomach dropped.

"Your office," he said, "is *intensely* boring."

That was a relief. Or a disappointment. Or both. How could it be both? Why did it even matter? I pushed those puzzling thoughts away and checked my e-mail. "Yeah, well, it reflects its owner."

Singer laughed. "I doubt that."

He wandered over to my desk. I kept my eyes on my screen. He picked up my single personal effect. The girls and I were still smiling up from the beach blanket. The jagged edge showed that someone had been lopped off. I'm sure that didn't look bizarre or anything.

"Your daughters?"

"Twins," I said. "They're fifteen. Do you have any kids?"

"A boy. He's nine." He replaced the photo. "I'm divorced. Are you married?"

"That's . . . a little complicated," I said.

Complicated? I was married. There was a certificate, in an appropriately labeled folder in a filing cabinet at home, attesting to the legal union of Aaron Peter Moore and Raney Jane Margolis, which occurred on April 17, 2002.

The situation may have been complicated. My marital status was not.

"Complicated," Singer said. "Right."

He looked like he was about to say more. Instead, he headed toward the door. "I've got to get back. Thanks again for the motion. Enjoy your lunch."

With a cheerful salute, he was gone.

An instant later, Wally tumbled in. "Was that Dr. Scholls?"

"What?"

"The guy who just sauntered out of your office. Is that Foot Fetish Man?"

"Enough with the foot thing, okay? Shoe repair was an inside joke."

Jonathan entered, grinning. "They have inside jokes! You know what that means."

"Raney and Schollsie, sitting in a tree," Wally chanted. "K-I-S—"

"He's a client, guys! You're being absurd." I began deleting e-mails.

Wally stretched out on the sofa. "Client or not, he's cute."

I looked up from my screen. "You think?"

"That athletic build? That strong chin?" Jonathan looked wistful. "I wish I had a chin."

"For sure," Wally said. "And I never say that about other men."

"Owing to your deep-seated homosexual panic," Jonathan noted.

"Exactamundo. But that guy?" Wally whistled. "I've got a half chub just thinking about him."

Jonathan cringed. I googled. Then I cried out in disgust.

"Out of here, both of you." I pointed at the door. "Some of us have work to do."

A WEEK before Thanksgiving I went to Knoxville, Tennessee, to depose a witness in a breach of contract case. Amanda accompanied me. It was her first deposition. The day could not have gone better. I was on my game, and it felt great.

Afterward, we waited for our plane in the airport bar. I sent a quick e-mail to the client letting them know we were in good shape for summary judgment. Then I turned to Amanda.

"What did you think?"

"I think law school doesn't prepare you for the law," she said. "That was intense."

"They aren't always that contentious. You'll get used to it."

She shuddered. "That guy was the worst."

"Who, the witness?"

"No. His lawyer. He acted so put upon, as if he couldn't believe he had to sit across the table from a woman. He kept lecturing you about the documents, and smirking at his client, like, 'Let's humor the little lady and answer her silly questions.' And he called you *dear*. Twice."

I poked at the bottom of my iced tea with a straw. "Did he?"

"You didn't notice?"

"Not really. I was too busy wiping the floor with his client."

Amanda got my meaning. "I know that's what matters. Still, it was so blatant. Weren't you bothered?"

"It said a lot more about him than it said about me."

"Right," she said. "But . . ."

"What?"

She was about to respond, but seemed to think better of it. She shook her head. "I'll go check on our gate."

The bartender refilled my glass. I called Aaron. When he answered, I said, "I get it."

"What's that?"

"We've changed. I've changed. We're," deep breath, "not who we used to be."

I heard him sigh. "Yeah."

It had taken a lot of frustrating, circular conversations, a lot of painful reflection, but I couldn't deny it any longer. Our marriage had always functioned so well. I didn't think it required much attention. I didn't tend to us.

The worst part? I didn't notice. Me, who was always on top of things, always in control. I'd been focused on being a great lawyer, a great mom. My marriage had been slipping away, and I wasn't even paying attention.

"I still can't believe it happened," I lamented. "We had a life. We had a marriage that was . . . capacious. It meant everything to me."

"We still do. Don't go past tense on me."

"I mean that it's changed. Everything we had has narrowed to this single point. It's all we talk about. It's all we are anymore."

"Because it's something we have to work through. Something we are working through. We'll get back to where we started. Stronger than ever."

He sounded so certain. Amanda appeared in the doorway of the bar, pointing toward the gate. It was time to board.

· · ·

I DESCRIBED the call to Bogard the next day.

"I accepted some responsibility," I said. "I acknowledged that Aaron's description of our marriage had some truth to it. That's progress, don't you think?"

"Tell me more about your conversation with your associate," he suggested.

"Why don't I ever get to decide what we talk about?"

"You do." He granted me a thin smile. "You just don't realize it."

I checked my e-mail, then dropped my phone into my bag. "She thought I should have made an issue out of my opponent's obnoxiousness. I disagreed. That was it."

"So you did notice his behavior."

"How could I not? I've been the recipient of it for years."

"Recipient of what, exactly?"

"Condescension. Excessive explanations. Gentle dismissal. The jokes and the jabs and the attempts to intimidate, subtle and otherwise. I work in a profession that tends to attract a particular type of man—arrogant, argumentative, combative. Sometimes—not all the time, but sometimes—that type of man is also the type of man who would prefer that a woman know her place, which to him is not on a bench, or at counsel's table, or across from him at a deposition. So yes. I noticed. But I didn't get worked up about it."

"I would think that sort of thing would rankle you," he said. "As a woman lawyer—"

"I'm not a woman lawyer," I said.

His gray eyebrows rose. "You're not?"

"No. I'm a lawyer who happens to be a woman."

"Explain the difference."

"There's no question that women are equal to men in every way that matters, right? But if we want men to accept us as equals—if we don't want to be interrupted and excluded and called 'dear'—we shouldn't go around defining ourselves by our gender. Woman lawyer. Woman therapist. Woman anything. That should take a backseat. Especially in the professional world."

"It sounds like you're suggesting women shouldn't complain about the problems you've identified."

"They shouldn't," I said. "There's no point."

The good doctor was perplexed. "You obviously care about these issues. Look at the case you won against that restaurant chain."

"What, Gaia Café?"

"Yes. Was that type of harm more serious in your view, and therefore worthy of pushback?"

"More serious?" I repeated. "It was certainly more harmful than anything I've experienced. The same goes for the abuse women have been suffering for decades in Hollywood, and in politics, and in the media, and which we're finally talking about. Still, it all stems from the same mind-set. One that perceives women as other, as lesser, as object. A mind-set held by many men—and some women too, I might add. Lawyers and judges might—on average—behave better than creepy restaurant managers and hideous movie producers, but many of them don't think about women any differently. Not really."

"Yet the lawyers and judges," Bogard persisted, "the subtle offenders—they don't deserve to be challenged?"

"Deserve? I don't know what they deserve. What I do know is that discrimination and harassment have legal remedies. I went to court. I presented evidence and won damages. What court is going to rectify mansplaining, Doctor? Who's going to issue an injunction against the 'dears' and the 'darlings' and the 'honeys'? Nobody. Because the root problem—the attitude—is fixed in place, and unless you can point to a specific harm, all the complaining in the world isn't going to get you anywhere."

"People can't be persuaded? You can't change minds?"

"People don't change. Not down deep."

Bogard was, unaccountably, not willing to let the subject drop. "Your associate may be looking to you as a role model. Doesn't that endow you with a responsibility to stand up to wrong attitudes, even if you're skeptical about the outcome?"

"I know what Amanda wanted me to do," I said. "She wanted me to call the guy out. To make a full-throated, rah-rah, how-dare-you-sir speech about what a pig he was being. Would that have made us feel better? Sure. Would it have shamed him, enlightened him, altered his beliefs in any way? No. To harp on the fact that we're being treated unfairly won't magically create fairness in the world. It will only distract us from what's important."

"Winning," Bogard said.

"Exactly. The answer is not to complain, but to ignore it. To work harder. The way to succeed," I said, "is to succeed."

Bogard chewed that over for a moment. Then he settled back into his chair.

"So you noticed what your opponent was doing, it annoyed you, and you suppressed your annoyance. You locked it up."

Clever Bogard. He'd managed to worm his way into my least-favorite subject. I raised my hands in surrender. "You got me. But I'm not the only person who puts on a game face at work."

"We're not talking about other people," he reminded me. "We're talking about you."

"What does *any* of this have to do with my marriage?"

"You suppress your emotions to be successful at work," he said. "Perhaps it's a mode you found harder and harder to switch off when you got home. That's consistent with Aaron's claim that you withdrew."

"I'm perfectly capable of distinguishing between my personal life and my work one."

"Are you?" he countered. "Look at your response when you learned about Aaron's infidelity. You reacted not like a hurt spouse, but like a litigator. And you attacked *his* professional reputation with particular ferocity."

"You can't say I wasn't expressing my feelings," I pointed out.

"You channeled them into action. That's not the same as acknowledging them."

I threw my hands in the air. "Fine, but I get it now! I accept what Aaron was saying. I shut down. I stopped sharing my inner life. Which gets you and me back to where we started—isn't that progress?"

"Not if you refuse to explore why it happened in the first place."

"Can we please talk about something else?"

Bogard gazed at me steadily for a moment. Finally:

"Why don't you drink?"

The tension broke, and I burst out laughing. What a game therapy is! Or maybe that's just how it was between Bogard and me. I'd change the subject when it didn't suit me, and sometimes he'd follow, sometimes not. He'd shift topics, trying to catch me out. Cat and mouse. No, two cats, batting around a ball of string: my convoluted, evasive psyche.

"I don't like the taste," I replied. "Or how it makes me feel."

"Or the loss of control, I expect."

I gave him a big smile. "We know how much I love control."

"You mentioned once that you don't swear, either. Why is that?"

"My grandmother disapproved. She was old-fashioned. Hated crude language of any kind. I didn't want to disappoint her, so I kept it clean. Later, profanity seemed unnecessary. There's always a better way to express anger or enthusiasm."

"Your life is filled with prohibitions," Bogard remarked. "Things you can't do."

"Don't do," I corrected him. "Won't do. It's a matter of choice."

"Conscious decisions," he noted. "Deliberate action. And most often, the decision seems to be no."

"I say yes," I said. "I say yes all the time."

"NO," I said to Singer, three days later, when he asked me out.

We'd run into each other at the gym of all places. I was coming out of the women's locker room. He was coming out of the men's.

"You!" I said.

"And you!" He smiled. "How are things?"

"Decent. Yourself?"

"Can't complain." He was wearing jeans and a black jacket. His hair was damp. He looked even less like a lawyer than usual.

"So you exist outside the office," he said. "I was beginning to wonder."

"Wonder no longer!" I said.

It came out way too loud. Dork.

Singer didn't seem to notice. We moved toward the exit. He shifted his bag so he could open the door. We stepped out into the chilly night.

"This weather," I said, and cringed again. Weather? That's really all you have to talk about?

"November's the worst," he agreed.

We walked down Sixth Avenue toward Forty-Fifth. I felt so awkward, painfully conscious of the movement of my body. I needed to say something. Anything. But what?

We stopped at the corner. "That suit you wore the other day," I said. "Is there a name for that color blue?"

"Do you want to get a drink?" he said.

What?

What?

"I—"

"Wait." He grinned. "Let's have chai!"

"No," I said.

Trying to soften it, I added: "I'm sorry. I . . . don't think that's a good idea."

"Is it because I'm a client?"

It was because I was married. But how could I say that now, when I hadn't said so before?

Why was everything so tangled? Why was he even asking?

"I'm sorry," I said again.

He looked at me searchingly. Then he smiled, and everything was easy again. "Don't be. And I don't mean to give you a hard time. I just have this feeling that . . ." He shook it off. "Never mind."

The light changed. He nodded uptown. "I'm heading this way. Talk to you soon."

Then he was gone.

SIXTEEN

"LET'S TALK ABOUT your sex life," Bogard said, a week later.

I pulled my phone out of my bag. Seven e-mails, two missed calls.

"Raney?"

"Haven't we covered that already?"

"Not yet. How many partners have you had?"

"Three. One in high school, more or less to dispense with the virginity thing, one freshman year of college, and then Aaron." I began typing a reply to a client.

"The first two were also men?"

"No, Doctor. One was a woman and one was a zebra. I dumped the zebra because it was lousy at spooning."

"The phone, Raney."

I sighed and dropped it. "Both were men. Boys, rather."

"How would you describe your sex life with Aaron?"

"It was good. We had sex twice a week, at a minimum. You have to admit that's not bad for a couple married almost sixteen years."

"It was good," he said. "Tell me what that means."

What was so hard to understand? "Good is . . . good. Our sex life was everything it should have been. Intimate. Satisfying. I made sure of that."

He looked interested. "What does that mean?"

I spread my hands. "Look at me, Doctor Bogard. I'm no sex goddess.

I don't look that way, I don't feel that way. Do I enjoy sex? Of course. And I know it's important. So I was always careful to make time for it."

"You're no sex goddess," Bogard repeated.

I really wished he'd stop repeating what I said with that intrigued look on his face. "All I'm saying is, I may come off as a little . . . whatever. Cerebral. Uptight. But I'm not. I like sex plenty. Even though . . ."

"Yes?"

I thought about how best to phrase it. "I guess sometimes I feel at a disadvantage. Sex is all everyone ever talks about. It seems to be all people ever do. I want people to have as much sex as they want, with whomever they want, in whatever configurations they want. But . . . don't we have better things to do with our time? I mean," I shrugged, "is sex all that?"

"You make it sound like we're a nation of sex addicts," Bogard said. "Popular culture is saturated with it, but there are plenty of opposing forces—religious, political—that condemn the kind of overt sexuality that's troubling you."

"It comes to the same thing," I replied. "The social conservatives who inveigh against transgender rights and pornography and suggestive dancing during the Super Bowl? They're as obsessed with sex as the people out there frantically humping in public."

"Again you're talking about other people," he pointed out.

"I'm sorry," I said testily, "but to explain what I'm thinking I occasionally have to refer to the rest of humanity. You want to know about Aaron and me? Fine. Sex was more important to him than it was to me. No big surprise there—he is a man, after all."

Bogard pondered that with a few slow, gray nods. Then: "You said you enjoy sex. What do you mean?"

"I mean that sex is fun. I don't have any hidden neuroses or buried traumas. I don't feel shame, I was never abused. Sex is—was—an enjoyable activity with my husband. A way to be close. It's a little ridiculous, but I—"

"Sorry," he said, "what's ridiculous?"

"Sex. Isn't it? I mean, the act itself. Aaron . . ." I hesitated, thinking how best to phrase it. "He took sex very seriously. He was always very focused, very intent. Yet it's such a bizarre enterprise. The thrusting, the moaning. And the facial expressions." I smiled. "Aaron did this thing sometimes, he would furrow his brow and bite his lower lip, as he was, you know . . . and sometimes I would have to look away so that I wouldn't smile. Then there was this circular thing he did, with his hips. It felt nice, but it was so deliberate. It made me think of Broadway musicals."

Bogard was staring at me blankly.

"I don't like musicals," I explained. "With a play, you can suspend your disbelief. But musicals are so artificial. Nobody belts out a tune during a crisis. Nobody breaks into a jig. The music interferes with the story. It's the same with sex. Certain movements and positions are so elaborate. They break the mood. I like sex that's loving and intimate. What do they call that? Vanilla. I'm a vanilla kind of woman. I don't think there's anything wrong with that. Do it, and get it—" I stopped myself. "Not 'get it over with,' of course, that's not what I was going to say. I mean . . . get it done. Keep it uncomplicated. Simple and straightforward."

"Simple and straightforward," Bogard said. "Uncomplicated."

"Right."

"But . . . you enjoy it," he said. "You enjoy sex."

"Sure," I replied. "Who doesn't?"

"LET'S TALK about our sex life," I said to Aaron.

"Okay," he said warily.

It was the next night, a Friday. The girls had disappeared into their room after destroying us at Monopoly.

"You've been telling me about the problems you saw in our marriage," I said. "Was sex one of them?"

"Yes," he replied.

I leaned back against the sofa cushions. "Wow."

"Raney, don't—"

"It's fine." I put my hands up. "I just didn't expect you to be so quick on the trigger."

"Sorry."

"Did you have sex with her because," I swallowed hard, "you didn't enjoy having sex with me?"

He reached for me. "We've been over this. I'm still attracted to you. I still want—"

"Was it better with her?"

"It was different."

I pulled away. "Which means it was better."

"Which means it was *different*. You and I weren't trying anymore. Our sex life had become a little predictable. Always the same. Which was good, and intimate, and I loved it," he added quickly. "I may have felt the staleness more than you did because sex isn't as important to you. But that doesn't excuse—"

"What do you mean?" I said. "Sex is important to me."

He hesitated. "Wouldn't you agree our libidos are a little mismatched?"

"Not necessarily."

Of course I agreed. I'd told Bogard exactly that. But now, here with Aaron, I felt compelled to dispute it.

He took my hands again. "You and I talk about everything, Raney. Except sex. You never tell me what to do. You never tell me what you want. More and more, I felt like sex was a chore to you."

"I don't have to tell you! You always know. And okay, maybe we weren't wild and crazy in bed, but at least we were *doing* it. We didn't have a sexless marriage, like some couples our age. We had sex twice a week, like clockwork."

"Exactly," Aaron said. "It was like clockwork."

I stared at him.

"I'm saying it shouldn't be so routine. It should be . . . I don't know. Fresh. Surprising. At least some of the time."

Twice a week. Like clockwork.

I'd been filling a quota.

I'd been doing everything wrong.

"We didn't make an effort to keep it interesting," he said. "Sometimes it felt like we were checking one more thing off a to-do list."

It took all my willpower to stay seated, to look into his eyes and listen to the things he was saying. They were like little knives, stabbing me in my most vulnerable places.

A chore. A to-do list. Like clockwork.

I finally found my voice. "Why didn't you ask me to change? Why didn't you ask for more?"

His look was so loving—which made this conversation all the more devastating. "You were obviously happy with the way things were. It's hard to be the one who asks for more. And you might not realize this, but your excitement feeds mine. I love nothing more than making you feel good. When you're not into it, my own interest flags."

I felt lost. "You want me to be, what? Wilder? More unpredictable?"

"This is my problem, too. And instead of doing the hard work of fixing this, I strayed. I don't want that. I want *you*, Raney. And I don't want you to be someone you're not. But maybe we could make an effort to reignite our passion. Try new things. Figure out what you really like. But only when you're ready."

AT SEVEN on Monday morning, I emerged from the elevator onto the thirty-second floor. I surveyed a vast warren of cramped cubicles hemmed in by banker's boxes, stacks of binders and cartons of paper. Photocopiers lined one wall, printers and scanners another. I heard shouting, laughter, ringing telephones. Distant music.

Lawyers rarely visit the paralegal floor. Partners never do. This is for the paralegals' benefit, believe it or not. They toil for us unceasingly, all hours of the day and most of the night. So we give them their own space, a sanctuary in which they can do things their own way.

Usually.

A small, balding man walked through the elevator bank, texting.

"Excuse me," I said. "Where does Cameron Utter sit?"

He saw me, and his eyes became impossibly large. "Uh . . ."

"Never mind. I'll find him."

I plunged between two rows of cubicles. Voices fell silent. The music stopped. Heads emerged from cubicle doorways, then shot back inside. You'd think I was the FBI, coming to raid a jihadi cell.

I found Cameron's workspace. He was sitting with his back to me, wearing headphones and dancing in his seat. I tapped him on his shoulder.

He turned, saw me and pulled off his headphones.

"You're firing me," he said.

"What? Of course not."

"Is this about the postage meter thing? That was all Hugo's idea."

"Who's Hugo?" I said. "What are you talking about?"

"Nothing!" He swiveled his chair to face me. "What's up?"

"You've been looking at sex, right? As part of your research into infidelity?"

"You bet."

"Can you give me an overview?"

"Sure." He started shifting around some papers and textbooks. "Do you want a seat?"

"I'm fine standing."

He hauled his binder into his lap. It had ballooned to four inches and was littered with flags, tabs and colored Post-its. He flipped through a few pages, then cleared his throat.

"Picture it, Boss. Virgin land, blue sky." His long hands swooped, shaping clouds and rolling hills. "Forests as far the eye can see. Mastodons roaming the fertile plain. The world is new."

"Mastodons lived during the Pleistocene," I said. "The world wasn't new."

He looked hurt. "I'm trying to set the scene here."

"Consider it set. What's the upshot?"

"Humans love sex," Cameron replied. "Boning is in our bones. We've evolved over the course of millennia to be joyful, enthusiastic, polyamorous sex havers."

"You're talking about men," I said.

"Men and women," he said.

"But men like sex more than women."

"No, they don't."

I crossed my arms. "I suppose you're going to tell me that women like sex as much as men do."

"Nope." Cameron grinned. "I'm going to tell you they like it more."

"ARE YOU sure you don't want a break?" Jared said. "Some water?"

I shook my head. "Let's keep going."

It was later that day. I'd come to the gym straight from a session with Bogard. I was once again enraged.

"Okay. This next move is a killer. I want you to stand with your feet together, your arms raised and core tight."

"My core is in my chest?"

Jared's brow crinkled. "Not as such."

I summarized for Bogard everything Cameron told me. "He showed me these studies suggesting that women underreport their masturbation and porn use. They have rich fantasy lives. They get more excited by the possibility of sex with strangers than men do. And they lose desire for their long-term partners far more swiftly than men."

I plunged on, rattling off facts and statistics, ignoring Bogard's puzzled expression. "My paralegal suggested that the conventional wisdom that men like sex more than women might be insidious cultural conditioning. We believe that women behave in certain ways, so we teach and persuade and shame them into behaving in those ways, then we turn around and say, 'See? That's how women are.'"

Bogard lost patience. "Again with other people! This is about you—what you want, and what you do, and how you think about yourself. These are the issues you should be examining."

"Now go into a low squat," Jared instructed me. "Keep your heels on the ground. Put your palms down, then jump into a plank, then jump quickly back into a squat, then jump up into a standing position. Good. Do it again."

"I *am* examining myself," I told Bogard. "Have I been brainwashed into not being interested in sex? If so, all I have to do is unbrainwash myself, and everything will be fine. But if it's something more inherent, then—"

"If," he scoffed. "You're launching yourself toward some solution without bothering to ask how you actually feel, and what you want."

I didn't say anything. What did I want? I wanted to fix our problems. I wanted my marriage back. But I was lost in a labyrinth, dark passageways twisting off in every direction. The harder I worked to find the exit, the farther away it seemed to become.

"Between you and Aaron, who usually initiated sex?"

"Neither of us. It was mutual. Unspoken."

"Did you climax regularly?"

"Not always, but often. Aaron always did."

He pounced. "What made you say that?"

"You were asking about orgasms."

"Yours," Bogard said. "Not his."

"Most people take these moves a little slower," Jared said. "You don't want to get your heart rate up too high."

"You complain I don't give you insights," Bogard said. "Here's one: when we talk about sex, you always turn the conversation to Aaron. And everything you say suggests a dynamic in which his pleasure was the focus."

"And . . . ten!" Jared clapped. "Let's take a . . . okay, eleven . . . twelve . . . thirteen . . ."

"That's ridiculous," I told Bogard.

"A few weeks ago you said you always made sure that your sex life was satisfying," he pointed out. "As if it was your responsibility."

"I'm his partner. I wanted to satisfy him."

"Did he satisfy you?"

"He always tried. I didn't have to come all the time to be happy with our sex life."

Bogard didn't say anything. I threw my hands in the air. "What do you want me to say?"

"What you really think," he replied.

"You seriously need to stop now," Jared told me.

I leaped up from my low squat, hands in the air. "I think I like sex!"
Jared stepped back.

Blood rushed to my head and I bent over. "I am . . . not . . . an aberration!" I was fighting for air.

"Uh, okay . . ."

"I'm interested in sex," gasp, "but not fascinated. Engaged, but
not," gasp, gasp, "obsessed. That doesn't make me a freak."

I straightened up. Bad idea—my vision went dark around the
edges. I bent over again. But I had to get my point across.

"Forget about the stupid studies." Gasp. "Whether it's nature or
nurture, this is who I am." Gasp.

My trainer gazed at me with wide, befuddled eyes. He had no idea
I was arguing with someone who wasn't there.

"I'm not totally uninhibited. But I'm not inhibited, either." Gasp.
"I'm . . . hibited."

"Hibited," he repeated.

"Yes." I straightened up at last. "I'm hibited. I'm just right."

"Um, good!" Jared said. "That's good. Let's get you some water."

"HIBITED," SARAH said the next day.

The skepticism in her voice spoke volumes. I put my head on the
table.

We'd met at our usual café on Sixth Avenue, now draped with
twinkling lights and fake icicles. Christmas was two weeks away.

"I need a Kleenex," Mercer said.

"That's not how you ask," she informed him.

"Please can I have a Kleenex?"

She reached into her bag and held out a packet of tissues. A grubby
hand rose from under the table and snatched it.

"Does he ever go to school?"

She snorted. "It's pre-kindergarten. I mean, it's New York City
pre-K—he's probably missing a session on personal branding—but
whatever. We'll muddle through. What's this about being hibited?"

"Can I ask you something?" I said.

She dumped a packet of sugar in her coffee. "No."

"Why not?"

"Because 'Can I ask you something?' never precedes a question." She tapped her spoon on the edge of her cup. "It always precedes a judgment. You should just say what you mean."

"Fine. Can I judge you about something?"

"Knock yourself out."

"Do you really like sex that much?"

"Yes."

"I'm hungry," Mercer declared.

"I'm Sarah. Nice to meet you."

"Please may I have a snack?"

She pulled a package of crackers out of her bag and passed it to him.

"I guess I thought you were unusual," I said. "Or exaggerating. Kind of overplaying your interest, you know?"

"Nope." She sipped her coffee. "I genuinely, unreservedly love to screw."

"So it's me, then. It's not Aaron. I'm the problem. I'm a freak."

She reached for my arm. "Honey, you're not. Some people like sex, some aren't so crazy about it. You've never shown a lot of interest." She chuckled. "Remember that time in law school, when you were trimming down there, and you thought your clitoris was a cancerous growth?"

"I didn't know it was that big!"

"Because you didn't know it was *there*."

Mercer poked his head out from under the table. "What's a clitoris?"

"Drink your juice," Sarah told him.

"Why are you being so hard on me?" I complained.

Her expression softened. "I'm not trying to be. How can I help?"

I looked gloomily into my chai. "Aaron said we had a relationship problem. We'd drifted apart, I'd closed myself off. At that point, part of me wished his affair was a sex thing—that he'd morphed into a middle-aged hound dog. That seemed fixable, containable. Now I find out we had a sex problem, too, and that seems equally complicated. Am I really not all that into sex, or am I so alienated from myself I don't know what I want? How do I figure it out?" I looked at her hope-lessly. "How am I supposed to *be*, Sarah?"

"May I have a toy please?" Mercer said.

"Oh for Christ's sake!" She grabbed her bag and threw it under the table. Then she pushed her coffee aside. "Can I make a totally off-the-wall suggestion?"

"Please do."

She looked me in the eye. "I think you should sleep with someone else."

I was aghast. It must have shown, but she pressed on.

"Sex is all about chemistry, Rane. Maybe you and Aaron aren't compatible. It happens, you know? Even with the most loving, oth-erwise in-sync couples. You want to know if you like it? Play around. After what he did, I'd say you have a pass. What about that guy who asked you out?"

"Singer? No! And he didn't ask me out."

Sarah looked confused. "You said—"

"I misinterpreted him. I'm sure he meant it as a work thing. But it doesn't matter. I can't, Sarah. I don't want to. Aaron and I are trying to work this out."

"Right," she said. "Okay. Well, it was only a suggestion."

SEVENTEEN

A FEW DAYS LATER, I walked into my suite after a client meeting. "Mickey Singer's got a real bug up his ass," Renfield announced.

"Sounds painful. Give him my condolences."

"I'm sure you're very comical. He's called three times in the last ten minutes." The phone rang, and she glanced at the display. "There he is again."

I went into my office and picked up. "Hey, Singer."

"You did it!" he cried.

"Is something wrong?"

"So bright, and yet so dim. Read the e-mail from the court."

I found it near the top of my inbox. The judge in the Hyperium case had granted defendant's motion to dismiss.

The defendant. That was us.

We'd won.

"They'll try to appeal, but if we throw a few thousand bucks their way, we'll be done with it." He paused. "Our general counsel wants to meet with you."

I felt myself starting to smile. "I'll have to think about it."

"How about Monday morning? That'll give you the whole weekend to sharpen your knives."

I laughed. "It's tight. But I should be able to manage it."

. . .

AARON MET me after work that night. We went to an Italian restaurant in the Village. As I watched him talking to the waiter, something in me just . . . let go.

I don't know if it was the good news at work, or the culmination of our conversations over the previous months, or a little of both, but at that moment, I knew the worst was over.

All my struggles—my agitation and overanalysis and relentless thought—suddenly seemed so unnecessary. Yes, he'd made a mistake. And yes, I'd suffered. We'd faced a dire test. But we were Aaron and Raney. We'd loved each other for half our lives. We were going to be fine.

Though there was one last thing I had to do.

I reached across the table and took his hand. "I betrayed you," I said.

He smiled when I touched him. Now he stopped. "Sorry?"

"What I did to you, the day I found out," I said. "The ways I punished you. I was hurt, and I lashed out, and it was totally wrong. There's more than one way to betray someone you love. It's taken me a long time to see that. I'm so sorry."

He squeezed my hand. "It's okay."

"You called it, right away—that was a sign that something wasn't right between us."

He started to respond, but I wasn't finished.

"There's more. You do so much for me, and I never acknowledge it. I wouldn't be who I am, and where I am, without you. I'm going to try really, really hard to open up, the way I used to. I'll have to get back in the habit. Maybe you can help me."

"I'd love nothing more," he said.

We smiled at each other. I wasn't angry anymore. I wasn't sad, or hurt, or confused. I was happy to be with him.

So when we arrived home and tiptoed up the stairs, it felt natural to face each other in the darkened bedroom. To kiss. To touch him again and inhale his scent. To feel the pulse in his neck. His jaw, slightly scruffy after a long day.

We undressed. Aaron was very hard. Were we going to do it the way we always did, me below, him above, face to face? Maybe we should try something new. I turned to pull down the sheets. I was bending over. We could—

He turned me around. Okay. We were doing it the old way. Made sense. We needed to ease back into it. Get reaquainted. We could try harder later. I sighed and arched my back.

How do you "try harder"? How do you spontaneously create lust? Seems like—

I told myself to focus. Aaron put a finger inside me, then two. He brought them to his mouth. He wet them and touched me again, because I wasn't quite . . . but soon I was, I was ready. We began to move together, Aaron thrusting, me pushing upward to receive him. He pressed his body close to me, as he always did, his face hovering above mine. My arms around him.

Was this how he did it with Deirdre? Close and slow, skin to skin? Or did she push him onto the bed? Did she hold his wrists over his head, as she straddled him, as he strained upward, ready to—

Stop. I tilted my hips upward. I wrapped my legs around his waist. He moaned. I kissed his neck. The meeting with Hyperium was set for nine o'clock on Monday. Marty thought it was a done deal. I wondered if Singer would be there. I wondered if—

Stop thinking. This is good. Tender and intimate. But should we be doing something new? Too bad I didn't have a bullwhip handy. There I go, cracking jokes. Bogard said my tendency to joke about sex revealed my profound discomfort with it. What did he know? I pulled Aaron's face close to mine. I kissed him, opening his mouth with my tongue. He groaned and bucked against me. He liked that. But what about me?

Who *cares* about me? It's hard to have sex when you're thinking about sex. Even harder when you're thinking about thinking about sex, and how you feel, and what you're supposed to feel, and how you feel about being told how you should feel, and how—

"Do you want me to touch you?" Aaron whispered.

"I don't think it's going to happen for me tonight."

"Are you sure?"

I kissed him, kissed his neck and chest. "It's okay."

Aaron came, calling out my name. I felt his heart beating fast as he lay on top of me.

"I love you, Raney," he whispered. "I love you so much."

I kissed his temple. "I love you, too."

ON MONDAY, Hyperium's general counsel and a handful of in-house lawyers joined Marty and me in the conference room on forty-five. Singer wasn't there. But I'd be seeing plenty of him in the future. I'd be seeing plenty of all of them.

We spent a few hours running through their most active litigations. We developed a plan for transferring cases from Rayburn. We were all pleased, all full of praise and compliments.

When it was over, and the door of the conference room closed behind them, Marty pulled me into a hug.

"You did it, Raney Jane! Congratulations."

I wandered back to my suite. Renfield wasn't around. I entered my office, but instead of taking my seat at the desk, I stretched out on the sofa. I put my hands behind my head.

I felt very, very good.

Wally appeared in the door, grinning like a wild man. "All hail the rainmaking goddess!"

I smiled up at him. "Word travels fast."

"Hyperium!" He pounded his chest. "That is *awesome*, Moore. *You* are awesome." He threw himself into a chair. "You're going to be managing partner someday."

Jonathan followed him in. "We should rename the firm."

"Fuck Hartwell," Wally scoffed. "Guy was a Nazi. Calder, Tayfield and Moore. I like it."

"You deserve this, Raney," Jonathan said. "Especially after the last few months."

I propped a cushion behind my head. "They've been rough. But I think Aaron and I are going to make it."

"I knew you would," Wally said. "You two are rock solid."

"Don't get me wrong. We're not one hundred percent over it. We still have work to do. I need to give more of myself to Aaron, not keep it bottled up inside. And then there's sex."

"No details, please," Jonathan said quickly.

I thought about the previous night. Our lovemaking was good, but I had to be more engaged. And I would be. Now that I knew there was a problem, I could fix it. We could fix it, together.

"Have you told him your big news?" Jonathan asked. "You two need to celebrate."

He was right. I needed to call Aaron and share my win.

Look at me. Opening up already.

I got up and walked toward my desk. Gaia Café and Hyperium. They were like bookends to my Very Bad Time. Not that I was going to forget about it. You're never done. Sarah had said that. You're never done, and you never should be done. Lack of vigilance—that had been part of the problem. I wouldn't falter again.

I thought back to the day after it happened, when Aaron and I argued across Brooklyn, and I told him he'd ruined everything. That he'd blighted the past, made our life meaningless. I was wrong. There was too much love remaining, too much happiness.

So we collected the pieces of our marriage and put them back together. Who knows? Maybe the result was stronger for the trials it had been through. Either way, I was ready to move forward.

My story was back on track.

As I reached for the phone to call him, it rang.

Let me stop. Right there.

Arm outstretched. Hand almost touching the receiver.

What if—

Oh, forget it.

What's the point? There is no what if.

There's only what happened next.

I hit speakerphone. "This is Raney Moore."

And a woman said, "This is Deirdre Nicholson."

PART THREE

EIGHTEEN

FOUR WEEKS LATER, on a blustery Monday afternoon, Marty tapped on my open door.

"Got a minute?"

I looked up from the memo I was drafting. "For you? Always."

He entered, stopping midway across the floor. "Look at this place!"

The contractor had finished renovations a few days earlier. My beige carpeting was gone, replaced by shining dark wood and antique rugs. The white walls had been wallpapered with a pattern of silver trees. I'd exchanged my staid, bulky furniture for a midcentury desk, a low-slung sofa and comfortable armchairs in bright orange and red.

It was warm and eclectic and fun. I loved it.

"You always said my office was plain," I reminded him.

"True. I just never expected you to do anything about it."

He headed for the window. "Of course, it's nothing compared to the other changes you've made." He glanced over his shoulder. "You look marvelous, by the way."

Marty was referring to my new wardrobe. On that particular January day, I was wearing a sleeveless sheath dress of emerald-green wool, a slim alligator belt and perilously high heels.

Or he was referring to my hair, which had been cut and defrizzed and restored to its original red-gold hue. Regularly tended to, it fell in soft waves around my face.

Or he was referring to my face, which now had color and definition. My eyebrows were neatly shaped. My eyes were rimmed with brown. My lips were dramatic and red.

Or he was referring to my glowing skin, my white teeth, my polished nails.

Or he was referring to all of it. Because I looked like a different person.

"Thanks," I said.

Marty nodded. "Yes. Lots of changes." He pivoted to the bookshelves, where he pushed a volume back into place. His attention shifted to a painting on the wall, borrowed from the firm's art collection. He roamed toward the sofa. Crossed his arms. Uncrossed them. He was uncomfortable.

But Marty was never uncomfortable. He was a paragon of being at ease in the world.

He sat down. "Is everything all right?"

"Everything's peachy."

"I worry about you."

"No need."

Unsatisfied, he rose and began another circuit of the room. "I know this is difficult, what you've been going through. To work so hard, to *try,* only to discover . . ." He inscribed a spiral in the air with one hand, heading upwards: *poof!* "It's horrible, and I'm so sorry."

He frowned at the rug. "What I'm saying is, people—even careful, levelheaded people—do rash things when they're in pain. What you've done is fabulous." Out came that expressive hand, waving in my direction, up and down. "But are you taking care of yourself, Raney Jane? Are you . . . being safe?"

I put down my pen. So Marty had heard the rumors. I was surprised it had taken this long.

"Perfectly safe," I assured him.

"Let me in, Raney. Talk to me. I can help you."

"Why do you think I need help, Marty?"

"Maybe because I don't know what's going on with you, and I always know what's going on with you. The way you look, where you're living, the car I've seen downstairs? It's richly deserved, but—it's not you."

"That's the point," I said, before I could catch myself.

"Oh, Raney."

"Thank you for your concern, Marty, but everything is okay. And I have a conference call in a few minutes, so . . ."

Ever the master of the graceful retreat, he raised his hands. "I'll butt out. Promise me this, though. You'll come to me if you need me?"

"I always do."

He left, and I dialed into the conference call. When it was over, I finished drafting the memo. Athena dropped off a few new outfits. I met with my team. I ordered a book Maisie needed for a history project. I texted Sarah to see if she wanted to go out on Saturday. I asked Renfield to reschedule my weekly facial and order me a box of pens.

Soon it was seven o'clock. I shut down my computer and pulled out my handbag (alligator, like the belt and the shoes). I freshened my lipstick and slipped on my coat.

Outside, the car idled at the curb. Jorge was polishing one of the chrome tail fins with a chamois. He opened the door for me and hurried around to the front.

"Heading to the hotel, Miz Moore?"

I relaxed into the plush red seat. "Yes, please."

Fifteen minutes later, we turned onto Sixtieth Street and pulled up to the large, well-lighted awning of the hotel. The doorman leaped to attention. I took the elevator to the lobby on the thirty-fifth floor. A young woman in a dark suit hurried past—when she saw me, she smiled.

"Good evening, Ms. Moore."

I stepped into the bar, a soaring space with a stunning view of the city. All of the patrons were facing that direction, admiring it—except one man, at a small table near the window, whose eyes were on the doorway. He saw me, hesitated, then raised a hand.

Dark hair. Chiseled features. Just like his profile picture.

I was pretty sure his name was Garth.

He smiled. I smiled back. I walked toward him.

Garth, I reminded myself. This one's named Garth.

NINETEEN

FOUR WEEKS EARLIER, I said: "I'm hanging up now."

Deirdre Nicholson said: "I wouldn't if I were you."

"THREE MONTHS?" Sarah cried, from the other side of the dressing room door. "It lasted three fucking *months*?"

Two hours after Deirdre called, I was struggling with a reluctant zipper. I heard the rattle of ice cubes, and Athena's silvery voice inquire, "More champagne?"

"Just a splash, thanks," Sarah said.

Athena called out, "How are you getting along in there, Raney?"

"Here I come."

As I emerged, she was easing the wine bottle back into the bucket. Sarah, Cameron and Amanda were crowded onto the leather sofa.

I held out my arms and turned around. "Well?"

Sarah set her glass down so she could cover her mouth. "Oh, honey."

Amanda was holding her phone to one ear. She watched me, eyes wide.

Cameron glanced up from the laptop balanced on his knees. "Hubba, Boss." Then he kept typing.

I turned to the three-way mirror.

I was wearing an asymmetrical gold lamé miniskirt, a red silk camisole, a black velvet bolero jacket and a pair of shiny, thigh-high boots.

"Your legs," Sarah marveled. "Your ass. My God, woman."

I swiveled, watching my reflection. "I look . . ."

"Amazing," Athena said.

Imagine that!

"Honestly, though," Sarah said. "Three *months*?"

IT HAD taken Wally and Jonathan a few seconds to place the name of my caller. Deirdre . . . Deirdre Nicholson . . .

Then it registered, and they shot out of their seats. I'd never seen Wally move so fast. I watched the door close behind them, wishing I could leave, too.

Instead, I braced myself and picked up the receiver.

"Just out of curiosity," I asked her, "how dare you call me?"

"He told you it only happened once, right? San Francisco?"

"Goodbye now."

"It was more than once. A lot more."

I felt a hollowness in the pit of my stomach.

"You're lying," I said.

"Check your in-box," Deirdre said.

"SHE'D SENT me five e-mails Aaron had written her," I told Sarah. "The first one from July. The last from September."

Cameron winced, but kept typing. Amanda studied the ground. I'd brought her with me to listen in on a conference call I couldn't miss. She didn't want to be there—once again a bystander to my marital operatics—but it couldn't be helped.

Sarah was watching me closely. "Did you read what he wrote to her?" I nodded. "And?"

I tugged at the hem of the miniskirt. I straightened the collar of the jacket.

"It lasted three months."

． ． ．

I CLOSED the fifth and final e-mail.

I felt calm.

It wasn't a precarious, pre-freakout calm. I was perfectly steady, perfectly relaxed. I drummed my fingers on the keyboard.

After a moment, I forwarded the first e-mail to Aaron's new account.

I'd put Deirdre on hold. Line one was blinking. I picked up the receiver. "Are you still seeing each other?"

"He ended it when you found out."

She was trying to sound businesslike. She just sounded bitter.

I forwarded Aaron the rest of his e-mails. "Why are you telling me this?"

"Because—"

"Never mind," I said. "I don't care."

"WHAT IS *wrong* with her?" Sarah fumed.

Inside the dressing room, I surveyed the ensembles arrayed along the walls. "She's hurting, I think. Spurned."

"Okay, fine, hell hath no fury and all that, but she's an awful, awful person."

"Maybe. I'm having a hard time getting worked up about it."

"No kidding. What's that all about?"

I came out of the dressing room wearing a lacy peasant blouse, a pair of crimson-colored leather culottes and a shearling vest.

"That needs to go in the Yes pile," Sarah said.

"The Yes pile needs its own zip code," I said.

Athena sailed in, smiling, with a stack of shoeboxes. "We can arrange that."

Amanda muted her phone. "They're talking about the motion for class certification."

"Tell them we'll take the lead."

She unmuted. "Calder Tayfield is happy to take the lead."

My own phone, which had been ringing regularly for the last two hours, now pinged three times in quick succession.

—Please pick up.

—Talk to me, Raney.

—Everything I told you about why it happened was true. Everything about us, and how much I love you. The only lie was how long it lasted.

I deleted them, as I'd deleted the dozens that preceded them.

"I'm so sorry, honey," Sarah said. "I know this is breaking your heart."

I inspected myself in the mirror. "I'm fine."

She looked at me closely. "How can you be fine?"

"Because when she told me, I wasn't surprised," I said. "Some part of me must have known all along. Think about it, Sarah. He happened to get caught the very first time? How likely is that? But I wanted to believe it. I chose to believe it."

If only I'd dug deeper into his e-mails when I had a chance. If only I'd asked Tom Nicholson more questions.

If only, if only.

Sarah's voice was full of trepidation when she asked, "What are you going to do to him?"

"Nothing."

"Nothing?"

"Not a thing," I said. "This time, it's about me."

I REPLACED the receiver. My eyes rested on the phone.

I heard a hesitant tapping. Wally and Jonathan poked their heads around the door. I waved them in, and they took their seats, looking like stricken schoolboys.

"Everything I told you a few minutes ago?" I said. "How much I've learned about myself, about Aaron, about my marriage?"

They nodded.

"Scratch that."

I summarized the phone call.

"Unbelievable!" Wally cried.

"That fucking *scumbag*!" Jonathan spat.

Their outrage swiftly turned into action.

"We'll handle your divorce," Wally said.

"We'll find you a gun," Jonathan said.

Wally eyed him. "Where are you going to find a gun?"

Jonathan shrugged. "I know a guy."

"You live in Summit, New Jersey," Wally said scornfully. "You don't know a guy."

"Walter—"

"Your whole life, you've never met a guy."

"Shut up, Fanucci! We're here for Raney right now."

"Right," Wally said. "Sorry."

I was still staring at the phone.

"What can we do?" Jonathan asked.

They leaned forward. My friends were eager to do anything, say anything, help in any way they could. I looked up.

"Tell me how to make men want me."

I LEFT the dressing room in a pair of flared white jeans, a cerulean silk plissé blouse and an ocelot-print faux-fur coat.

"Oh my lord," Sarah breathed.

Amanda was watching me closely, as if she were trying to puzzle something out.

Cameron consulted his phone. "Good news, Boss. The bank has transferred the funds to your new account. And the hotel says your suite will be ready by five."

—I'm sorry. I am so sorry.

—It didn't matter. Truly. She didn't matter.

Athena swooped in with an armful of coats and looked me up and down. "Love it, but we need accessories."

Sarah reached for my sleeve and flipped over the price tag. She smiled grimly. "I sure hope Aaron's selling a lot of paperbacks."

"More champagne?" Athena asked.

Sarah dropped the tag and held out her glass. "Just a splash."

WALLY AND Jonathan considered my request.

"The revenge fuck," Jonathan said. "A tad shopworn, but undeniably effective."

"You can't argue with a classic," Wally agreed.

"It's not about revenge," I said.

"Then what is it about?" Jonathan asked.

I didn't feel like explaining. I felt like getting started. "I'll tell you later. Right now, I need some tips. How do I get men to have sex with me?"

"By walking up to them and saying, 'Will you have sex with me?'" Wally said.

"It's that easy?"

"Easier," Jonathan said. "Just walk up to them. You don't even have to say anything."

"A few months ago, you said I've let myself go. How can you be sure anybody's going to want to?"

Wally stretched his long arms across the back of the sofa, ready to expound. "Here's the thing, Moore. People make a lot of jokes about how men are sex-starved savages, right? Far from being the paragon of animals, godlike in our apprehension, yada yada, we're little more than walking, talking, intermittently sentient sex organs. Ha ha, right? It's a big cliché."

"Which happens to be one hundred percent accurate," Jonathan said.

"Men do, in fact, want sex all the time," Wally continued. "Our dicks are nothing more than powerful, self-activated divining rods, pulling us toward any and all sources of pussy, regardless of danger, humiliation or the potential for wholesale financial ruin."

"Don't sweat it, Raney," Jonathan said. "You're not going to have a problem finding someone willing to sleep with you. Especially if you're making the first move. That's irresistible."

I HEADED back into the dressing room. "Let's work on my dating profile."

"You got it, Boss."

"I have to say I love your new attitude," Sarah remarked. "Why waste another second weeping over that asshole when you can go out and have some fun?"

Cameron called out, "Describe your dream first date."

I didn't have one. I wiggled out of the white jeans and nearly fell over. "Sarah?"

"Which site are you using?" she asked.

"All of them," Cameron replied.

"All of them?"

"The top ones, anyway. OKCupid, Match, Bumble, JDate, EDate, PDate, Fleek, Flook, Burnt, Turnt and Shakl."

"Shakl." She sounded intrigued. "I don't know that one."

When I came out of the dressing room, they were both absorbed in Cameron's laptop screen. Sarah looked up. I was wearing a black cashmere turtleneck, a plaid kilt and a yellow suede trench coat.

"Yes to that," she said. "A thousand times yes."

Amanda looked down at her phone. "I'm not getting good reception in here. I'll be out front." With a final, curious glance in my direction, she left the changing room.

Cameron said, "The first thing people notice about you is . . ."

I scrutinized my reflection. "My eyes?"

"Say lips," Sarah advised. "That will make men think of blow jobs."

Cameron looked at me. I nodded. He bent over his keyboard.

"Lips it is," he murmured.

· · ·

WALLY AND Jonathan were soon called away. They left reluctantly, and only after further offers of legal representation and weapons procurement. I watched the door close behind them.

All I had to do was ask? There had to be more to it than that.

I pressed the intercom button. Renfield appeared with her steno pad. I leaned back in my chair.

"A few things," I said. "First, I need you to find someone who can help me buy new clothes. Someone really good."

"A stylist?"

"Yes. Second, call Sarah and ask for the name of the guy who does her hair. Make me an appointment as soon as possible. Third, find the best place in the city for me to get a makeover."

Renfield glanced up from her notepad. "You want a makeover?"

"Whatever people do when they want a total overhaul. Skin, makeup, nails—set me up with everything. Fourth, I need a list of the best hotels—"

"I'm beginning to have the most terrible sensation of déjà vu," she murmured.

I told her what happened. I thought she'd stagger back, clutch her heart, holler and storm and swear. Instead she went very still.

"You're sure," she said.

I nodded.

"Positive," she said.

I nodded again.

She looked down at the list. Her brows drew together. She looked me in the eye.

"I know a guy," she said.

My colleagues and their assassins. It was touching, yet alarming. Renfield grew up in Bensonhurst. I was sure she did know a guy.

I asked her to cancel my afternoon meetings and call Cameron—he could probably help me figure out what else I needed to do. She finished scribbling and hurried out of the room.

Then the phone rang.

. . .

I LEFT the dressing room in a zebra-print slip dress, a purple calfskin jacket and a pair of gold stilettos.

"I think *I* want to have sex with you in that," Sarah said.

I heard a muttering, which grew in volume, accompanied by the clinking of glass and a familiar heavy tread. Renfield huffed through the doorway with a cardboard box. "I got all the testers I could find." She saw me and her mouth fell open. "Jesus Mary and Joseph!"

Cameron peered into his screen. "What are you most passionate about?"

"Put down gourmet cooking and exotic travel," Sarah told him.

"She hates to travel," Renfield said. "And she can't even make a cheese sandwich."

"It's for her dating profile," Sarah explained.

"Ah." Renfield nodded sagely. "Better skip the part about the cheese sandwich."

She plopped down on the sofa. Sarah handed her a glass of champagne. To me:

"You said you've already got a date for tonight? Who with?"

THE PHONE rang a second time, and a third. I didn't recognize the number.

What now?

Renfield picked up. A few seconds later, her voice came over the intercom. "It's a guy from Citywide Movers. Says he needs to talk to you."

I hit speakerphone. "Hello?"

"Ms. Moore?" A deep, accented voice. "It is Arnault. I helped you move to Brooklyn some time ago?" He paused. "Then move back again?"

"Arnault. Right."

He told me about a box found in a truck that hadn't been used for three months. He thought it was mine. He was very sorry.

I tried to remember what he looked like. Tall, dark, mournful?

"I can bring the box to you, or if you prefer I can—"

"Arnault?"

"Yes, Ms. Moore?"

"Would you like to have dinner with me tonight?"

"A MOVING man," Sarah mused. "I wouldn't have thought that was your type."

"He called at the right time. I figured I'd start there."

I went back into the dressing room and came out in a blue bias-cut devoré dress, a sheer ivory cardigan and a pair of gladiator wedge platform sandals.

"Who knew that's what you were hiding under those godawful suits?" Renfield said. She and Sarah raised their glasses and toasted me.

"Let's do perfume," I suggested.

"You betcha." Renfield pulled a slim bottle from the box she'd brought up and lifted her reading glasses from her chest. "This one's called," she squinted, "Black Opium."

She spritzed fragrance into the air. We all paused, sniffed, shrugged. She put it back in the box. My phone pinged.

—We've made so much progress. We're so much stronger than we were. Please pick up the phone, Raney. Please—

Delete!

"This one is called Love Bomb." Renfield spritzed. We grimaced. She put it back. My phone pinged again.

—Sorry I missed the big powwow today. Heard it went well.

Singer. Before I could respond, he added:

—You definitely owe me a sandwich. Possibly even a bag of chips.

"This," Renfield announced, "is Sex Party."

She spritzed. We all smiled.

"We have a winner!" Sarah said gaily.

"I gotta get out of the office more often," Renfield said. Then she hiccuped.

Sarah reached over to refill her glass. She glanced toward the doorway and froze. "Oh sweet Jesus look at that."

Athena had reentered the changing area, a bronze-and-black tunic draped over her arms. It had a long skirt and a neckline that plunged nearly to the waist. Sarah, Renfield and I bent closer. The gown was covered with thousands of metallic disks that shimmered like tiny fish scales.

"Any special events coming up?" Athena inquired.

"You would look great in this, Rane." Sarah stroked the scales with one finger. "Like some kind of badass warrior mermaid."

Cameron's phone buzzed. "Jorge's downstairs. We have an hour before he has to take it back to the showroom."

"Take what?" Renfield asked. "Never mind. I wanna be surprised."

I led my troops to the elevators. Then I remembered I was wearing several thousand dollars' worth of clothing that didn't belong to me.

"We're stepping outside, Athena. I'd better change back into what I was wearing when I came in here."

"Too late!" She smiled sweetly. "I already burned it."

"I *love* her," Sarah whispered loudly.

We crowded onto the elevator. "How about a status update?" I said.

Cameron checked his phone. "You're getting your teeth whitened tomorrow at eight, the nutritionist can start you on the detox at ten and the designer will stop by to take a look at your office at noon."

Renfield checked hers. "Olga at Bergdorf's will be ready to help you with makeup in an hour. On Wednesday, you're booked for a full day of appointments at the celebrity spa on Downing Street. And I got ya subscriptions to *Vogue*, *Elle*, *Marie Claire* and *Cosmo*." She glanced up. "That's the one with the sex tips."

"Was it this much fun last time?" Sarah asked.

Cameron: "Ha. No."

Renfield: "Last time was frankly very terrifying."

The elevator doors opened, and we wended our way through Fine Jewelry and Luxury Handbags. We walked through the double doors onto Madison Avenue and stopped.

"Holy Moses," murmured Renfield.

A red-and-silver car was waiting at the curb. It was a boat of a car, a yacht, luxurious, sensuous, with swooping tail fins, double headlights and a white convertible top.

Jorge got out of the driver's seat and stood next to us. We all stared.

"What is that?" Sarah asked.

"A 1959 Plymouth Fury," Cameron replied.

"How appropriate," Renfield muttered.

"Totally refurbished," he continued. "It has a 6-liter V-8 engine and automatic transmission. New upholstery, new brakes, new shocks, a custom—"

"Hush, man," Jorge said. "We just wanna look at it."

I don't talk much about my grandmother. As I've said, she was a quiet, self-effacing woman. Her stories of the good old days were few.

Unless you got her started on her Fury.

It had been an anniversary gift from my grandfather. She loved to recall the day she found it waiting in their driveway. She would drive my mother to school in it, even though they lived only a few blocks away. They took it all over the country on family vacations.

The car was long gone by the time I was born. When I was little, I dreamed of buying her another one, parking it outside our brownstone, seeing her face light up when she came outside. But by the time I could afford it, she'd passed away.

We were still staring. Passersby were slowing down to admire it.

Sarah: "This is insane."

Cameron, with enthusiasm: "Right?"

Jorge: "It rides so smooth. Like I was driving on a cloud or something."

Renfield: "How much does it cost?"

Cameron, checking his phone: "Eighty thousand dollars."

Jorge, Sarah and Renfield each made a noise like the wind had been knocked out of them.

I turned to Cameron and smiled.

"I'll take it."

TWENTY

IF I HAD ever imagined what it would be like to start jumping into bed with strange men—before I actually started doing it, I mean—I probably would have assumed awkwardness and discomfort to be the order of the day. My experience was limited. I didn't see myself as a free-and-easy sexpot. So the idea of taking some guy who I'd known for only a few hours, and . . . getting naked with him? Writhing around with him? Being *penetrated* by him?

That was nuts!

No surprise then that I was nervous at first. I survived my date with Arnault the French moving man only by subjecting him to a dinner-length interrogation about every aspect of his life. By donning my professional armor and treating him like a witness, I was able to avert painful silences and calm my hammering heart. He probably went to bed with me only to shut me up.

But there's the key.

He did go to bed with me.

We stepped into the hotel room. We faced each other. We touched—lightly at first, with hesitant looks.

Can I do this? Is this okay? Do you like this?

Once you begin, it gets easier. There are things to do, tasks that distract your anxious thoughts.

Hands roam. Kisses go deep. Clothing slips away.

It was fascinating. And slightly unreal—even as I went on more and more dates with more and more men. As I met them in bars and cafés. As I sat across from them in restaurants. As I learned how to flirt, how to gauge their interest, how to signal mine. As I rode up with them in elevators. As our clothes slipped away.

This is me? I thought. I'm really doing this?

It might seem like an unconventional reaction to the news that my husband hadn't been entirely forthcoming about his affair. But I'd tried everything else. I'd raged. I'd relented. I'd talked and listened, delved and explored. Joining the party—having sex myself, sex for sex's sake—seemed like the last available path toward the understanding I still craved. Not about Aaron, or my marriage—those were things of the past. This time, I was focusing on me, and my persistent confusion about sex. Could I like it? Should I like it?

And wanting. What was that all about?

Answer those questions, and I could move on. To what, I didn't know. But Bogard always told me to stop looking to other people, and to focus on myself. I was following the doctor's orders at last.

That's what I told myself, anyway.

I WENT out with Garth on a Monday in mid-January. I arrived at work the next morning around nine. I was wearing my faux-ocelot coat open to a velvet-trimmed blazer, a pair of fitted trousers, a blue silk shirt and ankle boots. My hair was slightly wavy from the light snow falling outside.

I breezed past Renfield's desk and into my office. She followed a few seconds later with the mail, a stack of phone messages and a client engagement letter. She waited while I skimmed the letter.

"He called again," she said. "Says he needs to talk to you about some bills he's getting."

"What did you tell him?"

She snorted. "To go screw, of course."

I signed the letter. "Good."

"You got that ACLU call in ten minutes. I'll buzz you when I've dialed in."

There was a partner lunch scheduled for one o'clock. A few minutes beforehand, Wally and Jonathan rolled in. "You coming upstairs?"

"Give me a second." I was writing an e-mail.

They each took a chair. I reread the e-mail, hit send and looked up. They were watching me with a strange expectancy. "Do I have something in my teeth?"

"Did you go out last night?" Jonathan asked.

"Yes. Why?"

"We're curious," he said.

"Intensely curious," Wally added.

"Did you . . . ?" Jonathan made an unmistakable gesture.

"Are you *serious*?"

"Our lives suck, Raney," Wally said. "We're so bored. So boring. Your personal sex revolution is the most exciting thing that's happened in a long time."

Jonathan nodded eagerly. "The glamorous new look? The parade of sexual partners? The luxurious sex pad? You're living the dream."

"Talk to us," Wally begged. "Tell us your dreams."

"My sex life used to make you cringe," I pointed out.

"That was the old you," Jonathan said. "This one is, you know . . ."

"Different," Wally proposed. "Let's just say she's different."

Andy Templeton leaned through the doorway. "You guys coming to lunch?"

Wally adopted the mock-heroic tone he sometimes used with Templeton. "All in good time, young Andrew. All in good time."

"We're discussing how to revamp the orientation program. I was thinking Moore could lead a panel on the acceptable use of firm computers."

"So witty, Andy," I said. "How long did it take you to think that up?"

"Get over it, Templeton," Jonathan said. "Everybody knows, and nobody cares."

"I'm not so sure about that," he replied. When none of us took the bait, he shrugged and left.

"So!" Wally slapped his knees. "Back to your sex life."

"Nice try." I stood up. "Let's go."

I WAS packing up that night when Cameron appeared in the doorway. I waved him in. He took a seat, smoothing down his tie. I shut down my computer.

"So," he said. "The dashing and magnetic Garth."

"Eh," I said.

"Really?"

"He was fine. Exactly as advertised. But," I picked a speck of lint off my trousers, "there's a sameness creeping in."

He cocked his head. "How so?"

"They're all lawyers or bankers or executives. They live in Gramercy or Wall Street or the Upper East Side. They like sailing or opera or museums."

"The bastards," Cameron said.

Fair enough. My dates were, with few exceptions, perfect specimens of educated, polished, eligible New York City manhood. They were handsome and fit and agreeable. They were what any woman would want.

But I wasn't learning anything. I wasn't getting it.

Cameron pulled out his phone. "Sounds like maybe you need more variety."

"Men who are younger, maybe? Or work in the arts?" I opened my bag and dropped in a few files, a legal pad, a binder. "Get creative."

"Sure thing." He typed quickly. "I'll adjust your profiles."

"LET'S TALK about your relationship with your paralegal," Bogard said.

I was in the middle of describing my date with Garth. "Cameron? Why?"

"It's somewhat unorthodox, wouldn't you agree?"

"He's highly efficient. I trust him. I consider him a confidant."

Bogard pressed his thin gray lips together. "Your firm hired him to assist you with legal work. Instead, he became an accomplice in your revenge against Aaron. Then, you set him to the task of researching infidelity and sex. After your second break with Aaron, you turned to Cameron to help engineer your new lifestyle. He procures dates for you—"

"He helps me vet them. To weed out the creeps and the weirdos."

"Vet them? These aren't job applicants. They're people you intend to be intimate with."

Bogard took every opportunity to telegraph his disapproval of my grand sexperiment. He was constantly prodding me to delve into the hows and the whys. I wasn't interested.

"I meet plenty of men on my own," I said. "There was that guy at a bar event, and Sarah's friend from college, and the man from Chicago I sat next to in the—"

"After each assignation, you and Cameron discuss what transpired," Bogard continued. "Often in detail."

"It helps to talk through my experiences with someone objective," I said. "Do a kind of postmortem."

Or as Cameron called it, a post *petit mort*-em.

He's very clever.

"How do you think he feels about his unusual portfolio?" Bogard asked.

"I imagine he prefers it to making photocopies and updating binders."

"He works for you. He might feel unable or unwilling to say no."

"I'm coercing him. That's what you're suggesting?"

"I'm suggesting we explore why you freely share details of your personal life with the people you employ. You've discussed Aaron's deception and your sex life in front of your associate and your secretary. You're an extremely professional person, yet you seem to have no regard for professional boundaries."

"What can I tell you? I've never spent a lot of time worrying about what people think of me. Anyway, everyone found out last time—"

"Because you roped them in."

"I refuse to be humiliated," I insisted. "I refuse to run and hide."

Bogard fixed his little gray eyes on me. "There's more than one way to run and hide."

Here we go again.

"If you act like you aren't hurt," he said, "people will believe you're not hurt. In moments of great turmoil, where others might crumble, you present the appearance of a person in control. Utterly indifferent to the opinions of others. It's an illusion, produced for those who might think you're weak. You open the treasure chest and say, 'See? It's empty.' But all the while, it has a false bottom."

"That's ridiculous!"

"Is it? If others think you're impervious, you can use their judgments to bolster yourself, rather than confront your own vulnerabilities."

"Why are you attacking me?"

For once, he gave me a straightforward answer. "Because you've stalled. You refuse to discuss your still-unresolved issues with emotions and sex. You won't investigate the real motivations behind this absurd plan of yours—"

"I've told you exactly what's behind it."

"—and you refuse to acknowledge that your reaction to the first disclosure of Aaron's infidelity and the second are essentially the same."

"Because they aren't!"

"The swiftness of your response?" he said. "Your refusal to communicate with him? Your dramatic tactics? Your apparent need to shock and awe?"

"My shoes are cuter this time." I stuck out my feet. "Look."

He wasn't amused.

"I'm not angry," I said. "There's a difference."

He frowned and sat back in his chair. "I'm not so sure about that."

TWENTY-ONE

ON THE TELEVISION, a man in a suit of armor dove into an Olympic-size swimming pool.

"Mom!" Maisie barked. "Quit hogging the popcorn."

I passed the bowl. My phone pinged.

—I had a great time on Monday.

It was Garth. I wrote back.

—So did I.

—What are you doing this weekend?

The armored man bobbed to the surface and began thrashing around in the water.

—Work is a little crazy right now. I'll be in touch.

"What Bill *doesn't* know," the announcer said, "is that the bottom of the pool is covered with thousands of powerful *magnets*!"

I looked up from my phone. "What's Bill trying to accomplish?"

Kate dug into the bowl. "If he survives this challenge, he can't be voted out of the RV."

"Why is that important?"

She looked at me as if I were simpleminded. "It's the whole point of *Roadtrippin'!*"

"And a potent yet subtle metaphor," Maisie said.

Kate rolled her eyes. "You think everything's a metaphor."

Maisie tipped the last of the popcorn into her mouth. "Because everything is."

It had taken the girls a few days to realize that once again, the world had changed. After the call from Deirdre and my shotgun makeover, I held them off with pleas of a work emergency. I needed to be prepared this time.

Two days after my date with Arnault, Jorge picked them up from school and drove them into the city. They tumbled into the suite, full of curiosity.

"Why are we here?"

"Why won't you talk to Dad?"

"Where did that car come from?"

"Mom! Your *hair*." Maisie reached out. "Kate—feel it."

But Kate was looking past me. "Oh my God."

The fine people at the Mandarin Oriental had offered me half a dozen suites. I'd chosen the Presidential: twenty-six hundred square feet on the fifty-third floor, two bedrooms, a study, a soaking tub, stunning views of Central Park and Midtown.

Kate and Maisie moved toward the window. I watched them. My daughters had never known a moment's deprivation. They were poster children for liberal, East Coast privilege—scions of the One Percent. But Aaron and I had never flaunted our wealth. Yes, we had a beautiful home, I used a driver, the girls went to private school. Still, compared to our peers, we lived modestly. We'd both grown up poor, so we saved our money instead of throwing it around.

Which means our daughters had never experienced anything quite like the Presidential Suite.

Kate tore her eyes away from the view. "What's going on?"

I sat them down at the long dining table. "Your father and I have hit a road bump. I'm going to be staying here for a while."

Maisie's bottom lip was already quivering. I reached for her hands. "We got through it last time, didn't we? I wish it wasn't happening again, but it is."

As always, Kate pressed for facts. "What is 'it,' Mom? What happened?"

"I don't think there's anything to be gained by sharing the details with you."

Maisie began shaking her head. "That means it's worse. It must be worse this time."

"You don't trust us to be able to deal with it," Kate accused.

"Honey, *I'm* having a hard time dealing with it. So, yes, I think you would, too. Anyway, what you're looking for is reassurance, right? A promise that everything is going to be fine?"

"Yes," they said.

"Your father and I love you more than anything in the world. And one way or another, everything is going to be all right."

They wanted more. I was loving and patient, but not forthcoming. As the weeks passed, and they shuttled between home and the city—a few nights with Aaron, a few nights with me—they adjusted. They were so resilient. So good. I was so lucky.

On the television, Bill thrashed around in the water. Underwater cameras showed a blanket of tiny black magnets rising toward him in an undulating wave. The effect was strangely beautiful. My phone pinged again.

—Bad news, counselor. I'm joining you for the hearing in LA on the 31st.

It was Singer. He was referring to an upcoming court conference in one of Hyperium's cases. I smiled and typed:

—Devastated.

—Me too. Unfortunately, the big boss wants someone trustworthy to go with you.

—To keep me in line?

—Exactly.

Bill was somehow managing to doggy-paddle. Maisie shook the empty bowl. "We need more popcorn. Who's working tonight?"

"Ernesto," Kate said. "Get some soda, too."

My unspoiled little angels had adapted well to life in the Presidential Suite.

Bill was two-thirds of the way across the pool and losing steam. A group of other contestants stood along one side, monitoring his progress. One of them was a young man with blond hair and a tan, angular face. Handsome, in a scruffy way.

I got a text from Sarah.

—Where do you wanna go on Saturday, hot mama?

The blond man hauled Bill from the water. Maybe that's what I needed. Someone young and pretty. Maybe that was the type of person who could help me figure it out.

Whatever "it" was.

I wrote:

—Let's go wherever really attractive men hang out. Like, professionally attractive.

—Have I mentioned how much I love the new you?

Bill lay on the edge of the pool. Strangled breathing issued from his magnet-encrusted helmet. An elderly woman stepped forward from the crowd to help him. As she bent down to pry open his visor, her gold crucifix floated toward him through the air.

"See?" Maisie looked at us triumphantly. "Metaphor, bitches."

. . .

TWO NIGHTS later, I got a text:

—Are you there?

—What's up, Herr Bug Doctor?!!

—Please come home, Raney.

—Please dream on, Aaron.

—I love you. I'm so sorry.

—lol

—Can we talk? Please?

—Nope. Busy.

—It's one in the morning. What are you doing?

—Lounging in bed after banging a Versace model.

—Be serious, please. Tell me how you're feeling.

—I'm great, Aaron. Thanks for asking.

TWENTY-TWO

THINGS SOMETIMES GOT WEIRD.

One Wednesday, I stayed late at work, preparing for a hearing. I finished typing up my notes and tried printing. Nothing happened. I tried again. Still nothing. I called the help desk.

The IT-type appeared in my doorway a few minutes later. I explained the problem and ceded my chair to him.

His fingers rattled across the keyboard. He said something I didn't catch.

"Sorry?"

"I said I like your boots."

I was wearing a pair of shiny, knee-high black boots with a four-inch heel. "Thanks."

"You're welcome." Eyes on the screen, he kept typing.

I moved around the desk and sat in one of my armchairs, watching him work. I'd never given the IT-type a close look before. He was in his early thirties, I guessed. Slender, with light brown hair. Interesting eyewear. A finely drawn, intelligent face.

He was pretty good looking, actually.

He was an IT-type, someone who pestered me. But of course, he was a person, too. A human being with likes and dislikes and opinions about boots. He had a name, Chase. I thought back to my last conversation with Bogard. I'd strong-armed this poor guy into helping me.

I'd treated him like an object that existed only to do my bidding. Law firms are hierarchies. Those at the top command, those below obey. It's a system everyone gets used to. Obviously I'd gotten too used to it. I felt terrible.

I heard a machine start up in the outer office. Chase pushed back from my computer.

"Your software is corrupted. I'll have to reinstall it tomorrow. For now, I've connected you to your secretary's printer."

"I'm sorry about what happened in September," I said.

"Oh." He blinked, startled. "Um, okay."

"I was wrong to involve you. I wasn't thinking straight. Which is not an excuse—I shouldn't have done it."

"I appreciate that." He was still sitting in my chair. There was an odd look in his eye. He was holding something back.

"I hope you didn't feel bullied in any way," I continued.

He shifted in my chair. "Bullied?"

"Coerced," I said. "You know—forced to do something you didn't want to do."

"Well, you're a partner." He tugged on his ear. "You guys can be a little much."

He shifted in my chair again. Crossed his legs. Was he nervous? Was I now coercing him into accepting my apology?

"That's what I mean," I said. "I'm afraid I was out of line."

"Abusing your authority," he suggested.

"I'm so sorry. Is there any way I can make it up to you?"

"You could do it again," he said.

"What?"

He didn't move. His eyes had a wild look, half terrified, half . . . Eager?

He shifted in his seat. Was he anxious? Or . . .

No.

No way.

I half rose so I could see over the top of my desk.

His khakis were definitely bulging.

I burst out laughing. I clapped a hand over my mouth.

"I'm sorry! I shouldn't laugh."

"Yes, you should!" he said breathlessly. "You should do whatever you want!"

"He did *not* say that!" Sarah gasped.

We were at a club a few days later.

"Oh, but he did."

A waitress sauntered by. Sarah ordered another drink. "What did you do?"

"What else? I took him to the hotel."

Where we faced each other at the foot of the bed.

"Are you sure this is okay?" I asked.

"It's not okay," Chase said. "That's why it's perfect."

I was so confused.

"Just to be clear, you *liked* it when I bossed you around a few months ago?"

"Loved it."

"But you acted so put out. So aggrieved."

"That was part of the fun," he said. "Now order me around."

"Kiss me." He did. We broke apart. I smiled at him. "That was nice."

"No it wasn't," he said.

"But . . ."

He stopped me with a meaningful look.

"That sucked!" I said. "Do it again." He did.

"May I undress you?" he asked.

"Sure." I tried to kiss him again, but he pulled back.

"Could you maybe be . . . a little more fierce about it?"

Fierce. He wanted more fierce.

"Undress me . . . worm?"

He took off my clothes. I reached down to unzip my boots. "I'd love it if you left those on," he said.

I looked up, my smile slow and dangerous. "Have you forgotten the magic word?"

"Please!" Chase whimpered. "Please leave the boots on."

I ordered him to strip. Finally, he stood before me, head bowed, nearly naked. I did tell Cameron I wanted more variety. I tugged at Chase's boxers. This wasn't exactly what I had in mind, but who knows? Maybe I'd love it. Though I had no idea how I was going to explain this to Bogard. He'd probably accuse me of—

It was at that point that Chase's penis vaulted out of his underpants like one of those snakes springing from a can of fake nuts.

I staggered back. "Whoa!"

"What's wrong?"

"Nothing," I said quickly. "You're just . . . extremely well endowed."

Understatement of the year. His penis was huge. It was like a thick, veiny sea creature. A fleshy calamity.

Chase shook his head. "I'm tiny."

"Huh?"

"Tell me," he muttered, "that I'm *tiny*."

"You're puny!" I cried. "You're a wee, elvish thing!"

He bent his head in shame. Yet his penis seemed to grow even larger.

"Keep being mean," he whispered.

"I can barely see it!" I shouted. "Where's my microscope?"

I brushed it lightly with my fingers. I wrapped my hand around it. I wrapped my other hand around it. There was still penis to spare. I felt like a longshoreman, hauling in rope.

"Seriously," I added, in a lower voice, "I don't think it's going to fit."

He looked up with a smile. "Let's give it a try."

Sarah was shaking with laughter. "I think I'm going to pee!"

"He wanted me to do that, too," I said. "I had to draw a line."

"Oh, God!" She wiped her eyes. "We should have known you're a born dominatrix."

Two men at a nearby table were eyeing us. I turned away. "I don't know. Surprising as it may seem, humiliating someone didn't really do it for me."

She looked like she was about to say something. "What is it?" I asked.

"I was just wondering. What *is* doing it for you?"

I poked my straw into my seltzer. "I'm still trying to figure that out."

"During all this sex you're having, how often do you come?"

"I've gotten close a couple of times, but . . ." I shook my head.

"Maybe you need to know people better first. Make sure you have an emotional connection before you jump into bed."

"I've tried that. I've gone out with some men three or four times. And we do connect. The sex is good. But it's not . . . important."

"Does it have to be important?" she asked. "Can't it just be fun?"

"Fun isn't really the point," I reminded her.

We were quiet for a while.

"I'm overthinking it," I said. "How do I stop?"

"It sounds kind of obvious, but you need to switch off your brain," she said. "Try to be present in a physical way."

People swirled and pressed in all around us. Music pulsed and lights flashed.

Stop thinking. Be present. Good advice, no doubt.

I'd keep trying.

From: Aaron Moore
To: Raney Moore
Date: Monday, January 29, 11:41 PM
Subject: You, Us, Everything

Dear Raney,

I have no right to bother you, but I feel compelled to reach out, to try to explain. I wish I could stop, but I can't seem to.

I don't know the right combination of words to bring you back. Maybe they don't exist. But there are things you need to know about what really happened. The full scope of the situation. These facts might not help you forgive me, but maybe they'll ease the pain you must be feeling. Pain that, once again, I caused.

I'm just going to lay them out, in a way that might speak to you.

1. The three months it lasted were the worst three months of my life. When I wasn't with her, I was wracked with guilt. When I was with her, I didn't feel all that much better.

2. Three months is misleading. I saw her maybe half a dozen times. Not trying to minimize it, but . . . just to be clear.

3. "It." "Saw her." These are euphemisms. Because I'm a coward.

4. I kept meaning to stop. As soon as it started I wanted to stop. But then I felt like I had obligations to her, too. Because of what I— we—had done. And the decisions I had made. I didn't want to hurt anyone. Of course, good intentions are meaningless when you act like a villain.

5. You and I talked about why it happened, we talked about us, but there were other reasons. Reasons too embarrassing to share. I was feeling old, Raney. Used up. I was between books and had too much time on my hands. Nobody ever looked at me the way she did. Nobody ever wanted me. I was a big nerd, you know? A dorky bug guy, for God's sake! It was flattering. I was someone different with her. I was—

Delete!

TWENTY-THREE

"SO," SINGER SAID. "Here we are."

I mustered an uneasy smile. "Here we are!"

"Here" was a sleek and gleaming restaurant, inside a sleek and gleaming L.A. hotel, where we were staying after our court appearance earlier that afternoon.

"Is Rahsaan feeling any better?" he asked.

My associate had accompanied us to California, providing excellent assistance, as always. He should have been with us now. Instead, he was heaving in agony in his room upstairs.

"Lox, in L.A.!" he moaned. "What was I thinking?"

"Come downstairs anyway," I said.

"You want me to eat right now? There's no way, Raney."

"I don't want to be alone with him," I confessed.

"Who, Mickey? He's great. And you . . . you . . ." Rahsaan covered his mouth and lunged for the bathroom.

"He's not well," I told Singer.

He unfolded his napkin. "Then my sinister plan worked."

I froze. "What?"

"I'm kidding. I promise that my efforts to get you alone don't extend to poisoning. Yet. Shall we order?"

He was joking. Of course. A waiter sidled up and poured water. I was uncomfortable, which annoyed me. I'd been on dozens of dates in the last six weeks. Some of them had been awkward, or boring, but I'd never felt ill at ease.

Get it together, I told myself. This is a business dinner, not a date.

"Let's do the chef's tasting," Singer said.

I glanced at him over my menu. I liked his suit. You don't see many brown suits. He reached for the wine list. He had good hands. Another waiter arrived and solemnly offered us three kinds of bread.

"The duck is supposed to be amazing," Singer remarked.

"I don't eat duck."

"I find that deeply troubling," he said.

"My apologies. But I had a pet duck when I was a kid."

"Name?"

"Gladys."

"I thought you grew up in Brooklyn."

"In Crown Heights. People had all sorts of pets there. I knew a family that kept a tapir in a fourth-floor walkup."

Yet another waiter arrived. We ordered. The waiter left.

"I think the plaintiffs will make a settlement offer within the next few days," I said. "Based on the judge's comments this afternoon, we should consider . . ."

Singer was shaking his head slowly.

"We're not talking about work right now," he said.

"Why not?"

He pushed his plate aside and rested his forearms comfortably on the table. "Because work, counselor, serves only one purpose: to be the thing you don't have to talk about all the time. You go to work, right? You do your work. Then, if you've done it well, you get to knock off and come to a place like this, where you can have an excellent time, talking about anything but work."

I laughed. "We are such different people."

"Too bad for you, because I'm the client, so I set the agenda. Would you like a glass of wine?"

"No thanks. What do you want to talk about?"

"You," he said. "Tell me your entire life story."

I started to demur. He waved a hand in the air. "Let's skip over the standard objections—I don't like to talk about myself, I'm not that interesting, blah blah blah. You've already name-checked Crown Heights, tapirs and domestic poultry, thereby piquing my interest. Also, we've got twelve courses coming. We have to talk about something."

I laughed again. He wanted my story? So be it.

I began with my parents, and what little I knew of them.

"I remember snippets, here and there," I said. "A birthday party. A day at the beach. But I don't know what's real and what I reconstructed from photographs."

"It was a car accident?"

"Drunk driver."

"Awful. Is that why you don't drink?"

"No," I said. "I thought you wanted me to talk. What's with all the interruptions?"

He smiled, a little sheepishly. "I'm a lawyer. Asking questions calms me when I'm nervous."

"Why are you nervous?"

"We'll get to that," he said. "Did you have any family other than your grandmother?"

"A few cousins on my dad's side, but they lived far away."

"She was his mother?"

"My mom's." I paused, remembering. "I never saw her cry. My grandmother, I mean. I never saw her sad. Now that I'm a mother, I can't imagine it. She put on a good show for me. She must have been tough."

"Runs in the family," he remarked.

Waiters began padding in and out of the room. So many waiters, so many plates, each graced with a tiny, sculptural bite. A sliver of fish atop a mound of pearlescent grains, surrounded by a pool of broth. A crisscrossed stack of vegetables sliced to translucence.

"That's amazing," Singer said, savoring something. "What is that?"

I could only guess. "Shallot?"

"Fennel, I think."

I attended firm dinners all the time, lavish events intended to impress clients or win business. I never paid much attention to the food. But now I did, and it was astonishing.

I told Singer about growing up in Brooklyn. High school. College. Meeting Aaron. Law school.

"I have an uncouth question," he said. "How old are you?"

"Thirty-eight in July. Why is that uncouth?"

"Some people don't like it. Thirty-eight. Your firm's website said you were admitted to the bar in 2003."

I smiled. "Do you stalk all your outside lawyers?"

"Excuse me, it's called *research*. Now I'm going to display my astonishing math skills and conclude that if you were admitted in 2003, you graduated from law school at . . . twenty-two?"

"I skipped a few grades early on."

"But if your daughters are fifteen, you must have—"

"Had them during law school," I said. Then I added, "They were an accident."

He leaned back, clearly surprised. Very few people knew that. Sarah did, of course, and Marty, but around the firm it was believed I'd simply wanted to start my family early.

Why did I just blurt it out to Singer? I was in a confessional mood, I guess.

"I got a bad cold at the start of my 2L year," I said. "It turned into an infection, and I had to take antibiotics. My husband—he was my boyfriend then—had just moved to California for graduate school. He came back to visit Columbus Day weekend, and . . . well, antibiotics and the pill don't mix so well."

I liked that Singer wasn't interjecting or making sympathetic noises. He was simply listening.

"Anyway, we decided to," I looked down at my plate, "to not have them. Aaron was a superstar in his program, applying for all sorts of foreign grants. I was intent on big things, too. We didn't even know if we wanted kids. But then I had a routine appointment, and found out that . . . there were two. Two heartbeats. At which point . . ."

Tears began to prick my eyes. "I shouldn't be dumping all this on you."

"Stop if you want, but not on my account." His voice was so kind.

I got a grip and continued. "Well, we couldn't do it. Aaron moved back East. We got married. The girls politely waited until after finals to be born. I finished law school and started at the firm. Aaron transferred to a different graduate program, but he'd lost momentum. It took him years to finish. He . . . gave up a lot."

We were silent for a while. A waiter swooped in and brushed the table free of crumbs. Another poured more water. Finally, Singer spoke.

"Way to kill the conversation, Moore."

I laughed, covering my face. "I'm sorry. I shouldn't have—"

"Stop apologizing! It's part of who you are. A surprising and fascinating part. You don't strike me as someone who makes many mistakes."

I smiled ruefully. It was true: up to that point in my life. I'd been pretty much error-free. So much so that it took a few weeks for me even to consider the possibility that something had gone very wrong. Sarah bought the test. She also held me afterward as I fell apart on our bathroom floor. I'd had to tell Aaron over the phone. Then there was the sickness. The decision, made over hours of tearful phone calls. Then he came back.

It was a calamity—a plan-changing, world-upending, life-altering mistake.

Until I met them.

"How many courses have we had?" I asked.

"Five, I think. No. Six."

"Plenty of time to cover my marital disaster."

"Oh boy."

I outlined the entire saga, though I left out the specifics of how I responded. It was too complicated to explain.

"Jesus, that's awful," Singer said. "How are your daughters coping?"

"Far more maturely than their parents. They're great."

"What did the e-mails say?"

Waiters had arrived with the next course, and I was trying to puzzle out what it was. I looked up. "Sorry?"

"The e-mails your husband sent to the woman," Singer said. "What did they say?"

I needed a minute to recover from my surprise.

"Do you know," I said, "you're the first person to ask me that? Even my best friend tiptoed around it. Everyone is too horrified."

He looked a bit abashed. "Sorry. I'm insatiably curious and utterly tactless. A winning combination. Feel free to tell me to go to hell."

"No, it's fine." I poked at a tiny carrot on my plate. "The funny thing is, they didn't say much of anything. Aaron writes—wrote—the best e-mails. They were always chatty and sweet. He really put himself into them, if you know what I mean. No surprise—he's such a gifted writer. Anyway, the ones he sent to her were fine, but . . ."

"They weren't him."

"No. And they weren't torrid love letters, either. They were friendly, they confirmed dates and places where they . . ." I glanced up at Singer, then down at my food again. "I'm sure there were a lot more of them—her husband said there were. But if these were the ones she chose to send me, if they were the most hurtful examples she could find . . ."

"The whole thing probably wasn't that serious," Singer said. "At least on his side."

"Except that it lasted three months. And he lied."

"Of course."

More waiters. More plates.

"I knew you weren't boring," Singer said at last, "but between the tragic youth, the unplanned pregnancy and the telenovela-level marital drama, well, let's say you've exceeded my expectations."

I laughed. "Now it's your turn to talk."

Singer grew up in the Midwest. Went to Brown, then UCLA Law. He told me about his son, his parents.

"Why did you get divorced?"

He hesitated before answering. "As a matter of fact, my wife had an affair."

I was mortified. "Oh," I said stupidly. "I'm . . . so sorry."

"Not your fault."

"No, but I was running on about my travails, as if I were the first person it had ever happened to, while—"

"It's fine," he assured me. "And anyway, the circumstances were different. My wife left me for him. They're still together, and very happy."

"Why did she leave you?"

He took a sip of wine. "You know the saying about law firm life—that it teaches you how to be a good lawyer and a bad person? It happened to me. I worked all the time. I drank too much. I was stressed out and grumpy. I didn't parent for shit. I was a real dick."

"I can't believe that."

His smile was brief, but grateful. "I like to think I've changed. I cleaned up my act. Went to therapy. Went in-house. Became a better father. I realized I was wasting my life working too hard and being dissatisfied. Slowly, painfully, I stopped." He smiled at me cheerfully. "And here I am."

A new course arrived, a ribbon of meat draped across a tiny potato, daubed with a bright green sauce. "Is this lamb?" I asked.

"I think it's veal."

I wrinkled my nose. "I don't like veal."

"You had a pet calf in Brooklyn, too?"

"I like your voice," I told him.

"Thank you. I like yours."

I cut into the meat gingerly. "There's nothing special about my voice."

"Of course there is. Your voice is vibrant."

"This is veal? It's delicious."

He picked up his glass and swirled the wine around before tasting it. "Your voice conveys what you're feeling. You've got a decent poker face, but a terrible poker voice."

"Singer." I put down my fork. "Stop flirting with me."

"You started it! With the voice thing?"

"You started it months ago."

"That's the problem," he conceded. "It's become a habit. I don't want to stop."

"Why not?"

He gave me a wide, innocent smile. "Because I have a huge crush on you, Moore."

"Singer!"

"You're blushing!" He laughed. "Who knew such a thing 'twere possible?"

"This is—"

"Inappropriate." He made a serious face. "I know. I think there's a section of the Hyperium employee handbook titled Thou Shalt Not Shamelessly Hit on Thy Outside Counsel. I might even have written it. Some people would think I'm being a horrible pig—"

"No, no," I said. "You're not."

"Well, that's the thing, Moore. I have the funniest feeling you don't really mind. Must be something in that voice of yours, or the way I catch you looking at me sometimes. I know I'm not supposed to say any of this, either. How dare I be so presumptuous and cocky and . . . *male,* right? But I think life is a little too short not to say exactly what's on one's mind. Don't you?"

I couldn't believe he was saying these things. Putting himself out there like that, unafraid of rejection, or what I might say.

"How can you come right out and admit that you have a crush on me?" I asked. "Aren't you—"

"Embarrassed?" He shrugged. "You've already rejected me once. And it's not like we didn't both know what was going on."

Had I known? I'd certainly done my best to deny it.

What was happening in this conversation? What was I supposed to do?

"Why do you have a crush on me?" I asked.

"Because you're smart and weird," he said. "And you can be hilariously mean."

"I'm not mean!"

"I don't meet many people who surprise me, but you surprise me. And of course, I find you incredibly attractive."

I looked into his eyes, then quickly away.

"You can do better," I said.

"Can I?" He propped his chin on his fist. "Tell me more."

Strategic error. I cast around for the waiters. "How many courses do we have left?"

"Three. Plenty of time for you to explain why you think I could do better."

"I just mean," I fumbled for my napkin, "you're intelligent. You obviously know how to enjoy life. And you're, you know. Good-looking."

He placed a hand on his chest. "Be still my heart."

"Singer," I said sternly.

He put both hands up, laughing. "I'll stop. I'm not really making you uncomfortable, am I?"

On the contrary. The last few minutes had been shocking, they'd thrown me off balance, left me feeling tongue-tied and foolish.

They'd been completely delightful.

Still, I couldn't let them go on.

"My personal life is a little challenging right now," I said. "I don't think this—you and me, you know, dating—is a good idea."

"I understand," he said. "And I will submit with good grace. I'm sure my crush will fade eventually."

Would it? Did I want it to?

"I'm sorry," I said.

"Don't be." He smiled at me easy as could be. "Aren't we having fun?"

TWENTY-FOUR

"HELP ME UNDERSTAND something," Sarah said.

I stared at my reflection in the full-length mirror. "I can't wear this."

She swept a makeup brush across her cheeks. "Here you are. Recently launched on a bonkers sex binge. Made over, done up, putting yourself out there in surprising and totally applause-worthy ways."

I was wearing a red leather miniskirt, a black-and-white-striped T-shirt, tall boots and a fur vest. "I look like a fool."

"Lo and behold," she continued. "Along comes a man. A man you find smart and interesting. A man who is objectively hot and openly available. A man who, notwithstanding your weird protestations, is clearly interested in you."

"But we work together, so—"

"You slept with an *IT guy*, Raney. 'We work together' is not a winning argument for you anymore, okay?" She made her eyes huge and swiped on mascara. "As I was saying. You and this man travel to another city. Circumstances force you to be alone together, during which time he banters with you. Flirts with you. Confesses his mad crush."

She capped her mascara and caught my eye in the mirror. "Why, why, *why* did you not take him upstairs and fuck his brains out?"

"Can we not do the whole exhaustive-analysis-of-my-motives-and-behavior thing tonight? I thought we were going to have fun."

"The whole exhaustive-analysis-of-your-motives-and-behavior thing *is* fun. Do you like him?"

"No! I mean, I like him, but I don't *like* him like him."

"Oh, God." Sarah raised a hand. "Put that answer right back in your Trapper Keeper, because you are so middle school right now I can't stand it."

I frowned at myself in the mirror. She nudged me. "You look fantastic. Let's go."

The Fury was waiting downstairs. As we emerged from the hotel, Jorge held open the back door. People on the sidewalk stopped and admired the car. Sarah took my arm, sashaying proudly.

"Raney?"

Aaron stepped into the light cast by the hotel's awning. My stomach lurched.

Sarah held my arm tighter. "Hi, asshole!" she cried gaily.

I found my voice. "What are you doing here?"

He stepped closer. "I need to talk to you. You won't answer your phone."

Sarah pushed herself between us. "Let me femmesplain something to you, Aaron, because you're obviously not getting it. When a woman ignores your calls and e-mails and texts, that doesn't mean she wants you to show up in person. It means she wants you to Fuck. Off."

"Hey." I touched her shoulder. "Wait for me in the car?"

She flounced into the backseat. Aaron watched, puzzled. "Is that hers?"

"It's mine."

He tore his eyes away from the Fury and noticed what I was wearing. "Why are you dressed like that?"

I adjusted the strap of my tiny purse. "Sarah and I are going clubbing."

He couldn't process that, so he moved on. "Raney, we have to come to some resolution here."

He started telling me about a couples therapist he'd found. I half listened. He looked tired. Was he busy with his next book? With the show? Was he still working with Deirdre?

Did I care?

I thought back to my realization, months ago, that I wasn't ready to give him up. That there was too much that was good about our life and our marriage.

What about now? Did I still love him? I looked at him, and I felt . . . Nothing.

I crossed the pavement toward the car. Aaron followed.

"This is not how we deal with problems, Raney. We talk. I did something terrible, I know. But I chose *us*. I want *us*. Doesn't that mean anything?"

He was drawing me in, trying to keep me talking. Even a screaming argument on a city sidewalk would have been preferable to total silence.

"I have to go." I ducked my head and got in the car, not looking back until we pulled away.

AND SO the days and nights passed. I worked hard. The girls spent two or three nights a week with me. I exercised with Jared, went out with Sarah, shopped with Athena.

And I slept with a lot of men.

I tried to follow Sarah's advice. To stop thinking. To focus on my sensations. Sometimes it worked. I felt more present, more engaged, more connected. Yet some part of me always remained detached. An observer. I was never swept away.

Was that all sex was? Was I expecting too much?

Thoughts like those nagged at me. Until I had a great idea.

"You're kidding, right?" Cameron said.

We were in my office one morning, near the end of February. "I'm completely serious," I said.

He practically leaped out of his chair. "Boss, that's . . . all due respect, but that's crazy talk right there."

"Why?"

He started pacing the room. He reached the window, then whipped around and headed back. I'd never seen him so worked up. "I guess I'm confused. We both know your track record is mega impressive. You don't need to pay someone to . . . to . . ."

"I don't want to *sleep* with a prostitute, Cameron. I want to talk to one. Learn from one."

He looked relieved, but only slightly. "It still seems extreme. There are books for that. Internet guides." He pulled out his phone. "What if I found you a sex therapist?"

"No talkers. I want a doer. Someone with experience." I paused. "Lots of experience."

He sank back into his chair. "Oh boy."

"I'm missing something, Cameron. I'm not getting it. I've hired a personal trainer to improve my body, and a stylist to improve my wardrobe, a decorator to enhance my surroundings. I've been scrubbed and peeled, whitened, brightened, detoxed. All of those experts helped me enormously. Why not a personal sex worker?"

"Because . . ."

He didn't have an answer. I felt a rush of optimism. I was on the right track at last.

He pulled out his phone. "I'll see what I can do."

TWENTY-FIVE

"YOU'RE BREAKING my heart," I said.

Jisun looked puzzled. "Wouldn't that require you to have one?"

We were sitting on a banquette in the cocktail lounge she'd chosen for her going-away party. My favorite associate was joining the U.S. Attorney's Office.

"I should have known you were interviewing," I grumbled. "So many doctor's appointments."

When associates, formerly the picture of robust youth and good health, suddenly acquire invisible afflictions requiring sustained medical attention? It means they're leaving the firm.

"I couldn't tell you the truth," Jisun protested. "You would have had me locked up."

"I still might." I patted her knee and stood. "But first, I'll get you another drink."

I wedged myself in next to Amanda at the bar. She was chatting with someone, but broke off to greet me. "Raney!"

"Having fun?"

"I'm having a great time!"

I tried to catch the attention of the bartender. As much as Jisun's departure stung, I consoled myself that I still had Amanda. I'd never worked with a first-year so naturally talented. She was brilliant, hard-working, unflappable. I was hugely impressed.

"You know why Jisun's really leaving, don't you?" she said.

The bartender skidded to a stop in front of us. I ordered, then turned back to Amanda. "Why's that?"

"Because the firm is a horrible environment for women," she said.

Her suit jacket was unbuttoned and her eyes were bright. She'd had a few. I kept my voice neutral. "In what way?"

"In the male-female way. The persistently sexist way. The way of men who are the *worst*."

Something about her expression, the bitterness in her tone, made my antennae go up.

"Amanda, if something has happened to you, you can tell me. We have procedures in place, and I promise—"

"You think I've been harassed or something?" She let out a short, sharp laugh. "No, although I've heard plenty of stories. What I'm talking about is far more pervasive. I think you know it, too. Even if you pretend not to, the way you did in Knoxville."

She was drunk, which meant this was a conversation for another time. I stepped back from the bar, but she held my sleeve.

"Here's a little secret, Raney. I joined the firm for one reason. To pay off my student loans. As soon as I wrote that final check, I was headed right back to the nonprofit world. But then something crazy happened. I fell in love with the work." She laughed again, this time in wonder. "I'm working with brilliant people, on fascinating cases, and getting so much experience. But the culture sucks."

"It's unfortunate that our profession attracts difficult people," I said. "You have to learn how to deal with opponents who are aggressive, and—"

"I'm not talking about opposing counsel, Raney, although they can be awful, too. I'm talking about lawyers at our firm. You know—the guys who work with us. Who are supposed to be on the same side. But who act like total jerks."

"Things are better than they used to be," I said.

"Oh!" She made her eyes theatrically wide. "Okay! I shouldn't complain, because the environment isn't totally toxic? Because we're not

Gaia Café, or Uber, or Fox fucking News? I should be grateful for the present shittiness, because the prior shittiness was so much worse?"

I said, as gently as I could, "You're never going to escape the fools and the oafs and the profoundly misguided, Amanda. Your best bet is to ignore them. Work hard. Be better than them."

"Why do I have to be better?" she retorted. "Why can't I be just as good?"

She'd taken my arm again. I gently disentangled myself. "Because that's the way the world is. And because it works. It worked for me."

She nodded slowly, giving me an appraising look. "Yeah. Let's talk about you. Do you know how psyched I was when I found out I was going to work for you? You're, like, a legend. You're so powerful and smart and accomplished, and you were going to be my mentor. Then, my first day, you got that phone call. Something horrifying happened, and where anyone else would have fallen apart, you dominated it. You've been that way ever since. You're bulletproof."

If only she knew. "I don't think you have an accurate idea of—"

"But then," she continued, ignoring me, "I started seeing things differently. There was the deposition, and that crazy day at Barneys. And all the other things you've done to change how you look. All for men."

"How about you don't bring my personal life into this?" I said.

"Why not? You brought me into your personal life. And now I want to know. If all you did to succeed was be yourself, like you told me that first day, well, who is that? Someone who lets it all roll off her, or someone who changes herself to accommodate what men want? Are you above the fray—or are you complicit?"

"Complicit?" I had to laugh. "Because I don't call out trivial sexism?"

"It's not trivial. Not when it's a constant drip, drip, drip, every day."

"Complaining about it won't change anything."

"How do you know? If you really care about women sticking around, you should be standing up for us. You should be showing us that you think the way we're being treated is wrong, and that—"

"You want some mentoring?" I snapped. "Get over yourself. Men won't change simply because you want them to. You need to forget about your grievances, forget about being a woman and do your job."

"That's what I'm trying to do!" she cried. "I only want to work, but I have to face this bullshit. Men falling silent when I enter the room. Talking over me. Ignoring me. Making stupid jokes. Making comments about how I look. Because they see me as a woman first, before I'm anything else. You think I want special treatment? I don't! I—"

"Aaaaand we're done here!" Rahsaan materialized, slipping his arm around Amanda's shoulders. "Nothing like a little diatribe from the tipsy first-year, right, Raney?"

He led Amanda away.

AN HOUR later I was ready to go. I said goodbye to Jisun and wended my way to the front of the bar, greeting a few partners and associates along the way. I was still a little shaken by my encounter with Amanda. I shouldn't have spoken so sharply to her. Still, complicit? Changing myself to accommodate what men want? In my off hours, for my own purposes, maybe. At work? Never.

I was reaching for the door handle when I felt a tap on my shoulder. I turned to see Rob Preskill, an associate who'd worked for me a few years earlier, during his second summer of law school. He joined the firm after he graduated, but chose corporate over litigation.

"Hey, Raney!"

After Amanda's diatribe, it was nice to see a friendly face. I smiled at him. "Hello, traitor."

He laughed. "You're still bitter I switched departments?"

"Of course. But what's new? And why do you look so good?"

"My girlfriend kept nagging me about the growing pudge, so I trained for a marathon." He patted his flat belly. "It had unintended benefits."

"She must be very happy."

"You'd think," he said. "But she still dumped my ass."

I laughed, then covered my mouth. "Sorry! That was rude."

He shrugged. "She was rude first."

We smiled at each other.

"So," Rob said. "What's new with you, Raney?"

I kissed him in a taxi on the way to the hotel. I kissed him in the elevator going up to the suite. He was voracious, hands everywhere. I laughed. Then we were kissing again.

We stumbled into the suite. I led him to the sofa. I held his face. I felt him. I felt myself, feeling him. My breathing, my body. I was there.

"This is not happening," he murmured.

I unbuttoned his shirt. "Is it so hard to believe?"

"Yes!" He pushed my skirt up, yanked my panties aside, and thrust two fingers inside me. I gasped. He thrust them deeper. He kissed my face, my neck. I pushed off his jacket and unbuttoned his shirt.

Was I getting it? Maybe I was getting it at last.

"Let me show you the bedroom," I whispered.

"No. I want you right here."

He pulled off his shirt. I felt his shoulders, his chest. His skin was cool.

More kissing. His hands, skimming. Our bodies stretching out. A knee between mine. Legs parting.

Then he was inside me. He began to move. One full stroke. Then another.

"Oh, God," he whispered. "Oh God that feels good."

I found his rhythm. We looked into each other's eyes. His were shining and so, so . . . what? Sincere.

How did I feel? I felt . . . I felt . . .

Nothing.

He was kissing my throat and murmuring something. I stroked his back.

But I was gone.

How could I not be into this? Rob was attractive and smart. I knew him well. I liked touching him and being touched by him. But a veil had come down between him and me, or between me and my body.

Used to be I wasn't present, I couldn't focus, I was distracted.

Now I was present, focused, undistracted. But I still wasn't there. And I didn't know how to be there.

"Rob?" I put my hand on his chest. "I think we should stop."

MARTY KNOCKED on my door the next morning. I looked up from the memo I was editing. "What's another word for *futile*?"

"Vain." He wandered in. "Fruitless, ineffectual, pointless."

I scribbled "fruitless" in the margin. "Thanks."

He headed for the bookshelves, where he inspected the titles. "The general counsel of Hyperium called me yesterday. You've got a very satisfied customer on your hands."

"Glad to hear it." I circled a typo.

Marty walked to the door and shut it. "I have to ask you something."

I waited.

"Did you take an associate home last night?"

"No."

He exhaled, visibly relieved. "Good."

"I took him to the Mandarin Oriental."

"Raney Jane." Marty sat down, all seriousness now. "You shouldn't do that."

"You know a better hotel?"

"Don't be clever."

"Why shouldn't I 'do that,' Marty?"

"Whatever you're after, all these," he waved at me vaguely, "changes of yours, these new habits? You need to keep them out of the office."

I tapped my pencil against the blotter. How easily I could have relieved his mind. Explained that my "changes" and "new habits"—none of it had worked. I couldn't understand sex. I didn't get desire. So I was done.

I could have said all this. But I didn't care for Marty's tone.

"I'm not Rob's supervising partner, Marty. I haven't broken any rules."

He stood again. He paced. "I've given you a lot of leeway. I didn't say word one about that business last fall, the stunt you pulled on Twitter—"

"What does that have to do with anything?"

"I don't know!" He whirled around again, hands up, helpless. "I don't know what's going on, because you won't tell me. I care about you, and I want to help, but you're shutting me out."

"Did you ask Victor Fleming if he needed help when he had an affair with his secretary? Did you ask Alex Curry to keep it out of the office the year his wife left him, and he slept with half the summer associates?"

"Fleming and Curry," Marty said drily. "Two buffoons in the grip of humiliating midlife crises. That's who you're comparing yourself to?"

I picked up my pencil. "I'll take that as a no."

Marty sighed, defeated. He walked to the door.

"Have it your way. But please. Be more discreet."

I STEWED over our conversation on my way back to the hotel that night. I loved Marty. He was my hero and my teacher and my guide. But on those rare occasions when he acted too much like an overprotective father, I had an unfortunate reaction: I acted too much like a petulant child.

Keep it out of the office? I'd show him.

I pulled out my phone.

—Let's have dinner on Saturday.

It took Singer a few seconds to respond.

—Sorry, who's this?

—Raney Moore, of course!

—Impossible. You've stolen her phone. You've kidnapped her.

—Give me a break.

—Good luck finding anyone to pay a ransom.

—Forget I asked.

—Wait! Yes! Yes to dinner!

—Yes?

—Yes please.

TWENTY-SIX

I STOPPED BY Sarah's house before my date on Saturday. Jorge had the day off, so I drove the Fury to Brooklyn myself. While I was backing into a space in front of her brownstone, she emerged, wearing a too-big overcoat and a kerchief over her hair. She began sweeping a dusting of late winter snow off the stoop.

I got out of the car. "How's life on the gulag?"

She leaned on her broom. "That's a fire zone. You're going to get a ticket."

I decided to take my chances. Inside, she tossed her peasant getup in the closet and looked me up and down. "Is that what you're wearing?"

I was in a pair of jeans and a black sweater. "I didn't feel like getting dressed up."

"You're not wearing makeup, either. What the hell?"

"I'm done," I said. "The clothes, the hair, the sex—it was all a giant waste of time. This is my last hurrah. I don't even know why I'm doing it."

Sarah looked like she was about to say something. She stopped, pressing her lips together. "You can't go out looking like that. Come on."

She stomped up the stairs. I followed. "Where are the kids?"

"Tad and his new girlfriend took them to Vermont." She led me into her room.

"Is that why you're cranky?"

"No." She flipped a light switch and entered the closet. "I am not cranky because the kids are with Tad and," she made her voice high and mincing, "*Audrey*, who is thirty and thin and infuriatingly nice and they probably already love her more than they love me." She yanked a few dresses off their hangers and tossed them onto a chair. "I'm cranky because Clem broke up with me."

"Clem?" I vaguely remembered him: glasses, boxers. Young. "I didn't realize things were serious between you two."

"That's what's so frustrating! They weren't. We've seen each other now and then over the past few months. Very casual, no big deal. Last time, I just *happened* to say something innocuous about how I enjoyed spending time with him, and he got this freaked-out look on his face. Like I suggested we start picking out curtains for the nursery or something. The next day he texted me that he thought we should 'cool things off.' Try the wrap dress."

I held it up in front of the mirror. "I'm not crazy about the collar."

"Then try the green one." Sarah left the closet and threw herself on the bed. "You know the worst part? Doctor Feuerstein accused me of engineering the whole thing."

"What?"

"Get this." She rose up on one elbow. "I told him what had happened, and he got this absorbed look on his face—"

"I *hate* that look!"

"It's the worst, right? But so he does it, and he wonders—he never asks, he always fucking *wonders*—whether I, quote, subconsciously pressure men into commitment, in order to provoke them into rejecting me, all for the purpose of reconfirming my deep-seated feelings of inadequacy."

I pulled the green dress over my head. "That's very complicated."

"Right?"

"Also, you don't have deep-seated feelings of inadequacy."

She flopped onto her back. "Tell my motherfucking shrink that."

I turned back to the mirror. "Here's something deeply inadequate."

"Stop slouching."

I straightened up. "Ugh. Even worse."

"You look great. But if you don't like it, try the orange one."

Why was I there? What was I doing? All at once it seemed pointless, pathetic. Humiliating. "I'm calling this off." I reached for my jeans and pulled out my phone. "Why am I even going on this date—because Marty lectured me? Singer probably doesn't even want to. All that flirting was—"

"Drop the phone, Raney."

I looked up from the screen. "Huh?"

"Drop the phone," Sarah said, with deadly quiet, "or our friendship is over."

"But—"

"Shut up!" she shouted. "Just shut up for one *goddamn* second!"

I dropped the phone.

She leaped off the bed and got right up close to me. "You are done talking, Raney Moore. You know why? I've had enough." She jabbed a finger in my face. "I. Have had. Enough."

Her eyes were fierce. Her finger was menacing. I leaned back.

"I'm sorry about Clem. I shouldn't have come over. I'm—"

"Did I say you could talk?"

I shook my head meekly.

"Then be *quiet*! This isn't about Clem. This isn't about me. It's about *you*, Raney. You, and your total and complete inability to have any fun."

"Fun?"

"Don't do that!" Her finger started jabbing at me again. "Don't say it with that dour, constipated look on your face! Fun is good, Raney. Fun is *fun*. And what we're doing right now? This should be fun. You're about to go out with a man who's witty and entertaining and hot. You and I could be lounging around my bedroom, talking and laughing. We could be doing your nails, and swilling chardonnay, as we gossip about where you're going to go, and what he's going to say, and how big his dick might be. Instead, you mope in here like a whiny baby, acting like this whole thing is a giant chore."

"I have a complicated relationship to pleasure, okay?"

"Oh, no." She wagged her finger at me. "You don't have a complicated relationship to pleasure. You have *no* relationship to pleasure. You think it's unimportant. You're wrong. Pleasure is critical, Raney. It is necessary to life. Watching you these past few months? I'm mystified! You do the right things—you make yourself look gorgeous, you find a beautiful place to live, you ride around in that insane car. You've created this fantasy life for yourself, but you don't enjoy it. My God, woman, the only thing you actually cop to liking is fucking *chai*!"

"My goal hasn't been to enjoy myself—"

"Of course not!" She stepped back, throwing her arms wide. "You had a *plan*. Your plan to solve the mystery of Aaron's infidelity. Or the mystery of you. Or the mystery of sex. Frankly, it's never been clear to me—but then, I don't think it's been clear to you, either. Because your plan, Raney? Never made any goddamn sense."

She was pacing the room now, muttering and gesticulating. I hadn't seen her this worked up since the last time she'd been in front of a jury.

"People get cheated on all the time," she said. "It's sad, but true. And in response, sometimes they go out and screw around, too. It's not healthy, it's not mature, but it's understandable. You know what they *don't* do, Raney? They don't turn it into an *intellectual exercise*. They don't devise a fucking . . . sex regime. They don't have objectives and action items and flowcharts."

"I never had a flow—"

"Quiet!" she hollered. "You know why they don't treat sex that way? Because *that's not how sex works*. It's messy. It's not goal oriented. It isn't kale, Raney—you can't learn to like it. But you sure as hell tried, didn't you? You spent all this time screwing random guys, executing your sex drills like some weird little sex general. And you still didn't like it." She clutched her head. "You're the most sexually repressed slut I've ever met!"

I pulled off the dress. "I can't believe you're shaming me about this."

"Don't," she warned me. "You know I'm not shaming you. I'm trying to explain that your plan was doomed because you can't control sex the way you control everything else."

"I wasn't trying to control it! I was trying to—"

"Understand it," she said. "Right. Of course, understanding is just another form of control. Of managing the unmanageable. Of beating the thing that had beaten you."

"Why are you being so hard on me?"

She clasped her hands, shaking them at me. "Because I don't know what the hell else to do! I have been watching and listening and offering advice. I can't take it anymore, Raney. You don't see what's so obvious."

I reached for my clothes. "I suppose you do."

"Yes!" she said. "I see *you*, Raney. I see how you look at yourself in the mirror, with your cute body and your pretty face and your amazing clothes. I see you enter that hotel suite and just . . . drink in the luxuriousness of it all. I see you wanting to be delighted, dying to *bask* in it, but you won't let yourself."

I pulled my sweater over my head. "You're being so presumptuous right now."

"Because it's not about that, right? All that good stuff is only a means to an end. Attracting men. Sleeping with men. But why, Raney? That's what doesn't compute. Why are *you* having so much sex with so many men?"

"I'm not. It's over. Tonight is my—"

"Last hurrah." She nodded. "Nice try dodging the question, but I haven't forgotten how to pin down a witness. Why the sex spree?"

I was dressed and ready to go. "I'm sorry I've been so tiresome these last few months. I won't burden you with my problems anymore."

She stepped in front of the door. "Tell me why, Raney."

"Please move, Sarah."

"All that sex," she said. "All those men. Was it revenge? Was it something else?"

"I've already told you—"

"Why, Raney? Why did you do it? Why why why why why?"

"Because I wanted to!" I shouted.

We were silent for a moment, staring at each other, breathing hard.

"What did you say?"

"You were hectoring me! I didn't mean it." I started to move around her.

She held my arm. "You did mean it. You said you wanted to."

"I wasn't thinking."

But now I was. Why had I said that? What did it mean?

Sarah could see the wheels turning. She held me tighter. "For God's sake, don't think now! Keep talking!"

"I wanted to have sex," I said. "I wanted to see what it was like."

As I spoke the words, I knew they were true. They had that unmistakable clarity, that clutch of recognition. Like when a face in a crowd clicks into place, and suddenly an old friend is smiling at you.

"You love sex," I said. "So does Aaron. So do lots of people. I think I wanted to try it. When everything fell apart with Aaron, the second time? I had an excuse."

I sank down on the bed. So did Sarah. "Why didn't you say that's what you were doing?"

"I didn't know," I said. "I couldn't admit it to myself."

"So you concocted a plan."

"It was one big rationalization." I shook my head. "A giant cover-up."

"The clothes. The makeover."

"I thought I had to do all that to make men want to sleep with me. You were right—I loved how I looked. But I couldn't admit it. I couldn't admit anything."

I fell silent, lost in a torrent of thoughts. Sarah whacked me on the arm. "Do you know what's happening right now? This is an epiphany!"

"It is?"

She whacked me again. "You're having a motherfucking epiphany!"

She was about to give me another whack, but I shied away. "Sorry. Keep going. You secretly wanted to have sex."

"Yes," I said.

"With a bunch of random men."

"No," I said.

"And so then you . . ." She blinked. "Wait, what?"

"I didn't want to sleep with them. Not really."

"Then why did you?"

"Because they didn't matter. If they rejected me, I wouldn't care. That's why I avoided the one person I actually wanted."

"Singer," she said.

I nodded. "But I couldn't admit I wanted him. What if I did, and he didn't want me back?"

"Why wouldn't he want you back?"

"Because I look like a frog," I said.

"I don't . . ." She squinted, shook her head, uncomprehending. "What?"

"I'm plain," I said. "Nobody could want me."

"But . . ." Sarah ran her fingers through her hair. "We're going to talk about how profoundly wrong that is in just a second, but back up. So what if he didn't want you back?"

"Then I wouldn't get what I wanted," I said. "I'd lose."

"You hate to lose," Sarah said.

"Exactly! Better to say I don't want. Then, if I don't get the thing I want, I can say, 'Oh well. I didn't want it anyway.' So I decided not to want."

I was realizing the truth of the words as I said them. Things I'd never articulated before, never even thought.

"And you thought you wouldn't get what you wanted because of . . . how you look?"

"I always thought I was ugly, unwantable. So a long time ago, I convinced myself that wanting wasn't my thing."

"Oh, Raney," she said softly. "You aren't ugly."

"I've always said I didn't care about how I looked. But I cared so much I couldn't bear it. I locked it away, but it kept bubbling up. I couldn't help asking Aaron what Deirdre looked like. I pretended not to care when Wally and Jonathan said I'd let myself go. I hired all those people to help me look better for the purpose of making men want me. Because I thought it was about what they wanted, not what *I* wanted. I act like I'm impervious, like other people's opinions don't matter. But all along, they've ruled me."

"You think?"

"I know, Sarah! I let other people affect what I wanted because I was ashamed. And competitive. If I couldn't win, I wouldn't play."

"What was winning, exactly?" she asked.

I thought about it a moment. "Never being rejected."

We were quiet for a while.

"I am *such* a mess," I said.

Sarah gave me a little nudge. "News flash. You're human."

I understood everything. What I'd done, why. How I was doomed to fail.

"It was always two steps forward, one step back. I wanted to have sex, so I threw myself into it. But I was still scared, so I chose men who didn't pose any risk to me. When I finally asked Singer out, I immediately started undermining myself."

"Why? You know he likes you."

"What if he changes his mind? What if he gets to know the real me?"

"Jesus," she said. "Let's hope that doesn't happen."

We looked at each other and burst out laughing. Big, helpless, hopeless peals of laughter.

We laughed and laughed.

Eventually we calmed down. Sarah caught her breath. "Oh, boy. That was refreshing."

"It felt good to say all those things!" I said. "Really, really good!"

She pulled me into a hug. "You are such a freak!"

"What do I do now?"

Her eyes narrowed. "You'd better be joking."

"Right, right, sorry! I know what to do."

"Of course you know, idiot!" She pushed me off the bed. "Go do it!"

TWENTY-SEVEN

I GOT CAUGHT in traffic coming back into Manhattan. How had it gotten so late? I raced up the West Side. Amsterdam Avenue was a torment. A few blocks from the restaurant I lost patience and parked in the first spot I found.

I was almost half an hour late. Would he still be there?

I spotted Singer from the doorway, at a table in the center of the small, crowded restaurant. Chin propped on one hand, he was twirling a wineglass.

He saw me and started to rise. "Well well well. Look what the cat—"

I pushed him back into his chair.

"I want to have sex with you," I said.

His eyes went very wide.

I was breathless from my dash up the street. "I wanted to sleep with you the moment I met you," I gasped. "But I couldn't admit it. So I slept with all sorts of other people instead."

"Sorry, you—"

"You're the one I want, Singer! But I denied it. I didn't go out with you, because I really, really wanted to go out with you!"

He tried to guide me into my seat. I stepped back.

"I don't want to sit down. I want to explain this to you. I thought I didn't know how to want. I just wasn't letting myself!"

"Raney . . . slow down."

"I've been so afraid, my whole life. But I'm not afraid anymore. And what I want," I took a deep breath, "is you. I think about you all the time. I pretend I don't enjoy texting with you and talking to you on the phone. I pretend I don't love how you make fun of me. I pretend I'm not interested in you, when I'm so, *so* interested. I ignored and explained away all your flirting, even your outright confession. I convinced myself there was no way you could *really* want me. So I didn't let myself want you. Because that mattered. You wanting first."

Singer was standing now, the table between us. I couldn't read his expression. Was he amused, appalled or simply incredulous?

"Can you do better?" I said. "That's what I told you, and maybe it's true. But it doesn't matter. You can do me. And I wish you would. Because I want to do you."

"I know that," he whispered. "So does the entire restaurant."

Everyone was staring. Even the waiters clustered at the back.

"I don't care," I told him. "You know what else I don't care about? Whether you want to sleep with me. I mean, I hope you do, but it has no effect on how *I* feel. I used to let all sorts of people dictate what I wanted, but I'm not going to do that anymore."

"I think that's wise," he said.

Something about his smile brought me back to earth. I took a step back.

"Oh no. I screwed up. You don't want to sleep with me. You think I'm crazy."

"I do think you're crazy," Singer said. "But I still want to sleep with you."

"Great!" I grabbed his hand. "Let's go."

I DRAGGED him, laughing, out of the restaurant. He looked up and down the street. "I don't see any cabs. Should we—"

I kissed him. I reached up, bringing his face down to mine, and I kissed him. I opened his mouth with mine, and I kissed him. I pressed my body against his. I tasted him. I breathed his breath. I felt him responding, his mouth, his fingers in my hair, on my shoulders. I bit his lower lip. I felt his teeth with my tongue. I reached inside his coat. My hands moved down his chest, along his sides, to his waist. I found his belt and I pulled him to me. He lost his footing and stumbled. I felt his huffs of laughter in my mouth. I drank them in.

Had I ever kissed anyone in my life before? Kissed, I mean, not been kissed? Seeking instead of responding? Wanting, instead of waiting to be wanted?

We broke apart. He looked down at me, disbelieving. "Is this really you?"

"It's me! Come here."

"We're causing a scene on Columbus Avenue, Ms. Moore. Fortunately, I live only a few blocks away."

"Do you have a bed?"

"I have three."

"We only need one."

He slipped an arm around my waist. "That remains to be seen."

SOMEHOW, WE made it to his building. We lingered inside the entryway, near the mailboxes.

We were good with each other right away, playful and easy and giving. I reached inside his coat again. I loved how he pressed into me, how he responded.

"Raney," he breathed.

How did I feel? Words failed me. Thoughts failed me. I wasn't thinking. Wasn't wording. No ironic asides or nagging color commentary. That critical little voice, audio guide to my psyche, had nothing whatsoever to say.

I DIDN'T notice much about his apartment. It appeared to have the requisite walls, floors, a ceiling. I pulled off his coat, his jacket, unbuttoned his shirt, unbuckled his belt and yanked it off, unbuttoned and unzipped his pants. He laughingly submitted, hands up, ducking low to catch my mouth and kiss me when he could.

"Let's go into the bedroom," he said.

"Where are we now?"

"We haven't made it past the foyer."

I let him lead me, touching, kissing, into the apartment. Into his darkened bedroom. He pushed my coat off my shoulders. He pulled my sweater over my head. He unbuttoned my jeans. Slowly, so slowly. Kissing me all the while. He undressed me so well I couldn't stand it. I wanted to put my clothes back on so he could undress me all over again.

"Turn on the light, Michael. I want to see you."

He was kneeling, kissing my stomach. He stopped. "What did you call me?"

"Michael."

I couldn't call him Mickey. I'd feel like a pedophile.

"You never call me Michael."

"You want me to call you Singer in bed?"

He pushed me back onto it. "Of course! I love how you say my name. You're so skeptical. It drives me wild. Look at you." He caressed my breasts. I sighed and arched my back. He bent and kissed me. "Every time you say 'Singer,' I get an erection. It's very inconvenient, professionally speaking."

"I had no idea."

"Seems like we've been keeping a lot from each other." He slipped his hand between my legs. He put his mouth on my breast. I collected my thoughts.

"There is something else I have to tell you. I've never really allowed myself to enjoy sex. Now . . . oh, that's really good." He was kissing the base of my throat. My collarbone. "I'm trying to say that this is new for me. Letting go, I mean. Enjoying it. Not the having-sex part. Obviously I've been doing a lot of that—"

"So I've heard." His mouth was close to my ear. I felt his knee part my legs.

"I want to do it right with you. But I'm worried I won't . . . be very good. At sex. I guess I'm asking you to be patient, if it's not, you know, spectacular, right off the bat. I'd like to keep trying, and—"

"Raney," he said.

"Yes?"

"Shut up."

"Okay."

And in one long, smooth stroke, he entered me.

AFTERWARD, HE murmured in my ear, "You faked that."

"I did not!"

He caught my hand and kissed the palm. "All that thrashing and crying out? It was too much. Though I did appreciate the incoherent narration."

"Why are you teasing me?"

He pulled me on top of him. "I thought you loved that."

"I do." I kissed him. "This is fun, Singer! Did you know it would be this much fun?"

"I had an idea, but you're right. This is unusually fun. Are you hungry?"

"Starving."

He jumped out of bed and left the room. I watched him go. I stretched out, arms above my head, legs splayed wide. I could feel my lips curving into a huge, goofy grin.

So *that's* what all the fuss is about!

I hadn't been ironic or wry, cool or calm. I had felt my body, every part. My toes curled—they really did. I grabbed the sheets and twisted them. I took. I gave. I played. I laughed.

I was there.

I was there at last.

I heard a rattle of dishes, and Singer returned, with bread and butter, and small cold tomatoes. Sparkling water, salty olives, little dishes of cured meat. Strawberries and creamy white cheese. We set upon it as if we hadn't eaten in weeks. It was the most delicious food I'd ever tasted.

"Sadly, I'm out of chai," he said.

I wanted to talk about what had just happened.

"I really liked that thing you did with your tongue," I said. "About midway through?"

"I'm so glad."

"And when you flipped me over, and pulled me to my knees, and entered me from behind?" I said. "I've never done that before, and I've always wanted to. The only drawback was that I couldn't see your face. But actually, that's also what I liked about it. Just feeling your hands, you know, and your cock, and the way you kind of held me down, and were so forceful—"

"Your powers of description are getting me all worked up again, Moore."

"Isn't that a shame." I pushed the dishes aside.

"Although I also feel as if I'm getting a performance review."

"I need you to lie down on your back so that I can explore every inch of your body," I told him. "I haven't done that yet and I really want to."

He stretched out. I straddled him. I felt him grow hard underneath me.

He smiled up at me. "In my wildest dreams—and trust me, I've had a few—I never imagined our date would turn out quite like this."

"Are you glad?"

He laughed his big, joyful laugh. "What a question."

I kissed him again. I was so completely happy.

"Can we do everything, Singer? I mean, everything?"

"Yes, Moore," he said, pulling me down to him. "We can do everything."

TWENTY-EIGHT

PICTURE IT.

Virgin land, blue skies. Mastodons roaming the fertile plains. The world was new.

New for me, anyway.

One shouty conversation with Sarah, one cascade of revelations, and my treasure chest lay in splinters around me. I was whole and happy and free.

Where had I been all my life? Hiding, even though I thought I had nothing to hide. Terrified, even though I'd come off as so brave. In the space of a few minutes, my insecurities had been revealed, then banished. I had cracked the code, solved the riddle of myself. My reward?

Orgasms. Lots and lots of filthy orgasms.

But it was about so much more than sex. It was about everything I wanted but was afraid to ask for. Everything I felt, but squirreled away from the judgments of others, and myself.

The old me would have cocked a skeptical eyebrow at all this soaring self-revelation. She would poke at the premises. She would nitpick and deny.

She was such a drag.

Not fair. She had done her best. And I was grateful for her flailing attempts to fix what ailed her. If she hadn't been who she was, I wouldn't be me.

I thought I was so smart, but I was clueless. I thought I was in control, but I was a mess.

And that was okay! Because everybody is clueless, and everything's a mess. I understood that, and my understanding had set me free. It was time for me to breathe, to live, to be human.

To embrace the mess.

ON MONDAY morning, the elevator doors opened on forty-five. I strolled down the hall, into my suite, past Renfield's desk, into my office.

Before I could drop my bag, Jonathan poked his head in. "What's that noise?"

"What noise?"

He stepped into the room. "Were you . . . whistling?"

I shrugged off my coat. "Was I?"

Singer and I hadn't gotten out of bed until Sunday afternoon. I headed back to the hotel after dark, weary and sore, but not at all sated. I knew every inch of him, and he knew every inch of me. Inches I didn't even know I had.

Talk about virgin territory.

Jonathan scrunched up his long nose. "Something's different."

"Nothing's different." But I couldn't stop myself from smiling.

Jonathan cupped his mouth with his hands. "Fanucci! Get your ass in here!"

Wally shambled in. He took one look at me and stopped. "Whoa."

"Right?" Jonathan said.

I was starting to get worried. "What is it?"

"You're glowing," Wally told me. "You have a distinct glow."

"First you were whistling," Jonathan accused, "now you're glowing. You're holding out on us."

I sat down behind my desk. "Something happened. I had a kind of . . . revelation."

I'd been looking forward to telling them. Jonathan and Wally had stood by me through my worst time. I knew they'd want to hear how everything had been so unexpectedly, beautifully resolved.

"I had a date on Saturday," I began.

"Was it with a woman?" Wally asked.

"Beforehand, I . . . what?"

"You had sex with a woman, right?" he said. "And it was amazing?"

"How does it work?" Jonathan asked

They waited expectantly. They were almost slavering.

"You guys are unbelievable," I said.

"You said you had a revelation!" Jonathan protested.

"Not that kind of revelation, clown boy!"

They exchanged a disappointed glance.

"It wasn't even really about sex," I continued. "I mean, it *was*, but it was also about me. I grasped some home truths."

"Did you grasp Schollsie's home truth?"

"Jonathan!"

"She did!" Wally grinned and pointed. "Look—she's laughing!"

"Whistling, glowing and laughing," Jonathan said. "We have a hat trick!"

Renfield came over the intercom. "Your ten o'clock is in the conference room." I stood up and grabbed a legal pad.

"Wait!" they cried. "You can't leave us hanging like this!"

"I'll tell you everything at lunch. I promise."

SINGER GREETED me at the door of his apartment that night. I felt his hands slip around my waist, inside my coat. He pulled me close. My waist hadn't been touched like that in years, not in that wanting, needing, new-greeting way.

Later, lying in his bed, I said, "Remember when we met, back in September?"

He rose up on one elbow, smiling at me. "As if I could forget."

"I was awful, but you hired me anyway. What were you thinking?"

"If I recall, my predominant thought was, please please please let her be single."

I laughed. He pulled me into his arms. "Keep in mind that the decision wasn't really up to me. But your reaction was perfect. We wanted ferocity, and fearlessness. As for myself? I was instantly besotted."

"Ferocity. That was the allure?"

"My God, yes! You were not afraid to tell me exactly how smart you were, and exactly how stupid I was."

"But I was so . . . meh."

I felt his lips on my temple, his breath in my hair. "The last thing in the world you were," he said, "was meh."

Later still, lying on his side, he said, "I have a question about your job."

"I thought we weren't supposed to talk about work."

"Only when food is in the vicinity. Post-coitally it's fine."

"All right then."

"If you were so afraid of rejection, how could you become a litigator? It's all about winning and losing, and the outcome is never guaranteed."

"Yes, but it's not personal. If you work as hard as you can, if you're excellent, you haven't lost, even if the outcome didn't go your way. Anyway, even at work I worried and fretted and got agitated about outcomes."

"Do you think success at work was bad for you as a person?"

This was a question I'd been mulling over since my big epiphany. The two sides of my life—professional, personal—how did they feed on each other?

"Yes," I said. "At least, the way I did success. The longer I wore my game face, the more I began believing it was really me—that what I was concealing was less important. Mattered less." I paused. "My therapist was right all along."

"I hate it when that happens," Singer said.

"It's like you said once—the law firm made me a good lawyer and a bad person."

" 'Bad person' is a little harsh, don't you think?"

"What if I'd stayed that way?" I wondered. "What if I hadn't picked up the phone?"

"Perish the thought." Singer rolled onto his back. "Now, fascinating as this discussion has been, it's time to talk about me."

I trailed my fingers along his chest. "We've been neglecting you."

"You wanted me *so* badly. And you had to repress it. Wasn't the urge to jump my bones an overwhelming daily torment?"

"It would have been. If I had known it existed."

"And how do you feel about me now?"

"Eh," I said.

He pulled me toward him. "Try again."

"I like you."

"How much?"

I kissed him. "A lot."

ON FRIDAY morning, Cameron appeared in my doorway. I was on a call, but waved him in. He sat down and waited. The call ended.

"Hi," I said.

"Hi."

"Sorry I haven't been in touch for a while."

"No problem." He pulled out his phone. "So, that thing we discussed, a little while ago? About me helping you find a . . . uh, professional, to discuss sex and so forth? I've done some research, and—"

"No need," I said.

He glanced up.

"You can cancel all my dating profiles, too."

He blinked, taken aback.

"I figured it out, Cameron."

"You mean . . ."

"My plan worked. Not in the way I expected, but . . ." I smiled. "Yes."

"Boss, that's amazing! Congratulations!"

"I couldn't have done it without you."

"Oh please." He waved that away. "I was just doing my job. Or," he amended, "*a* job."

I felt a twinge. "About that. I've been in a really weird place. I'm sorry if anything I asked you to do, or anything I said, ever made you uncomfortable."

"Uncomfortable? Boss, please. I got to read about the sexual pro-clivities of hunter gatherers, shop for classic cars and hone my online dating game. I had a blast." He paused. "But I guess this means it's back to the paralegal salt mines for me?"

"I'm afraid so."

"Ah well." He stood and stretched. "It was fun while it lasted."

I'd never noticed how tall Cameron was. Skinny, too, but in a graceful way. In fact, he was adorable, with his blue eyes and curly hair and goofy charm.

Funny how I'd missed that.

He headed to the door. "Don't be a stranger, okay, Boss? Whistle if you need me."

With a wave, he disappeared.

"THIS ALL goes back to the fact that you're an orphan," Sarah re-marked, a few days later.

"Naturally," I said.

"I'm serious." She reached for the sugar. "Your world was lonely, and uncertain. But there was one thing you could control. Yourself. Maybe keeping a lid on your emotions wasn't about succeeding. It was about surviving."

I thought it over. "Huh."

"You're welcome." She stirred her coffee. "Now let's gossip about your friend's dick."

I laughed. "It's top-notch."

"Glad to hear it. And the sex?"

"Astonishing, constant and ridiculously fun."

She reached across the table to squeeze my hand. "Yay for Raney!"

"I'm *there*, you know? I never used to be. I was always hovering, critiquing, assessing. Never swept away."

Sex wasn't a chore anymore. It wasn't like clockwork—unless clock-work meant wanting Singer every second of every hour.

I was insatiable. I was focused. I was intent. I took it seriously, and found it ridiculous. Because it was.

Ridiculously fun.

As it turned out, I was a little bit of a sex goddess.

Sarah glanced around the café contentedly. "Remember how we used to meet up like this, and you were always so dour and irritable and down on yourself?"

"Was it awful?"

"Sometimes."

"Hey!"

She laughed. "Relax. If I had to endure a few gloomy lattes to get this—you, sitting here looking so happy and relaxed and beautifully . . . *laid*? It was worth it."

She raised her coffee. I raised my chai. We clinked glasses.

TWENTY-NINE

IT WASN'T ALL fun and games and self-congratulation. I had some hard work to do.

The next Monday, I took Amanda out to lunch. She'd been avoiding me since her outburst at Jisun's party. She picked up her menu. She put it down again. She glanced at me, then away.

"I'm not angry, Amanda."

"You should be." She spoke all in a rush. "I am mortified by the things I said to you. I was drunk, but that's no excuse. In fact, it makes everything worse. I was so unprofessional. If you want to transfer me to another team, I'll understand. Maybe—"

"You were being honest," I said. "I appreciate that."

"But the way I did it—"

"You were a little rambunctious," I conceded. "But as you know, I'm no stranger to outsize reactions."

That earned me a weak smile.

"We do need to talk about a few things," I continued. "You accused me of being complicit in the ways the firm makes your life difficult."

"I was wrong. You're not complicit."

"Complicit is too forgiving," I agreed. "I'd say I was more of an active participant."

She looked at me curiously.

"I entered the firm straight from school," I told her. "I'd never held a real job before. I thought the professional world would be like the academic one. Work hard, do your best, be present and eager and engaged, and you'll do well. I soon learned that there were other, less clear-cut signifiers of who was going to succeed. Where you came from. How well you spoke. Whether you played squash or tennis or golf. Who you knew. And whether you were a woman or a man."

"So you felt it, too," she said.

"Along with everything else you mentioned. The diminishments, the assumptions. The sexism disguised as gallantry. The sexism that didn't wear any disguise at all. It was all new to me, and I had no idea how to handle it. At school, you surround yourself with the like-minded. You tune out what you don't want to hear."

"You can't do that out here in the wild," Amanda said.

"If I was all business, I was perceived as a humorless robot. If I tried to be playful, I wasn't taken seriously. If I accepted praise, I was cocky. If I demurred, I was weak. I couldn't be harsh, or pleasant, or mean, or nice, without being judged for it."

"What did you do?"

"Like you, I loved the work, notwithstanding the hard time I was having. I wanted to excel, and I wanted to be treated with respect. As a person, as a woman. When I realized I couldn't have both—at least, not without a fight—I settled for excelling. I locked my resentments away—something I was already pretty good at. I thought I was doing it for myself. But I was doing it to accommodate other people—exactly as you pointed out."

"But, it did work," she said. "I mean, you succeeded."

"Did I? I knew an injustice was being done—to me, to other women—but rather than push back, rather than stand up and say, 'This is not okay,' I capitulated. I suppressed an essential part of who I was, then I turned that suppression into a work philosophy I preached to others. Women have to lower their expectations, I said. They have to be better, get over it. For someone who spends a lot of time thinking about truth and fairness and the evils of sexism, that's appalling. And it's the definition of complicity."

Amanda was quiet for a while. At last she said, "Thank you for telling me this. It means a lot."

"I'm glad. But I have an ulterior motive." I reached into my bag and pulled out a legal pad. "We need more people like you at the firm. More women. I came up with a list."

"A list?"

"A plan of attack," I said. "How we're going to change attitudes. Change the culture."

"But at Jisun's party, you said—"

"That people don't change. Let's say I've recently seen persuasive evidence to the contrary. I think Calder Tayfield is the best place to work in the world. But we can make it better. I want to correct the problems that made Jisun leave and that are making you so unhappy you get drunk and lose your marbles at your supervising partner. So let's complain. Let's make some noise."

Amanda began to smile. "Are you sure about this?"

I smiled back. "What's the worst that could happen?"

ON THE television, a dozen beautiful women paced back and forth inside a Lucite cube. They were wearing bikinis, stilettos and handcuffs.

"These top supermodels haven't eaten in *four days*!" the announcer cried.

"I read somewhere that we're living in the golden age of television," I said.

"Shh," Maisie said.

"Can't we watch something good?"

"We are, duh," Kate said.

A man covered in chocolate frosting entered the cube. The models closed in.

My daughters watched, rapt. I thought back to my conversation with Amanda. I had known her only a few months, and I'd already let her down. I'd been Kate and Maisie's role model for years. Had I failed them? Had I given them the wrong signals about how to be a woman, a human? Had I—

"Mom," Maisie muttered. "The staring."

"Have I warped you?" I blurted out.

"Not lately," Kate said. "But cheer up. Tomorrow is another day."

I switched off the television. They turned to me, puzzled.

"I know I give you a hard time," I began. "I'm dictatorial. I nag. Lately I've turned your lives upside down. But I've always tried to be a good mother. I've done everything in my power to ensure that you're happy, healthy, good people."

"You're great, Mom," Maisie said. "You know we think you rule."

"That's what I'm worried about. I project this aura of invincibility. I don't want you to think you have to act the same way. I never want you to hide how you feel."

They exchanged a confused glance.

"We know you're powerful and all that," Kate said, "but we've never really seen you as, like, omnipotent."

"Maybe the people you work with do, but we know you better," Maisie added. "We notice things."

"What kind of things?"

"Like how you only harangue us when you're freaking out about work," Kate said. "How you're always sneaking in and checking on us. How you compulsively tidy when you're agitated."

"I do?"

"There are good things, too," Maisie said. "The little smiles. The way you drum your fingers when you're excited. The way your voice goes weird when you're happy."

It sounded like my superhero costume had a few holes in it. This was good news.

"Sure," Kate continued, "you don't confide everything to us, or try to turn us into your best friends, like some moms do. But that's okay. We knew you had Dad for that."

"We'd come in, and you'd be lying with your head in his lap, telling him your troubles," Maisie said.

I nodded. "Right."

"Who do you tell your troubles to now?" Kate asked.

They were curious, of course. But I couldn't talk about any of that. Not yet.

I reached for their hands. "Thank you. I was worried I'd been a terrible role model."

"No way," Kate said. "And anyway, it's not all on you. We have Dad."

"You're both crazy . . ." Maisie began.

"But together you make, like, one sane person," Kate said. "You're a good team."

"Were," Maisie corrected her. "Were a good team."

"SO THAT'S the story," I said. "I wanted to stop by to let you know how everything worked out."

"This strikes me as rather abrupt," Bogard remarked.

"It is, but with good reason. And I appreciate what you've done. Our talks revealed exactly what you suggested they might. Things about myself that I wasn't aware of. Things I needed to know. I couldn't have gotten where I am without you."

Bogard steepled his gray fingers. "And where are you?"

"Here." I spread my hands. "Problems solved. Questions answered. I've faced my insecurities. I've stopped denying what I want. I'm expressing how I feel and allowing myself to be vulnerable. I recognize how much I was relying on other people's perceptions of me to reinforce my own. I've completely conquered my discomfort with sex."

"And you discovered, what," Bogard said, "that this man was the one you wanted all along? What does that mean? You wanted to sleep with him?"

"Yes. And more. I wanted to . . . know him. Be with him."

"Are you in love with him?"

"No!"

Bogard blinked, startled. I don't know why I was so vehement. I was smitten with Singer. In my bed, in my life, he was exactly as he had been before—smart and funny, at ease in his skin, happy. I thought about him constantly. Within minutes of leaving him, I wanted to be with him again. I liked how he walked. How he talked to waiters. The glasses he wore when he read in bed at night. The sounds he made when he came. His apartment. His cooking. His laugh, of course. His body. The feel of his hair in my fingers. How he smelled. His skin. His intelligence. His warmth. His eyes.

I liked, I liked.

But love?

"Would it be wrong to be in love with him?" Bogard inquired.

"Yes," I said. "No. I don't know. I don't want to think about this right now."

"A sign," Bogard noted, "that you probably should."

Sure, eventually. But today? Bogard was doing his best, but I wasn't going to be drawn into another of our roaming, circular discussions.

"I'll deal with it later," I assured him. "Right now, I'm happy. And I'd really like to stay that way."

"WHAT ARE you thinking about?" Singer asked that night.

I said, "I'm making a mental list of all the places I want to sleep with you."

"An organized sex fiend. I approve." His hand skimmed my belly. "Tell me what you've got."

"Number one. On a grassy lawn, under the stars."

"Natural, but not too natural. I'm in."

"Number two. In the ocean. Number three. In the backseat of the Fury."

"We could combine those two," he said. "I've got some scuba gear in storage."

"Number four. The house where I grew up."

"The one that's been condemned?"

I raised my head so I could see him. "Is that weird?"

"Not if you want to roll around in black mold. Next?"

"This one's embarrassing," I said. "In a library."

He laughed. "Neither embarrassing nor surprising. Next time we pass a branch you can drag me in and have your way with me in the stacks. What else?"

"I suppose I should choose some romantic foreign cities," I said.

He scoffed at that. "Anyone can make love in Paris or Rome."

"You're saying we need a challenge. A place where great sex would be a real accomplishment."

"Exactly. A place like . . . Ptuj."

"Ptuj," I said.

"It's in Slovenia."

"How do you know that?"

"I know a lot of things," he said.

"Ptuj. It's sounds extremely unerotic."

"Trust me, it is." He put his hands behind his head. "There's also Uzhhorod, in the Ukraine. And Slupsk, of course."

"Who can forget Slupsk?"

He reached for his phone. "I'm going to google it. I bet they have a hell of a library."

He was spending the next day with his son, so at midnight I got a cab back to the hotel. We coasted through empty streets. At a red light, I looked out the window. My heart stopped.

Aaron was looking right back at me.

Then the illusion dissolved, and I was looking at an advertisement on a news kiosk. He was smiling, wearing a dorky safari hat, a butterfly perched on his finger. A new season of *The Bug Doctor* was coming soon.

He looked so boyish. Maybe that's what happens to people we meet when they're young. They become frozen in time, their freshness an indelible part of how we see them.

Aaron noticed me at that party, all those years ago. He chose me. But had I chosen him? Would I have wanted him, if he hadn't wanted me first? Was I attracted to him, or simply grateful?

Maybe these were the wrong questions to ask. Attraction did come, love did grow.

And here we were.

I thought of something Sarah once said. About how furious she'd been that Tad had cheated—until she realized she no longer wanted the thing that had been taken from her.

Did I want Aaron? Would I have lost my mind and tried to destroy him if I didn't? Or was that my well-documented competitive streak—my unwillingness to lose, even when I wasn't all that interested in the prize?

The light turned green. The cab rolled down Columbus, leaving Aaron, and my questions, behind.

THIRTY

THE FOLLOWING MONDAY, an instant message popped up on my computer screen.

    CCrowley: How are you?

Chase. I'd noticed him hanging around the outer office a few times over the last week, but I'd always been on the phone or with someone.

    RMoore: Fine. You?
    CCrowley: Good. Wondering whether you needed any upgrades?
    RMoore: No, thanks. My systems are operational.
    CCrowley: Fully operational?

Points for tenacity, I guess.

    RMoore: Working at maximum capacity.
    CCrowley: Let me know if that changes.

IT WAS mid-March by then, and an impending blizzard was dominating the news. This, folks, was going to be the big one. It was christened

Spring Storm Juno. Referred to as a snowpocalypse. A snowmaggedon. On one evening news program, a snowlocaust.

Somebody must have gotten fired for that.

As the clouds gathered, the city shut down. School was canceled, public transportation suspended, courts and businesses closed.

Snow started falling at midnight. It stopped at two. We got a total of four inches.

Most people took the next day off anyway. Midtown was beautifully plowed and almost entirely deserted. I hadn't seen Singer in three days—he'd had a bad cold. At noon, I texted him.

—Invite me over?

—Wish I could, but I have Alex.

His son. I hadn't met him. Singer had suggested it, tentatively, but it felt way too soon.

He wrote again:

—Tomorrow?

—Ok.

I didn't want to wait until tomorrow. I wanted to be with him now. I wanted to spend a long afternoon in his bed, having sex and talking and watching the snow not falling outside.

Wally ambled in. "Get your coat, li'l lady! I got us a reservation at that Brazilian steak joint on Fifty-First Street. We're going to stuff our faces with skewered meat until they kick us out."

"Or we collapse from acute gastrointestinal distress," Jonathan added, coming in behind him.

"Tempting. But I'll pass."

Wally stretched out on the sofa. "Come on, Raney. We want to hear all about your consciousness-raising sessions."

"My what?"

"We heard about your meetings." Jonathan grinned. "Ladies' Night with Raney Moore!"

A few days earlier, I'd asked Amanda to gather a group of women associates for a chat. I'd also begun dropping in on some of the other women partners. Everyone had stories. Everyone was eager to talk about unconscious bias and bad habits, and how we could change the atmosphere at the firm.

"We heard you lit candles and offered a prayer to the moon goddess," Jonathan said.

"Then you led a drum circle."

"After which all the attendees miraculously sprouted armpit hair."

"It's too bad you weren't there," I said. "Some of our associates are dissatisfied in ways the partnership doesn't realize."

"Associates are always dissatisfied," Wally said.

"You do realize we have a culture that isn't welcoming to women, don't you?"

"Culture?" Jonathan smirked. "Like the ballet?"

"We work at a law firm, Raney. It's an equal opportunity hellhole."

"No it isn't," I said. "It's—"

"They don't like the culture?" Wally continued. "Lead the way. Explain that the key to happiness is finding a hot client to sleep with. They'll stop complaining about the culture."

"And billable hours will skyrocket," Jonathan noted.

I stared at them both. "You think I found happiness through a man?"

"Uh, didn't you?"

"No. The happiness came first. The understanding. Only then could I—"

"Whatever. We can debate this over giant skewers of charred steak." Jonathan stood up. "Shall we?"

"Another time," I said. "Have fun."

They left. I continued cleaning off my desk. Wally and Jonathan were clowning around as usual, but it was annoying. Did they not see the problems at the firm? Or did they not want to see them?

Or did they not care?

I threw a letter into the recycling bin. They thought I was being humorless. I could tell from their faces. Well, maybe I needed to be. Maybe the time for joking was over.

I was irritable. Restless. I didn't want to be at work. But I didn't have a good alternative.

I sent an e-mail to Cameron, asking for help with an upcoming deposition. He appeared at my door within moments, and I started explaining what I needed.

"I'd like a pleadings binder, organized chronologically," I said. "I'd also like a correspondence binder. Then, I'd like you to—"

"Hang on a sec," he said.

He typed furiously. He bit his lip. I watched him.

Cameron had a nice mouth.

He reached up and tugged on an ear. Good hands, too.

He was young. And energetic. A little loopy.

I wondered what it would be like to sleep with him.

Whoa, I thought. Cameron? No. No, that's . . .

True, he's adorable, but I couldn't. I shouldn't. I have Singer.

I have Singer. What does that mean?

I said I was besotted. I didn't just like him, I *liked* him liked him. I found him wonderful in every way.

Maybe I did—

No. Not possible. I wasn't trading one man for another, no matter what people like Wally and Jonathan thought.

So if I wasn't in love with Singer, why was I acting like it? Denying any interest in other people? Denying what I might want?

Singer and I weren't exclusive. We'd never had that talk.

Cameron cleared his throat. "Is that it, Boss?"

"Scratch all that," I said. "Arrange the materials chronologically. Make a detailed table of contents that tells me where everything is. I need to make this easy." I paused. "Much like myself."

He looked up from his phone, startled. "Was that a . . . double entendre?"

"How was it?"

"Good!" he said. "Basic, but good."

I wasn't in love with Singer. And I was going to prove it. I was going to establish once and for all that my happiness, my new self, my revolution, was *my* doing, and not the result of union with the Right Man.

"Boss?"

I'd been gazing at Cameron as I pondered. Now he was gazing back.

I didn't look away. Neither did he.

IN THOSE tumultuous months from September to April, I did a lot of reprehensible things. I lashed out. I melted down. I made some terrible decisions. Some of what I did was understandable—a product of my heartbreak and fear and utter estrangement from myself. I behaved badly, but not unforgivably. For the most part.

But of all the rash, inexplicable, reckless things I did during that time, there was one thing I truly regretted.

The thing I did next.

I DIDN'T regret it right away, though.

"He was amazing!" I gushed to Sarah on the phone the next day.

"Cameron the paralegal?" she said. "This is who we're talking about?"

"I see why you like young guys now."

"Yeah, but not ones who work for me."

"It's fine," I assured her. "He won't talk."

"Okay, but . . ."

"But what?"

"I don't know," she said. "It's not like you to flout the rules like this."

And it wasn't like her to be so disapproving. I thought she'd be delighted. I thought it would be like those times she called to brag to me about her conquests.

"What happened to Singer?" she said. "Did you have a falling out?"

"Are you trying to make me feel bad about this?"

"Of course not! I'm . . . surprised, that's all."

"It was an impulse decision. It didn't mean anything."

"Okay," she said. "Well, I'm glad you had fun."

From: Aaron Moore
To: Raney Moore
Date: Tuesday, March 27, 1:09 AM
Subject:

Dear Raney,

I'm beginning to understand that you're not coming back. I know it's my fault—still, it's hard to accept that our marriage is over.

It's late. I'm having trouble sleeping. Who cares, right? But it's hard, being in this big house without you. Remember the night we moved in? The girls were, what, seven? We couldn't figure out how to light the stove. We had to drive around forever to find pizza.

Remember the fall when I was at Stanford, and we watched movies over the phone? I kept a list of everything we rented. I just pulled it out. Can you believe we watched *Crocodile Dundee in Los Angeles*? Talk about desperation.

I guess I'm feeling nostalgic tonight.

Here's another memory. Something you said to me once, early on. That you'd felt alone all your life. But with me, you weren't alone anymore. I was so happy. I was going to make sure you never felt alone again.

This is killing me. I'd better stop.

Love,
Aaron

THIRTY-ONE

I COULDN'T PINPOINT the hour, the day, the week it started, but at some point, Marty and I stopped getting along. We had always been in and out of each other's offices. He was the first person I turned to for advice. I was the first person he called when he had a special project. But lately, he didn't drop by as much. His e-mails were short and to the point.

After a partner meeting on the second of April, hostilities spilled into the open.

I'd just returned from the conference room on forty-eight when he strode into my office and shut the door.

Hand still on the knob, he said, "In the future, please tell me in advance if you want to add an item to the agenda. That way, I can make sure the subject matter is appropriate."

"The subject matter was perfectly appropriate."

His face was dark with anger. "What on earth, Raney? You just delivered a diatribe about how the firm is riven with sexism, how that has to change, and change has to come from the top."

"It wasn't a diatribe."

"You've obviously been speaking with some of the women partners—they were nodding along. And you've been meeting with associates?" He threw his hands in the air. "What is this, a coup?"

"I should have warned you," I conceded. "I hadn't intended to bring it up, but Horner made that dumb joke about women who talk too much, and—"

"Did you see how they were looking at you? Horner and Anton? Fanucci and Tate? It was like you'd grown a second head."

I didn't respond. Marty wandered to the window. He returned and took a seat.

"Listen, I know what you're talking about, Raney Jane. Men can be assholes. But the rest of the partnership? They don't have a clue."

"They need to get a clue, Marty. They're part of the problem."

"But the examples you gave were such little things. Jokes and interruptions and tone? Being told to smile? Is that really such a big deal?"

"That's a selective summary," I countered. "How about the big dinner last month with Morehouse Capital, where a bunch of hedge fund managers ranked the attractiveness of our female associates, and our partners sat by and said nothing? How about the partner—whom I didn't name—who drove a married associate out of the firm by sending her poems and repeatedly confessing his love? Or the associate who got drunk and assaulted the paralegal at a team event? Or—"

"Okay, yes," Marty said. "But those are isolated incidents."

"To you, maybe. To women? They're part of a pattern. And a culture."

"A culture," he repeated. "Our supposedly 'toxic' culture. What does that mean, Raney? What does it encompass? I call you 'dear.' Am I harassing you now?"

"That's different and you know it. You said you knew what I was talking about, Marty. You said you got it. So why are you arguing with me?"

"Because you need to pick your battles."

"Pick my battles," I said. "Be accommodating. In other words, fulfill their idea of what women are like."

" 'Their,' " he said. "Them and us. It's come to that?"

"Here's something interesting," I said. "You applaud me when I fight for the rights of waitresses and line cooks. But when I object to the treatment of my own employees, I'm causing trouble."

He only shook his head and turned away.

"Every workplace has these problems, but this is our workplace, Marty. We can make it better."

He turned back to me then, and he was the old Marty, gentle and imploring.

"What's really going on, Raney Jane? I don't mean to harp, but I hear things, and, well, they concern me. Is this sudden zest for female empowerment somehow connected to"—he waved vaguely in my direction—"everything else?"

It wasn't. And it was. Two branches from the same root. How could I explain that? Why should I have to?

Anyway, Marty didn't want explanations. He didn't want to help. He wanted a return to the status quo.

"My personal life is none of your concern," I said.

He was hurt. Then his face hardened. He stood and headed for the door.

"As you prefer. But keep in mind that you aren't the head of this firm. If you've got something you want to say, run it by me first."

I CALLED Sarah as I left work that night. I needed to vent.

"You would have thought I was the first person ever to suggest that law firms are bastions of male privilege," I fumed. "Or that sexism is still a problem in the world. People have been talking about these issues for a long time—and not only in the law. Other firms are taking steps—we should too, or we'll be left behind."

"Right," Sarah said.

"He tried to make it all about me, which was really infuriating," I continued. "Like I'm not entitled to speak up, because I never have before. Or that my complaints should be ignored because they're by-products of other changes in my life. I'm beginning to wonder if part of why I've succeeded is that I never really threatened them. The men,

I mean. I worked hard, but in my own neutered way. They didn't think of me as a woman. But now that I show myself to be one, they're up in arms. Especially when I make the slightest gesture toward questioning their vaunted prerogative."

I was expecting some indignation, but she was silent.

"Sarah?"

When she spoke, she seemed to be choosing her words with care. "I'm sure you're right about the environment of the firm, and you know I love a good conspiracy as much as the next girl. But . . . Marty kind of has a point."

"What do you mean?"

"You aren't really yourself lately, Raney."

This again.

"I don't think he's questioning you because you're a woman, but because you're . . ."

"What?"

"Acting like a sex-crazed teenager," she said.

"Excuse me?"

"People get freaked out by the unfamiliar. He's worried about you."

"I'm having fun. I'm living my life. I'm doing what you wanted me to do."

"Which is great," she said. "But don't forget—you're still married. That's something you need to deal with. And fortunately you're in a position to deal with it. You've found someone you really like."

"My goal isn't to replace one man with another, Sarah."

"What is your goal?"

I didn't answer. I hadn't thought about it. For once in my life, I didn't have a plan, or a strategy, or an objective. Why was everyone having such a hard time with that?

It had been a long, busy day. I was stressed. I think that's why the conversation took the turn it did.

"Are you bothered that I'm actually enjoying myself?" I said. "Are you jealous?"

"What?"

"You were always the fun one. The one who slept around and loved to talk about it. Now that I am, too, it feels like you're becoming a little puritanical."

"Puritanical," she said. "Really."

"I thought you'd be happy for me," I said. "I thought that you'd get it. I guess I was wrong."

"Okay," she said. "Well, this has been interesting, but I hear Mercer calling. I'll talk to you later."

She hung up.

THIRTY-TWO

A FEW DAYS LATER, an old case reared its head. I needed a file from my office at home, so I had Jorge drive me out to Westchester after work.

The girls were bickering at the kitchen table when I walked in.

Maisie saw me and gasped. "Who died?"

"You seriously need help," Kate told her.

"I'm getting something from upstairs," I told them. "I'll be right back."

As I left my office, I saw light coming from the master bedroom. Inside, Aaron was on the bed, reading *The New Yorker*. He was wearing a faded button-down and his clunky glasses. A lock of hair fell over his forehead. He brushed it back. He smiled at something. Turned the page.

He didn't see me. I stood there, and I simply looked.

I'd spent weeks freezing him out, telling myself he was a stranger, a liar, a deceitful conniver with unfathomable motives. He wasn't. He was a human being. Full and complicated and contradictory, full of virtues and flaws. He had a story, just like me. He had whole worlds inside him. Needs and wants and yearnings.

He wasn't good or bad, right or wrong. He was normal. Mortal.

I felt a rush of tenderness toward him.

He saw me and scrambled to sit up. "Hi!"

I stepped into the room, holding up the folder I'd come for. "Just grabbing something."

"Oh. Right. Well, it's good to see you."

I sat on the bench at the end of the bed. He watched me, wary, curious.

"I saw your picture on a newsstand the other day."

"What? Oh." He laughed, embarrassed. "Those stupid ads."

"You looked cute. How's the new book coming?"

"Slowly. But I'm keeping at it." He was encouraged by this un-expectedly amicable conversation. "You look wonderful, by the way. Have you—"

"I get why you did it, Aaron."

He drew back, uncertain. I got up and shut the door. When I re-turned, I sat on the edge of the bed, closer to him. I put a hand on his leg.

"You wanted. And you wanted me to want you. I didn't. Not in the way you needed."

"What are you saying? That you . . . you never loved me?"

"Of course I did," I assured him. "With all my heart. But some-where along the way I stopped showing it. I always had this protective shell. You got past it, more than anybody else. But it kept growing. And I . . ."

"Don't cry, Raney."

"I'm not!" I laughed, brushing the tears away. "I mean, I am, but I'll stop."

His eyes were so expressive. I felt a flash of attraction for him. He was so familiar, yet totally strange. I looked around the room. Dresser and nightstand and lamp. Bathroom door. Window. I used to live in this room. And this bed—it was *my* bed. The site of so many long talks with Aaron. So many kisses good night, so many see-you-in-the-mornings.

So much sex.

We used to do it twice a week. Like clockwork.

I looked at Aaron. I looked him up and down.

What would it be like now?

"Did you enjoy sleeping with Deirdre?"

He started a little, shocked by the question. "Of course not."

"Aaron, come on."

He sighed. "It's hard to talk about, given everything that's happened."

"I know you're sorry now, but you did it for months. It couldn't have been torment."

He was not at all sure where I was going with this. Neither was I. I took the magazine he was still holding and tossed it on the floor.

"Wasn't it exciting? Exploring a new body? All those voluptuous curves?"

I removed his eyeglasses and set them on the nightstand. "Kissing someone, for the very first time? It must have been thrilling."

"What's . . . happening right now, Raney?"

Good question. Why was I flirting with my estranged husband?

Easy answer. Because I wanted to.

"Was she good?" I brushed his lips with mine. I felt him inhale sharply. I took his lower lip between my teeth and pulled. I kissed his neck, the line of his jaw. He tried to kiss me back, but I pushed him back. I felt his hands on my waist. I slapped them away. I unbuttoned his shirt.

"Did she know that you love this?" I nibbled on his earlobe. "And this?" I raked my fingernails gently down his chest. He reached for me again. I pushed him onto his back and straddled him. I kissed him deeply.

"This is really strange," he murmured.

"Should I stop?"

"God, no." He reached for me again, trying to pull me down. I grabbed his wrists and held them above his head, stretching out on top of him.

"Did she make you this hard?" I reached down and stroked him with one hand. He groaned. I kissed him, my mouth open. I unbuttoned his pants, reached inside, stroked him again.

I pressed down on him again, kissing him, touching him, until finally I whispered in his ear, "Did she do *any* of this, Aaron?"

"None of it! It was nothing like this!"

"No?" I sat up. "That's too bad."

I jumped off the bed, tugged down my skirt and headed for the door.

Aaron lay there, stunned. He raised his head. "Raney? What . . . where are you going?"

"Back to the city." I paused in the doorway and smiled at him. "Have a good night."

SINGER MET me at the hotel the next day. He'd been traveling, and we hadn't seen each other in almost a week.

He held my face in his palms. "I missed you."

I kissed him. "Show me."

Later, he was in the bathroom when my phone pinged. It was Aaron.

—Hi there.

—Hi.

—The firm's big party is next week, right? Am I still invited?

I was feeling lazy, sated, generous toward the world.

—Do you want to come?

—I do.

—Then come.

Singer returned. I was hoping he'd get back in bed, but he bent to collect his clothes. "Duty calls. Are you free tomorrow night?"

I smiled at him. "As a bird."

He reached under the bed, and something crackled. "What's this?"

When he straightened up, he was holding a condom wrapper.

We both looked at it.

How? I thought. Who?

Then I remembered. Cameron.

Singer looked so vulnerable, standing there naked, a torn piece of plastic in his hand. I sat up, covering myself with the sheet.

"Were you . . . is this . . . new?"

I forced myself to meet his eyes. I nodded.

"So, you've been with someone else. Since we . . ."

I nodded again.

"What does that mean?"

"Nothing," I said quickly.

He lowered himself to the edge of the bed. "How can it mean nothing?"

"I don't mean nothing. I mean, we've never really talked about—"

"Right." He nodded, looking down at the carpet. "I guess I thought, after everything that's happened, the things you said to me the night we . . . I mean," he looked up now, "you and I are so good together."

My phone pinged. It was Marty.

—I got a call from Jim Schleifman at Hanover. He has a new case.

—Great. Forward it to Stephen.

"Singer, what I do with other people—"

"Can I ask you something?" he said.

I thought back to a conversation with Sarah. Singer is about to judge me for something.

"Is this just about sex for you, Raney?"

"What? No!"

"Am I, whatever. A good lay? One of several?"

"No! I mean, I love having sex with you—"

"That's not all we're good at, Raney. We talk. We connect. There are moments when I feel like . . ."

He bowed his head, defeated. When he looked up, his expression was pained. "Do you care about me at all?"

"Yes!"

"How much?"

"I don't know," I confessed.

"You don't know." A flicker of irritation crossed his face. "All your pitiless self-scrutiny, and you haven't reached that topic yet?"

My phone pinged again.

—Can you handle it? I know your plate is full with Hyperium et al

I almost laughed in disbelief. Could I *handle* it? Marty wrote again.

—I was thinking of giving it to Templeton

—Sure, Marty. Give it to Templeton. We can always afford to lose another client.

"Can you put down your phone?" Singer said testily.

I did. "I'm sorry. I didn't know this would matter to you. I didn't think."

Of course I didn't think. I didn't allow myself to. As long as I didn't think, I could do whatever I wanted.

My phone pinged again.

"I should go," I said. "Can we talk about this later?"

"You have to work." He headed for the bathroom. "Of course. Go."

THIRTY-THREE

I GASPED. My eyes flew open. I'd been dreaming someone was chasing me down a dark country road.

It was my first nightmare in weeks. I hadn't even noticed they were gone.

I blinked, breathed, calmed my pounding heart. I reached for my phone on the nightstand. It was Thursday, April 12, the date of the firm's long-awaited bicentennial party.

It would also turn out to be the single worst day of my life. But I didn't know that yet.

I rolled onto my back. That's when I felt it: an itch, between my legs. I scratched. If anything, that made it worse.

In the bathroom, I inspected myself with a mirror. Two mirrors. Everything looked normal. I e-mailed Renfield to make an appointment with my gynecologist.

When I came out of the bedroom, the girls were sitting side by side at the dining table.

"Good morning," I said.

"Why is there a second toothbrush in your bathroom?" Kate asked.

Oh no.

"What were you doing in my bathroom?"

"Answer the question, Mom."

Unprepared. Once again, I was caught unprepared.

At last, I said, "It belongs to a man I've been seeing."

"Who is he?" Maisie asked.

"Nobody."

Kate pounced. "Then why does he keep a toothbrush here?"

"He doesn't. Not normally. He must have left it by accident. And I don't mean he's nobody. You don't know him. He's—"

"Is he your 'road bump'?" Kate was struggling to keep her voice steady. "Is he the reason you moved out?"

"Is he why you made yourself so pretty?" Maisie was holding back tears. "And why you're so weirdly happy all of a sudden?"

"No! He—"

"You promised us everything would be fine," Kate said. "You told us you and Dad were working it out."

"Oh, honey. I never said that."

"You came home the other night. You were upstairs for a long time," Maisie said. "We thought . . ."

She began to cry. I reached for her, but she shied away.

My girls were utterly clear eyed, scarily smart. They were cynical teenagers! How could they have believed Aaron and I were working out our problems?

Because they were fifteen. Because they were hopeful. Because they couldn't possibly understand any of this.

"You should have been honest," Maisie sniffed. "You should have trusted us."

"I never meant to lie to you."

"Yeah?" Kate stood up. "Good job. Say hi to Nobody for us."

She flung herself out the door. With a final, betrayed look, Maisie hurried after.

FORTUNATELY, THINGS improved as soon as I got to my gynecologist.

Ha. No. They got so much worse.

By the time I was hurrying into the office on Central Park West, the sun had disappeared. Soon I was hunched on a padded table, rubbing my crotch with one hand and checking my e-mail with the other. Various clients had written to say they were looking forward to the big party.

My phone pinged. It was Aaron.

—I'll swing by your office at six, ok?

Wait, why? Of course. He was joining me for the gala. More complications. Before I could respond I heard two quick knocks, and a pale young woman in a white coat hurried into the room.

"Ms. Moore? I'm Dr. Melanie." She stuck out her hand, not bothering to look up from my chart.

Dr. Melanie? I didn't know any Dr. Melanie. I wanted Dr. Emmons, the stooped and genial codger who'd tended to my genitals for several decades.

"Dr. Emmons couldn't make it in today." She busied herself at the sink. "Why don't you tell me what's going on?"

"I woke up with a terrible itch."

She reached for a paper towel. "Are you sexually active?"

"Yes." My phone pinged.

—Hi there. Can you have lunch today?

It was Singer. I hadn't heard from him in a few days. Despite the day's mounting problems, seeing his text made me smile.

—I'd love that.

—Sonya's? One o'clock?

—See you there.

Doctor Melanie rolled her stool toward me. "Lie back and put your feet in the stirrups. Thanks. Good thing you got in early. We're closing at noon, before the storm hits."

"Another storm?" I said. "It's April."

"I know, right? Thank you, climate change." She snapped on a blue mask. I opened an e-mail from Renfield.

Marty stopped by. He needs to see you.

"I'm inserting two fingers now. The snow should be starting any minute. They say this is going to be the big one. Spring Storm Novartis."

I glanced down at her through my parted legs. "Like the pharmaceutical company?"

"I guess so. Try to relax your pelvic muscles."

They're selling naming rights to weather now?

What a world.

"I'm inserting the speculum." I gasped as the cold metal slipped inside me. Why do gynecologists always think a warning is going to help?

Doctor Melanie took her time poking around in there. Then she glanced at my chart. "You're married, Ms. Moore?"

"That's right."

"Do you feel pain when you have intercourse with your husband?"

"We don't have intercourse."

Her forehead furrowed. "You said you were sexually active."

"I am. Just not with him."

If that fazed her, she didn't show it. She removed the speculum and wheeled back. "You can sit up."

I rearranged my flimsy gown. "What is it, a yeast infection?"

"No," she said. "It's chlamydia."

"That's not funny."

"It's not supposed to be."

I stared at Doctor Melanie. She stared back.

"Chlamydia," I said.

She nodded.

"That's . . . it's . . . I've got an . . . STD?"

"An STI," she corrected me. "We call them infections now. It's less pejorative."

Less pejorative. Okay. So, I shouldn't have been overwhelmed with shame, horror or humiliation, right?

I covered my face with my hands. "This isn't happening."

"There's a small chance it's gonorrhea. I took a culture, so we'll know soon."

I couldn't breathe. Chlamydia. Gonorrhea. Pretty words, when stripped of their meaning. They could be the names of low-emission cars. Or students in Mercer's Brooklyn preschool.

Focus, Raney.

"Are you sure?"

"Fairly sure. The good news is that treatment for both infections is the same." Doctor Melanie scribbled something on her prescription pad and tore it off. "You'd better head to the pharmacy. What with the storm coming."

I took the slip of paper from her. The storm.

The storm was coming.

I WANDERED Midtown in a daze. The wind was rising. I stopped at a Duane Reade. The pharmacist skimmed Doctor Melanie's scrawl, then glanced at me. I detected a flicker of curiosity. Or disapproval. Sure, it looked like an ordinary prescription for an ordinary antibiotic, but one of those doctor hieroglyphs probably spelled out "diseased tramp."

On my way out, I got a text from Cameron.

—Can you call me, Boss? We need to talk.

I felt queasy all over again. I'd have to tell him. I'd have to tell a lot of people. But first, I'd have to tell Singer.

I waited for him at a table by the window, where I downed three Tylenol and two hundred milligrams of doxycycline.

Chlamydia. *Chlamydia.* How was this possible? How had I gotten it? Who else had I given it to?

You're a professional, I told myself. You have two teenage daughters. You're nearly forty.

I'd gone too far. I'd thrown off the shackles of conventional behavior, and now I was going to pay. I was the fallen woman, marked with a big red C.

Just what I needed. A new narrative.

I looked toward the doorway, and Singer was there. Striding in on his long legs, smiling as he approached the table. He bent and kissed me on the cheek. I instantly felt lighter, better. Then I remembered what I had to tell him.

He sat down. "I'm so glad to see you."

"Me, too. But I have to—"

"Listen." He took my hands across the table as he smiled into my eyes. "I'm so sorry about the other day."

The other day? It took me a minute to remember what he was talking about. Oh, right. Our discussion of all the sex I was having with other people.

"You have no reason to apologize," I said.

"Yes, I do. You caught me by surprise, and I shamed you. I'm sorry."

"It's okay, Singer, really. I—"

"If there's an upside, it's that the whole thing made me do a lot of thinking. About you and me." He held my hands tighter. "I'm crazy about you, Raney. I want you to leave your husband. Maybe you're not ready to move in with me. You probably need space, and time. But I want you in my life. Permanently. What I'm trying to say," he took a deep breath, "is that I think I'm in—"

"I have chlamydia!" I blurted out.

"Has anyone told you about the specials?" the waitress asked.

I looked up at her. "We're going to need a minute?"

She wandered off. Singer's eyes hadn't left my face.

"You . . . what?"

I didn't want to announce it that way. But I couldn't let him say what he might have been about to say. Not before I had a chance to speak.

"I don't know how or," I swallowed hard, "who, but it's true. You should probably see a doctor as soon as you can."

My phone pinged. A text from Marty.

—I need you in my office right away.

"Raney."

I looked up from my phone.

"Please tell me you're joking," Singer said.

"I'm not. I'm so sorry."

My phone pinged again. It was Renfield, who never texted.

—Somethings cooking. Get yer ass in here.

"Can you please stop checking your fucking phone?"

Other diners glanced up from their meals.

"It's work," I said. "An emergency. I have to go."

He was outraged, disbelieving.

"I come in here, I pour my heart out to you, and your response? 'Guess what, honey? I've got a sexually transmitted disease!' "

"Infection," I said in a small voice. "They use the term—"

"Stop!" he cried. "Just stop!"

Why did I say that? Did I think it would help? What was wrong with me?

So much. So very much.

"I'm sorry," I said. "I'll call you later."

I GOT off the elevator on forty-five and went straight to Marty's office. The lawyers I passed greeted me briefly, eyes averted.

Marty was at his desk, paging through a folder of documents. "What's the big emergency?"

His eyes flicked to the sofa. Templeton was sitting there.

"Why don't you have a seat?" Marty suggested.

I crossed my arms. "I'm fine standing, thanks."

Marty closed the folder. He rested a hand on it. "Go ahead, Andy."

Templeton rose. "An employee came to me this morning. Apparently, a routine review of our servers turned up some alarming documents. The employee was uncertain how to deal with them, so he—"

I lost patience. "Spit it out, Andy."

He glanced at Marty. Marty offered me the folder. I opened it.

The first document was an e-mail from me to Cameron, alluding to the afternoon he'd spent in my bed.

I lowered myself into one of Marty's wing chairs and started reading. There were more e-mails. Calendar entries. Summaries of Cameron's research. Drafts of my dating profile.

Chase must have given these to Templeton. Was he getting back at me for the fact that I wouldn't sleep with him again?

I read through everything. Then I read it again. Or pretended to. I was buying time. At last, I placed the folder in front of Marty.

"This," I said, "is an outrage."

"I couldn't agree more," Templeton said.

"The employee Andy referred to wasn't doing a 'routine review,'" I told Marty. "He went searching for these things. How could you allow that?"

Marty pinched the bridge of his nose. "I didn't know any of this was going on, of course. But electronic files are property of the firm, Raney. You know that."

"You've kept your paralegal awfully busy," Templeton remarked.

I swung around on him now. "Don't even think of firing him."

"I wouldn't dream of it! Imagine the lawsuit we'd have on our hands."

I took a deep breath and focused on Marty. "I can't believe I even have to say this, but what happened was consensual."

"He's your direct report," Templeton pointed out. "It's a violation of firm policy."

"We're enforcing that policy now? I can think of, oh, ten or twenty other partners who should probably be informed. Why don't you get on that, Andy?"

"Because I'm on this," he replied, with infuriating calm. "And what you've done is much more serious."

Marty had been silent for a while, eyes on the closed folder. I needed to know what he was thinking.

"I can't believe you're condoning this . . . this witch hunt," I said. "Do you really have nothing to say?"

"He doesn't even know about the prostitute," Templeton said.

I turned on him now. "Excuse me?"

"The prostitute. The one you asked your paralegal to hire for you."

Marty's face went very still. "Is that true, Raney?"

"What?" I cried. "No!"

"We found a reference to it in the paralegal's e-mails," Templeton said. "I'm having it printed now."

"It never happened!" I cried. "It was only . . . an idea."

"An idea," Templeton said. "You've been having a lot of wacky ideas lately, Moore. Did I say wacky? I meant criminal."

"Tell me something, Andy. Do you only speak in clichés, or do you think in them, too? I've always wondered."

He ignored me. "More erratic behavior, Marty. It's becoming a real pattern. Remember that Internet business in the fall? It's a miracle she wasn't caught. You can't keep letting her get away with it."

"Why are you here?" I demanded. "You are such a waste of space."

Marty's voice was very quiet as he asked, "Did you hire a prostitute, Raney?"

"No!"

"I'm calling an emergency meeting," Templeton announced.

Marty sighed. "Nobody's calling a meeting."

"You think you can get me kicked out?" I laughed. "Good luck."

"She's violated half a dozen rules, Marty. She's exposed us to liability. She's probably broken the law. You read what's in that folder. The way she talked about men, objectified them, denigrated them? What if this leaked? A partner at one of the nation's most powerful law firms, renowned for fighting for women's rights, also happens to be a harasser and an opportunist and a closet sexist. In this political climate? The press would have a field day. Clients would run away screaming."

"You're a moron," I said.

"And you're a whore," he replied.

"Enough!" Marty shouted. "Enough! Andy, go."

Templeton strode out, not bothering to conceal the triumph on his face.

"Marty—"

"Sit down."

I did. He gazed at me sorrowfully. "Raney. What the hell?"

"How could you let him talk to me like that, Marty? When a man acts this way, he's having a midlife crisis. When a woman does, she's a sinner and should be—"

Marty raised a hand. We were silent for a moment. His shoulders slumped. He rubbed his face. He looked like the oldest man in the world.

"Walk me through this," he said. "You've slept with three employees. You ordered two of them—and others—to conduct unauthorized and potentially illegal activities on your behalf. You're having a relationship with a client." I started to protest, but he cut me off. "Don't ask me how I know. I just do. My point is this. Any number of men at this firm have had midlife crises, Raney. Any number regularly behave like entitled assholes. You, my dear? Have surpassed them all."

I said nothing.

Marty rose and went to the window. Looking out, away from me, he said, "I think you should take a leave of absence."

It was like a punch in the gut. Stop working? That was unthinkable. Impossible.

"If you take a leave for a few weeks, apologize, maybe agree to get some counseling—"

I was on my feet. "There's nothing wrong with me!"

"I don't care!" Marty cried. "To be perfectly blunt, Raney, all that matters to me right now is appearances. Andy is right—this doesn't look good."

"He needs two-thirds of the partnership to force me out. He'll never get that, Marty—I make this place way too much money. He won't even find another partner to second his motion for a meeting."

Marty sat down, placing his hands flat on his desk. "Let's say you're right. The partnership stands behind you. Do you think Templeton is going to let it die? You've made no secret of your disdain for him over the years. He's the one who will leak this to the press. He will hurt you, Raney Jane. And that's the last thing in the world I want."

"I find it interesting that none of this was a problem until I started making noise about pervasive sexism at the firm."

"Goddammit, Raney, you know the one has nothing to do with the other!"

"Should I sue on my own behalf, or do I have enough female lawyers for a class action?" I put a finger to my lips, thoughtful. "I'll have to do some research."

I was sure that would set Marty off. I wanted him enraged, as furious as I was. Instead, he gave me another of his tender, hopeless looks. The ones that killed me.

"I only want what's best for you, Raney Jane. I always have."

"I'm not going to scurry away in shame and let Templeton think he's won, Marty. I can't let him or anyone else dictate how I should behave. I've come too far for that."

"Then skip the party tonight," he pleaded. "If both of you calm down, this could blow over."

It was tempting. But I couldn't.

I stood a little straighter as I said, "I am a partner of this firm. I have as much a right to be there as anyone."

"You're putting me in an impossible position! What am I supposed to do?"

"Be on my side," I replied. "But apparently that's too difficult. So I'll defend myself."

I walked out.

THIRTY-FOUR

I WENT BACK to my office. I made calls and drafted e-mails. I read, wrote, revised and approved. I worried and fretted and surreptitiously scratched my crotch. At four, Amanda stopped by with a letter.

"Looking forward to the party?" she asked.

"Mm-hmm." I skimmed what she'd written, signed it and gave it back to her.

"Thanks." She headed to the door, then stopped. "By the way. I'm going to be a little late tomorrow. I have a doctor's appointment."

It was the way she said it. The way she failed to meet my eye.

I fell back in my chair. "Amanda. No."

To her credit, she dropped the pretense. "I'm sorry, Raney. It's just not working out for me here."

"But you converted me. I'm working on the problems you pointed out."

She sank into a chair. "The male partners have been talking about what you said at a meeting a few weeks ago. Let's just say it hasn't been complimentary. They aren't listening. They don't care."

She was right. They didn't care. About her or about me. Why was I pleading with her to stay when my own career was in jeopardy?

I caught myself. Nobody listens to Templeton. You're fine.

"I'm almost thirty," she said. "I can't invest much more time in a place where I don't belong."

"It sounds like you've made up your mind."

"I've only started looking." She paused. "I'm sorry you had to find out this way."

"I'm sorry I had to find out at all."

She frowned unhappily and walked to the door. "I'll see you at the gala, okay?"

"Sure," I said. "See you there."

AT SIX, I closed my door and got ready. I wiggled my way into the bronze-and-black gown Athena had shown me during our first Barneys extravaganza—the one with the plunging neckline and metallic scales. I put up my hair. Renfield came in and took one look at me. "Zowza."

I rooted around in my makeup bag, but couldn't find any lipstick. She stumped out and returned with a gold-sequined pouch. She removed a tube and uncapped it.

"Go like this." She leered at me horrifically.

I eyed the stub of brownish-pink color. "How do you know that's going to look good on me?"

"It's Rose Potpourri, by L'Oréal," she said. "Looks good on everyone."

"Everyone?"

"Remember my sister Elaine's memorial service, how everybody said she looked so beautiful in her casket, better even than when she was alive?"

"Rose Potpourri?"

"Brought a tube to the funeral home myself," Renfield said proudly. "Woulda put it on her, too, but that jagoff little undertaker wanted all the glory."

I sat patiently as she performed her magic.

"Any news?"

She knew what I meant. "He's been making calls, according to his secretary. Nobody's agreed to second him. Blot." I took the tissue she held out and pressed it to my lips.

"What if someone does?"

She snorted. "Never gonna happen. Everybody loves you. I have no idea why, seeing how you're such a royal pain in the ass, but there's no accounting for taste."

Two knocks. Aaron stood in the doorway. For an instant, I forgot everything. The strife, the heartbreak. My professional peril and the bacteria tormenting my nether regions.

He looked so handsome. I always loved him in a tuxedo.

"Raney!" He laughed in wonder. "You look . . . beautiful."

"Thanks." I turned to Renfield. "Text me if you hear anything?"

She nodded, then bent to kiss me on the cheek. "Try to have fun tonight, will ya?"

Snow was falling as we hurried through the revolving doors. The Fury was waiting. We got inside. Aaron gave me an odd look. "So, this car . . ."

"Impulse purchase." My phone pinged. It was a text from Marty.

—Barfeld has seconded Andy's motion. We're having a preliminary meeting tomorrow morning.

—I'll be there. With my lawyer.

Jorge pulled away, and we were immediately stuck in traffic. "This city," he muttered.

I felt Aaron's eyes on me. "You seem tense. Is everything okay?"

"Everything's fine." I crossed my legs, carefully arranging the pleats of my gown. The itching had abated for a while, but now it was returning with a vengeance. I opened my bag.

"Can we talk about what happened the other night?" he asked.

I tapped Jorge on the shoulder. "Do we have any bottled water?"

"Sorry, Miz Moore. I forgot to restock it."

"The way you—" Aaron broke off as I dry-swallowed a pill. "What is that?"

I coughed, pounding my chest. The metallic disks on my dress shivered. "Doxycycline."

My phone pinged. Rahsaan.

—I'm trying to finish the Wexroth memo before I head to the museum. Who am I addressing it to?

"Raney?" Aaron said.

I replied to Rahsaan. Then I realized I hadn't heard from Kate and Maisie all day. Were they still upset? How upset? "Where are the girls?"

"Staying with a friend," Aaron said. "Why?"

"Which friend?"

"They didn't say."

"You weren't curious where your daughters might be sleeping?"

He looked at me curiously. "It's Maisie and Kate. I'm sure they're fine."

They were hurt, furious, confused. Who knows what they might do? I texted them both.

—Can you please let me know where you'll be spending the night?

"We can't keep going like this, Raney. Radio silence, then you came home, and we started talking, finally making some progress, until you . . ." Aaron glanced at the back of Jorge's head before continuing in a lower voice. "It was like you were a different person."

Buddy, you have no idea.

Ping!

Kate: We're staying at Audra's. Where will YOU be spending the night, Mother?

Aaron's phone buzzed. She'd added him to the group text. He read it, puzzled. "Why is she asking that?"

"They're upset with me."

Me: At the hotel, of course. I'll see you tomorrow. I love you.

Jorge navigated around Columbus Circle. Snow splattered against the windows.

"What is it you want, Raney? Should we try counseling?"

"Do we have to talk about this now?"

"I think we do. The uncertainty is killing me. And I don't think it's good for you, either. You're so on edge. I want us to find a way through this. But . . ."

Ping! It was Singer.

—I need to talk to you.

"We aren't communicating. I have no idea where your head is at."
Ping! Marty.

—Apologize, Raney. Agree to get help. You can make this go away.

Ping!

Kate: You won't see us tomorrow. We're not coming into the city for a while.

Ping! Rahsaan.

—Do you want 3 copies or 4?

Ping!
Ping!
Ping! Ping! Ping!

My mind was being pulled in a dozen different directions. I responded to Singer first:

—I can't call you right now. Did you go to the doctor?

I sent it and began a reply to Marty.

"We will talk, Aaron. I promise. But I've had a really hard day, and I need to focus on—"

"What does your text mean?"

Aaron was peering at his screen, brow furrowed.

"What text?"

"The one you just sent." He held his phone up. It read:

Raney: I can't call you right now. Did you go to the doctor?

More texts began appearing below it.

Maisie: Huh?

Kate: WTF, Mom?

Comprehension dawned—slowly, terribly. I sat back in my seat. Jorge lost patience and swerved into another lane. My head bumped against the window. "Sorry!" he called out.

"Raney? What's going on?"

"I didn't mean to send that to you," I said.

"Who did you mean to send it to?"

I looked down at my phone. Texts were still coming.

Ping! Ping! Ping!

I could lie. Say it was for Sarah, or Marty. Or an associate who was ill. But I didn't want to lie. I was so scattered. So frazzled. Lying felt like too much work.

So I said, "I meant to send it to a man I've been seeing."

Aaron's face went blank.

"A man," he repeated. "A man you've been seeing."

I nodded. He looked around the car, down at his screen. He read the text again, as if he might find some different meaning there.

"Who is he?" Aaron said at last.

"Someone I work with."

"I don't believe you."

"It's true."

Aaron shook his head. He looked at his screen again. "Why do you ask him if he went to the doctor?"

"Because," I took a deep breath, "I may have given him chlamydia."

Aaron froze, just for an instant. Then his face darkened with anger. "This is all a big joke to you, huh?"

"I'm serious, Aaron."

He threw his hands in the air. "There's no man. You won't give me a straight answer about anything!"

He didn't believe I could have met someone else. Slept with someone else. He found it unfathomable. I felt my anger rising.

"There is a man, Aaron. There have been quite a few, in fact."

Jorge's eyes met mine in the rearview, then darted away.

"Quite a few. Really. Can we stop playing games and have an adult conversation now?"

"You want to have an adult conversation?" I snapped. "You got it. I've been having sex with other people. A lot of sex. With a lot of other people."

"Raney, stop! I know you. You wouldn't do that. You don't even like sex that much."

At which point my anger exploded. My new life, my fantasia of happiness and pleasure, had curdled into a nightmare. In my rage and dismay, I could see only one source for all my troubles. The man sitting beside me.

This—everything—was Aaron's fault.

He'd complained about me not giving him enough of myself? Of keeping it all in, not telling him how I feel?

Fine. I'd tell him everything.

I slid toward him along the seat. I got right in his face, and I said:

"That's the funny thing, Aaron. Turns out I do like sex. I like it a lot. I just don't like it with you."

I waited. He thought he knew me? I knew him. How each feature telegraphed his feelings. There were his eyebrows, drawing together in confusion. Rising in disbelief. His dark eyes became wary, began to wonder . . . but no. His mouth drew down. He couldn't believe it. And yet . . . his jaw twitched. Eyebrows, back to confusion. Is this real? No. Yes. This is real. This is happening. It's not possible. It's not. But it is . . .

"Raney." His face crumpled. "How could you?"

As quickly as it came, my fury vanished, leaving me alone with Aaron. Who loved me. Whose heart I'd just broken.

Had he done it to me first? Sure. Did that matter?

At the moment, not at all.

We were stuck at a red light. "I'm sorry," I managed to say. "I'm so sorry."

I got out. I slammed the door.

This time, he didn't follow me.

THIRTY-FIVE

I RAN ALONG Central Park West, slipping and tripping in my ridiculous heels. The driving snow obscured all the signs. I turned down a side street and made for the well-lighted avenue ahead. Snow pelted my face and soaked my dress.

As I limped along, I reflected.

Things were going *really* well.

I had traumatized my daughters and devastated my husband. I had alienated my friends and mistreated a man I cared about. I had put my career in serious peril.

In short, I'd ruined my life, as I'd tried to ruin Aaron's months ago. With one small enhancement.

Venereal disease.

I stumbled blindly through the slush. At the corner, I waited as a cab crawled through the intersection. Something glowed redly above me. A neon sign.

It said: BAR.

I heaved the door open and went inside.

The place was dark and nearly empty. On a television bolted to the ceiling, tiny men kicked a ball around an emerald field. I approached the bar and pulled out a stool. The bartender—young, bearded, wearing a checked vest—slid a square white napkin in front of me. "What can I get you?"

I was cold, wet, drained and defeated. I was in a bar and out of ideas.

More than anything, though? I was sad.

What's the number one thing people do when they're sad?

Right.

"I would like," I said carefully, "a venti martini."

"This isn't Starbucks," the bartender replied.

"Just bring me the biggest one you have. Please."

I draped my coat on the stool beside me. I checked my phone. It was seven fifteen. The big shindig would have started by now. Marty must be relieved that I hadn't shown up.

The bartender set a large glass in front of me, full to the brim with clear liquid, a toothpick with two olives tipped jauntily along one side. I lifted it to my lips and took a sip.

I spat it out. "That's disgusting!"

A flicker of hurt crossed his otherwise impassive face. "It's a textbook martini."

"I don't doubt it. Can you make me something that tastes good?"

"What do you like?"

"I don't know. I haven't had a drink in twenty years."

His eyes widened above his bushy beard. "Oh shit. You're not an alcoholic, are you?"

"No," I said. "Just a lightweight with control issues. Right now I'd like to get extremely drunk. Can you help me with that?"

He selected a glass from the rack above his head. "You've come to the right place."

I glanced at my phone again. Nothing from Aaron, or the girls, or my associates, or Singer.

The world—my world—was going on without me.

The bartender set another drink in front of me. The martini had been daunting, with its severe stemware, its icy transparency. This one was glowing and crimson, in a curvy glass, topped with a slice of orange.

"Cheers," he said.

I picked it up and took a sip.

I took another sip. And another. I stopped sipping and started slurping.

I graduated from slurping to swigging.

I swigged and swigged. Until it was all gone.

I set the glass down. My mouth was tingling. I felt the loveliest sense of warmth and well-being, starting in my throat, melting down my chest, deep into my belly. It was as if I'd swallowed a space heater, or a snuggly blanket.

I felt my lips twitch. I was smiling. Then I was grinning.

"That was sensational!"

The bartender swiped the counter with a white cloth, a smile peeking from under his mustache. "Glad you like it."

"I don't like it. I love it! It's . . . it's . . ."

I struggled for the right expression.

"It's fucking *fantastic*!"

Something inside me loosened. I breathed deeply, filling my lungs.

"Fuck!" I cried. "*Fuck* that's good!"

"Wow," the bartender said. "Enthusiasm."

"What do you call this delightful beverage?"

"Sex on the Beach."

"Sex on the Beach." I pondered that. "Is it anything like sex in Ptuj?"

"Huh?"

"Never mind." I held out my credit card. "Keep them coming."

AN HOUR later, I'd had four more drinks and a bowl of strange-tasting popcorn.

"I'll have another," I said, when the bartender passed by.

"I think maybe you should slow down, Raney."

Horatio and I had become acquainted midway through drink two. We were old friends by now. Well, not really. I was a bedraggled woman in an eight-thousand-dollar evening gown. Horatio was an inscrutable bartender with a carnival-barker waistcoat and exceptionally thick facial hair. But I felt a connection. A spark. He made such delicious drinks.

I was a little bit in love with him.

"I'll take this one slow," I promised him.

As he placed it in front of me, I patted his hand. "Thanks, Horatio. You're a good pal."

"My name's not Horatio," he said. "But you're welcome."

"Hey!" I leaned back on my stool, clutching at the brass rail to stop myself from falling off. "You're a *bartender*! Aren't you supposed to listen to people's problems, and offer insights, and dispense sage yet practical advice?"

"I try to avoid it. Most people's problems are pretty boring. But what the hell? It's a slow night." He crossed his arms, waiting.

"Ah, forget it." I didn't want to bore him. I wanted to sit here quietly and drink my drink. Speaking of which . . .

I held up my empty glass. "May I have another?"

Horatio looked mildly disappointed. "I thought you were going to take that one slow."

"I did," I said. "Unfortunately, time sped up."

My phone pinged.

—Hi there. Everybody's asking where you are.

It was Amanda, texting me from the party. I reread her message fondly. Then I responded.

—What do you want, you filthy coward?

On reflection, that seemed harsh. I sent a second text.

—Oops! Autocorrect fail!

Amanda wrote again:

—There are some weird rumors flying around. Is everything ok?

—on the contrary, my dear. The fan has most decidedly hit the shit

There was a long pause. Then:

—Do you need help?

—Only help I need is hlep gettin on the outside of another one a these cokctails!

—Tell me where you are.

Horatio had wandered away to tend to another customer. "Horatio!" I shouted. "Horatio!" He moved toward me. The light was dim. It looked like he was swimming. Finally, he hove to.

"Horatio! What's the address of this fine eslab . . . estlab . . . establishment?"

He told me. I tried typing it, but my phone had become slippery. I handed it to him. I hadn't asked Amanda to come, I'd been positively indifferent. But now I was possessed of a burning desire to see her.

"Write, 'Make haste, young Amanda!' at the end of it," I instructed him. "I need her to know that. Make haste, young Amanda! Type—"

"Yeah yeah." He typed. "I got it."

"We'd better prepare for her arrival," I said. "Nine more drinks, please."

He poured me a glass of water.

"Horatio. I have to tell you something." I reached for his arm. He stepped back. I stood up, balancing on the rung of my stool. I reached for him. I lost my balance and sprawled onto the bar. He grabbed my arms and helped me back down.

"Relax, Raney, okay? Look." He pushed my phone toward me. "Your friend is coming."

—On my way.

"I have to finish my story!" This had become pressing, crucial. "The story of the night Aaron and I met. I didn't tell you all of it."

"You didn't tell me any of it. Who's Aaron?"

"He's my husband. Was my husband. 'Scomplicated. Just listen. The night we met? I left out one *very* important detail." I clutched the bartender's large hand with both of mine. "I got *drunk*, Horatio. We went back inside the house, after he showed me the beetle? And I had too much to drink. I was giddy. I wanted him to like me. I wanted to seem sophlisticated. Aaron took care of me. He got me home and stayed with me all night. No funny stuff, though." I shook my finger. "That was the last time I ever had a drink. Until now."

"He sounds like a nice guy."

"He's an asshole!" I shouted. "He's a fucking prick!"

"Whoa. Can you—"

"He's a cunting prick, Horatio. He's a sick sack of fucks!"

I enjoyed swearing. I thought I was good at it, too.

"He's a pricking, sucking, cunting bag of fucks!"

"I'm going to have to ask you to quiet down," Horatio said.

"I'm going to have to ask you to give me more of that ass-corn," I said.

He sighed. "It's truffle flavored popcorn. But okay."

"It tastes like ass," I said. "It's asstastic."

That was funny! I slapped the bar. "I have to tell Cameron." I sent him an e-mail.

From: Raney Moore
To: Cameron Utter
Date: Thursday, April 12, 8:38 PM
Subject:

Dear Cameron,

Asstastic!

Love,
Raney

The door opened, and a cold gust blew in. It gave me a great idea. I texted Marty.

—Additional agenda item for tomorrow's bullshit sexist scapegoating meeting. Let's buy naming rights to a blizzard! Winter Storm Calder, Tayfield and Hartwell.

He didn't respond. Probably too busy hobnobbing. Hobbing and nobbing. Schmoozing. That's a funny word.

"Schmooze," I said. "Schmooze. Schmoooooooooo—"

It was time to call my daughters.

I dialed Maisie.

"Hello?"

"You're the only good things left in my life!" I howled.

"Huh?"

"Don't abandon me!"

"Mom?" It was Kate now, slightly echoey.

"Something's weird," I heard Maisie say.

"Am I on speakerphone?"

"Yeah, Mom."

"You can do that on your phones?"

"It's kind of standard. What's going on?"

"My daughters," I whispered. "My loves."

A long pause. "Are you . . . ?"

"She can't be."

"I know, but *listen* to her. Mom, are you . . . drunk?"

I looked up. "Horatio, am I drunk?"

"Big time," he said.

I set the phone on the bar and bent close to it. "Big time," I said. I said it again, low and deep. "Horatio says big time. So, big time. Biiiiiiiig time. Big tiiiiii—"

"Mom, where are you? Are you safe?"

"Am I safe, Horatio?"

"You're fine," he said.

"I'm fine, girls! Horatio says so, and I believe him."

"Who's Horatio?"

"A wonderful man," I said. "I'm going to marry him."

"Uh," said Horatio.

"You'll love him. He makes the most wonderful alcoholic beverages."

"Where's Dad?"

"I lost him!" I burst into tears.

"You lost him?"

"I'm sorry, girls. I've been having a really hard time. Everything is fucked up."

I heard them both gasp. "*What* did you say?"

"There's no other word for it. Everything's fucked. Everything's totally fuckarooni."

"Okay, Mom? You need to call Jorge. He'll bring you to the house. We'll meet you there."

"I thought you hated me."

"We never hated you," Maisie said. "We were just really upset. But we had a long talk with Audra's mom. She told us what you've been going through makes a person kind of crazy. She was super helpful."

"She's a beautiful woman," I said. "Mrs. Audra."

"Mrs. Karnow."

"I'm going to send her a fruit basket."

"I'm sure she'll appreciate that."

My daughters still loved me! Relief nearly knocked me off my stool.

"Mom, give the phone to Horatio. We need to—"

I hung up. There was someone else I needed to apologize to. I texted Sarah.

—Whuzzup, homie?

After a minute or two, she replied.

—Who is this?

—Your old pal Raney! Raney Moore! Moore the Whore!

—Raney?

—I have a diseased vagina. All of my chickens are coming home to roost.

. . .

—My sexy, bacterial chickens.

My phone rang.

"Phlaney Bloore speaking!" I said. "Snoredy Core of Moordy Floore!"

"Raney? What's going on?"

"It's the end of the universe!" I cried. "The end of time!"

"Are you . . . have you been . . ."

"Drinking? Like a fish! Like the little dipping bird. Like a rock rolling down a hill."

"Oh Jesus. Tell me where you are."

"I'm sorry for being such an asshole the other day."

"*What* did you say?"

"On the phone, I mean. But also all the times I was an asshole in person. And via text. I don't want to fight with you. I love you."

"Oh, honey," she said. "I love you, too."

"But I was so nasty to you."

"A little bit. But we've been friends for twenty years. One little spat isn't going to be the end of us."

"Thank you," I sobbed. "You're wonderful. I don't deserve you."

"Probably not. Now, where are you?"

Apologizing felt good! I didn't apologize enough.

I hung up on Sarah and texted Singer.

—First I didn't believe in fun, because I was all about the meaning.
Then I finally understood the fun, but forgot about the meaning.
You're fun AND meaning.

I sent it. Then I reread it. What the hell was I trying to say?

—I like you. Like, really like you. Do I the other thing you? I don't know. I got scared. I wasn't ready to start a new narrative. Not before my old one had ended.

I sent that one, too. I watched the phone for a long time. He didn't respond.

I put my head down on the bar.

After a while I felt a touch on my shoulder. It was Amanda!

I grabbed her arm. "It's fucking amazing to see you!"

"Oh my God," she murmured.

Under her heavy coat, she was wearing a sparkling blue gown. I held her away from me so I could admire her. "You look beautiful! Especially your boobs."

I tried to open her coat for a better look, but she took my hand. "Raney, what have you been drinking?"

"Sexes on the Beaches!" I cried. "Thousands of 'em!"

"She's had seven," Horatio said. "But I stopped adding alcohol after the fourth one."

I drew back. "Horatio. Thou hast betrayed me."

"My name's not Horatio," he told her. "Just for the record."

"I love you," I told Amanda.

"I love you, too. Listen, your friend Sarah called the firm trying to track you down. I'll wait with you until she gets here, okay?"

I pulled Amanda onto a stool and slammed my fist down on the bar. "Seventeen drinks for my lovely young friend!"

"She needs to stop hitting the bar," Horatio said to Amanda.

"One more drink and I'll stop," I promised.

Amanda nodded. Horatio reached for fresh glasses. "She's your re-sponsibility now."

He made us drinks. I sipped mine. "It's so much better with alcohol," I declared. "So fucking much fucking better." I took another sip. "Fuck."

"Oh boy," Amanda said.

That reminded me of all the things I had to tell her.

And it pissed me off.

"Oh boy? Oh *boy*?" I smacked her on the arm. "You of all people shouldn't say that! It's gendered *bullshit*. It's linguistic *sexism*. It's men, worming their way into our brains, the way they worm their wormy ways into every other fucking thing. They've sunk their penis-shaped claws into hundreds of words. Useful words. Words we need. But to use them, we have to talk about men. Think about it, Amanda. Hu*man*. Business*man*. Bogey*man*. Per*son*. Fe*male*."

Examples were rushing through my brain. I couldn't stop them.

"Treason!" I cried. "Tamale! Broth!"

"Broth?" Amanda said.

I clutched her arm. "The bros got the broth, Amanda! They got the broth!"

"You're kind of hurting me."

"Sorry." I released her. "I'm glad you're here. I figured it all out. Men. Women. Work. The whole shitbang. Shebang."

Because I had. It had come to me in an instant, and I was ready to share it with her.

"Men have these divining rods between their legs," I said. "That's what gives them access to sources of immense power. All the power in the world. Are you going to drink that? You are? Okay. Anyway, yes. Men have always had this power. They've kept it for themselves, guarded it jealously. They're not going to relinquish it. We have to make them, Amanda. We have to prune those divining rods. We have to," I slashed my hand through the air, "cut off their dicks!"

"We should call your driver," Amanda said.

"You want to start with Jorge? Great! You get the pinking shears." I slid off my stool. "I have to pee."

I walked to the back of the bar, mind spinning, truths flying at me. Men and women. Men versus women. Women versus men. The problem was so complicated—but so easy! It was about tradition and culture and propaganda and biology. It was about being a subject, and being an object. Men being the default. Women being raised to defer, to apologize. To react, rather than act. It was about people lacking imagination, and empathy, about everyone being so jealous of their own prerogatives, so reluctant to admit error and so afraid.

So. Fucking. Afraid.

Like I'd been afraid, my whole life.

Everybody needed to stop being afraid, and start being honest, and open, and just . . . love one another.

The floor was moving. Pitching back and forth. Was I on a ship? I reached for a wall. I saw the sign for the bathroom. Land ho!

In the stall I hiked up my dress and sat down. I glanced at my phone. I had a voice mail.

I nearly cried out with joy. Someone had called me! Someone still loved me! Was it Singer? I fumbled to press Play.

"Hi, Ms. Moore. This is Melanie Seton, from Doctor Emmons's office? I had some second thoughts after you left the office this morning, and ran a quick test here. Turns out you were right. You don't have an STI. It's a severe yeast infection. I think what happened is—"

I dropped the phone. I staggered out of the stall and lay down on the cold tile floor. I closed my eyes.

When I opened them, Amanda was standing over me.

"He didn't call," I whispered.

She crouched down. "Hang in there, Raney."

When I opened my eyes again, Amanda had become Jorge.

"My Jorge," I said. "How I treasure you."

"Hey, Miz Moore. Let's get you out of here, okay?"

He walked me to the front. The door blew open, and a snowy figure hurried in.

"I'm sorry it took me so long," Sarah said. "Are you—"

"He didn't call!" I wailed. "I don't have the clap, but I don't have Singer, either!"

I fell into her arms, weeping. She held me while Jorge paid Horatio. Then Amanda helped me on with my coat. My friends. How kind they were. Jorge stood ready to hoist me in his arms, but I had to walk out of the bar myself. Out into the world.

Out into the rest of my disastrous, ruined life.

A life that had been so well-crafted, so satisfying. So complete.

I emerged into a shocking wind. Sarah, Jorge and Amanda trailed behind. As I crossed the sidewalk, a man bumped into me.

"Whoa!" He staggered a little, clutching at me.

I shoved him away. "Watch where you're going."

"Easy, honey. You bumped into me."

"No, *honey*," I retorted. "You bumped into me."

"Whatever." He looked me up and down. "You should try smiling. You'd almost be pretty."

He'd been walking with two or three others. They guffawed. I looked deep into his eyes. They were blue. His hair was dark. His teeth white and even.

"It's you," I whispered.

"Who?" Sarah said.

"Derek Frasier. We sat next to each other in second grade." I took a step toward him, poking him in the chest. "He's an asshole."

Derek held his hands up. "What are you talking about?"

"Miz Moore, this guy's like twenty-two. I don't think—"

I pushed Jorge aside and grabbed the front of Derek's coat. "Who the fuck do you think you are? Calling me a frog? Telling me to *smile*?"

"Lady, I don't—"

"Raney!" Sarah cried. "No!"

Too late. I reared back and swung as hard as I could at his sneering face.

The *crack!* as I made contact was extremely satisfying.

Even though it might have been my hand breaking.

Derek stumbled back, clutching his nose. Blood seeped through his fingers. His eyes bugged out.

"You hit me, you crazy bitch!"

"You had it coming," I said. Then I smiled. Just like he wanted me to.

That was the last thing I remembered.

PART FOUR

THIRTY-SIX

I OPENED MY EYES.

The air around me was hot, but my body was icy cold. I was sitting on a concrete floor, back against a tile wall.

I ached everywhere. My head throbbed. And my hand . . . I tried moving my fingers, until a bolt of pain persuaded me to stop.

An overhead light flickered. I rubbed my eyes, blinked, opened them wide. The place was packed with people. Nearby, a tall woman in nurse's scrubs was pacing and chewing her nails. A young girl was huddled in a ball, weeping drunkenly. Another young girl drunkenly comforted her. To my right, an elderly woman slumped against the wall, snoring gently.

Through the press of bodies I saw bars, a passageway beyond. A man strolled by in a uniform.

Of course. I was dreaming.

Soon a wrecking ball would come bashing through those bars, or a spaceship would land, or the cell would tip into a volcano, and I would gasp awake. Blink. Calm my pounding heart.

Then I remembered.

Templeton. Marty. Aaron. Horatio. Derek Frasier—who wasn't Derek Frasier at all.

This was no nightmare.

There was a woman to my left, a round-faced little elf with bright yellow hair. She was sitting cross-legged, chewing her bottom lip and staring into space.

"How long have I been here?" I asked.

"Do I look like I keep the motherfucking visitor's log?" she retorted.

"Is there a visitor's log?"

With an outraged huff, she turned away.

Through the pain and mental fuzziness, I felt my anger begin to stir. So I was in jail. I'd been in jails before, interviewing inmates for my ACLU case. Somehow, I'd gone from litigating the defects in the criminal justice system, to entering that system. The men—all those pompous, self-righteous, hypocritical men in my life—were going to love this. I was exactly where they wanted me. In a cage full of trouble-some women.

Metaphor, bitches.

It was so unfair. I wouldn't have hit that oaf if I hadn't been drunk. I wouldn't have been drunk if I hadn't been under attack from all sides. And I wouldn't have been attacked from all sides if the *men* hadn't felt so threatened.

I was the woman punished for speaking up. For challenging the status quo. Talk about an insidious narrative. Talk about—

"Don't be an idiot," I said out loud.

The sleeping woman whimpered and slumped against me. The tiny blonde glared at me.

"Not you," I said.

I closed my eyes and rested my head against the wall. I wasn't the victim here. I had abused my power. I had taken my newfound libera-tion as license to do as I pleased, regardless of the consequences. I had downed those drinks and thrown that punch.

My predicament wasn't about Women and Men. It wasn't about sexism. And it definitely wasn't about other people.

It was about me.

I buried my face in my hands. I was going to lose my job. I loved the firm. It was the only place I'd ever worked, the only place I'd ever wanted to work. Being a partner there was my identity. My world. And it was all going away. If Templeton's charges hadn't been enough to oust me, my arrest for assault would surely do the trick.

I gazed around, despondent. The pacing nurse was talking with another woman. Their voices rose and fell in agitation. The drunk girls had quieted down. From farther back in the cell came a bark of laughter, the hum of conversation. The overhead light buzzed. The place stank.

I heard a noise in the distance, coming from somewhere outside the cell. There was shouting and clanging in the corridor. The women arrayed along the bars craned their necks to see.

Soon, a pair of guards dragged a woman into view. She was weeping and thrashing around. One guard unlocked the door, and the other pushed her in. She stumbled a few steps and fell to her knees, close to my feet.

She raised her face, and we looked at each other. She was bruised. Her clothes were torn. Her hair was a mess. My cellmates immediately started protesting.

"Quiet down!" the guards shouted.

I struggled to my feet. "What did you do to her?"

One of the guards just rolled his eyes.

"She's hurt," I said. "She needs help."

"Oh, she'll get help." They laughed.

"Hey!" I shouted. Their laughter died. Heads swiveled in my direction.

"Do your jobs," I told the guards. "Or you might not have them for much longer."

That got them laughing again, harder than ever. They left the cell. The nurse knelt beside the new woman. A few others tried to make her more comfortable. But she was scared, and didn't speak English. Eventually she huddled in a corner, and everyone left her alone.

I was fully awake now. Restless. I wanted to do something.

"This place sucks," I said.

My blonde neighbor snorted. "You don't say."

I turned toward her, too quickly. My brain thudded painfully against the inside of my skull. Didn't matter.

"What are you in here for?"

"Why the fuck should I tell you that?"

"I'm a lawyer."

She looked me up and down. "You sure?"

"Positive."

"What happened to your hand?"

"I punched a man."

She looked impressed. "You might be my kinda lawyer. I'm Lola."

We shook, awkwardly, with our left hands. "Why were you arrested, Lola?"

"I jacked a cockatiel," she said.

"I have no idea what that means."

With a kind of aggrieved patience, she elaborated. "I committed grand larceny in the fourth degree upon the person of my landlord's nasty-ass bird, due to its inability to shut the fuck up, like, ever."

"Alleged," I said automatically. "Alleged grand larceny."

"Yeah, well, I did the whole alleged building a goddamn alleged favor. We were like zombies from the sleeplessness." She gave a righteous little jerk of her head. "Bunny had to go."

"Grand larceny," I said. "You're sure?"

She nodded.

"Was the bird worth more than a thousand dollars?"

"That raggedy-ass thing? Please."

"Then you didn't commit grand larceny."

Lola's smile transformed her face. "No shit?"

I smiled back. "No shit."

HOURS LATER, I was led out of the cell and up several flights of stairs to a small interview room. It was painted a sickly green, furnished with a metal desk and two chairs. The guard waited outside—I could see his stubbly neck rolls though the grilled window.

The door opened, and a man hurried in. He was youngish, pale and paunchy, wearing a stained tie and a put-upon expression. He tossed a file folder onto the desk and pulled out a chair.

"Ms. Moore? Matt Bergman. I'm the assistant district attorney handling your case."

"Why am I here? None of the other women have been brought out of the cell."

"They'll come up in about an hour, when arraignments start. I'm trying to get you out of here before that." He opened the file. "I've spoken with your attorneys—"

"Who?"

He looked up. "Amanda Hewes and Sarah Kellerman."

"Excellent. I'd like to see them."

"They're waiting upstairs. I thought I'd go ahead and present our offer to you now, so that—"

"I need to get back to the cell." I stood up. "Can you have my lawyers meet me down there?"

Bergman passed a hand over his face. "Ms. Moore, I'm sure you're overwrought, but if you could try to focus. My boss clerked at your firm during law school, years ago. He's got fond memories of the place. We're offering you a deal."

"I'm not taking any deal."

He squinted at me, perplexed. "You're facing a serious charge. Assault in the second degree is a—"

"I'm not guilty."

"I have witnesses. And a complainant with significant injuries. I can convert the criminal complaint into a desk appearance ticket, and you'll walk out of here in twenty minutes. All you have to do is agree that," he picked up a sheet of paper and began to read, "on the evening of April twelfth, you did willfully and with—"

"I'm not agreeing to anything."

He dropped the sheet of paper, exasperated. "We're trying to do you a favor. Why are you being so difficult?"

I didn't like Bergman's superiority, his air of harassed importance. I didn't like how he was wasting my time. And I definitely didn't like his tone.

"If you think I'm being difficult now," I said, "wait an hour."

"Huh?"

The guard opened the door. "The women are causing a racket downstairs. Say they want to see their lawyer."

Bergman sighed. "You know the drill. They'll be assigned someone from Legal Aid as soon as they come upstairs."

"They say they've retained a lawyer." The guard pointed at me. "Her."

THIRTY-SEVEN

THE BRIDGE OFFICER called out, "CR-164271, People versus Rona Evans."

A bailiff led my next client—the agitated nurse—into the drafty, grungy courtroom. I pulled a file from the stack on the table and scanned its contents.

I leaned toward Amanda, seated at counsel's table beside me. "I need the elements of criminal mischief in the third and fourth degrees."

She started typing on her phone. I turned to Cameron, perched behind us in the first row of the gallery. "I need the factors judges use when determining bail."

He got busy, too. On the bench beside him, Emily from the ACLU was huddled with the reporter.

"So the problem is bad lawyering?" he asked.

"Not at all," Emily said. "Most lawyers want to represent their clients effectively. Defects in the system prevent them from doing so. For example . . ."

"Counsel," the judge boomed. "Maybe we proceed?"

I rose and stood next to Rona, giving her shoulder an encouraging squeeze. "Yes, Your Honor."

For the fifth time that morning, the bridge officer inquired, "Do you waive the reading of the complaint?"

For the fifth time I said, "We do not."

The bridge officer sighed. The judge glowered. Bergman, seated at the table to my right, looked at me with loathing.

I was having a blast!

A criminal arraignment is a pure formality. The defendant stands before the judge, enters a preliminary plea and is either granted bail or held without release. The process typically lasts two to three minutes. A five-minute arraignment is painfully long. A fifteen-minute one is unheard of. That morning, court had been in session for ninety minutes, and we'd completed four.

It wasn't entirely my fault. Bergman had argued that I shouldn't be allowed to represent my cellmates. We spent twenty minutes debating the issue before the judge decided in my favor. My first cases went slowly, as I familiarized myself with the process and the jargon. But now I was getting the hang of it.

And I had help. When I finally managed to see Amanda and Sarah, I had them call Cameron, who raced downtown with office supplies, aspirin and suit jackets to cover our evening gowns. Amanda also called Emily, who hurried right over, eager to drum up publicity for our indigent defense lawsuit. Sadly, Sarah had only been able to stick around for two cases before leaving to pick up the kids.

"Never change, maniac." She hugged me goodbye. "I love you. Call me when it's over."

The bridge officer read the charges against Rona in a dull monotone. Bergman beckoned to me irritably. "It's a breach of etiquette to force a reading of the complaint."

"My client has the right to hear the charges against her. How else can we fight them?"

"This isn't trial! We've got two objectives here—serving the required legal notices and determining bail. You're deliberately slowing this down!"

"I'm being an effective advocate. You should try it sometime. Because this thing?" I held up the complaint against Rona. "Is a piece of garbage."

"We're here gathering information," Emily was telling the reporter.

"My co-counsel, Ms. Moore, was in the Tombs all night, interviewing prospective plaintiffs."

"And now she's representing them?"

"We're trying to illustrate how different the outcomes can be when lawyers have the resources to advocate effectively for their clients."

The reporter scribbled rapidly. Then he peered up at me. "Why is she wearing an evening gown?"

"I'll have to get back to you on that," Emily said.

The bridge officer finished reading and sat down. I stood. "Your Honor—"

"No no no." The judge shook a finger at me. "It's not your turn, Ms. Moore. Mr. Bergman, do you have any notices?"

"Yes, Judge." He shuffled around some papers. "We're serving a seven-ten-thirty-one-a and a one-ninety-fifty."

The judge regarded me warily over his reading glasses. "Ms. Moore?"

"Your Honor, we're serving a cross one-ninety-fifty. I'd also like to note for the record that we'll be moving to suppress evidence from the line-up, and—"

"Ms. Moore, this is neither the time nor the place to—"

"We'll also be moving to dismiss the complaint."

Bergman couldn't help himself. "On what grounds?"

I was skimming the statute Amanda had called up on her phone. "It fails to state all of the elements of the crime. Nowhere does it claim that the damage my client is alleged to have inflicted on the complainant's motor scooter exceeds two hundred and fifty dollars."

Bergman flipped rapidly through his copy. "That's an inadvertent omission, Judge. I'll file an amended complaint, and—"

The judge shuffled his papers, casting an annoyed glance at Bergman. "This is the second defective complaint this morning, Mr. Bergman."

"Mr. Bergman's 'omission' is the difference between a felony and a misdemeanor for Ms. Evans," I said. "A preliminary review of my other clients' files shows similar flaws."

"We'll get to that, Ms. Moore. Mr. Bergman, do you have a statement with respect to bail?"

"We ask that it be set at five thousand dollars, Judge."

"We strenuously object, Your Honor." I scrolled down Cameron's screen as Rona whispered in my ear. "Ms. Evans has extensive ties to the community. Three generations of her family live in the city. She has two children in the New York City school system. She works as a registered nurse at Montefiore Medical Center. She is the opposite of a flight risk. Moreover, I can personally guarantee her appearance, as we'll be working together on a civil rights lawsuit concerning the circumstances of her arrest. I'd also like to point out—"

"Enough," the judge said wearily. "Enough." He paged through the file in front of him. He held a whispered conference with his courtroom deputy. Then he removed his glasses.

"I'm releasing the defendant on her own recognizance."

Rona beamed. In the back of the courtroom, someone cheered.

"Clean up the complaint and refile it today, Mr. Bergman."

"Yes, Judge."

"I've offered to negotiate with Mr. Bergman for a reduced charge," I said. "He refuses to discuss it with me."

"Ms. Moore, your interjections are most unhelpful." The judge paused. "Why on earth won't you plea-bargain, Mr. Bergman?"

"Ms. Moore is intentionally gumming up the works, Judge. This courtroom has slowed to a crawl. Cases are piling up on our end, and—"

The judge's eyes narrowed. "I'll worry about the management of my docket. I suggest you do your share to expedite matters. And Ms. Moore. No more wasting time."

"Of course not, Your Honor."

I smiled at Bergman. He murdered me with his eyes.

The next defendant was from a different cell. I moved aside for his lawyer. I felt a tap on my shoulder and turned. Marty was standing there.

"What the hell are you doing?"

He'd found me. No surprise, I guess—the man had the instincts of a bloodhound. But his presence could mean only one thing: my partners had decided my fate.

"A little pro bono work," I said. "How was the gala?"

Marty was staring hard at Emily, trying to place her. She smiled at him. "Hey, Marty!"

The reporter perked up. "Marty Rauschenberger?"

"That's right," Em said, a glint of mischief in her eye. "Calder Tayfield's managing partner."

The reporter stuck out his hand. "Kevin Mooney, *New York Times*."

Marty took in the notebook, the ID badge, the air of eager inquisitiveness. He didn't flinch or even blink. Unless you knew him as well as I did, you'd have no idea he was dying quietly.

Marty hated publicity. Especially the negative kind. The kind that generates headlines like "Partner at White Shoe Law Firm Charged with Assault in Drunken Rampage."

"I'd love to get a quote from you about the firm's decision to get involved in this case," the reporter said.

"Raney," Marty said.

Amanda handed me a complaint. "Our next client. Check out the fifth paragraph."

"Raney," Marty said.

"I'm a little busy," I told him. "Let's catch up later?"

As all this was happening, other defendants were being led into the courtroom. Prosecutors and defense lawyers were standing up, speaking and sitting down again. Marty jerked his head toward the side of the room. I followed him. Might as well get this over with.

He angled himself so that his back was to the reporter. He took a deep breath, struggling to keep his cool.

"Let's recap, shall we? From what I understand, on your way to the museum last night, you stopped at a bar. There, you downed seven or eight drinks. Upon leaving, you accosted a stranger on the street, accused him of bullying you thirty years ago and broke his nose. Hours later, you rejected a plea deal that would have allowed you to walk out of here essentially scot-free. Instead, you chose to remain incarcerated, apparently so that you could stand up in open court—looking, you'll excuse my candor, considerably the worse for wear—in order to represent a pack of prostitutes, petty thieves and other miscreants."

"Alleged miscreants," I said. "Other than that, you nailed it. Mind if I get back to work?"

"Don't move." He glanced back at the reporter. "Why in God's name is the *Times* here?"

"Em called them. She thought a sympathetic article would put pressure on the state to settle our indigent defense case."

"Does he know you've been arrested?"

"Not yet. But who knows? Maybe it'll add a touching human interest angle."

That was as much as Marty could take. "Goddammit, Raney Jane! Did you stop for an instant to consider the reputation of the firm, or your own reputation? Why couldn't you fall apart like a normal person? Why do you always have to be so extreme?"

"I'm an erratic person," I conceded. "I should really get some help."

He ignored that little dig. "Do you realize the trouble you're in? You've been charged with a *felony*. You could go to jail. Fortunately, I just persuaded your rather tiresome victim not to assist the prosecutor. Do you know how much I had to pay him to do that?"

Marty had taken my arm as he spoke. I jerked away. "Feel free to deduct it from my final paycheck."

"Oh for God's sake," he said. "You're not going anywhere. Wally and Jonathan pulled your clients aside at the party last night and told them a movement was afoot to oust you. Everyone threatened to follow you wherever you went. Templeton was forced to drop the entire thing."

To my surprise, I found I couldn't speak.

"You'll be delighted to know that half your partners love you, and the other half are terrified at the prospect of facing you in court one day." Then his eyes went soft. "You're safe, my dear."

Safe. I was safe.

Tears pricked my eyes. I wiped them away.

"Good," I said. "Then I quit."

Amanda approached. "We're up next."

"Amanda and I are starting our own firm," I told Marty.

"Uh," she said.

"Don't be ridiculous."

"You hung me out to dry, Marty! You stood by and let me be shamed, and insulted, and—"

"You were completely out of control!"

"Yes I was," I said. "All the more reason for you to stand by me. It's easy to support someone when they're following the rules like a good girl. You always told me you were there for me. You said all I needed to do was ask. But when I really needed you, when I finally asked? You turned your back on me."

The bridge officer called out, "CR-167195, People versus Jade Hallenbeck." I moved past Marty and took my place at the podium.

The morning proceeded. Bergman issued notices. I issued cross-notices. He argued for bail. I argued against it. Emily interviewed potential plaintiffs for our lawsuit and offered the occasional word of advice. Cameron did research. Amanda reviewed the complaints and assisted on strategy.

I kept talking.

"My client wasn't read her rights."

"We're going to need discovery."

"The complaint fails to allege all of the elements of the crime of assault."

". . . of forgery."

". . . solicitation."

". . . petit larceny."

". . . health care fraud."

". . . prostitution."

"Nowhere does the State allege the value of complainant's elderly tropical pet," I said.

Bergman was furious. So was I. One of my clients hadn't been read her rights. Another had been roughed up during a search. Others shouldn't have been arrested at all. They'd been subject to harassment, illegal searches, discrimination.

The judge was deeply annoyed—until he learned that a reporter was present. He stopped hollering at me and started hollering at Bergman. Why was the documentation sloppy? Why were so many of the charges excessive?

I happened to be looking back at the gallery when the door opened and Aaron slipped in. He scanned the room for me. Our eyes met.

I'd just gotten a complaint dismissed. My headache was gone. I was having fun.

Without thinking, I smiled at him. He smiled back.

The bridge officer called out, "CR-164532, People versus Raney Moore."

Bergman leaned toward me with an evil grin. "You're going *down*."

"I take it you're representing yourself, Ms. Moore?" the judge said.

"I am. And if I may—"

"I beg your pardon, Your Honor." Marty entered the well of the courtroom. "I'm Martin Rauschenberger, of the firm Calder, Tayfield and Hartwell. I am Ms. Moore's counsel."

"No he isn't," I said.

Marty smiled genially at the judge. "May I confer with my client for a moment?" He grabbed my arm. "Knock it off."

"I don't need to be saved, Marty. Not by you or anyone else."

He dropped his head. He sighed.

"I should have stood up for you," he said. "I should have told Templeton to go to hell the minute he walked in my office. Your behavior was utterly outlandish, but no worse than the stunts other partners have pulled over the years. I suppose I couldn't accept that you were the one doing it, and that you wouldn't confide in me."

That was all I needed to hear.

"I'm sorry, too," I said. "I showed terrible judgment. I was arrogant, and reckless, and incredibly stupid. I don't know why I couldn't talk to you. I just couldn't."

"Please don't leave the firm, Raney Jane. I don't know what I'd do without you."

"We need to deal with our problems."

"What do you want, Raney? What's going to satisfy you?"

I was ready with my answer. My full-throated, rah-rah speech.

"This is going to sound corny and ridiculous, but I want to work at a place where I don't have to hide who I am. Where nobody does. Where we air our grievances and treat each other decently. I want to kick ass *and* cry. To be respected *and* real. We have to set expectations for how clients and partners and associates behave, and make clear that our tolerance for shittiness is extremely limited."

"That all sounds wonderful," Marty said. "And it will never work."

"It's utopian and goofy," I agreed. "And no, it won't work—unless we try. But if we do try, we can make improvements. We can be good lawyers *and* good people, Marty. I know it."

He studied the ground for a moment. He rubbed his bald head. When he looked up, my spirits rose.

Marty was in dealmaking mode.

"No more sleeping with the support staff," he said.

"Done."

"No more personal business on the firm's dime."

"No problem."

"We'll arrange a series of partner meetings," he said. "We'll convene a working group. We'll do studies and hire consultants and whatever else you think we need. You're in charge. I'm still skeptical, but you have my support."

I squeezed his hand. "Thanks, partner."

"Mr. Rauschenberger?" the judge boomed. "We're waiting."

Bergman wasn't happy to learn he no longer had a cooperating victim. After a lot of huffing and puffing, he agreed to reduce the charge to disorderly conduct. I got off with a fine and a stern warning from the judge.

The gallery cleared. I looked for Aaron, but he was gone. Amanda scooped up the files of our new clients from the table.

"I'm sorry about last night," I said. "Dragging you away from the big party, everything you had to deal with? I'm appalled at myself."

"We've each had a drunken tirade." She smiled. "I'd say we're even."

"Please don't leave the firm, Amanda. I can fix this. I can make a start, anyway. But I need your help. I need a mentor."

She laughed. I kept pressing.

"Give me a year. Or even six months."

"I can do that," she said. "It means a lot that you want me to stick around."

"You won't be sorry."

"Or bored." She held up the files. "I'll take these back to the office. See you Monday."

The next stop on my apology tour was near the door of the gallery, where Cameron was hovering.

"Thanks for helping out today."

"I wouldn't have missed it, Boss."

"Were they hard on you?" I was thinking about Templeton, the paralegal supervisors and the rain of fire that must have come down on his head.

"I definitely received what you might call a stern talking-to, but I bore it manfully. And honestly? Now that word about our 'special project' has spread far and wide, my cred among the other paralegals is," he pointed a thumb skyward, "stratospheric."

The rumors. How would I ever live them down?

"Listen, Cameron. I'm sorry. About everything. The things I asked you to research, the claims I made on your time, the . . ."

I trailed off. He looked at the floor.

"I didn't . . ." I swallowed hard. "You didn't feel like you . . . had to sleep with me, did you?"

"*Had* to? Boss, are you nuts? I've been into you forever."

"Forever?"

"Okay, maybe not forever, but a long time. At least since that day back in September, when you went all Third Punic War on your husband. I think you're amazing. I—"

All at once he seemed to process what he was saying. He blushed harder than ever.

"I just mean," he mumbled, "I was, uh, pleased to be asked."

"That's a relief. Still, given the circumstances, maybe you should transfer to another team."

His eyes widened with horror. "God, no. Anyway, I'm not sticking around much longer." He shifted from foot to foot. "I didn't get a chance to tell you yet, but I'm going back to school."

"Not law school?"

"Ha! No. Psychology, as a matter of fact. With a concentration in," he blushed, "human sexuality."

I felt myself starting to smile. He grinned.

"I'm going to be a sex researcher, Boss. All your doing—no pun intended. Actually, pun fully intended. But I'm not leaving for a few months. So if you need anything," he blushed again, "you know where to find me."

He saluted me and loped out of the room.

WHEN I emerged from Central Booking, the afternoon light was failing. Aaron was waiting. We looked at each other across a patch of slushy sidewalk.

"Hi," I said.

"Hi," he said.

There was too much to say. Meaning that, for a while, neither of us said anything at all.

Finally, he broke the silence. "You did a great job in there. I always love watching you in court, but that was something else. I bet your parents would have been proud."

"I suspect their methods were slightly different."

He smiled. "Maybe."

"Did Sarah tell you I was here?" He nodded. "How are the girls?"

"Fine. Waiting at home."

We looked at each other in silence for a moment.

"Miz Moore!" Jorge hustled around the corner. "I got the car. Can I drive you somewhere?"

We crunched across the snow. I wobbled in my heels—Aaron held out a hand and steadied me. Then he let go.

"I found a spot on Center Street," Jorge said. "It should be right . . ."

We turned the corner in time to watch a tow truck pulling away with the Fury.

THIRTY-EIGHT

JORGE ALMOST CAUGHT up with the truck. But the street was too slippery. He skidded and fell. It turned onto Chambers Street, the Fury bumping and rattling behind it. Jorge knelt in the middle of the street and watched them disappear, the picture of Old Testament desolation.

Then he jumped up and stormed back to the now-empty spot. "This is *bullshit*!" he shouted. "Tow companies pull this all the time. Hauling off cars that are legally parked? It's fraud. It's a crime. There's nothing wrong with this spot. I found it fair and . . ."

The sign above the spot was white with snow. Aaron shook the pole it was attached to, and the snow fell away. It was a handicapped spot.

Novartis strikes again.

Jorge's outrage became abject horror. "Oh, no."

"It's not a big deal," I said.

"Not a big deal?" he cried, wild-eyed. "But that car. It's . . . it's . . ." He was too choked up to continue.

I took his arm. "Let's get her back, Jorge."

The Manhattan sheriff's office was a few blocks away. Aaron and I had to run to keep up with Jorge. Aaron gave me a curious glance.

"The car makes him very emotional," I explained.

We arrived at the office on John Street. After waiting in a long line of other restless and aggrieved New Yorkers, we reached the window, where we learned that I couldn't get the car unless I could prove I owned it. I couldn't prove I owned it unless I had my insurance and registration. I didn't have my insurance and registration.

"Because they're in the *car*," Jorge told the haggard, speckled clerk. "Where, like, normal human people keep them."

She didn't care what normal human people did with their vehicular paperwork—we weren't getting the Fury back without mine. We argued. We begged. We showed her the keys. She wasn't impressed. After a few more minutes of abject pleading, she finally admitted that I could call my insurance company, which would fax the information over.

Jorge pulled out his phone and looked at me expectantly.

"I don't know who insures it," I admitted. "I just signed the papers, I didn't . . ."

He looked like he was about to lose his mind.

My own wasn't working properly, which is why I hadn't immediately realized how to solve this problem.

"It's State Farm, dummy," Renfield said, when I called. "What the hell's going on, anyway? I'm hearing rumors that are even more nutso than usual."

"I'll tell you everything. But first, can you fix this?"

She called the sheriff's office, spoke directly to our tormentor and sent a fax. Ten minutes later we walked out with a vehicle release form.

"Renfield's a godsend," Aaron said.

"She speaks fluent clerk," I agreed.

We got a cab. Jorge sat next to the driver, hunched forward, gnawing on his nails and jiggling one knee up and down. He wouldn't be at peace until he was behind the wheel of his beloved Fury.

Aaron and I were in the back.

I looked at him. He looked at me.

Where to begin?

"Why did you come?" I asked. "Today, I mean. After last night, how can you even bear to look at me?"

"I didn't think about it," he said. "I just came."

"I've put you through hell, Aaron. I've said and done the worst possible things to you."

"We both have," he reminded me. "But I promised I'd always be there for you, remember? I haven't exactly succeeded, but I'm still trying."

"We've made such a mess of things," I sighed.

"I know."

"Why didn't you tell me the truth, from the very beginning?"

He looked down at his hands. "Because I was desperate for us to get back on track. Because I knew the truth would make you think the whole . . . thing, meant more to me than it did. And of course, because lying was easier. It felt safer."

"You were probably worried about what else I might do to you."

He smiled a little. "The thought did cross my mind. But the truest, most basic reason? I couldn't risk losing you again. You used to talk about what I did for you, how you needed me. I don't think you ever understood how necessary you were to me. Are to me. You're so smart, so honest. You're such a good person. So strong."

"I was never strong."

He took my hand. "You were. You are. You got me through graduate school. You encouraged me to keep going all those times I didn't see the point. You had an unbelievably stressful and time-consuming job, not to mention two babies, but you read my dissertation over and over again. You helped me not feel totally defeated when I couldn't get a tenure-track job. You supported us when I was making no money. You raised two wonderful daughters. Everything I was to you, you were to me. I wrote my first book for you. I write everything for you. You're the only person I ever want to impress."

He took a deep, shaky breath. "That's why I couldn't tell you the truth. I couldn't bear to lose any more of your respect."

We were quiet for a while. I looked down at our joined hands. I said: "I'm glad you didn't tell me."

He started, shook his head. He couldn't have heard me right.

"I'm glad you lied, Aaron. If you hadn't, I never would have found myself."

"Tell me what you mean."

"My whole life, I've put forward an idea of myself as this powerful, tough person. I did it to quell my anxiety, to make me feel strong. But little by little, I began to believe in that version of myself. Everybody around me thought that was the real me—I figured, maybe it was. I think that's part of why I pulled away from you. I didn't confide in you anymore because I didn't think I needed to. Meaning that by being self-sufficient, by not making myself vulnerable, I made us vulnerable."

Aaron tried to interject, to reassure me, but I kept going.

"That's where matters stood, all through our attempts at reconciliation, all through my efforts to understand what had happened. I was beginning to see that there were things going on inside me I wasn't aware of, things I needed to let out, but I couldn't. I didn't know how. Until a few weeks ago, when I . . . woke up. I grasped some truths about myself that I'd never admitted, beliefs I held, things I wanted, ways I wanted to be. All these recognitions came tumbling out, and everything changed. I felt like I was living for the first time, really being myself."

He had been listening carefully. Now he gave me an uneasy glance. "And so, is that when you . . ."

"Slept with other people? That actually started earlier. But it's related. I slept with people I didn't care about to avoid acknowledging what I really wanted. Or rather, who I really wanted. One particular person."

Aaron was staring at the floor of the cab, nodding. "And did you . . . did you . . . sleep with him?"

"I did. But then I went overboard. I'd hidden the truth from myself for so long, deprived myself of what I wanted—I think I felt entitled to do whatever I pleased. I got greedy, and careless. I believed I was freeing myself. That I'd finally stopped managing my life, and started living it. I was still hiding things from myself, still denying the truth. And I was such a jerk. Especially to you."

As I spoke, Aaron had slowly pulled away, retreating into himself. I reached for his hand.

"I'm sorry I shut you out. I'm sorry I came on to you last week in that weird way. But most of all, I'm sorry about what I said last night. It was unforgivable. And wrong. I loved making love with you. I just didn't let myself enjoy it as much as I could have."

"I wish I'd helped you," he said mournfully. "I wish I was the person who . . . made you realize how much you loved it."

"You couldn't do that for me, Aaron. Nobody could. I had to do it for myself. Anyway," I added, "you did help. You cheated on me."

"Jesus, Raney!"

"I mean it. If you hadn't, I would have lived the rest of my life not really knowing myself. Painful as it was, what you did saved me."

We sat in silence for a while. Then he asked, "Where does this leave us?"

Before I could answer, the cab pulled into the tow pound on Pier 76, and Jorge gave a little cry. The Fury was parked next to a maintenance shed, surrounded by an admiring circle of men in overalls. He leaped out and raced over.

"I'll be right back," I said to Aaron.

"She's fine!" Jorge called out. "Not a scratch on her!"

A bent and crusty old fella with a baseball cap and a leathery face stepped forward. "Who's the owner?" I gave him our paperwork, and he limped into the shed.

Jorge was beaming, bouncing on his toes. "Can I ask you a question?" I said.

"You bet."

"Every driver I've ever had has quit after a few months. They say the hours are terrible, I'm too difficult. Why did you stay?"

He scuffed at a bank of dirty snow with his shoe. "Driving's a pretty boring job, Miz Moore. Hauling rich people around, listening to them complain? Having to apologize when they blame you for the traffic, and the weather, and, like, whatever else is wrong in their lives? You never do that." He grinned. "And you keep things interesting."

The old man returned with our paperwork. I handed it to Jorge. "She's yours."

He'd been gazing lovingly at the Fury. He turned back to me, startled. "Huh?"

"I want you to have the car. I don't need it anymore."

He still wasn't processing. "What now?"

"The car is yours, Jorge."

He stepped back. "Get the fuck outta here!" He clapped his hands over his mouth.

I laughed. "It's okay."

He looked at the car. He looked at me. His eyes were wide. "Oh my God! This is some *Karate Kid* shit right here!"

Then he lifted me into the air, nearly squeezing the life out of me. "You're the best! I promise I'll take good care of her."

"I know you will." He put me down. "I'll see you Monday. In a normal car."

He grinned. "Bright and early." Then he jumped into the Fury and took off.

Back in the cab, I directed the driver to the hotel. Aaron turned to me. He seemed energized, eager, full of purpose.

"I've sat in here for the last ten minutes, thinking through everything you've told me. And I realized something, Raney. I don't care about what you did. It doesn't change anything. We've made a mess of things, but I don't want us to end. Let's try one more time. I know we can get back to where we were."

"No, Aaron. We can't."

He gripped my hand. "Don't say that!"

"You want us to return to the status quo, right? That's what I wanted when I came home, and we resolved to work it out. I thought that if I listened hard enough, and talked hard enough, if I studied the problem and figured out where we went wrong, I could get us back to where we started."

"Can't we?"

"We never could have gotten back there. You changed when you had your affair. I changed when I had to deal with it. I learned things about myself, and us. I can never be the Raney who loved the Aaron who would never cheat. Those people are gone."

He buried his face in his hands. "This is all my fault."

I touched his shoulder. "Things aren't supposed to change, right? That's what everybody believes when they fall in love. That we're solid, and strong. That we're going to be the ones who make it. It doesn't always work that way. I wasn't supposed to pull away. You weren't supposed to have an affair. I wasn't supposed to fall in love with someone else."

He looked up, devastated. "You . . . you love this guy?"

I'd tried to avoid thinking about it. At every opportunity, I'd pushed the idea firmly away. Just like I'd pushed him away. Maybe permanently.

"I love you, too," I said.

"How is that possible?"

"I don't know. It just is."

"I don't understand. How can this be *us*, Raney? How can we be *here*?"

"This is what happens when something happens in a marriage, Aaron. You pull one thread, and the whole thing might unravel."

He stared bleakly out the window. I watched him, feeling that old, familiar tug at my heart. For so long, I'd obsessed over the question of who my husband was. How could he be the man I loved and the man who'd betrayed me? The boy at the party and the man in a hotel with another woman?

But then, who was I? Uptight lawyer, or drunken brawler? Dutiful wife, or happy sex fiend?

The cab approached the hotel. I gathered my bag and wondered what I should do next. Immediate goals were easy: bath, food, sleep. But what about the big stuff, the life stuff? I could (a) start over with Aaron, make an effort to show him my true self. Or I could (b) rush to Singer and beg his forgiveness, tell him I'd figured it out, I was ready to be with him. Or I could—

(c) stop thinking about men all the damn time.

Finding a man, keeping a man, choosing one man over another. Honestly, why does it always come back to men?

The bros have the broth. They can't have my story.

Not right now, anyway.

Because what I'd been through, the ways I'd triumphed and suffered, the good and the bad, the horribly misguided and the deeply weird—it was never really about men. It was about me. Who I was and what I wanted.

So what did I want?

At that very moment, sitting in that cab, what the hell did I want?

The answer, when it came, was surprising, though it shouldn't have been. It was my constant, my consolation. The cure for what always ailed me. The thing that made me me.

I wanted to work.

AND SO I worked. And I lived. I hassled my children. I sparred with my therapist. I exasperated my friends. I still swaggered, and I still staggered. I loved, and I let go. I was alone for a long time. I figured a few things out, including that I would never figure everything out. Still, that doesn't stop me from trying.

Now it's another Monday morning, another perfect September day. The elevator doors open on forty-five. I stride the familiar halls. I drop my bag and wake up my computer.

I take stock. I get to work.

I send and receive, draft and delete, argue and complain and explain.

I am me. I am happy.

And so it goes, until a few minutes before eleven, when my phone rings. I recognize the number and reach for the receiver.

I pause, hand resting on the worn black plastic.

Answering the phone. Such a simple act to set so much in motion.

I think of everything that's come before, everything leading to this moment. Everything I've been, and done, and everything still to come.

Renfield picks up. A few seconds later, her voice comes over the intercom.

"It's yer husband."

Yes, it is. And that makes me laugh, because I still can't quite believe it. I'm still laughing when I pick up the phone.

"Hi, Singer," I say.